AZURICA

Power Crystal

Once a Star Darling has granted her first wish and returns to Starland, she receives a very special treasure—a beautiful Power Crystal.

WATCH

Wish Pendant

A Wish Pendant is a powerful accessory worn by a Star Darling. On Wishworld, it helps her identify her Wisher and stores the ever-important wish energy.

Gemma

Gemma loves to talk, and she has an opinion on just about everything.

She is easygoing, extroverted, and funny. But her honesty can come off as tactless and offensive, and she gets distracted easily.

SCATTERITE

Power Crystal

Once a Star Darling has granted her first wish
and returns to Starland, she receives a very
special treasure—a beautiful Power Crystal.

EARRINGS

Wish Pendant

A Wish Pendant is a powerful accessory worn
by a Star Darling. On Wishworld, it helps
her identify her Wisher and stores the
ever-important wish energy.

Clover

Clover is very patient and has strong willpower and self-discipline. She's creative and loyal to those close to her, but she can be a little standoffish and reserved with people she doesn't know.

Power Crystal

Once a Star Darling has granted her first wish and returns to Starland, she receives a very special treasure—a beautiful Power Crystal.

BARRETTE

Wish Pendant

A Wish Pendant is a powerful accessory worn by a Star Darling. On Wishworld, it helps her identify her Wisher and stores the ever-important wish energy.

Adora Finds a Friend

Clover's Parent Fix

Gemma and the Ultimate Standoff

Shana Muldoon Zappa and Ahmet Zappa

with Zelda Rose

Disney Press

Los Angeles • New York

Printed in the United States of America
Reinforced Binding
First Paperback Edition, September 2016
Adora Finds a Friend First Paperback Edition, June 2016
Clover's Parent Fix First Paperback Edition, July 2016
Gemma and the Ultimate Standoff First Paperback Edition, August 2016

1 3 5 7 9 10 8 6 4 2

FAC-025438-16218

ISBN 978-1-4847-8293-4

For more Disney Press fun, visit www.disneybooks.com

SUSTAINABLE
FORESTRY
INITIATIVE
Certified Sourcing
www.sfiprogram.org
SFI-01415

Halo Violetta Zappa. You are pure light, joy, and inspiration. We love you soooooo much.

May the Star Darlings continue to shine brightly upon you. May every step upon your path be blessed with positivity and the understanding that you have the power within you to manifest the most fulfilling life you can possibly dream of and more. May you always remember that being different and true to yourself makes your inner star shine brighter. And never ever stop making wishes.

Glow for it. . . .
Mommy and Daddy

And to everyone else here on "Wishworld":

May you realize that no matter where you are in life, no matter what you look like or where you were born, you, too, have the power within you to create the life of your dreams. Through celebrating your own uniqueness, thinking positively, and taking action, you can make your wishes come true. May you understand that you are never alone. There is always someone near who will understand you if you look hard enough. The Star Darlings are here to remind you that there is an unstoppable energy to staying positive, wishing, and believing in yourself. That inner star shines within you.

Smile. The Star Darlings have your back. We know how startastic you truly are.

Glow for it. . . .
Your friends,
Shana and Ahmet

Student Reports

NAME: Clover
BRIGHT DAY: January 5
FAVORITE COLOR: Purple
INTERESTS: Music, painting, studying
WISH: To be the best songwriter and DJ on Starland
WHY CHOSEN: Clover has great self-discipline, patience, and willpower. She is creative, responsible, dependable, and extremely loyal.
WATCH OUT FOR: Clover can be hard to read and she is reserved with those she doesn't know. She's afraid to take risks and can be a wisecracker at times.
SCHOOL YEAR: Second
POWER CRYSTAL: Panthera
WISH PENDANT: Barrette

NAME: Adora
BRIGHT DAY: February 14
FAVORITE COLOR: Sky blue
INTERESTS: Science, thinking about the future and how she can make it better
WISH: To be the top fashion designer on Starland
WHY CHOSEN: Adora is clever and popular and cares about the world around her. She's a deep thinker.
WATCH OUT FOR: Adora can have her head in the clouds and be thinking about other things.
SCHOOL YEAR: Third
POWER CRYSTAL: Azurica
WISH PENDANT: Watch

NAME: Piper
BRIGHT DAY: March 4
FAVORITE COLOR: Seafoam green
INTERESTS: Composing poetry and writing in her dream journal
WISH: To become the best version of herself she can possibly be and to share that by writing books
WHY CHOSEN: Piper is giving, kind, and sensitive. She is very intuitive and aware.
WATCH OUT FOR: Piper can be dreamy, absentminded, and wishy-washy. She can also be moody and easily swayed by the opinions of others.
SCHOOL YEAR: Second
POWER CRYSTAL: Dreamalite
WISH PENDANT: Bracelets

Starling Academy

NAME: Astra
BRIGHT DAY: April 9
FAVORITE COLOR: Red
INTERESTS: Individual sports
WISH: To be the best athlete on Starland—to win!
WHY CHOSEN: Astra is energetic, brave, clever, and confident. She has boundless energy and is always direct and to the point.
WATCH OUT FOR: Astra is sometimes cocky, self-centered, condescending, and brash.
SCHOOL YEAR: Second
POWER CRYSTAL: Quarrelite
WISH PENDANT: Wristbands

* • • * • • ✴ • • * • • *

NAME: Tessa
BRIGHT DAY: May 18
FAVORITE COLOR: Emerald green
INTERESTS: Food, flowers, love
WISH: To be successful enough that she can enjoy a life of luxury
WHY CHOSEN: Tessa is warm, charming, affectionate, trustworthy, and dependable. She has incredible drive and commitment.
WATCH OUT FOR: Tessa does not like to be rushed. She can be quite stubborn and often says no. She does not deal well with change and is prone to exaggeration. She can be easily sidetracked.
SCHOOL YEAR: Third
POWER CRYSTAL: Gossamer
WISH PENDANT: Brooch

* • • * • • ✴ • • * • • *

NAME: Gemma
BRIGHT DAY: June 2
FAVORITE COLOR: Orange
INTERESTS: Sharing her thoughts about almost anything
WISH: To be valued for her opinions on everything
WHY CHOSEN: Gemma is friendly, easygoing, funny, extroverted, and social. She knows a little bit about everything.
WATCH OUT FOR: Gemma talks—a lot—and can be a little too honest sometimes and offend others. She can have a short attention span and can be superficial.
SCHOOL YEAR: First
POWER CRYSTAL: Scatterite
WISH PENDANT: Earrings

Student Reports

NAME: Cassie
BRIGHT DAY: July 6
FAVORITE COLOR: White
INTERESTS: Reading, crafting
WISH: To be more independent and confident and less fearful
WHY CHOSEN: Cassie is extremely imaginative and artistic. She is a voracious reader and is loyal, caring, and a good friend. She is very intuitive.
WATCH OUT FOR: Cassie can be distrustful, jealous, moody, and brooding.
SCHOOL YEAR: First
POWER CRYSTAL: Lunalite
WISH PENDANT: Glasses

****

NAME: Leona
BRIGHT DAY: August 16
FAVORITE COLOR: Gold
INTERESTS: Acting, performing, dressing up
WISH: To be the most famous pop star on Starland
WHY CHOSEN: Leona is confident, hardworking, generous, open-minded, optimistic, caring, and a strong leader.
WATCH OUT FOR: Leona can be vain, opinionated, selfish, bossy, dramatic, and stubborn and is prone to losing her temper.
SCHOOL YEAR: Third
POWER CRYSTAL: Glisten paw
WISH PENDANT: Cuff

****

NAME: Vega
BRIGHT DAY: September 1
FAVORITE COLOR: Blue
INTERESTS: Exercising, analyzing, cleaning, solving puzzles
WISH: To be the top student at Starling Academy
WHY CHOSEN: Vega is reliable, observant, organized, and very focused.
WATCH OUT FOR: Vega can be opinionated about everything, and she can be fussy, uptight, critical, arrogant, and easily embarrassed.
SCHOOL YEAR: Second
POWER CRYSTAL: Queezle
WISH PENDANT: Belt

Starling Academy

NAME: Libby
BRIGHT DAY: October 12
FAVORITE COLOR: Pink
INTERESTS: Helping others, interior design, art, dancing
WISH: To give everyone what they need—both on Starland and through wish granting on Wishworld
WHY CHOSEN: Libby is generous, articulate, gracious, diplomatic, and kind.
WATCH OUT FOR: Libby can be indecisive and may try too hard to please everyone.
SCHOOL YEAR: First
POWER CRYSTAL: Charmelite
WISH PENDANT: Necklace

* • • * • • ✦ • • * • • *

NAME: Scarlet
BRIGHT DAY: November 3
FAVORITE COLOR: Black
INTERESTS: Crystal climbing (and other extreme sports), magic, thrill seeking
WISH: To live on Wishworld
WHY CHOSEN: Scarlet is confident, intense, passionate, magnetic, curious, and very brave.
WATCH OUT FOR: Scarlet is a loner and can alienate others by being secretive, arrogant, stubborn, and jealous.
SCHOOL YEAR: Third
POWER CRYSTAL: Ravenstone
WISH PENDANT: Boots

* • • * • • ✦ • • * • • *

NAME: Sage
BRIGHT DAY: December 1
FAVORITE COLOR: Lavender
INTERESTS: Travel, adventure, telling stories, nature, and philosophy
WISH: To become the best Wish-Granter Starland has ever seen
WHY CHOSEN: Sage is honest, adventurous, curious, optimistic, friendly, and relaxed.
WATCH OUT FOR: Sage has a quick temper! She can also be restless, irresponsible, and too trusting of others' opinions. She may jump to conclusions.
SCHOOL YEAR: First
POWER CRYSTAL: Lavenderite
WISH PENDANT: Necklace

Introduction

You take a deep breath, about to blow out the candles on your birthday cake. Clutching a coin in your fist, you get ready to toss it into the dancing waters of a fountain. You stare at your little brother as you each hold an end of a dried wishbone, about to pull. But what do you do first?

You make a wish, of course!

Ever wonder what happens right after you make that wish? *Not much*, you may be thinking.

Well, you'd be wrong.

Because something quite unexpected happens next. Each and every wish that is made becomes a glowing Wish Orb, invisible to the human eye. This undetectable orb zips through the air and into the heavens, on a one-way trip to the brightest star in the sky—a magnificent place called Starland. Starland is inhabited by Starlings, who look a lot like you and me, except they have a sparkly glow to their skin, and glittery hair in unique colors. And they have one more thing: magical powers. The Starlings use these powers to make good wishes come true, for when good wishes are granted, the result is positive energy. And the Starlings of Starland need this energy to keep their world running.

In case you are wondering, there are three kinds of Wish Orbs:

1) GOOD WISH ORBS. These wishes are positive and helpful and come from the heart. They are pretty and sparkly and are nurtured in climate-controlled Wish-Houses. They bloom into fantastical glowing orbs. When the time is right, they are presented to the appropriate Starling for wish fulfillment.

2) BAD WISH ORBS. These are for selfish, mean-spirited, or negative things. They don't sparkle

at all. They are immediately transported to a special containment center, as they are very dangerous and must not be granted.

3) IMPOSSIBLE WISH ORBS. These wishes are for things, like world peace and disease cures, that simply can't be granted by Starlings. These sparkle with an almost impossibly bright light and are taken to a special area of the Wish-House with tinted windows to contain the glare they produce. The hope is that one day they can be turned into good wishes the Starlings can help grant.

Starlings take their wish granting very seriously. There is a special school, called Starling Academy, that accepts only the best and brightest young Starling girls. They study hard for four years, and when they graduate, they are ready to start traveling to Wishworld to help grant wishes. For as long as anyone can remember, only graduates of wish-granting schools have ever been allowed to travel to Wishworld. But things have changed in a very big way.

Read on for the rest of the story. . . .

Adora Finds a Friend

Prologue

TO: Sage, Libby, Leona, Vega, Piper, Astra, Adora,
Clover, and Gemma
FROM: Cassie
INSTRUCTIONS: Auto-delivery of this holo-letter
scheduled for Reliquaday, in three starhours' time

Dear Star Darlings,
Greetings and salutations, friends and fellow
Star Darlings. You may be wondering why I'm
sending a holo-letter when I've just seen you all at
the ceremony. (Starkudos, Tessa, on a successful

mission!) There are many answers to that question. And I'll get to the most important one at the end of this holo-letter. So keep reading.

In short, I am writing to clarify the dangerous situation on Starland and, in doing so, explain my own actions. Wait! Don't delete this letter! Please hear me out! (This means you, Sage and Libby, who have turned a blind eye to Lady Stella's involvement.) And don't roll your eyes. (This means you, Adora! I do not overreact to problems.) I am not imagining that Starland is in major trouble. It is. I am not imagining conspiracies or villains. They exist.

To support my stand, here are the issues in no particular order:

The Issues on Wishworld: Problematic Missions

Why do the Star Darlings even exist? As we all know, Lady Stella brought us together to test her theory that if the wishes of young Wishlings were to be granted by young Starlings, this special combination would produce an even greater amount of positive wish energy than older Starlings could ever collect. And now, since we know that Starland is having a serious wish energy crisis, our wish missions are even more important than ever.

Why are our Wish Missions—even the successful ones—always in danger until the last starmin? We've been trained and schooled and are starmendously capable, yet something always goes wrong. And that does not even take Leona's mission into account. Not only was her Wish Pendant destroyed, making it impossible for it to absorb any wish energy, but she almost didn't make it back on her shooting star! And she obviously (sorry, Leona!) didn't get her Power Crystal.

The Issues with Star Darlings: 1) Fighting within Our Group and 2) Strange Behavior
(Both designed to keep us from acting together and from acting at all!)

Specifically:

Why were we fighting with our roommates? The poisonous flowers from the Isle of Misera that were placed in our rooms.

Why were all the Star Kindness Day compliments changed to insults? That one speaks for itself!

Why were we all acting so odd and not even realizing it?
Because of the poisonous nail polish from the Star
Darlings–only mani-pedi party! Whoever created
the polish knew this strange behavior would
interfere with our missions. Not to mention it was
starmendously embarrassing for everyone (Libby's
falling asleep anywhere and everywhere; Scarlet's
skipping anywhere and everywhere; and probably
the worst: my bragging anywhere and everywhere).

Additional Star Darlings Issues: the Band and
the Star-Zap

*Why was Leona's band named the Star Darlings, with
tryout info sent to the whole school?* To bring our secret
group into the starlight is my guess!

Why was my Star-Zap not working properly?
So someone could intercept Star Darlings
communication. Again, that's my guess.

My Issue with Lady Stella: She Is Responsible
for All This
(Again, Sage and Libby: hear me out.)

Specifically:

Why was Scarlet kicked out of the Star Darlings and replaced with Ophelia? To sabotage a mission, of course.

And who set that in motion? Lady Stella! She switched admissions test results so it looked like Scarlet had low scores and Ophelia's were high as the moons. (Starkudos to Scarlet. Impressive work, really!) Then she instructed Ophelia to lie—about being an orphan, about being a gifted student, everything! And that information, Star Darlings, came from Ophelia herself.

And that, finally, brings me to the real purpose of this holo-letter.

The Real Purpose of This Holo-Letter

Why did I write it? Scarlet, Tessa, and I have decided to explore the Star Caves, deep beneath our school. We are looking for clues in the very labyrinth Lady Stella introduced us to—clues about the headmistress, clues about our missions, clues about anything and everything. (Yes, Gemma, your sister, Tessa, is with us, even though she just came back from her mission and is not a fan of dark, dank, spooky places.)

I have a feeling something big will come out of our search. We are just now setting off. But if you are reading this, it means we have not made it back. We are still underground, in the tunnels, maybe trapped and most definitely in trouble. So . . . help! Find us as fast as you can!

Yours in jeopardy,
Cassie

CHAPTER
1

"*Mmmmmm, hmmmm, mmmm, hmmmm.*" Adora hummed tunelessly, alone in her dorm room.

It felt nice to have the room all to herself. Still, it was a little strange that Tessa, her roommate, wasn't there.

The two had just come back from a Wish Mission. It was Tessa's mission; Adora had yet to be chosen for her own mission to Wishworld. But Adora had been sent to help when the situation looked dim. Really, Tessa had been so caught up in her Wisher's emotions that she hadn't been able to see the orchard for the ozziefruit trees. Luckily, Adora had set her straight. So thank the stars, the trip had been successful and quite exciting.

After the Star Darlings ceremony, where Tessa had

gotten her Power Crystal, Adora had expected her to come straight back to their room. Tessa was quite the homebody, after all. And there were her virtual galliope, Jewel, to feed and her micro-zap waiting to bake yummy astromuffins.

But Tessa hadn't so much as stopped off at the room as far as Adora could tell. She was probably catching up with her younger sister, Gemma. And Adora planned to take full advantage of her alone time.

She had been right in the middle of an experiment when she'd been called on to help Tessa. She'd been itching to get back to it for over a starday now. It combined her two biggest passions: science and fashion—specifically sequins.

Adora wanted the sequins to be extra twinkly. That alone wouldn't be so difficult. But she wanted that newfound sparkle to bring out each sequin's color, too, to make the shades themselves brighter, warmer, and more radiant.

The gold sequins Leona favored had to become even more brightly golden; Cassie's silvery pink ones even more silvery pink; Clover's an even deeper, more brilliant purple. And Adora's goal was to do it with just one formula.

She wanted the formula to work with every shade under the suns, and that was twelve in the Star Darlings group alone. Add all the different tones at Starling Academy, or, furthermore, all of Starland itself, and the numbers were starmazing!

Adora had already removed natural elements from glittery yellow calliope flowers, fiery red florafierces, and other plants and trees. Now she needed to add twinkle-oxide—with a spark of glowzene for good measure—to each mixture. The combination had to be just right so the formula would react with any Starling shade.

Luckily, it was Reliquaday, the first starday of the weekend, which gave her plenty of time to test her ideas. Adora would be logical and methodical, as always. But she wanted to get it done sooner rather than later so the sequins could be sewn onto outfits the Star Darlings band members planned to wear for the upcoming Battle of the Bands on Starshine Day.

"*Mmmmm, hmmm, mmmmm.*" Adora hummed, pouring 5.6 lumins of twinkle-oxide into a beaker. "*Mmmm, hmmmmm.*" She turned on her personal bright-burner to 179 degrees Starrius and waited for the mixture to heat. "*Mmmm.*"

Alone in the room, Adora felt free to sing to her heart's content. Her music skills were nothing to brag about, but Adora wasn't much into the arts, anyway. For her, it was science, science, science—and fashion, fashion, fashion.

Adora planned to be a style scientist, maybe the first on all of Starland. And she'd show everyone she could be the brightest in both style and science.

Adora's parents owned a trendy clothing store in Radiant Hills, the ultraexclusive community in Starland City where Libby had grown up alongside glimmerous celebrighties and famous Starlandians.

Adora herself had lived in a perfectly nice neighborhood of modest, comfortable homes. She couldn't complain. She and her parents had shared a simple one-level house where they each had their own workspace to create designs to sell in the store. Even as a wee Starling, she'd had a microscope and a star-sewing machine and had come up with lustrous new fabrics for her parents to use in their clothing designs.

Adora pushed back sky-blue strands of hair that had fallen out of her loose bun, and adjusted her knee-length glittery lab coat and gloves. She checked her pockets, making sure the extra test tubes she always carried around were closed up tight.

Finally, with great care, she straightened her safety starglasses. Safety first, she knew from prior experience.

Just this staryear, Tessa had mixed a batch of glo-range smoothies. Adora, meanwhile, had been working on special fabric that would sparkle extra brightly when it got wet. She'd combined orangey lightning in a bottle with starfuric acid and was ready to soak the fabric. The mixture did look a bit like the smoothies, Adora had to admit. So it was no wonder Tessa had reached for the wrong container and lifted it to her lips, about to take a sip. Adora had to make a running dive to knock the liquid out of her hands.

Right after that, Adora had established rules, including clearly separating food from experiments and wearing safety starglasses. The second one was particularly important, Adora realized a starsec later, when—

Bang! Her sequin mixture fizzled and sparked, overflowing from the beaker and spilling onto her workspace. Immediately, the smoking liquid disappeared, thanks to the self-cleaning technology featured in all Starland dwellings.

Adora's side of the room in particular was squeaky clean and spare—some might say sterile and uninteresting—with a neat desktop and lab space containing carefully arranged beakers and test tubes. Even the "fashion section" had neat cubbies for bolts of fabrics and a carefully polished star-sewing machine.

She did like an orderly room, with minimal possessions. Tessa, on the other hand, had a moonium knickknacks—along with plants and herbs and old holo-cookbooks.

Adora didn't quite understand. She didn't get attached to things. *Out with the old, in with the new,* she thought frequently, deleting old experiment notes and equations. She was thinking that now, in fact, as she struck the sequins formula from her holo–lab notes.

"*Starf,*" Adora said, eying the now blank screen. She'd have to start over, maybe lowering the brightburner to 147 degrees. But that was okay. That was what science was all about—trial and error and patience.

And that was all part of the lightentific method, Adora's personal approach to experimenting: Ask a question based on observation. Come up with a reasonable hypothesis (a guess, really) to answer the question. Create an experiment to see if the guess was correct and analyze the results. Finally, draw a conclusion. Either the experiment worked or it failed.

But Adora wasn't one to accept failure.

"*Mmmmmm.*" Adora's voice grew more powerful as

she started on a new hypothesis. It was a relief, really, to be loud. She had been so frustrated when no one had been able to hear her for so long, only later realizing the poisonous nail polish was causing her to whisper. At least it had been better than giggling nonstop, like Sage, though. Or pulling practical jokes, like Astra had done. No one liked it when their drinks were switched at the Celestial Café!

Adora was carefully carrying fresh batches of the mixture to the bright-burner when her Star-Zap buzzed.

Should she ignore it and just keep concentrating on her experiment?

Part of her wanted to do just that. But with all the strange goings-on lately, it could be an important message. Or maybe it was an announcement for the next mission!

"Oh, moonberries," she said, using Tessa's favorite expression as she set down the beakers. She'd just have to check. She reached for her Star-Zap and glanced at the screen.

A group holo-letter from Cassie? she thought. That was a little bizarre. Why would Cassie write a long letter when she could just talk to the Star Darlings or send a brief holo-text?

Adora tapped the screen and the letter appeared in

the air, floating at eye level. Quickly, she read the note, then read it again just to be sure: Cassie was with Tessa—and Scarlet—and they were trapped in the Star Caves. There Adora was, happily going about her experiment, pleased as sparkle-punch to have the room to herself, while Tessa had been in trouble the whole time.

Every problem had a solution—scientific, mathematical, or otherwise. It just took a cool, clear mind to figure it out. But Adora had to leave the room, step away from Tessa's knickknacks and holo-photos from the farm, to think things through. Calmly, she went outside.

"Adora! Thank the stars you're here!" Leona shouted, rushing down the hall, her golden curls bouncing behind her. "Did you see Cassie's holo-letter?"

"Shhh!" hissed Adora. She glanced pointedly in the other direction, where two third years were getting off the Cosmic Transporter and eyeing them curiously.

"Just the SDs being SDish," one said with a laugh.

Ask just about any Starling Academy student and she would say *SD* stood for *Slow Developers*, a nickname given to the twelve girls because they all attended a special class for extra help. Little did the students know, however, that *SD* was short for *Star Darlings*. And the "extra help" was lessons in information about Wishworld that they used on actual Wish Missions.

Adora shrugged off the label and the idea that anyone would think she was a weak student. It just went to show you how dim other Starlings could be, she thought. Particularly those girls still hanging around the hall, trying to eavesdrop on her conversation with Leona.

"We should all get together to talk about the holo-letter," she told Leona. "Right now."

"Must be an SD assignment," one of the eavesdropping girls said. "A sloooow assignment." Happy with their insults, the girls moved on.

"Of course," said Leona in a calmer voice. "I'll holo-text everyone right away. We should meet in my room. It's the perfect place. You know I have my own personal stage? So it's all set for a group discussion. Whoever wants to talk can use the microphone."

"Right," said Adora, though she didn't think they really needed a microphone. What they needed was a plan.

CHAPTER
2

Adora was sitting crisscross starapple sauce, as they used to say in Wee Constellation School. Most of the Star Darlings gathered in Leona's room sat the same way. Of course, Piper went one better, putting her feet *on top* of the opposite legs and placing her hands palms-up in a meditative pose. It wasn't the most comfortable position, Adora knew.

She'd actually tried it when she'd joined Piper in a meditation class. She'd wanted to test the effectiveness of being in the moment, of being aware of each movement. Adora had left with a healthy respect for mindful thinking—and sore legs.

The girls were grouped around Leona's mini star-shaped stage, waiting while Leona searched for her microphone. "I know it's here somewhere!" Leona shouted, flinging starbrushes, shoes, and accessories everywhere.

The room was bathed in a golden light, filtering through gauzy starlight curtains. Adora couldn't help wondering if she could capture that exact shade for Leona's sequins.

Adora's eyes swept over the other Star Darlings, and she noted their coloring. Sweet-looking Libby, with her jellyjoohle-pink hair, leaned forward worriedly. Sleepy Piper half closed her seafoam-green eyes.

Fiery red-haired Astra—a perfect match for the florafierce extract, Adora realized—dusted off her star ball uniform.

"You know, I got Cassie's message right in the middle of the Glowin' Glions star ball game," she was saying to Piper, "and when I was leaving, I spotted Leebeau in the stands!"

Adora frowned. She'd heard about that boy, Astra's "biggest fan," who went to Star Preparatory, the school across Luminous Lake. Astra had met him on a starbus, on the way to visit an orphanage during the search for the missing Ophelia. And she'd been keeping an eye out for him in the stands at every game since.

There might be some scientific explanation for

Astra's interest in the boy. That would be fascinating to pursue. But it didn't quite figure into Adora's game plan.

"So he's finally here," Astra continued, "and I had to leave! And miss the rest of the game!"

Piper nodded sympathetically. "If you're destined to see him again, it will happen."

Surprisingly, Astra nodded. "It's true. This is an emergency situation."

"Yes!" Adora agreed, standing to address the group. "So what are we going to do about it?"

"Ahem!" Leona cleared her throat, hurrying over. "I found the microphone." She tapped it to make her point, and the thudding sound echoed loudly. "If anyone wants to speak, just signal me and I'll give you the mic."

"Just wait a starsec, Leona," Adora said. "We can't start yet. Where's Gemma?"

Just then, there was a knock at the door. Leona opened it from across the room with a flick of her wrist, and Gemma bounded inside.

"I can't believe Tessa would do this!" she cried, her ginger eyes flashing. "Going down into those creepy caves? If I went down there, she'd be saying, 'It's too dangerous, Gemma. You need to be careful, Gemma. What were you thinking, Gemma?'" Glittery orange tears trickled down Gemma's cheeks. "I'm so worried about Tessa. About them all! What were they thinking? What were—"

"Star excuse me, Gemma," Leona interrupted. "I have the stage . . . I mean, floor . . . I mean, microphone. And we need to begin a real discussion, now that we're all here—except for Cassie, Tessa, and Scarlet, of course."

Scarlet and Leona were roommates. They were a combustible mix, worse than sparkle-oxide and phenol-twinkle. And while Adora and Tessa had their differences, those two definitely did not get along.

As if on cue, Scarlet's skateboard slid down her ramp-like wall, rolled across the room to Leona's side, and came to rest right by the stage.

Piper gasped. "It's a sign. We need to hurry up and do something. Scarlet needs us!"

Sage nodded vigorously. "Yes! Why are we sitting around like a bunch of Starlings in their twilight years?" She jumped up impatiently. "Let's go."

Gemma was already halfway out the door.

"Whoa," said Adora. "Slow down, you two. We all want to find our friends. But we need to approach this methodically and thoughtfully, not like a bunch of bloombugs during a full moon."

Vega nodded, her short blue hair bobbing. "That's

right. It's like a puzzle. We need to fill in the missing pieces to see the whole picture. We know they went down hoping to find some clues about Lady Stella. Now they're in trouble. We need to rescue them." She paused. "And here's the missing piece: how?"

"The only way I know down to the Star Caves is through the secret passage in Lady Stella's office," Astra mused aloud.

The girls exchanged nervous glances. Adora paced back and forth, thinking.

Some professors would have access to the office: Lady Stella's inner circle, those teachers who knew about the Star Darlings and gave special lectures to their class, for instance. But no school visitor—no matter how glimmerous, no matter how famous, no matter how important—was allowed into Lady Stella's office without her personal invitation. As for students, it was strictly forbidden. Bot-Bot guards roamed those halls at all starhours.

Adora didn't know what would happen if a student was caught. Would she be expelled? Refused admittance to any other school? She didn't want to find out.

"Let's analyze this," Adora said out loud. "Maybe the girls didn't go down through Lady Stella's office. Maybe they found another way. Does anyone have thoughts on that?"

Leona spoke into the mic. "Scarlet."

"What?" said Sage. "What does that even mean?"

"It means," Leona continued, "that she's always been fascinated by the caves. From the very first time we went down, Scarlet couldn't wait to go back. Whenever we got a holo-text that a Wish Orb was ready, her glow would flare with excitement. Honestly, I've seen her smile more in those caves than just about anywhere else. She might have found another way down there."

"Once, Scarlet went left when everyone else was going right," Astra added. "I grabbed her arm, thinking that she just wasn't paying attention. But maybe there's something more there. Maybe she was trying to explore on her own."

"Hmmm." Adora pondered the idea. "I believe she does enjoy the caves. I noticed a bitbat land on her shoulder one time, and she actually petted it. So maybe she has gone down on her own before, most likely through a different entrance." Adora shook her head, clearing her thoughts. "But we don't have time to waste trying to find it. I think we are going to have to go down there the only way we know—through Lady Stella's office. So how do you propose we get inside?"

"Well, we certainly can't ask Lady Stella," said Leona. "She's probably the one who trapped them!"

Adora looked around the circle. Astra tapped her foot, shooting off sparks of nervous energy. Gemma chewed on a fingernail. Even Piper had shifted into a tense, upright position.

"Listen," Adora said calmly. "There's a chance this has nothing to do with sabotage or anyone purposefully trapping them."

"That's right," Clover said. She tipped her ever-present purple fedora in a hats-off gesture to Adora. "They might have gotten lost and now they can't find a way out. That would be scary for them, sure, but not very dangerous.

"My family is so big I once got left behind and no one even realized it! We were traveling from New Prism to Solar Springs with the circus, and I was getting supplies for our star-swallowing act when the circus swift train took off without me. My uncle Octavius had to teleport back to pick me up."

Adora always found Clover's circus stories interesting. (The Flying Molensas not only used scientific equations to figure out trapeze trajectories; they also wore starmazing outfits.) But right now they needed to focus on the task at hand: rescuing their friends.

"So we need to come up with a plan to get into Lady

Stella's office," she said out loud. "Without getting caught."

"I think we should choose a leader," Libby added. "Someone to be in charge."

"So we don't have endless discussions," Clover cracked, "like this one."

"Like a team captain!" Astra said eagerly.

"Or light leader," Libby told the group. Everyone knew that she intended to run for class office one day. "I say we take a vote."

"I nominate Leona!" said Leona.

"You can't nominate yourself!" Astra exclaimed. "But if someone would like to nominate me, I think I could do a starmendous job. I understand group dynamics and winning, and—"

"How about we don't nominate anyone and just all vote anonymously?" said Adora. She quickly set up a survey site on her Star-Zap, then made a few adjustments for the group to vote.

Immediately, everyone tapped in their responses. Only Adora waited, thinking for more than a starmin. She considered Astra first, then Libby—who had shown leadership by suggesting the election—then everyone else equally. But in the end, weighing all the evidence, she clicked on a checkmark next to her own name.

Libby did a quick tally. "Adora!" she announced.

"Starkudos," said Astra quickly. "You'll make a great leader."

Adora hadn't really expected to win. Those things tended to be popularity contests. Sure, Adora thought she was popular in her own way. After a hard day's work at the lab, she liked to socialize as much as the next Starling. But that didn't mean she had many close friends.

Adora was certain that a good number of Starlings thought she could be a little cold and unfeeling. But she disagreed. She was just calm and logical. She didn't let feelings get in the way of decisions. And apparently, that was the best approach right then.

"You won't be sorry," she told everyone.

"I know," said Gemma, reaching out to touch her hand. "You'll get everything under control."

Adora nodded. "But I don't want to be the lone voice."

"Surely *my* voice should be heard," said Leona. She grinned graciously. "Even if this time I'm only a backup singer."

"All right," said Adora. "I propose another vote. Should I choose one or two girls to go with me down to the caves? Or should we all go together?"

That time, no vote was necessary. Everyone shouted, almost in unison: "Together!"

Adora looked at Astra and grinned. "Let's do this the Glowin' Glions' way."

Everyone moved onto the stage, drawing closer and placing their hands in the center of the group, one on top of the other.

"But instead of a team name," Adora continued, "let's say—"

She didn't even have to finish the sentence.

"Star Darlings!" they all cried.

CHAPTER
3

Quickly, Adora reviewed the situation. So far the Star Darlings had decided:

1) to make the rescue a group effort, and
2) to sneak into Lady Stella's office to take the secret entrance to the Star Caves.

Now she had to put her lightentific method to use.

Generally, she would start by thinking, *If I did A, then B, I'd most likely get C.*

First she sent a scout to Lady Stella's office to see if she was there. The result was inconclusive. Rather than take a chance that the headmistress was inside, Adora came up with a plan. In this case, her hypothesis was:

(A) If we make sure Lady Stella is not in her office, we could (B) sneak inside and open the secret entrance and (C) rescue Cassie, Tessa, and Scarlet.

Step One: determining Lady Stella's location.

Of course, there had to be a conclusion at the end of the whole process, an answer to the bigger questions: Had the girls been trapped on purpose? And by whom? But Adora thought those questions would have to wait. First things first, and the first thing in this case was the rescue.

Everyone was still in Leona's room, looking at Adora expectantly. "Okay," she told them in a firm voice. "We'll divide into pairs to scout around for Lady Stella."

Her eyes settled on Libby. "Libby," she said "You come with me. Everyone else, find a partner."

While the others milled around, Adora took out her Star-Zap and opened a holo-map of Starling Academy. The school was in the shape of a five-point star, with the Little Dipper and Big Dipper Dorms clustered in one point. Faculty housing was in the point to their right, at the very tip. *Libby and I will go there*, Adora decided. *Now, how far should the others spread out?*

She peered at the holo-map intently. She was so absorbed in the task that she didn't notice someone standing next to her until she felt a tap on her shoulder.

"Um, Adora?" said Gemma. "I don't have a partner." She blinked rapidly, trying to hold back tears.

Adora stared at her, uncomprehending. The girl was overwrought. She needed to get in control.

Of course Adora realized Gemma was upset about her sister. But really, it did no good going into a star-tizzy. Besides, Gemma should have been the first to pair up; the girl never hesitated to approach anyone and start chattering away.

For stars' sake, if it was me, Adora thought, *I'd be just as happy to work alone. In fact, it would be easier.* Already she half regretted having Libby come with her. She'd just tell Libby and Gemma to go together.

"Gemma," she said, "you and Libby—"

"Can go with you!" Gemma's face lit up. "Oh, star salutations, Adora! I'll just run to the Lightning Lounge and scrounge up some snacks before we go. I know Tessa will be hungry!"

Before Adora could stop her, Gemma was gone.

Adora sighed. This was going to be a long step one.

Not long after, the Star Darlings dispersed, each pair heading in a different direction. Adora had assigned Astra and Sage the Radiant Recreation Center and the surrounding area; Piper and Vega the Illumination Library and class-rooms in Halo Hall; and Leona and Clover the band shell, the Celestial Café, and the nearby orchard.

She'd told everyone to set their Star-Zaps for reminders to meet at the hedge maze in precisely one half starhour.

Vega had nodded in agreement. "The hedge maze is perfect," she'd told the others. "It's a great place to meet in secret."

Stepping onto the Cosmic Transporter, Gemma linked arms with Adora and Libby. "Come on," she urged. "We were the last to leave, so we need to hurry!"

Adora didn't bother to remind Gemma why they were last: she and Libby had had to wait for her to get back with ozziefruit and astromuffins. But teacher housing wasn't too far away, so they hadn't lost much startime.

Just starmins later, the three girls hopped off the transporter and found themselves in front of a small holo-sign. The flowing print read simply FACULTY.

If Adora hadn't been looking for some sort of sign, she might have missed it. There was nothing else to indicate there were homes there.

Adora saw boingtrees and druderwomp bushes, along with the Crystal Mountains in the background, looming beyond Luminous Lake. That was all. But Adora knew for a fact that teachers lived there. It said so right on the sign, not to mention the map. Indisputable proof. But she'd never actually been to that part of campus before. It was all new to her.

"This is odd. Where are all the houses?" she asked. "Have either of you been to a professor's home?"

Libby and Gemma shook their heads. "We're only first years," Gemma reminded her. "Don't older students usually get invited for twinkle tea? I thought by third year everyone had been here at least once."

Adora hoped Gemma would stop at that, but unsurprisingly, she continued talking. "I know Tessa has been here a bunch of times. She never made it seem like a top secret location. All the other third years talk about their visits. Have you at least been invited, Adora?"

Adora almost blushed an icy blue. But she didn't. By sheer force of will, she held herself in check. "I meet with teachers all the time. After class. In the Astro-Energy Lab. Or the Sparkle-Transfer Space. I just don't have time for twinkle tea or leisurely conversation."

Adora realized she hadn't quite answered Gemma's question. If she had, she would have said, *No, I've never been invited.* She had her theories about why. The science teachers thought she was too frivolous, too interested in clothes and fashion. And the art teachers thought she was too factual and serious-minded to discuss painting and wish-energy sculpting. Besides, she told herself, she wanted her grades to reflect her work, not her student-teacher relationships.

She paused, frowning. "It never occurred to me it would be hard to find."

Now Adora did blush. She usually had all contingencies covered, all what-ifs thought out. Not knowing what else to do, she stepped forward to examine the sign. Finally, she noticed the hand scanner on a nearby boingtree.

Is this area open to all students? she wondered. *Or do you need special permission?* Would her palm open some sort of door?

Adora groaned. How could she have been on campus for three years and not know any of that?

Well, there was only one way to find out. She placed her hand on the scanner, and it glowed blue. Directly ahead of the girls, shimmery leaves parted like a curtain to reveal a small suburban neighborhood.

Homes of all colors, shapes, and sizes circled a village green. Lampposts, bright rainbows arcing from them, bordered the green.

"Why do these houses look so familiar?" Libby asked.

Adora gazed intently at the homes. Libby was right. There was something about this place . . . something recognizable that made her feel she'd seen it before. Maybe she'd been somewhere similar . . . seen the houses in some other form . . .

She snapped her fingers. "I've got it!" she cried. She pointed at a stunning umber-colored home with silver-white trim and long elegant lines. It seemed so inviting, so warm and open, Adora wanted to walk right inside. "Does that remind you of anyone?" she asked.

Libby smiled. "Professor Eugenia Bright!"

Professor Eugenia Bright taught Wish Fulfillment. She was so lovely and welcoming—just like the house— that Starlings signed up for her classes starmester after starmester.

"And that must be Professor Dolores Raye's right next to it," said Adora.

That home was small, tidy, and off-putting, with a sign that read KEEP OFF THE STARGRASS.

Windows flanked its front door so it resembled a face with large-framed glasses perched on its "nose." And it seemed, Adora had to admit, like a boring place to live.

"It looks just like her!" Gemma giggled. Unlike Professor Eugenia Bright's lectures, Professor Dolores Raye's Wishful Thinking class—covering the nuts and bolts of wish energy manipulation—was cut-and-dried, all business with little spark.

"And guess who lives there!" Adora pointed to a short, squat home that gave the impression it was falling apart. Shutters hung slightly askew, and wispy purple grass escaped the confines of the yard, like hair from a bun.

Suddenly, the front door swung open. The girls all jumped as Lady Cordial stepped outside, checking her Star-Zap and hurrying as if she'd just received an important message.

Z-z-z-z. Adora's own Star-Zap buzzed at the same time. She gave it a quick look, already knowing it was a holo-reminder to meet the Star Darlings at the hedge maze.

Just then, Lady Cordial tripped over a glimmervine. Her purse fell to the ground, and all its contents spilled onto the walkway.

Libby rushed to help. "Lady Cordial! Let me get those things for you!"

"Oh, my s-s-s-s-stars," Lady Cordial stuttered. "What are you girls doing here?" She stooped down to gather her things, accidentally knocking Libby farther away.

Adora bent down to help.

"No! I can do it myself!" exclaimed Lady Cordial. Clearly, she was embarrassed by her clumsiness.

"Star greetings, students and teacher!" Professor Findley Claxworth was fast approaching. His long, loose paint-splattered smock swung in the breeze. His lavender eyes, a perfect match for his hair and glasses, twinkled merrily.

Everyone liked the affable art professor. Adora had taken his Aspirational Art classes—Introduction to, Advanced, and Exceptionally Advanced. She liked him, too. But she feared he was one of the teachers who thought she spent too much startime focused on the scientific end of art and design.

Professor Findley Claxworth smiled warmly. "Ladies," he said, including the Star Darlings in the greeting.

Libby's and Gemma's glows deepened with pleasure.

"Star greetings, Professor Findley Claxworth," said Adora.

Lady Cordial barely nodded, too busy closing her purse and clucking in embarrassment at her clumsiness.

"To what do we owe the pleasure of your company?" he asked the girls.

Gemma and Libby stepped back to let Adora take over.

"We're tracking flutterfocuses for my Comparative Creatures class. I think they flew over here. Libby and Gemma are just helping me." Adora was lying, and Libby and Gemma knew it. She only hoped Lady Cordial and Professor Findley Claxworth didn't.

Adora rarely lied, and she doubted she was very good at it. As a scientist, Adora believed in truth and accuracy—both in experiments in the lab and in life outside the lab. How could she consider herself a true scientist—not to mention a good Starling—if she allowed facts to be altered to fit her own needs?

But every once in a while, it needed to be done.

"That's interesting," said Lady Cordial distractedly. "I didn't notice any s-s-s-s-swarms. But I've been inside most of the day, going through admissions applications. Next s-s-s-s-staryear's incoming class looks like a s-s-s-s-strong one."

"Oh!" Gemma piped up, suddenly interested. "Are there any applications from Solar Springs, my hometown?"

Adora felt sure Lady Cordial wouldn't give out that kind of confidential information unless it was by accident. She was too thoughtful and by-the-holo-book. But Adora knew the sweetly bumbling head of admissions was certainly capable of slipping up. To save her any more embarrassment, Adora turned to Professor Findley Claxworth and changed the subject. "Are you working on something right now?"

"Why, star salutations for asking, Adora," he said, clearly pleased. "I'm just about to start my new piece. And I'm thrilled to have an audience."

He waved his arms, and a small white house that looked like a blank canvas built on easel-like stilts lit up with a soft glow. Adora noted the neat garden in front. Then she realized the flowers were really lightpaint cans.

Professor Findley Claxworth snapped his fingers and the cans rose into the air. He pointed to one. It swung back and forth, splashing bright yellow lightpaint against one side of the house. He snapped again and the other cans flung vibrant blues and greens. He fluttered his fingers and the dripping lightpaint transformed into a field of bluebeezel flowers under setting suns.

"S-s-s-s-so lovely," Lady Cordial stammered.

"Just experimenting," Professor Findley Claxworth said modestly.

Experimenting! Adora had to focus on her own light-entific method. They had to find out if Lady Stella was home.

"And I'm just leaving." Lady Cordial interrupted

Adora's thoughts. "S-s-s-s-star apologies, girls. Next time you visit, I'll have you over for twinkle tea and astro-muffins." With one final nod, she disappeared through the leaves.

"Anyone like to try another side of the house?" Professor Findley Claxworth asked. "I have plenty of lightpaint left."

"Yes!" said Libby and Gemma, stepping forward.

"Yes, we'd all love to try," Adora said firmly, "but we have to find those flutterfocuses!" She turned to Gemma. "*Tessa* is in my Comparative Creatures class," she added, stressing Tessa's name. "She needs this information, too."

"Of course!" Gemma's eyes flashed. Her voice rose in agitation. "Tessa! The project! We don't have time for anything else!"

Suddenly, silence descended, as if a blanket had been thrown over Starling Academy, muffling all sound. The distant whir of the Cosmic Transporter, the faraway hum of the startrack, all the regular every-starday noise—the kind you didn't notice until it ceased—stopped. The light of the rainbow lamps shut off with a click.

The Starlings stared at the lampposts in disbelief. Another energy outage! They'd been happening more and more frequently.

"One, two, three . . ." Adora counted the starsecs, and at twenty-seven, the lights blinked back on.

"Really just a blip!" said Professor Findley Claxworth almost cheerfully. "And it helped me see my painting in a different light. It definitely needs a hint of purple to balance the colors more—" Then he seemed to catch himself. "Of course, these blackouts are terrible. Just terrible."

He smiled once more at the girls. "I hope to see you all in my next starmester classes. Adora, look into Art of Wishing. It's a high-level elective!" And he slipped inside his house.

Gemma grabbed Adora's arm. "Oh, my stars! Did you hear him? The professor actually likes the outages! He could be behind the energy shortage, the one who's trying to mess up our missions."

Libby gasped. "Maybe he thinks we'd all create more art if Starland ran out of energy! If we didn't have Star-Zaps or transporters or swift trains, we'd all slow down and really look at things." She shook her head, confused. "Not that it would be bad to focus on art."

"Let's not think about good or bad, or why or why not," Adora said. "And let's not jump to conclusions! We can discuss art versus science all starday long when Starland is on track again."

She paused to check her Star-Zap. They really had to leave. They'd spent way too much time there already, and the other Star Darlings might be waiting.

"But right now, let's find Lady Stella's house."

CHAPTER
4

Adora led the two younger Starlings around the village green to look at the row of houses facing the Crystal Mountains. She kept her eyes open for the headmistress's house. Lady Stella had a classic kind of beauty. She wasn't flashy—not like that globe-shaped house with hydrongs of stars shooting out the chimney. Or that hot-pink one with bright yellow shutters opening and closing as if it was rapidly blinking.

Lady Stella was stately; she moved in a calm, unhurried way. Adora had admired her from the starmin they'd met. She couldn't really be guilty of sabotage, could she? That would be truly devastating.

Something caught in Adora's throat.

Odd, thought Adora. *Am I coming down with star pox?*

She pushed the possibility out of her mind and concentrated on Lady Stella.

She'd been reserving judgment on the headmistress, determined not to brand her innocent or guilty until all the evidence was in and the findings were incontrovertible. Still, thinking about Lady Stella's powerful, dignified presence made Adora long for her to be innocent.

One olive-colored house caught her eye. It stood in a far corner, tucked between two rare and beautiful kaleidoscope trees that were constantly shifting colors. Its lines were simple yet elegant, its color understated but glowing. A calm golden-white light radiated from its windows.

"That must be it," she whispered. Libby and Gemma nodded.

Adora took a holo-pad out of her coat pocket and quickly sketched a flutterfocus. "This can be our cover if we see anyone else," she added.

"On the farm, Tessa always chased flutterfocuses." Gemma began to prattle, as if they were really working on a class project. Adora let her talk as they skirted other houses. But when they drew closer to Lady Stella's home, she held up a hand for silence. Then she pulled them behind a kaleidoscope tree.

"Hush. We need to be quiet now. Lady Stella knows too much about our classes and homework for the flutter-focuses to work."

She peered through the color-shifting leaves. Lady Stella was nowhere to be seen.

"Are you sure this is her house?" whispered Gemma, beginning to panic once again.

"*Shhh!* Do you hear that?" Adora hissed. Straining to listen, they caught the faint *click-clack* sounds of snipping scissors.

"It's coming from the backyard," Libby said in a low voice.

The three girls nodded at one another. Then they crept along the side of the house until they reached a corner. Peering around, they saw Lady Stella.

She was standing in front of a large, lovely garden ringed by goldenella trees. Glittery yellow calliopes mixed with orange chatterbursts. Coral-colored roxy-linda flowers twined around the purple zelda blooms. Glitterbees buzzed between rows, and a sweet fragrance wafted through the air.

A glowzen pairs of scissors hovered near Lady Stella, as if at rest.

Lady Stella sipped from a tall glass of sparkle juice. Then she waved one arm at the scissors. The scissors seemed to bow, then flew from flower to flower, snipping off brittle leaves.

Lady Stella worked at a leisurely pace, directing the scissors while more tools hovered nearby, ready to work. Clearly, the gardening had just begun.

"The garden is huge," Libby whispered. "This could take a very long time."

Adora agreed. "Lady Stella won't be going to her office at all this afternoon. We need to tell the others. To the hedge maze!"

★

"Okay, who had the bright idea to meet here?" asked Gemma, pouting a bit.

Adora, who was standing next to Gemma in front of the maze, held back a smile. "It was me. Bet you wish you had paired with Vega now."

Somehow, Vega always knew her way around the maze. A world-class puzzle solver, she actually enjoyed taking tests and figuring out answers. Adora had tried to get Vega's input on an experiment or two over the staryears, but Vega had made it clear she didn't like the guesswork involved. She liked tried-and-true answers, resolutions that had been studied for eons.

"Don't worry," Adora said, trying to reassure

Gemma and Libby, neither of whom had spent much time in the hedge maze. "We'll find our way sooner or later. It's all a matter of trial and error."

Linking arms with the younger Starlings, Adora led them through the maze entrance.

Inside, the tall hedges seemed to tower even higher. It was impossible to gauge location or get a sense of direction. Paths curved this way and that, twisting and turning at every step.

Should we go right? Adora wondered. *Or left? Forward? Or back?*

It didn't matter that she'd visited just the other starweek and had found her way in two shakes of a glion's tail. The maze changed constantly. One starday you could guess correctly and walk straight to the center. But the next, the same path would take you stars knew where. At least with the Glowin' Glions game going on that day, it would most likely be empty.

Star-Zap mapping functions didn't work there, and not everyone enjoyed the challenge. If you panicked—like Gemma was about to, Adora guessed—you could pick one of the red flowers that were placed strategically on every wall and open an exit.

Adora, Gemma, and Libby wandered aimlessly, Gemma growing more fidgety with every dead end.

"Let's head back to the entrance and start over," Adora said, turning everyone around. The next thing she knew, they were standing in the center of the maze.

Vega and Piper were already there.

Piper was relaxing in a comfy lounge chair with a headrest of soft pillows. She reached into a deep pocket of her long flowing dress and took out a sleep mask.

Why does she always carry sleep masks? Adora wondered. *Why close your eyes to the worlds when a universe of possibilities stands right in front of you?*

Vega, meanwhile, sat stick-straight on a stone bench, staring at them with a relieved expression.

"You're finally here!" she cried, jumping up. "Piper and I have been here so long she's falling asleep."

"Not quite," said Piper, taking off the mask. "I'm just using the time to regroup." She turned to Adora. "I'm getting a strong vibe: the others are close by."

Vega hurried toward the path. "I'll poke around and see if I can find them. Be back in a starsec."

Adora had barely settled into a seat when Vega returned with the rest of the Star Darlings.

Leona flung herself onto the lounge chair, squeezing in next to Piper. "Scoot over, Piper. I need to rest my weary bones." She lifted one foot to examine the sole of her delicate golden sandal. "Scarlet and her combat boots would have done better tramping all over Starling Academy and through this maze. I am so done!"

Piper adjusted a pillow for her. "Star salutations," Leona murmured.

"Don't get too comfortable," Adora warned. "We should move quickly. Lady Stella is busy at home, but—"

"We have to tell you about the faculty housing," Libby said excitedly. "It's so starmazing."

Sage looked at Libby eagerly. Everyone else regarded her with amused expressions. "We've all been there," Astra said.

"Well, how could we be sure?" Gemma asked. "Adora—"

"Let's get back to Lady Stella," Adora said quickly. "She's gardening. I'm not sure when she'll finish. And we don't know who else may be near her office. So we should divide into small groups, again, to avoid suspicion."

She noticed Gemma and Libby edging closer to Vega.

"We'll all leave the maze together," she added. "Vega, you go first."

With Vega leading the way, it took only a starmin to exit the hedge maze. Outside, Adora decided to stay on her own. It seemed simplest; that way she could avoid any complicating opinions or outbursts.

She made a wide circle around Halo Hall, not seeing

a glimmer of another Starling. She thanked her lucky stars for the star ball game. Quickly, Adora ducked into a side entrance. Glancing over her shoulder—still no one in sight—she hurried down a gleaming starmarble hall. She had just turned a corner when she spied Leona and Sage ahead. *Might as well stick together,* she thought, rushing to catch up.

Just as she reached the others, a Bot-Bot swooped over their heads, stopping to block their path.

Adora caught her breath. Was it a security guard?

"Mojay! What are you doing here?" asked Sage.

Mojay? That didn't sound like any Bot-Bot name Adora had ever heard before. Not willing to say anything aloud in case the Bot-Bot was recording, she turned to Sage and raised her eyebrows.

"Oh, Mojay is really MO-J4, but that sounds so . . . um . . . robot-like!" Sage finished. "He was my tour guide when I first came to school. And we've developed a bit of a . . . um, friendship."

The Bot-Bot seemed to smile.

"That's so cute!" said Leona.

To Adora, this was quite startling. All Bot-Bots were polite and—she hoped—programmed to be well meaning. But she'd never seen one with a personality before.

"I'm on security detail," Mojay explained. "Are you

girls here to look for a lost holo-textbook? I spotted a few in the Astral Accounting lecture hall." He winked. "I won't tell your professor. Promise."

"Star salutations!" Adora said before Sage could say a word. "We'll look there right now!" She pulled Sage and Leona down the hall.

"Wait!" called Mojay. "Astral Accounting is the other way."

Adora hit her head. "Of course, you're right!" The three girls turned in the other direction and kept walking until Mojay was gone.

"You didn't need to lie," Sage complained. "Mojay is totally trustworthy."

"You never know," Adora told her. "We need to be careful." Still, it pained Adora to lie once more. Even little light lies went against her scientific, accurate-to-a-fault mindset. But right then it seemed necessary.

Adora glanced around cautiously. "And if there's one Bot-Bot guard, there's bound to be more."

The three girls pressed themselves against the wall, then continued toward Lady Stella's office. The other Star Darlings were quietly moving up behind them as they neared the door.

Adora grinned. *Almost there. Just a few more steps.*

Suddenly, she spied another guard, coming from the opposite direction.

She stopped short. "Oh!" cried Sage, bumping into her from behind. A chorus of "ohs" followed as, one after the other, the still-moving Star Darlings bumped into the ones who'd stopped.

"We're like a clown act from the circus!" Clover joked. Everyone laughed—until they saw the guard.

"What are we going to do?" cried Gemma.

"Calm down and go back around the corner until it's all clear," said Adora. "I'll try to distract it."

As the Bot-Bot neared, Adora slipped away from the others, running up and down halls to make a U-turn and approach the Bot-Bot from behind. She carefully took out the test tubes she was carrying, mixed them together, and threw them against the wall, knowing there would be an explosion.

Bang! It worked!

The Bot-Bot swiveled around. It swooped to the wall, examined the broken glass and liquid mixture, and took a sample before it all disappeared. *Good*, thought Adora. It would take the specimen to the school lab for analysis. That should take some time.

Meanwhile, Adora raced back to Lady Stella's office.

By then the girls were crowded around the door. Each girl placed her hand on the scanner, and each time it beeped and turned red.

Of course the door is locked, Adora told herself sternly. *Why didn't I think of that earlier?* And the Bot-Bot was already back, flying toward them once again. She needed another distraction.

But she'd used up her bag of scientific tricks. Now what?

CHAPTER
5

"Halt!" the Bot-Bot guard called out to the Star Darlings.

In her head, Adora ran through a list of ideas, explanations of why they were there. Then she logically discarded each one. Finally, she had it.

"How about a starring role in 'Fainting on the Floor While Searching for My Homework'?" she whispered to Leona.

"I accept," said Leona.

Quickly, Leona strode to the center of the hall, away from the other Star Darlings, and clutched her head.

"Moons and stars!" she cried. "All of a sudden, I don't feel well. I was trying to find my Astral Accounting holo-textbook . . . but now I don't know where I am. Everything is a blur!"

The Bot-Bot snapped to attention.

Leona staggered farther from the girls—and the door—then collapsed on the floor.

Meanwhile, Adora led the others around the corner to hide.

"Do not worry. I am programmed to aid in emergency situations," said the Bot-Bot tonelessly.

"Please, please," Leona said softly as it hovered above her. "Get help."

"I will not leave you. I will call for more Bot-Bots."

"No!" Leona sat up quickly. Then she realized her mistake and lay back down. "No, please," she whimpered.

"I'll give her a gold star for acting," Adora said, watching from her hiding place.

"I need you to get help," Leona continued. "Make sure the EMBs bring a stretcher. Don't signal them— bring them here so there's no misunderstanding."

That's good, Adora thought. *Getting Emergency Medical Bots might take a while.* Of course, that was what she'd thought about taking the explosive mixture to the lab!

"Bring them . . ." Leona paused. "And my mother."

"Your mother," the Bot-Bot repeated.

Adora clapped a hand over her mouth to keep from laughing.

"Where is your mother located exactly?"

"Probably in the shoe store," Leona gasped.

Adora knew Leona's family worked in the shoe business—not show business. Locating that one tiny shoe store would prove difficult for the guard. Leona really was a starmendous improviser.

"There are no shoe stores in Starling Academy."

"It's in Flairfield."

Adora elbowed Clover. Flairfield was floozels away.

Leona shut her eyes and lay very still, barely breathing.

"Miss?" said the Bot-Bot. "Miss? I am not programmed for these kinds of decisions."

Leona stayed quiet.

The Bot-Bot floated above her uncertainly, then took off in the direction of Health Services.

Immediately, Leona popped to her feet. She met Adora and the others back at the door.

"We don't have much time," Adora whispered loudly. "Who knows when that guard will come back?"

"And what if it actually brings my mother?" Leona added.

Adora didn't answer. She and the others stared at the door. There didn't seem to be much else to do.

As every Starling Academy student knew, individual wish energy manipulation didn't work on locked doors.

Still, Adora thought, they didn't know for a fact that a group of nine advanced students, working together, couldn't open one small locked door.

"Let's try doing this all at once," she suggested. Everyone stared hard at Lady Stella's office door. "On the count of three," she continued. "One, two, and—"

All the Star Darlings focused, seeing in their minds' eyes the door whooshing open.

It didn't move a star inch.

They tried again and the result was conclusive: they couldn't do it.

Astra pulled Adora aside. "When Libby and I were on Wishworld, we got locked out of the auditorium, and she used her Power Crystal to open the door."

Adora rubbed her hands excitedly. "Good thinking," she said. Adora faced the group. "Okay, anyone who has a Power Crystal, take it out now and we'll see what they can do."

Libby, Astra, Sage, Vega, and Piper hurriedly took out their crystals.

"Show-offs," muttered Leona, stepping back.

Get over it! Adora was about to tell her. *So your Wish*

Pendant burned to a crisp while you were coming home after your mission. So you didn't bring back wish energy or receive your Power Crystal. Figure out what you can do now!

Instead, Piper spoke up. "Leona," she said almost sternly, "you should be sending positive thoughts. That could be your way to help."

Adora did believe in positive energy; she'd seen its effects for herself. Once, when her star-sewing machine had some sort of breakdown, she'd visualized it rethreading, concentrated fiercely, and somehow the machine had righted itself.

"Gemma, Clover, and I will add our positive thoughts, too," Adora said. So five Star Darlings placed their Power Crystals on the door while four others sent out positivity vibes.

The door stayed shut.

The girls tried again and again, but each time their energy grew weaker. Finally, they gave up.

"Well," said Leona, "guess those little old Power Crystals aren't as powerful as you thought."

"You're right," said Adora dejectedly. *Why do the Power Crystals work on Wishworld, but not on Starland?* she wondered. *That is very curious.* She examined the door one last time, just to make sure. It was still closed tightly.

She gazed out the window and saw a group of Bot-Bots heading toward the building entrance. They carried a stretcher.

"The EMBs are here," she told the others. "We need to leave and come up with another plan."

She heard a noise, a soft thud of some sort, close behind them. She whirled around to see Leona giggling—in front of the open door!

"How did you do that?" she asked.

"I leaned on it and it slid open!" said Leona.

"This way," the guard called to the other Bot-Bots. "The student is around the corner."

Adora peered inside the office. "It's empty," she whispered. "Hurry!"

Quickly, the girls slipped inside and closed the door behind them.

"Where is the student in distress?" one EMB asked in a level voice. On the other side of the door, Adora raised a finger to her lips, signaling the others to keep quiet.

"I do not know," said the guard.

There was the sound of some movement. Maybe the EMBs were putting down the stretcher to search the area.

"She was here just a few starmins ago," the guard added.

"GR-D3," the EMB said, "you just returned from a technical support appointment, did you not?"

"Maybe," said the guard.

"You cannot even answer that. Clearly your rewiring tune-up was faulty."

"Yes," the guard agreed. "Star excuse my false report." Then there was silence.

"They left," Adora whispered. She glanced around the office. There was the familiar silver table, where they'd gathered many times for Star Darlings meetings.

There were the huge picture windows and the holo-bookcase. And there were the other Star Darlings, of course. But the room seemed empty without Lady Stella. It was uncomfortable—maybe even wrong, Adora considered. It was almost a lie to be there without permission, and it was strange not to have Cassie, Tessa, and Scarlet with them.

The girls stood close together in the center of the room. They looked at one another guiltily. Gemma gripped Adora's hand, her face flushed orange with fear and concern.

"It's all right," Adora said calmly. "But let's not linger. There's the desk."

Of course everyone knew the desk was there. Everyone knew it had a secret drawer, with a button to open a hidden door, the entrance to the Star Caves. Adora just felt she had to say something to get everyone moving.

As a group, the girls shuffled closer to the desk, then stopped. No one wanted to go to the other side, where Lady Stella usually sat so regally, her back straight, her expression calm and reassuring.

Adora almost changed her mind. What if she told everyone they should leave, not mess with Lady Stella's desk, and find another way to rescue their friends? She shook her head to clear it. No, they had to do this—now. "Maybe someone should open the drawer?" she said, still a little hesitant.

No one stepped forward.

Finally, Leona said, "For stars' sake, let's just get it over with!" She edged behind the desk and opened the drawer.

"Oh!" she gasped. Her golden glow paled, and her eyes widened in shock.

"What?" cried Adora. "What is it?"

She hurried to the other side, but Leona half closed the drawer and blocked her view.

"It's n-n-n-nothing," Leona stammered. "Everything is fine. I just saw a twelve-legged rainbow orb spider in there."

"Oh," said Gemma, looking interested. "Can I see?"

"No!" Leona said quickly. She peered back inside. "It's gone already." She smiled a little shakily. "You know me. I can't stand the sight of any creepy crawly." Then she reached into the drawer and pressed the button.

Behind them, the hidden door in the back wall slid open. Again, the girls exchanged glances. *This is it*, Adora thought. She set her Star-Zap on flashlight mode, and the others followed her lead. Then she started down the curving metal stairs, the line of Star Darlings behind her.

CHAPTER
6

"**Wait!" Adora called** up the stairs just as the last girl, Astra, was about to close the door behind them. "We need to keep the door open so we can get out when we're done."

"Okay," said Astra. "I'll do it."

Of course Adora trusted Astra. The Starling had, after all, recently come back from a successful mission. How difficult could it be to leave the door open just a crack? But Adora liked to control every experiment as best she could, and that went stardouble for times like those. She hurried back up the steps, waving the others forward.

Adora checked that the door was open, just a bit,

then turned to leave. But she heard a soft murmur. Voices drifted through the crack.

"Wait!" she whispered. "It's Lady Stella! And she's talking to someone."

Adora stood on the top step uncertainly. Should she and Astra catch up with the others? Or should they eavesdrop and maybe learn a thing or two about Lady Stella? She decided to listen in.

"Can you hear anything?" Adora whispered to Astra.

Astra cocked her head, concentrating. "Not really." She reached into her sports bag and took out two empty water bottles. She handed one to Adora. Then she placed the other one against the wall, the bottom against her ear.

"Don't laugh," she told Adora softly. "It transmits the sound and helps you hear. I caught my little brother eavesdropping on my parents this way!"

Adora lifted the bottle. She could hear a little more clearly, it was true, but it was still more mumbling than actual words.

Then the bottle slipped from her hands. It clattered to the solar metal steps. The voices stopped, and Adora froze. She and Astra stood as still as statues. Finally, the voices continued. Adora bent to pick up the bottle. Then a thought struck her: what if she had to sneeze?

All of a sudden, as if the mere thought of sneezing could make it happen, she felt a tingle in her nose. *For stars' sake*, she thought. *This is ridiculous.* She clamped two fingers on the sides of her nose as Astra looked at her curiously. Finally, the feeling passed.

"Are you all right?" Astra whispered. Adora nodded, gesturing that they should listen through the water bottles again. *More star craziness*, she thought.

But Lady Stella and her visitor must have moved closer to the back wall. Adora could hear them more clearly now.

"This is happening even faster than I imagined," Lady Stella was saying. "Starland is losing energy every starday."

The headmistress sounded the same as ever, calm and steady. If she thought the energy shortage was a serious problem, wouldn't she be anxious? And if she was engineering the whole thing, wouldn't she sound more pleased?

A second voice answered. "On my end, wish energy scientists have been working hard to . . ." Adora heard the rustle of clothing as the Starling moved farther from the door, her voice fading. Adora could just make out the words *Cosmic Transporters . . . swift trains . . . energy supplies . . . a true crisis.* Then the voice sounded a bit more clear: "Two schools have temporarily shut down. And more may follow. It may be time to tell them. You can't keep it secret any longer."

Tell who what? Adora wondered.

Lady Stella spoke next, but Adora couldn't catch anything at all. Astra grabbed Adora's arm. "I recognize that other voice!" she hissed.

"Who is it?"

"I'm not sure. I don't think I know her, really, or have heard her say more than a few words before. I have to hear more."

Astra paused. "Or maybe I could just . . ." She flicked a wrist so the door opened a tiny bit wider. Then both girls peered through the opening. They saw Lady Stella's back and a figure in a lavender cloak facing her. Astra leaned closer. Suddenly, the door whooshed shut.

"Odd," Adora heard Lady Stella say. "I thought that door was closed. . . . I must have left it open when I *mumble mumble.*"

Did Lady Stella think she'd left the door open when she trapped Cassie, Tessa, and Scarlet? Or was she talking about something else entirely, like checking Wish Orbs?

It was so starmazingly confusing.

"Adora? Astra? We're waiting."

The Star Darlings were calling to them softly from the foot of the stairs. They couldn't waste any more time trying to listen. Adora squared her shoulders. They had to rescue their friends. And hopefully, when they did, Scarlet would know of another way out of the caves. Because now they were trapped, too.

★

The stairway to the caves wound round in spirals. At any given moment, Adora couldn't see past the step she stood on. Finally, she reached the bottom, pushed past the other Star Darlings, and once again led the way.

Plop . . . plop. The sound of dripping water grated on her nerves. Sage, behind her, stepped on her heel.

"Star apologies," Sage told her. "But maybe you could go a little faster?"

"Yes!" Gemma called down from behind them. "This is a rescue mission, you know!"

It was true that Adora didn't like to hurry. She walked the same way she thought: slowly and methodically. Haste, in the long run, interfered with reaching correct conclusions. Still, Adora moved a little more quickly. She wanted to help Tessa, Cassie, and Scarlet as much as anyone else did.

Finally, she reached a split in the cave. Now which

way should they go? Remembering other visits, she turned left. Slowly but almost surely, she led the girls down one long tunnel into the next. Really, it wasn't so bad down there. Even without Lady Stella's guidance, they were moving along.

Adora was congratulating herself on her leadership skills when she bumped smack into a boulder blocking the way. Could they squeeze past it?

She examined the passage more closely. Not even the thinnest Starling in Starland could get through. They'd have to take a detour.

Adora took the group to the right. She made a second right, then a third. By her calculations, that should have taken them around the boulder. Instead, they wound up in the same spot—directly behind it.

This time, they'd go left, Adora decided.

"You know," said Leona a few starmins later, when they found themselves stuck behind the boulder once more, "maybe this is some elaborate practical joke." She shot an angry look at Astra. "And no one likes a practical joker."

"What? Don't give me that solar flare, Leona. You know those jokes were out of my control. And do you think I'm having fun wandering around these tunnels? My star ball game must be over by now. Coach Geeta will bench me for a double starweek because I left in the middle. And I don't even know who won!"

Astra checked her Star-Zap to see if she could get the score, but the screen stayed dark. "*Starf!*" she said. "I forgot. Star-Zaps don't work underground."

"Except for the flashlights," Adora corrected Astra— accuracy was always important!—as she plowed ahead, mentally crossing off tunnel routes they'd already taken.

Then she stopped short. How could they possibly be behind the boulder again?

"If *we're* getting frustrated," Gemma said, hiccupping back a sob, "I can't even imagine what Tessa, Cassie, and Scarlet are going through. You know, Tessa likes wide open spaces. She's probably feeling claustrophobic."

Gasping, Gemma clutched her own throat. "I'm feeling it, too! I remember when Tessa and I were wee Starlings, and we got stuck in a Flash Vertical Mover. We didn't have any wish energy manipulation skills yet and—"

"*Starf!*" someone yelped.

"Sage?" Adora said, swiveling around. "Was that you?"

"Yes," Sage said with a groan. "I stubbed my toe."

Secretly, Adora was grateful that Sage's cry had at least ended Gemma's story. All the whining and bickering was distracting. And they really had to find the others.

"Piper!" she called, waving the Starling to her. "Can you sense if the girls are nearby?"

"Why, Adora!" Piper said, sounding surprised. Astra could hear the smile in her voice. "You're asking me to use my intuition? I'm flattered."

"Just do it," Adora said calmly. "I've used up all my reasoning skills, and you know I have an open mind. Besides, I think everyone has just about had it."

Piper closed her eyes and swayed dreamily. Adora tapped her foot impatiently. Finally, Piper opened her eyes. "I do sense another being."

"You do?"

All the girls leaned toward Piper eagerly. "She's coming closer. I believe we just need to wait." She paused, concentrating. "It might be Tessa or Cassie or Scarlet." She closed her eyes again. "Then again, it might be—"

"A bitbat," said Adora, stepping back as the small winged creature swooped in front of the girls.

The bitbat fluttered its wings, hovering in place. It held Adora's gaze for a moment. Then it went down the line of Star Darlings, stopping in front of each girl. Most stepped back, trying to put some distance between themselves and the creature. But Leona stared at it intently, actually edging closer.

"Leona!" said Adora. "What are you doing? You don't like bitbats, remember? You're always saying you're afraid they'll get caught in your hair."

Leona started to toss her curls, remembered herself, then pulled her hair back with both hands. "Of course I don't like them! But maybe this bitbat is the one that landed on Scarlet that time and it's trying to tell us something."

Leona looked at the bitbat again, then shook her head. "Forget it. That's crazy."

"Maybe; maybe not," said Adora. "The only way to find out is to give it a chance."

The bitbat flew to Adora, gave a funny little nod, then took off slowly down the tunnel back the way they'd come. Adora followed close behind, and the others filed after her.

The tunnel twisted again and again. Adora lost track of their path. *Stars crossed this works*, she thought.

At last the bitbat paused in front of a sheer stone wall.

"Well, this is just starmendous," Leona said crossly. "There's nothing here. What a waste of time."

Adora shook her head. "We don't know that yet. Cassie?" she called. "Tessa? Scarlet?" Her voice echoed eerily through the chamber.

The girls held their breath, waiting. But no one answered.

Adora sighed, disappointed. "Come on, bitbat," she urged. "Show us why you brought us here."

The bitbat swooped close to the wall, its wings brushing the stone. It moved around on the wall, almost in a pattern. . . .

"It's making a rectangle!" Adora exclaimed.

With every bitbat movement, the gray stone brightened, until Adora realized they were looking at a holo-screen.

The bitbat bowed, then flew away. They all stared at the screen, wondering what on Starland it could possibly mean.

"This is it," Piper said with certainty. "Tessa, Scarlet, and Cassie are on the other side of the wall. I can feel it. They just can't hear us."

Adora snapped her fingers at the holo-screen. She waved her hand in front of it. She placed her palm at different spots, hoping a hand scanner would appear. The screen stayed blank.

"Let's try our Power Crystals," Libby suggested.

"Yes, they were such a startacular success before," Leona said.

"Don't be sarcastic." Adora shook her head. "You never know."

Libby, Sage, Astra, and Vega waved their Power Crystals, but again, nothing changed.

Leona couldn't seem to help herself. "Like I said . . . big success."

Leona appeared to be correct. But Adora had a hypothesis and she wouldn't give up: if they activated the screen, they would find their friends. But how?

She searched again for a button, a lever, a scanner. They all set their Star-Zaps on the strongest flashlight mode, and she looked again, hoping to find something she'd missed. But there was nothing.

"Hey!" said Vega suddenly. "What about a password?"

"Great idea, Vega," said Adora. "Let's each try a word or phrase," she suggested. She knew it was a moonshot, but it was better than just standing there, doing nothing.

Piper stepped forward. "Dreaming is believing."

"Password denied," said a Bot-Bot voice as the phrase appeared on-screen, as well.

"Well, at least we know there is a password," Adora said reasonably.

Leona went next. "Wish Pendant," she practically hissed.

Nothing.

"We're never going to guess it!" Gemma cried. "It could be anything under the stars!"

Adora whirled around to calm Gemma, and her Star-Zap flew out of her hand and crashed to the floor. "Oh, moonberries!" she snapped, using her roommate's favorite new curse.

The holo-screen lit up. "Password accepted," said the voice, and a door slid open.

Inside, Cassie, Scarlet, and Tessa huddled on the ground.

Tessa jumped up, rushing to meet them. "Thank the stars you're here!" she cried. "Did you bring any food?"

CHAPTER
7

Everyone talked at once, and it was impossible to make out what anyone was saying.

"Wait a starmin!" Adora held up a hand. "Let's settle down and find out exactly what happened. Cassie, since you sent the holo-letter, why don't you explain?"

Cassie gestured at the room, which was filled floor to ceiling with shelves of ancient holo-books. "Okay, but come inside. I have to show you something important."

"First things first," said Tessa, looking expectantly at her sister.

Gemma handed Tessa the container of ozziefruit, along with some wrapped astromuffins.

Tessa flung her arms around her sister. "Star salutations, Gemma! You're the best sister ever! I'll tell Mom I was the one who left the barn door open that time when all the galliopes ran off."

"Good," Gemma said. "Because it *was* you."

Adora and the rest of the Star Darlings joined Cassie and Scarlet inside the room. With twelve girls and hydrongs of books, it was a tight squeeze. Scarlet stood to the side, careful to keep her distance as best she could. But Cassie pulled her into the center of the group.

She quickly explained how Scarlet had found another entrance to the caves through a supply closet, and how her special bitbat had brought them to the room.

"Hey!" said Gemma. "That must have been the same one we saw!"

"Anyway," Cassie said, "we found this." She held out an ancient-looking holo-book with a five-point star pulsing on the deep purple cover. "It's hard to read. The writing is dim and in some old-fashioned style. But there's one part . . ."

Her voice trailed off as she flipped through the pages. "Here!" She stopped about halfway through, and a holo-picture rose in the air, showing twelve girls in a circle. Each Starling had her own Wish Blossom. Energy from the flowers was flowing into the circle's center, gathering in a ball of light.

"I can't see from back here," complained Leona. "What does it say?"

"The writing explains a prophecy," Cassie explained. "An ancient oracle that predicts the future." She pointed out some words as they hovered in the air. "This part tells about twelve Star-Charmed Starlings who have a special gift: the ability to grant wishes and gather powerful wish energy."

"Twelve?" Adora said slowly. "So that must be us. We're the Star-Charmed Starlings!"

Adora smiled at Scarlet. If she had to take sides in the Leona versus Scarlet battle of the roommates, she might just choose the serious loner over the social flutterfocus. Who else would have explored the tunnels and found that room?

Without thinking, the girls drew together in a circle. Even Scarlet reached out to hold hands with Sage and Clover. They looked at one another in awe and disbelief.

"There's more," said Cassie. "The oracle says we save Starland."

The rest of the Star Darlings gasped in unison.

"Save Starland? From what?" Clover asked.

"I don't know," said Cassie.

Adora stared. Could that be what Lady Stella had been talking about in her office?

It was all so unbelievable that Adora found it difficult to take in. A moonium thoughts flew through her mind, lightning fast.

Why us? she wondered. Adora admired, respected, and basically liked all the other Star Darlings. Really, they were starmazing. But for them to be chosen like that, above all others on Starland . . . it took her breath away. Sure, they had been selected to go down to Wishworld ahead of the rest of their classmates. That was special enough. But the thought that they were actually part of an ancient prophecy . . . and that they were supposed to save Starland . . . from something—that was overwhelming news, indeed. It was a privilege, of course, but a huge responsibility, too. They had the weight of the worlds on their shoulders.

Still, it was an opportunity to change the course of Starland. Adora had always hoped to make a difference, to improve the planet with science *and* fashion. But this was something much, much bigger.

"Talk about being in the starlight," Leona said. She shook her head in disbelief. "We're the twelve Star-Charmed Starlings."

The words sounded like Leona, but she spoke so quietly that Adora turned to study her for a moment. Ever since they'd started their rescue mission, Leona's glow had been pale. Something was definitely bothering her.

Adora gazed around the room to see how the others were taking the news. Sage and Libby were whispering excitedly, but everyone else seemed overwhelmed. Vega had a blank expression, as if this didn't fit into her practical worldsview. Adora understood. Being selected to go on Wish Missions was one thing. But this took the Star Darlings to a whole other level—a cosmic one!

Finally, Cassie spoke again. "And this all brings us back to Lady Stella. She must know about this ancient oracle. She brought us together, after all. So why is she keeping this secret from us? Is it part of an evil plan?"

"It has to be!" Scarlet said loudly.

"Then why did she form the Star Darlings at all?" Sage countered.

"Well, if we're part of an ancient oracle, there's a good chance we would have come together on our own anyway," Cassie said seriously. "My theory is that Lady Stella organized us so she can keep an eye on us, control us . . . driving us apart on Starland with poison flowers and nail polish . . . interfering with our missions on Wishworld."

Scarlet took a deep breath and flung her hood over her head. "She could be keeping us from actually saving Starland," she said.

Adora weighed Scarlet's and Cassie's words. They made some sort of sense.

"I disagree!" cried Libby. "Lady Stella could just as easily be keeping everything secret to protect us. Too much knowledge could make us panic. It's a lot of pressure knowing the fate of Starland rests in our hands, isn't it?"

Adora nodded slowly, eyeing Gemma, who still held tightly to Tessa's hand.

"All that knowledge could have have jeopardized our missions," Sage added, "making us second-guess our every move—and put us in danger! Luckily we didn't know—"

"Ahem," said Clover. "Some of us haven't had a mission yet."

"Oops!" said Sage. "You know what I mean." She smiled broadly at Clover, then Gemma, then Adora. "You'll do starmendously, I know it! There's nothing to worry about at all."

"Yes, just the future of Starland," Scarlet added with a wicked grin. "No big deal, right?"

The girls erupted into arguments, some speaking in support of Lady Stella, some against. Adora listened to the debates, not judging, just thinking.

When there was a lull, Tessa stood up. "I really want to leave now. Can we all agree on that?"

"Yes, let's go back through the supply closet," Adora told everyone. "Lady Stella may still be in her office."

Everyone stood. But just as they turned to leave the room, the door slammed.

"Not again!" groaned Tessa. "Is it on a timer or is someone sabotaging us?"

The Star Darlings hurried to the door, pushing, pressing, waving Power Crystals, and flicking their wrists in a panic.

"Let's stay calm," Adora said quickly.

Cassie, next to her, turned paler than usual and whispered, "But we're all here. Who will rescue us now?"

"We'll have to find our own way out." Adora moved around the room, peering into all corners. "Maybe this is like Lady Stella's office, with a secret door."

"You know," Cassie said, joining her, "my uncle has written lots of detective novels. And in one of them, *The Trouble with Twilight*, there's a bookcase that spins around on a platform. The characters pull out a certain holo-book and it triggers the revolving bookcase, taking them into another room."

"Come on, Cassie," said Adora, shaking her head. "That's just fiction. The bookcase is a literary device to move the action along. We need to deal with real devices. Fact, not fiction."

Then a holo-title caught her eye: *The Great Escape*. Could it be? She pulled it off the shelf expectantly.

Cassie gasped.

"What?" Adora said a little impatiently. There was no revolving bookcase. Nothing even moved.

Silently, Cassie pointed to the empty space on the shelf—and the wall behind it. There was a hole in the wall, right at eye level, perfect for peeping.

Immediately, Adora peered through it. "Moons and stars!" she cried. "I see the Wish-House!"

She looked more closely. Yes, there it was: the tall windows, the glass roof, golden waterfalls of pure wish energy running down its sides.

Everyone rushed over, jostling a bit to get a better look. "There's got to be a way into the cavern," Adora said. She turned to Vega, who was good at figuring out the hedge maze. Maybe she could figure this out, too. "Any ideas?"

Vega rolled up her sleeves and moved random holo-books off the shelves. Nothing changed, but a satisfied expression crossed her face.

"Look!" she said. "There's a door around that peephole." Quickly, the Star Darlings pushed aside the remaining holo-books.

"A door!" said Tessa. "Do you think we can open it?"

"Not with your silly Power Crystals, I bet," said Leona. Then, before anyone could say or do anything else, she blinked at the wall. *Whoosh!* The door opened smoothly.

The girls wriggled over and under the shelves, making their way through the opening.

Adora was the last one through, and she joined the rest of the Star Darlings in the Wish-House, closing the door behind her. They stood there silently, staring. Lady Stella was already there, her back to them.

"Lady Stella!" Adora said with a gasp.

The headmistress whirled around. "Oh, my stars," she said, surprised. "I just sent you girls a holo-text saying a Wish Orb had been identified. When no one came to my office, I thought I'd check on the orb before you arrived. How in the stars did you get down so quickly?"

CHAPTER
8

How indeed? The Star Darlings all looked at each other, unsure of what to say. Adora took a deep breath.

"Well," she began, allowing herself to blush a shade of sky blue, "when we got your holo-text, it just so happened we were all together. You, um, must have left the door to your office open, so we let ourselves in. But you were nowhere to be seen. So star apologies, Lady Stella, but we used the secret drawer to open the passage. And here we are."

There wasn't one lie in the whole speech! Well, maybe some little light lies. *But still, not bad if I do say so myself,* Adora thought, relieved she'd managed to stick to a fuzzy kind of truth.

Lady Stella looked a bit doubtful and seemed about

to say more. But then the sunlight streaming into the cavern brightened dramatically—Adora had asked herself startime after startime how that worked underground—and Lady Stella bowed her head. "It must be time. Come, girls."

The Star Darlings moved to the center of the Wish Cavern and gathered around the grass-covered platform.

Adora's mind, usually so focused, buzzed with ideas, theories, and possibilities. That secret room . . . had someone tried to trap them there? Or was the door on a timer? And why was Lady Stella keeping so many secrets? Who had been that mysterious visitor in her office?

Adora's thoughts switched to the upcoming mission as the platform opened and a Wish Orb floated up into the room. The glittering ball could choose her, Adora knew. But she wouldn't get that special feeling so many of the others had at the sight of their orbs. She just didn't have that intuitive sense.

A couple of Wish Orb presentations before, in fact, she'd felt a definite tingle. *This is it*, she'd thought. *This Wish Orb is mine. I'm going on the mission!* But instead, the orb had settled right into Cassie's waiting hand.

Now she didn't have the slightest sense the orb would stop at her. It hovered between Gemma and Clover, and Adora sighed. She'd just have to wait until next—

Suddenly, the orb dipped and moved, swaying as if blown by a breeze. It first flew to Cassie, who unthinkingly reached out for it but then drew back her hand. Then it continued, moving a bit jerkily, to stop directly in front of Adora.

Adora held out her hands, and the orb landed on her palm as softly as a flutterfocus.

"The orb has chosen," Lady Stella said, just as always. Adora felt everyone's eyes on her, and she smiled. Each girl smiled back, even Scarlet, but Adora felt the tension in the room. They'd just learned the fate of Starland was in their hands—*and* they'd been trapped underground!

The gravity of the situation hit Adora like a load of starbricks. She'd be traveling mooniums of floozles away to a distant planet, away from her family and friends and everything she knew in the middle of a wish energy crisis. What if she got trapped there?

Adora brushed aside the thought. She would handle anything that came her way with logic and clarity, and it would turn out all right.

"That's it, then, girls," Lady Stella said with a sigh. She gathered herself and moved gracefully to Adora's side. The headmistress reached for Adora's hand and gave it a reassuring squeeze. Adora couldn't help herself:

she squeezed back. And for a moment, all doubts about Lady Stella flew out of her mind.

Aboveground once more, Adora hurried to get ready. She had to choose some Wishling clothes from her Wishworld Outfit Selector and compose a reminder list of everything she needed to do on Wishworld. Chronological order would be best, she thought—from folding up her shooting star to identifying her Wisher to collecting the wish energy.

Another list spelling out Wishworld tips would be helpful, too: keep track of the Countdown Clock, monitor energy levels, use the Mirror Mantra, figure out her special talent.

Adora walked into her dorm room, already starting to holo-type, her eyes on her Star-Zap. "Tessa?" she called. "Are you here?"

"We're all here," said Cassie.

Adora looked up with a start. The Star Darlings were grouped around the room, leaning toward her expectantly, as if they'd been waiting for her.

"What's going on?" she asked.

"Don't go!" said Leona, rushing over and flinging her arms around her tightly.

Adora waited a moment and then carefully removed herself from the embrace. She took a few steps back.

"Do you know how dangerous this mission could be?" Leona said, taking a few steps forward. "Someone is trying to stop us! Who knows what they will do?"

"Lady Stella *is* very powerful," Vega added.

"Anything could happen," Scarlet said.

"Stay home and bake astromuffins with me," Tessa cried.

All those Starlings in agreement! That was concerning. Clover wasn't telling any circus stories or cracking any jokes. And Cassie—smart as a glow-whip Cassie—was nodding seriously.

Adora looked at Sage and Libby, the strongest Lady Stella supporters. "What do you two think?"

They exchanged looks and Sage spoke up. "We want you to be safe. We don't want you to go, either."

Adora sat down at her lab table, her back to her friends. This was starmendously unusual. Everyone had come to her room to try to convince her to stay on Starland. Adora had read about this sort of gathering in a scientific holo-journal just the other starday. *Instarvention*, it was called.

In the holo-article, an astro-energy scientist on a quest to spot the mythical Galliope Comet could not stop looking through her telescope. She missed meals, bright days, even her own wedding. Finally, her family lifted her from her observation post, removed the telescope from her hands, and fed the scientist her favorite food—gamma-chip clusters—until she saw reason.

Reason, Adora said to herself. A key concept. Was it reasonable to go on the mission? Adora was nothing if not rational. She'd weigh the evidence.

First and foremost, no Starling had been hurt on Wishworld . . . at least, not yet. There had been Leona's return trip to Starland, during which she almost hadn't made it back . . . but that had been more of a cosmic fluke, Adora thought, since it hadn't happened again.

Plus, if she didn't go, Starland would definitely be in worse shape than it was now. There'd be no chance for extra wish energy. If she did go, she could very possibly help.

Besides, Adora felt confident she could reason her way out of any situation. As Lady Stella said, that was her strength: analyzing problems and figuring out solutions.

The good outweighs the bad, Adora decided. She turned to face the Star Darlings.

"I'm going," she announced. "And no one can convince me otherwise." She took a deep breath. "As one of the twelve Star-Charmed Starlings, it's my responsibility."

CHAPTER
9

The next morning, everything happened quickly. Right after breakfast, the Star Darlings headed to the Wishworld Surveillance Deck. Lady Cordial gave Adora the traditional Wishling backpack and keychain, and Lady Stella gave her last-minute instructions. *A cover-up?* Adora wondered. *Or a safety check?*

"Remember to figure out your special talent as quickly as possible," Lady Stella said. "That could make all the difference."

"I'll do my best," Adora agreed. Maybe that had been the problem with Leona's mission: she hadn't used her special talent. Adora put that at the top of her checklist.

Lady Stella smiled down at her. "Adora," she said

softly, "much rests on your mission. Rely on your strength: your ability to study situations with an objective mind, your aptitude to examine any circumstance from a distance. And remember to recite your Mirror Mantra when your energy is low: 'Use your logic. You are a star!' You will do fine and make us all proud."

Adora nodded. If Lady Stella's concern was just an act, she was an accomplished actress.

Next Adora made sure her Wish Pendant—a sky-blue watch with a star-shaped face—was securely fastened. Then the Star Wranglers strapped her to a shooting star and she took off, with barely a good-bye.

The journey through the universe was a bit bumpy, with plenty of time for the Star-Zap's outfit selector function to change her clothes. She'd chosen rolled-up denim shorts, a sky-blue sleeveless T-shirt, and sneakers designed with bright blue sequin circles.

Finally, she changed her appearance, reciting the lines "Star light, star bright, the first star I see tonight: I wish I may, I wish I might, have the wish I wish tonight."

"There," she said, gazing into her Star-Zap mirror, totally satisfied. She'd lost her shimmery glow, and her blue hair had turned a light brown. She looked washed-out and dull—perfect for Wishworld.

When she landed in a field of clover, no Wishlings were in sight. So she folded her star, placed it carefully in her backpack for the return trip, and gazed around.

It was peaceful and quiet. Just then, Adora had an idea. She stepped carefully around the field, looking for a four-leaf clover.

There! She spotted one! Quickly, she plucked it out of the ground. How lucky could one Starling get? And while she normally didn't believe in luck—perseverance and hard work paid off more in the end, she thought— she certainly wouldn't discount it now.

She'd learned in her Wishling Ways class that Wishlings used these clovers to make wishes—similar to those fluffy white flowers they blew on. So you never knew when one would come in handy. Besides, if she didn't use it, she could always give it to Clover for a souvenir.

She was still bending over close to the ground when she heard voices. She froze. All of a sudden, cool, confident Adora wasn't sure what to do. She'd just gotten back from helping Tessa on her mission. She'd navigated the route, found Tessa, and done her best to make a difference, all with ease.

But now she was the one responsible for success or

failure. It crossed her mind that she could be the first to complete a mission without another Star Darling helping out on Wishworld. That would be starmazing!

"This way, campers!" someone called.

Adora lowered herself to the ground so she was hidden in the long grass and clover. She peered across the field.

A straggly line of wee Wishling girls was following a bigger girl—not quite an adult, but older than Starling Academy students.

"Let's march, campers!" the girl called out. "Left, right. Left, right, left."

The little girls stomped their feet and did their best to follow the directions. But the line looked even worse than before.

"Jenny!" one said loudly. "Are we going straight to lunch?"

"You bet, campers!" Jenny sang out, not turning around. "Our nature hike is ending just in time."

Adora knew all about camp. For as long as she could remember, she'd gone to star camp over the Time of Lumiere break, during the warmest season on Starland. She fondly remembered making lightyards in stars and crafts and singing "Moonbaya" around the campfire.

Adora realized that school must be out and the Wishlings were enjoying their summer vacation.

The camp group disappeared into the distance. Adora decided to follow while she checked her Star-Zap for directions to her Wisher. *It must be someone at the camp*, she thought.

Sure enough, the directions told her to cross the field like the campers, then take a short trail through a wooded area. Adora stopped at the edge of the trees. A rustic complex spread out before her in a large open space.

There were playing fields off to one side. Games were winding up, it seemed, and many centered on nets.

There was that one called "basket of balls" that Astra had talked about. And another with a long net stretched across a rectangular court, where Wishlings hit a small green ball back and forth using smaller nets. Some shouted "Service!" before hitting the ball, as if they expected a Bot-Bot waiter to come and take their food orders.

It all seemed rather silly to Adora.

Adora looked at the other side. Large tents, built on solid wood platforms, ringed half the clearing. Beyond the trees she spotted a lake with a small sandy beach, floating docks, and canoes that looked too heavy to hover like the ones back home.

Large ramshackle buildings filled the center of the clearing. Each building had a sign in front: OFFICE. NURSE. MESS HALL.

Then she thought she must have misread one of the signs. She paused and read it again: " 'Mess hall.' "

Adora knew Wishling homes didn't have self-cleaning capabilities. Maybe at camp they just threw all their garbage into that one building.

A stream of Wishlings was heading into the mess hall as she watched. No one carried trash.

Then she spied the group of wee Wishlings she'd seen earlier. They were hurrying inside. Could they possibly be eating lunch there? She made a mental note in her Cyber Journal: *There is a strong possibility that Wishling campers eat garbage.*

Adora edged closer to the mess hall. She looked through a window and was relieved to see Wishlings sitting at picnic tables, eating what appeared to be regular Wishling food—not scraps of paper or old torn socks.

She was just about to amend her observation when one girl called out, "Where's the bug juice?"

Adora shivered. She'd just stick to water there. And she'd keep the observation in the journal, just in case.

Just then, a man hurried past, talking into a device like a Star-Zap but much clunkier. "Uncle Hal to Chef Jeff! Uncle Hal to Chef Jeff! Come in, Chef!"

Adora heard a crackling sound, and an indistinct voice answered.

"Running late," the first man continued. "Do not start lunch without me. Repeat: do not start lunch. First-day protocol must be maintained: Uncle Hal announces camp rules and greets campers. Repeat: first-day protocol must be maintained."

Adora was fascinated by this Wishling male, not a type she'd seen before.

The man—Uncle Hal—wore a T-shirt with a picture of a big brown creature on it. The creature had four legs and what looked like a big empty coatrack attached to its head. Beneath the picture, there was writing: *Director, Moose Lake Camp.*

Uncle Hal wore a big floppy hat, too, along with baggy shorts and white socks that went up to his knees. His nose was covered with some sort of white cream.

Uncle Hal stopped short when he noticed Adora by the mess hall. "Young lady!" he called out. "Did you just arrive? I need to make sure our campers and staff are accounted for. That's my job and my privilege."

Adora waved at a group of girls about her age walking

past. One girl, with short curly hair, waved back and smiled.

"I'm with them," she said, not answering his question.

"Oh, you're a CIT," Hal said, flipping through pages on his clipboard.

"Hmmm. It seems like everyone checked in already. Odd. What is your name?"

Adora looked him in the eyes and said, "My name is Adora. I'm a CIT." (She almost giggled. What did that even mean?) "You don't see my name on your list. But it doesn't matter."

"Hmmm," the man said again. "Your name is Adora. You are a CIT. I don't see your name on my list but it doesn't matter." He sniffed the air and lowered the clipboard. "Welcome, Adora. Do you smell prune bran muffins?"

Adora had learned about lots of foods in her Wishers 101 class. But prune and bran? Those were new ones.

"Never mind," Uncle Hal continued. He grinned, and Adora couldn't help smiling back. He was goofy and a little self-important but nice. "You can call me Uncle Hal."

Without waiting for a reply, he went on. "Right now, it's time for lunch." He puffed out his chest a bit. "Of course they won't start without me."

Adora snuck a look at her Star-Zap, trying to figure out if her Wisher was inside the mess hall. No, her Wisher was—

"Adora!" Uncle Hal said sternly. "There are no cell phones at camp. You should know that."

"Oh! Of course!" Adora said quickly.

"You must bring it to the office. They'll hold it for you there. And you can pick up your camp T-shirt at the same time."

"Yes, I'll do that before lunch," Adora told him. She had no intention of letting the Star-Zap out of her sight for one starmin. It was too important a tool.

Uncle Hal nodded, then strode off to the mess hall. Idly, Adora wondered if he was indeed anyone's uncle.

Smiling, Adora walked away, checking her Star-Zap. It directed her to the waterfront. Quickly, Adora made a detour to pick up the shirt—marked with the words *Counselor in Training.*

So that's it, she thought. *CIT!*

After stuffing the shirt in her backpack, she hurried to the lake.

It was pretty there. The water was a soothing shade of blue. A circle of tall, leafy green trees provided shade. And the brightly colored canoes were lined up on the side of the beach. She walked closer, peering all around.

Where was her Wisher?

Adora looked down at her watch. It glowed slightly. She was getting close. She edged to the canoes. Her Wish Pendant brightened.

"Hello?" she called. "Anybody here?"

No one answered, but Adora thought she heard a noise.

She walked to a large silver canoe and squinted at a shadow between the seats.

It was a girl, sitting on the canoe's bottom and leaning back so she was almost lying down. She had big green eyes and straight brown hair that fell to her shoulders, and she wore a Moose Lake CIT T-shirt.

Yes! Adora's Wish Pendant glowed with a brilliant light. She'd found her Wisher!

"Hello," Adora said.

The girl in the canoe turned away, as if she couldn't bear to face her. "Are you looking for me?" the girl asked quietly.

"Yes," said Adora, stepping into the canoe. It wobbled a bit, so she quickly sat down in the nearest seat at the other end. "I'm Adora."

The girl mumbled a response.

"What?" said Adora loudly.

The girl said even more quietly, "My name is *mumble mumble*."

"Speak up!" Adora said a little brusquely. This was getting tiring. What was so difficult about saying your name?

The girl sat up, her fair skin turning a bright red. "My name is Hannah."

"Okay," said Adora. "So, Hannah. Do you want to get lunch?" Traveling through space had made Adora very hungry, and she thought she could feel out her Wisher as they ate.

Hannah shook her head.

"Why not?"

Hannah shrugged, then slunk back down to the bottom of the canoe.

Well, if this Wishling could wait to eat, so could Adora.

She considered the situation: what would be the fastest way to identify the wish? If she took care of everything quickly, she'd be back home in the blink of a star—*and* be the first Star Darling to grant a wish all on her own. That would be something.

Adora favored the direct approach. What if she just asked outright?

"Hannah, do you have a special wish?"

"Huh?" The girl was so startled that she spoke loud and clear.

"Do you have a special wish?" Adora repeated. She sat back, waiting patiently—except that she couldn't stop tapping her toe.

Hannah drew herself into a ball, her arms hugging her legs. She looked for all the worlds like a Starland pricklepine curling up for protection.

Adora sighed. This wasn't going well at all. "Clearly, you're a shy Wish—I mean, girl." She smiled widely, if a little falsely. "Some of my best friends are shy."

That was the truth. Adora considered Cassie a friend. Yes, Cassie was outspoken about her conspiracy theories, and she'd managed a Wishworld mission just fine. But she'd barely spoken to anyone her first double starweek at school. And she'd dreaded going on a mission until that poisonous nail polish had made her annoyingly braggy.

Maybe this girl was new at camp. Maybe she needed to be drawn out of her shell. That wasn't Adora's strength, but she'd give it a try.

"I'm new here," she told Hannah. "Is this your first time at camp, too?"

Hannah shook her head. "It's my fifth summer," she whispered.

Well, there went *that* idea. Suddenly, Adora had another idea. She reached into her backpack for the four-leaf clover. "Here," she said, handing it to Hannah.

Hannah's eyes widened. "A four-leaf clover. For good luck!"

"Go on," Adora urged. "Make a wish."

Hannah blushed, turning her back to Adora. "I-I-I . . ." she stuttered. Then she stopped.

Clearly, Hannah wanted to make a wish. She just didn't want to make it in front of Adora. "I'll step away," said Adora, pleased with herself for understanding the situation so well.

She climbed out of the canoe and walked to the edge of the lake, deliberately leaving her Star-Zap—set on record—on the canoe bottom.

She waited a bit, counting—"one Starland City, two Starland City"—until she reached a hydrong, then returned to Hannah.

"Oops!" she said. "I left my cell phone here. I'm not even supposed to have one! I'd better bring it to the office."

Adora moved out of Hannah's earshot, then played the recording: "I wish I had the confidence to make friends," Hannah said, her voice thin and quiet.

Wish identification accomplished! Adora allowed herself a starsec to savor her success.

If she could help grant the wish right then, she'd definitely have the record for fastest time. "Not that I'm competitive," she added to herself under her breath. She turned back to Hannah.

"So," she said brightly, "I really think we should go to the mess hall. There are some girls there who seem really nice. You seem nice, too. Maybe we can all be friends!"

Hannah stood up, rocking the canoe. "You were eavesdropping!"

Adora groaned. Now they were back in that fuzzy area of truth versus lies. Was it okay telling a little light lie to grant a wish? In all fairness, that was a technicality. Strictly speaking, Adora had heard the *recording*, not Hannah as she was making the wish.

"Star—I mean, I'm sorry, Hannah," Adora said. "It was none of my business." (That actually was a lie. Hannah's wish was most certainly her business.)

Hannah sank onto a canoe seat. "It's all right, I guess. You're new here. You'd like to make friends. I understand. But you see, I did have friends here. Two best friends. We started camp together the first year we were old enough for sleepaway. We were close right from the start. Uncle Hal called us the triplets. Every summer was fun. And we kept in touch during the school year, too."

Hannah's voice caught, and she paused. She squeezed her eyes shut, holding back tears.

Adora nodded encouragingly. But she couldn't resist a look at the Countdown Clock on her Star-Zap. She was definitely on track for breaking the wish-granting record.

"But this year, my friends didn't come back," Hannah continued. "One is traveling with her family. The other decided to go to science camp instead."

Science camp? Really? Why couldn't that girl have been my Wisher? Adora wondered. It would have been a much better match. This Wishling was a wreck!

"And my parents didn't tell me any of this until the day before camp started," Hannah whimpered. "So I had to come! And now I'm here alone."

Finally, tears slipped down her cheeks.

"Well, you're not really alone," Adora said logically. "You're surrounded by girls your age and other people. Were those other CITs here other summers, too?"

"Some," Hannah admitted.

"And do you like them?" Adora prodded her.

Hannah shrugged. "I guess so," she said.

"So just go up to them and talk. They're in the mess hall right now!" *There*, she thought. *Problem solved. Wish granted.*

"It's not that simple," said Hannah.

"It can be," Adora insisted. "You're talking to me, right?" Then she added quickly, in case Hannah thought that she could be her new friend, "You should know I'm only a . . . a TCIT—a Temporary Counselor in Training. I'll be leaving very soon."

"I didn't know that was allowed," said Hannah eagerly. "Maybe I can be a TCIT, too, and leave with you?"

This isn't working at all, Adora thought exasperatedly. "Uncle Hal said he'd make an exception for me, just this once. It turns out I have a family emergency. Something really bad happened. To my house. And we have to . . . to move and . . . and . . . other stuff!"

Adora stopped, realizing she'd just told outright lies. She'd expected to tell some. After all, she couldn't be on a strange planet and fit in without lying. But she hadn't thought they would be such big fat ones.

"Oh!" Hannah cried harder. "You're going through something terrible. And here I am, so worried about myself and my problems! I feel horrible."

This was even worse. Awkwardly, Adora put her arms around the Wishling. "There, there," she said. "Don't cry."

Hannah sobbed.

Adora raised her voice and said, "Don't feel bad on my account. Really." These lies were definitely backfiring! "I have another idea for how you can make friends. And it will make me feel better if you feel better."

"Okay." Hannah wiped her eyes.

"Do all the CITs share a tent?"

"Yes."

"So it will be like a sleepover every night!" Adora exclaimed. "You'll definitely make friends. You know, whispering in the dark, sharing secrets." Adora didn't know much about sleepovers, actually. But that's what happened when Libby had one right before Piper's mission.

"I chose the bed in the corner, away from everyone else. I'm too far to whisper. So that's not going to happen." Hannah sniffled.

"What about your CIT job? Won't you be working with other girls?"

"No, I'm helping with arts and crafts. Uncle Hal is in charge, and I'll be his assistant. That's why I'm just hanging around today. There aren't any special activities until tomorrow." She sniffled louder.

Oh, starf! Was Hannah going to burst into tears again? Why was this Wishling so emotional? They were such an unlikely match!

"You should just leave," said Hannah, sensing Adora's annoyance. "Go on. You can hang out with the other CITs." She reached to the ground, tracing a sad face in the sand.

Adora frowned. Now Hannah didn't even want to talk to her. She'd rather draw starmojis in the sand.

Just then, Adora heard a strange buzzing. From the corner of her eye, she spied a tiny winged creature flying around her head. Peering closer, she saw it had a yellow-and-black-striped body and looked a bit fuzzy—like a glitterbee without the sparkle.

Two more Wishworld insects flew down from some sort of nest in a nearby tree. They joined the first, and then even more swarmed closer. *Bzzzz, Bzzzz.*

Adora held out a finger, hoping one would land on her so she could observe it more closely.

"What are you doing?" Hannah jumped out of the canoe. Her voice rose in panic.

What was with that Wishling? One starmin you could barely hear her speak; the next she was practically shrieking. It was like Hannah was on an emotional star coaster.

"Obviously, I want to get a closer look," Adora said, trying not to snap. It would be an interesting observation to add to her journal.

"Those are bees! You're going to get stung!"

Stung? Glitterbees were sweet and gentle. On Starland, no insects or bugs had stingers, and it took a moment for Adora to realize what that meant. She sat very still and considered the situation. Should she stay close to the bees as an experiment? What would a Wishworld bee sting feel like? Would it be worth it to be able to make an accurate observation?

In the end, Adora decided against it. And that was just as well, since the bees were flying over to Hannah, attracted to her movements.

The bees circled Hannah as she moved left and right, trying to dodge each one. Some landed on her arms and legs. One landed on her nose.

"Ouch! Ouch! They're stinging me!" she cried, batting them away.

Adora started running toward the dock. "Follow me!" she cried. Hannah followed close behind her. "Now jump in!" Adora commanded. Hannah hesitated for a split second, grabbed her nose, and leaped.

A moment later, she popped to the surface. "That was really smart," she told Adora as she paddled to the shore. She shook herself. "I just wish I had taken my sneakers off first."

"You did what you had to do," said Adora. "I'm glad it worked."

Hannah held out her arms. "Look at all those bee stings," she said. "They really hurt."

Adora examined the red bumps individually. Curious, she touched the one on the end of Hannah's nose. Hannah flinched.

Adora watched the bump get smaller . . . and smaller . . . and smaller . . . until it disappeared.

"Hey, my nose doesn't hurt anymore!" said Hannah.

Adora touched another sting, on Hannah's arm. That one disappeared, too.

"That's crazy!" said Hannah, holding out her other arm to show Adora more stings.

Adora touched the red spots one by one. They all disappeared.

"Wow!" Hannah said. "How did you do that?"

Thinking quickly, Adora spotted a bottle on a nearby picnic bench and picked it up. The label read SPOT-ON SUNSCREEN. Adora had no idea what sunscreen even was. But when she opened it, it looked like the cream Uncle Hal had been wearing on his nose. She figured it wouldn't hurt Hannah. And it wouldn't hurt to tell just one more little light lie.

Adora ran one finger along the bottle's cap. "I just put this on the bites!"

Hannah looked confused but shrugged. "I guess sunscreen helps bee stings, too."

Adora grinned. She'd just discovered her special talent: she could heal bee stings!

Then she noticed a scratch on Hannah's arm. "Can I try to make this better, too?" she asked.

Hannah nodded. So Adora smeared a bit of lotion on her arm, carefully touching the scrape, and like magic, that disappeared, as well.

She could heal scrapes and scratches and who knew what else!

But she had to get back to the matter at hand. "I'm glad I could help you," she told Hannah honestly. "That's why I'm here."

Hannah looked at her doubtfully. "There's no sunscreen that can fix friendships." She looked like she was about to cry again.

This wasn't going to be easy.

CHAPTER
11

A short while later, Adora was standing in the bathroom, which was a small building by the CIT tent. She gazed at her plain reflection in the mirror. Already she felt tired. Her energy levels must be getting low—and so soon into the mission! Dealing with Hannah and her emotions certainly took a lot of strength.

Adora had told Hannah she needed to "freshen up" before lunch. But really, she'd just wanted to refresh using her Mirror Mantra.

She leaned in close to the mirror and recited her lines: "Use your logic. You are a star!"

Immediately, Adora saw her reflection shift to her shimmery Starland self, all sparkle and glow. Adora grinned. She did indeed feel refreshed. Satisfied, she stepped away from the mirror and called, "Hannah!"

Of course her Wisher was too nervous to go to the mess hall on her own. She was waiting for Adora outside. But Adora wanted to say her Mirror Mantra again, this time away from the mirror, with her Wisher. That would definitely give them both strength.

"Coming," said Hannah in a small voice, knocking tentatively before she walked in.

Really, how timid could one Wishling be?

Slowly, Hannah walked inside, looking shyly at the floor.

"Come on, Hannah," said Adora. "Look at me so we can talk!"

Hannah lifted her downcast eyes. "Oh!" she gasped, falling back against the door.

Adora frowned. What was her problem now?

"Y-y-you're all sparkly!" Hannah stammered. "And your hair: it's blue!"

"What?" That couldn't possibly be true. Adora's heart thudded in her chest. Even in her shock, Adora took note of her rapid pulse. It was certainly an unusual state for her and worth reflecting on. "You're serious?"

Hannah nodded.

Slowly, Adora turned to face the mirror. It was true!

Her skin still shimmered, and her blue hair actually sent sparks flying into the air, a reaction to her heightened sense of danger. She recalled being taught that a Wishling should never see your true appearance. This was bad—very bad.

"Who—what—are you?" Hannah whispered.

Adora made a split-second decision. She would tell Hannah everything. But first: privacy. Like a science experiment gone haywire, this situation needed to be contained as quickly as possible.

She rushed to lock the door. It took her a moment to figure out the mechanism. When she whirled around, she saw a panicked Hannah slipping into the bathroom stall farthest away. Hannah closed the stall door with a click.

"You locked me in!" Hannah cried. "What do you want with me? Wait! Don't answer. Just don't come any closer! I have . . . I have . . ." Adora heard her rummaging around. "A toilet plunger! And I'm not afraid to use it!"

Adora took a deep breath. Then she knocked softly on the stall door.

"Hannah? Open up the door so we can talk. I may look different. But I'm still Adora. I won't hurt you."

"How do I know that? I need proof."

Adora could understand that. "Tell you what. I'll

unlock the outside door. Then I'll go in another stall, in case anyone comes in. You can leave whenever you like."

"Okay," Hannah said softly.

Quickly, Adora unlocked the door and sat down in another stall. *This is just too weird,* she thought, sitting on the uncomfortably hard seat. Why couldn't Wishlings come up with technology to make objects conform to individual bodies and preferences? And now she had to explain to her Wisher why she was glowing. What had gone wrong? None of her Star Darlings classes had ever covered a situation like that one!

Adora heard Hannah's door open. She half expected the girl to rush outside. Instead, the Wishling moved closer and stood outside Adora's door. "Go on," Hannah said.

Hannah hadn't run away. That was good. Now to explain. There was only one logical way to proceed: she had to tell the truth. "I'm from Starland," Adora began. She talked about her world, about Starling Academy and the Star Darlings and the energy crisis.

When she paused for a moment, Hannah said she could open the door.

Adora went on to explain what her mission was and how she had traveled to Earth. When she took a breath, Hannah said she could come out.

Hannah's eyes were wide. "It sounds unbelievable," she said, "but something is telling me that you're not making this up." She laughed. "Maybe it's your sparkly skin and your glittery blue hair that convinced me!"

The two girls leaned against the sinks as Adora finished her explanation. "So I discovered my special healing talent. That wasn't, ah . . . sunscreen. It was just me. What is sunscreen, anyway?"

"It's lotion that protects your skin from harmful sun rays," Hannah told her. Adora looked at her in shock. Imagine needing protection from a light source!

"Anyway," Adora concluded, "I know that you're my Wisher. So I need to help make your wish come true."

"Starland . . . Wishworld . . . granting wishes." Hannah shook her head in wonder. "I would like to help. Do you think if I just say, 'Okay, I'm good at making friends now,' you can get the wish energy and leave?"

"I don't think so," Adora said doubtfully. "It probably needs to be a genuine wish-come-true." She shrugged. "But let's try it anyway."

She held out her arm, bringing her Wish Pendant watch closer to Hannah. She smiled as the Wishling proclaimed loudly, "I feel so confident! I realize now how easy it is to make friends!"

But no rainbow of colors whooshed from Hannah

to the watch. She didn't give off one tiny spark.

"That was nice of you to try," Adora said. "But it's useless."

With those words, her heart beat faster once again. She didn't like those feelings. She was nervous. Upset. Clueless. She didn't have the starriest idea how to fix the situation.

What had she done to make things go horribly wrong? How would she ever be able to grant a wish when she couldn't even leave the bathroom?

Suddenly, the door to outside swung open. Hannah quickly but gently pushed Adora back into the stall. Adora hastily locked the door, then pulled up her feet when she realized even her sneakers were sparkling.

She heard footsteps. Someone said, "Hi, Hannah. I haven't seen you yet! How have you been?"

Hannah mumbled a soft, awkward response.

Adora opened the door very slightly, peeked out, and saw the girl who had waved earlier. She was so friendly. Why couldn't Hannah see that? It would make everything so much easier!

The girl finished quickly and left the bathroom without saying another word.

"Now what?" said Hannah in a normal-sounding voice when Adora came out again.

"I really don't know," said Adora. For the first time ever, she had no next step, no hypothesis to test.

"Well," Hannah said, "you need a hiding spot. You can't stay in this bathroom forever."

"I do have a tent," Adora said, wondering why she hadn't thought of it earlier. Why, oh why, wasn't she thinking straight?

"Great!" said Hannah. "You can set it up in the woods."

"Well, it is kind of big," Adora explained, "but it won't need to be hidden. It's invisible to Wishlings." She thought for a moment. "But I guess it shouldn't be too close so nobody will bump into it!"

"You can put it behind the CIT tent!" said Hannah.

Adora could, in fact, leave the bathroom. So why was her heart still racing? And why was her mind still a muddle?

The whole mission was more difficult than she could have imagined. Forget about finishing in record time—what if she never finished her mission at all?

A lump formed in Adora's throat. She couldn't swallow. She thought back to the previous day, when she'd suspected she was getting sick. If it really was star pox, she'd be in deep trouble. Who would take care of her on Wishworld?

Then one tear rolled down her cheek. *Oh!* Adora realized with a start: She wasn't sick. She was crying. It had been so long she'd almost forgotten what it felt like.

Hannah stared at Adora's pale blue tear. "It's like liquid glitter," she marveled. Then she patted Adora's arm. "It's okay. Just wait here."

Hannah brought back a long terry cloth robe. Adora slipped it on, the bottom sweeping the floor. She pulled up the hood so it covered her head and face.

"Lead the way," said Adora. "And fast."

The girls hurried outside, not pausing for a moment—not even when Uncle Hal called out, "Hannah! Why weren't you at lunch?"

"Not hungry!" Hannah squeaked out.

A distance behind the CIT tent, Adora opened her backpack and took out her folded-up tent. Immediately, it popped up to its full size.

"When are you going to pitch the tent?" Hannah asked.

For a moment, Adora was too confused to answer. Pitch a tent? Was that some kind of Wishling sport?

"The tent is right here, set up and everything," Adora said. "Remember you can't see it?"

"Can I go inside?" asked Hannah.

Again, Adora didn't know. They were really in uncharted waters. What if she wasn't allowed into the tent? What if Hannah could go inside but was still visible to Wishlings? Either way, they'd never get anything done.

"I'll try to lead you inside," Adora finally told Hannah. She opened the flap, took Hannah's arm, and steered her through the opening.

Inside, Hannah opened her eyes wide.

Well, at least she can see the interior, Adora thought. And it was impressive, if she did say so herself.

The star-shaped room was large and plush. Thick blue carpeting covered the ground from one end to the other. In the very center stood a huge bed, covered with fluffy pillows, all tinted a lovely shade of sky blue. Adora took off her backpack and dropped it to the floor.

Hannah stood for a moment with her mouth open. "This is unbelievable!" she said.

"Remember, you can't tell anyone about this!" Adora said warningly.

"Who would I tell, anyway?" Hannah replied. "Remember? I don't have any friends."

Adora felt sad for her.

Hannah walked around the perimeter, examining

the paintings of Starland that hung in every point. Looking at the pictures, Adora felt an unexpected pang in her stomach. That time she knew she was sick—homesick.

"This is amazing!" said Hannah. "But am I invisible, too?"

"I don't know!" Adora said. She peered outside. The girl from the bathroom and her friend were leaving the CIT tent and moving closer. "But we're about to find out."

"Uh-oh, that's Jess and Allie." Hannah quickly sat on the floor, putting her head in her hands, as if she was upset.

"I'm striking a pose," she whispered. "If they see me sitting in the middle of nowhere all alone, they won't even think it's strange."

The two girls walked past as if Hannah and Adora and the tent weren't there at all.

Adora and Hannah collapsed in a fit of giggles.

"We figured that out," Hannah said, catching her breath. "Maybe we can figure everything else out, too."

"Star salutations, Hannah," Adora said, still smiling. "That means 'thank you.'"

Hannah had snuck into the mess hall and returned with sandwiches, fruit, and cookies. She'd even brought Adora bug juice, which Adora learned wasn't made from bugs after all. In fact, it tasted a lot like starberry juice.

Now it was dark outside the cozy tent, and the girls were still trying to come up with a plan.

"I have to go to the CIT bonfire," Hannah told Adora. "But I'll come back later to make sure you're all right."

Adora sighed. Somehow it seemed she and her Wisher had switched places. She was supposed to make Hannah feel better, not the other way around.

Still, she appreciated everything Hannah was doing for her. And while her Wisher was at the bonfire, Adora would go back to her logical way of thinking. She would come up with a foolproof plan for Hannah to gain the confidence she needed to make friends.

Of course, the plan couldn't take Adora outside . . . so maybe she had better figure out how to fix her appearance first.

Oh, moonberries. Her mind was in a muddle once again. What should she try to take care of right then? And how would she accomplish any of it?

Adora leaned back on her pillows and stared at the

tent ceiling, waiting for inspiration. She yawned loudly. It had been quite a starday. She was starmazingly tired.

Across the tent, a lone mirror hung between a holo-photo of the Crystal Mountains and an artist's rendering of a florafierce field. All she had to do was walk across the floor, gaze at her reflection, and say her Mirror Mantra. That would definitely make her feel better. She really needed energy! But then she realized that she needed that strength just to reach the mirror.

Slowly her eyes began to close. She'd just rest for a few starmins. . . .

CHAPTER
12

"Adora, wake up!"

The next thing Adora knew, someone was shaking her shoulders and bouncing up and down on her bed.

She sat up quickly. "Cassie!" she exclaimed. "Am I late for Astral Accounting?"

Wait! Cassie wasn't even in her Astral Accounting class. And how had she gotten into her room, anyway?

Then it all came back in a rush: Adora wasn't in the Big Dipper Dorm. She was in a tent on Wishworld, and her mission was going starmendously wrong.

She'd been hoping she could handle it all on her own, but there was her helper Starling. Adora would not be the first Star Darling to complete a mission on her own after all.

Adora was pleased to see Cassie but a little put out at the same time. "I haven't even been here one day," she said with an edge to her voice. She glanced at her Star-Zap, which was sitting on a nightstand. "My Countdown Clock says I have lots of time left. You could have waited a little longer."

Cassie smiled at her gently. "Your energy levels were so low everyone was alarmed. Besides, look at you! You're shimmering and glittery and everything a Wishling is not. Something is really wrong. That must be draining your energy. You definitely need some help. That's why I'm here, Adora. Not to make you feel bad."

Adora slumped back against her pillows. Cassie was right. It actually felt good to have her close by, frowning in sympathy. Adora gazed at her friend: no sparkles, no glitter. Wishworld plain as could be. Adora would never have believed she'd ever be envious of dull skin and hair. But she was!

"Star salutations, Cassie," she said.

Cassie reached out for her hand. "How did it happen?" she asked. "How did you change back?"

"I don't even know," said Adora miserably. "I was in the bathroom, saying my Mirror Mantra. One starmin I had no sparkle; the next I was as shiny as a newborn Starling."

Again, a tear rolled down Adora's cheek. *This is ridiculous!* Adora thought. *I'm an emotional swift-train wreck.*

"You poor thing," Cassie said. She hugged her close for a moment, then looked at her thoughtfully. "We'll figure it out."

"Oh, Cassie!" Adora burst out crying. "Don't mind me. I'm just so glad you're here." *If sweet, sympathetic Cassie had taken on this mission,* Adora thought, *she'd have gotten Hannah to open up on her own, without resorting to trickery with a recording device!* She had a sudden thought. "Cassie, what was your Wish Mission?"

"To help a Wishling who wanted her teacher to appreciate her," Cassie replied.

"So you and your Wisher were a good fit?" Adora asked.

Cassie thought for a starmin, her brow furrowed. "Now that you mention it, I don't think we were! Or at least, we wouldn't have been. She was a real class clown. It only worked out because I was so"—she blushed Wishling pink—"um, braggy at the time."

Adora grabbed Cassie's hands. "Cassie, I think that our Wish Missions were mixed up!"

"Really?" said Cassie.

"Yes," replied Adora. "My Wisher is very sensitive. I almost don't understand her."

"Well, it makes sense, I guess," said Cassie. "Something seems to go wrong on every mission."

Adora pointed to her sparkly self. "And on this mission, more than one thing!"

"Well, maybe we can reverse your appearance," Cassie said.

Adora leaned forward eagerly. "Maybe we can!" She got out of bed, gave a small yawn, and began to move more quickly. "Let's re-create the scene. I was standing in front of the mirror, wearing my backpack." She grabbed her backpack and threw it over her shoulder, the key chain swinging.

"Then I said my Mirror Mantra."

Adora gazed deeply at her reflection and said, "Use your logic. You are a star!"

Immediately, Adora felt wide awake. But there was no appearance change. If anything, her glow grew stronger.

"That's okay," she told Cassie. "Trial and error. Scientists live by it."

"What if you said it backward?" Cassie suggested.

"Good idea!" Adora paused a moment, composing the mantra in her head, then said, "Star a are you. Logic your use."

Nothing.

Then she tried another approach. Instead of looking

in the mirror, she turned her back to it and said the mantra again. But Adora could tell by Cassie's expression that that hadn't worked, either. Neither did saying it backward while facing backward.

"Maybe we should go back to the bathroom," Adora said.

"I don't think we should take a chance that anyone sees you," Cassie said. "We can try a few more things first. I know the Power Crystals didn't make a difference on Starland, but on Wishworld, Astra's really did open a door. Say your Mirror Mantra, Adora, and I'll wave my crystal."

Cassie held out her lunalite, a cluster of teardrop-shaped jewels glowing with pink moonlight.

This has to work! thought Adora. She closed her eyes and said her Mirror Mantra one more time while Cassie waved the crystal all around her. Then she held her breath, expecting to feel the change from the tips of her glittery toes to the top of her sky-blue head.

Nothing!

Just then, Hannah walked into the tent. She and Cassie gasped at the same time. "Who is that?" they both cried.

"It's okay, Cassie. It's my Wisher. I told her everything," said Adora. Then she turned to Hannah. "This is my friend Cassie," she explained. "She's a Star Darling who's here to help." She filled Hannah in on what they'd been trying to do to reverse her appearance.

"Hmmm." Hannah thought a moment. "What did you do to look human?"

"I recited the 'Star Light, Star Bright' poem," Adora said. She grinned. "Good thinking, Hannah! Let's try that."

Adora recited the poem, but there was no change. "Should I say it backward?" she asked Cassie.

"Let's try the Power Crystal again while you say it the regular way first," said Cassie.

That time it worked! Once again, Adora looked like a Wishling—no glow, no sparks.

Quickly, she hugged Cassie, then Hannah. "You are the best Wishling ever!" she cried.

"Well, you're the best Starling," Hannah replied. She smiled at Cassie. "No offense."

Once again, Adora and Hannah burst into giggles. "I don't know why I'm laughing like this!" Adora said, clucking like a glow-hen and snorting. She had never been much of a giggler before she'd met Hannah.

Hannah pushed Adora so she faced the mirror and could see her own laughing expression. "Has anyone ever told you you're *Adora*-ble?" she asked.

Adora laughed so hard her sides ached.

"Okay, okay," Cassie finally said. "Your appearance is fixed. Now we can concentrate on the wish."

Immediately, Adora sobered.

"If you don't mind my asking, what is it?" Cassie said.

Adora and Hannah exchanged looks. "You tell her," said Adora. "It's your wish."

Hannah nodded. "I wish I had the confidence to make new friends."

Cassie gazed searchingly from Adora to Hannah. "You mean you don't want to be afraid to talk? You want to feel secure enough to be friendly and open? So you can make friends with people you don't really know?"

Hannah sighed. "That's it exactly. How did you know?"

"Because I know exactly how you feel." Again, Cassie glanced from Adora to Hannah. "And I have great news for you!"

Adora knew Cassie had had a hard time when she first got to Starling Academy. An orphan without siblings, Cassie had traveled often with her uncle, a best-selling novelist, and had a private tutor. So when she'd arrived at Starling Academy, she hadn't felt comfortable with other students—at first. *Hannah and Cassie really have a lot in common*, Adora thought. But right then, she just wanted Cassie to get to the point.

"So?" she prodded.

"Adora, you've already helped grant Hannah's wish. It's just that neither of you realize it."

Adora gripped Hannah's hand. "What is Cassie talking about? Did you make friends at the bonfire? You've been spending so much time with me, how did you even manage it?"

Hannah's eyes opened wide. "I didn't make friends at the bonfire. I made a friend right here."

Cassie grinned. "You bet your stars you have! Adora, you granted Hannah's wish by opening up to her and needing *her* friendship. You gave Hannah confidence. And just look at you two!"

She pointed down, and the girls noticed they were still holding hands. "You've bonded. You're real friends."

"Oh, my stars," said Adora, finally realizing it for herself. "We do have fun together."

Hannah giggled. "We are real friends," she agreed. "So what happens now?"

"Now your wish energy is supposed to fly through the air in a colorful stream, straight into my Wish Pendant."

Everyone looked at the watch expectantly.

When nothing happened, Adora rubbed her hands together, pacing back and forth. "Maybe you're not entirely there yet," she finally said to Hannah. "You need proof you're a friend worth having."

Hannah groaned. "So now I have to knowingly make a friend?"

Adora grinned. "Yup! But let's wait until morning. It's so late now everyone must be sleeping. You'd only make enemies if you tried now!"

That night, Adora stayed up for hours, thinking things through. If everything worked out, she'd be back on Starland before too long. And she still didn't know what to think about Lady Stella.

By the time the sun rose the next morning, she wasn't any closer to a conclusion. So finally, she closed her eyes.

She and Cassie slept through breakfast and well into the day while Hannah worked at the arts and crafts cabin. Right before lunch, the Starlings met her at the agreed-upon spot: a picnic table outside the mess hall.

Adora was so certain Hannah's wish would be granted that she'd packed up her tent and all her belongings.

"Okay," she said, getting right down to business. "Here come Jess and Allie. Call them over."

"Right now?" said Hannah. "Can't we have lunch first?"

"Now," Adora said firmly.

Hannah ducked her head, leaning down to scratch her knee. *A nervous gesture*, Adora thought, and her heart went out to her. This was difficult for Hannah. Just because Adora could march right up to the girls and start talking didn't mean it was easy for someone else.

"Do it fast," she advised. "It will be easier that way." She glanced at the girls. "And they seem to be in a hurry."

"Hey! Allie! Jess!" Hannah called loudly.

The girls stopped and looked at her in surprise.

Hannah sidled closer. "Um . . . what's going on?" she said much more softly.

"We have to see the nurse." Allie's voice sounded strained. "Look!" She and Jess held out their arms. Red blistery rashes streaked their skin. Jess scratched hers, making it look even worse.

"It's so itchy," Jess complained. "It's got to be poison ivy."

She glanced at Adora and Cassie curiously. "Oh," said Hannah, "Adora and Cassie are visiting for the day." She smiled. "They're my friends."

Jess nodded absently. "Well, that's nice. But we've really got to run. We must have gotten poison ivy at the bonfire. We woke up with the rash this morning, and we should get it taken care of as soon as possible."

The girls started to edge away.

Adora looked around, hoping for an idea, a way to get them to stay, and she noticed Hannah's knees. They were red and blotchy, too. "You have that poison ivy thing, too," she whispered loudly. "Tell them!"

"Oh!" said Hannah, raising her voice even louder than before. "I have it, too! On my knees!"

Everyone bent closer to look. "You're right!" said Allie. "Isn't it awful?"

"It is," Hannah agreed. "But you know, Adora has some amazing lotion for rashes and bug bites." She winked at Adora. "Maybe it would work on poison ivy, too."

The sunscreen! Hannah wanted her to pretend to use it so she could heal the rash—and maybe help the girls bond even more. Luckily, Adora had the bottle in her backpack. She'd been planning to examine its chemical makeup back on Starland. There wasn't much left. She hated to use it. But it had to be done.

She rifled through her backpack, feeling around for the bottle, pushing aside the tent, the camp T-shirt, and other Wishworld specimens she'd picked up. "Here it is!" she said triumphantly.

She poured out just a smidgeon.

"Is that enough?" asked Jess anxiously.

"Enough for all of you!" Adora said cheerfully.

She crouched down and applied the lotion to Hannah's knees first, then to Allie's and Jess's poison ivy patches. She made sure to hold her hand over each spot.

Starsecs later, all three girls were smiling. "Thank you!" Allie said. "That is amazing stuff!"

"I know, right?" said Hannah. "By the way, be careful by the canoes. There must be a beehive nearby. I got stung there yesterday."

"You did?" said Allie. "I am totally afraid of bees."

Adora and Cassie stepped away as the three Wishlings compared their camp histories of bites, stings, and rashes. Then they moved on to camp plays, swim tests, and Color War.

Color War? Adora didn't remember that one from Wishling History class. Hopefully, the war was pretend, since this was just camp, after all.

Then Hannah turned to Adora and smiled so widely that Adora knew her Wisher's wish had come true. Right on cue, wish energy streaked through the air, streaming into her Wish Pendant. Adora and Cassie watched, openmouthed. It was startastically beautiful.

"Let's all go to lunch together!" Hannah said, waving at the Starlings to join the group.

"Great!" said Allie.

"Hannah, I need to talk to you for a minute," said Adora.

"We'll save seats, Hannah," Jess said as she and Allie headed toward the mess hall.

"Well, that went great!" said Hannah happily. "I just know I'll be friends with those guys." She looked at Adora. "You don't seem very excited."

"Oh, I am," Adora said. She sighed. There was another of those little light lies. But that would be her last on Wishworld. "It's just that now my mission is over and we have to leave."

Hannah's face fell. "You won't even stay for lunch?"

Adora was about to say yes, but Cassie elbowed her. "It's time to go back," Cassie said gently.

"Of course." Adora tried to sound brisk and unemotional, the way she normally would. But her voice broke. "You are a true friend, Hannah," she told her Wisher. "I haven't laughed this hard since I was a wee Starling." Two big tears rolled down her cheeks. *Again!* thought Adora. That was really too much. "I'll always remember you."

"And I'll remember you," said Hannah.

Adora knew that wasn't true; Hannah wouldn't remember a thing. All Adora had to do was hug her Wisher and Hannah's memory (and everyone else's) would be wiped clean. She'd have no idea who Adora was and would certainly not remember anything about Starland. Adora thought it kinder not to tell her.

"I almost forgot!" Hannah said. "I made you something in arts and crafts." She reached into her pocket and drew out a long multicolored braid. "It's a friendship bracelet," she explained.

"I love it!" exclaimed Adora. She held out her wrist and Hannah fastened the bracelet.

"It's time to go," Cassie reminded her.

Half smiling, half frowning, Adora hugged Hannah. When she moved away, Hannah looked at her blankly.

"Are you new at Moose Lake?" she asked.

Adora shook her head. "No, we're just visiting to see if we'd like to work here next summer." *Oops!* That was definitely the last little light lie.

"Oh, you would love it here!" Hannah said, smiling. "Everyone is so friendly!"

Who knew? Maybe Adora hadn't lied. Maybe somehow she'd find her way back. She could be one of Hannah's summer friends who came back year after year.

Adora wanted to believe it so badly she almost did.

"Good-bye, Hannah," she said as she and Cassie walked away.

"Wait!" called Hannah. "How do you know my name?"

It took all her strength, but Adora didn't turn around. She just looked ahead toward the clearing, where she and Cassie would unfold their shooting stars and take off for home.

Epilogue

Adora was sitting between Cassie and Tessa in Lady Stella's office. Somehow, she'd wound up by the two Star Darlings with whom she'd shared missions. Fitting for the Wish Orb ceremony, she supposed.

Adora noted the mood around the table. Everyone was subdued. They all spoke in hushed tones, even when they congratulated her, as if acting too happy would make the Starland situation worse.

Adora was quiet, too, thinking wistfully of Hannah and Moose Lake Camp. She touched her bracelet. *Why do they even call it Moose Lake?* she wondered. She hadn't seen any actual creatures that looked like the camp logo. Uncle Hal should really change the name to Bee Lake Camp. Or Clover Lake. Or even Poison Ivy Lake.

"Star greetings, Star Darlings," said Lady Cordial, interrupting Adora's thoughts as she glided into the room. Everyone nodded in a tense way, not quite meeting her eyes.

Abruptly, Adora was brought back to Starland. "What happened while we were gone?" she whispered to Tessa.

"Well . . ." Tessa settled in like she was about to tell a long, involved story. "Leona has been acting all strange and quiet. Gemma told me she even canceled band practice. Leona said she needed to think, of all things! Not sing! And there have been a few more blackouts. They're happening more and more often. But really nothing major."

Not too long before, one energy outage would have been news. Now it was almost expected. And the shortage would only get worse. Yes, Adora had had a successful mission. Yes, she'd collected wish energy. But with outages happening so frequently, it was clear it would not be enough.

Lady Stella gazed around the room. "Girls, your colors seem muted. Please know I am here for you. You can talk to me if you wish, anytime, anyplace."

Next to Adora, Cassie stiffened. *She doesn't believe a word Lady Stella is saying,* Adora thought. *But she wants to.*

"Adora," Lady Stella said, "well done, despite the obstacles you faced. Starkudos to you. As you all must realize, though, as important as these energy-collecting missions are, they may not be enough to turn the tide that has begun. But let us not lose hope."

Then Lady Stella brought out Adora's Wish Orb. The glowing ball floated to Adora, then shifted into the loveliest flower Adora had ever seen: the blue sky-winkle, its corona petals blazing like the Wishworld sun and glittering with stardust.

Slowly, a crystal rose from its center. It was a shimmering stone of blue cylinders hanging together like icicles under a golden dome. Just holding it made Adora feel stronger.

There were some halfhearted oohs and ahhs. Quietly, the girls filed out of the office. In silent agreement, they all returned to their rooms.

Adora stretched out on her bed, happy to be back. She eyed the sequins experiment still spread out over the lab table. Maybe she'd get to it later. Maybe she wouldn't. Right then fashion could wait. Energy science would be her focus.

Across the room, Tessa pulled out astromuffins from her micro-zap. Absently, she put them aside, not bothering to take one—or offer Adora one, either. *Everyone is trying to figure out Lady Stella and the energy problems,* Adora thought. And it was taking its toll. Maybe that was why Leona was staying quiet, too.

As if she had summoned the Star Darling with her thoughts, Adora's Star-Zap buzzed with a holo-text from Leona. It was to the Star Darlings group, and Adora read it quickly: *Come to my room right this starmin! I have something to tell you.*

Adora sighed. Why couldn't she have talked to them when they were all together at the ceremony? Leave it to the star-diva to make a big deal out of nothing. *Forget about Leona thinking deep thoughts about wish energy,* Adora thought, annoyed that she'd have to leave her room before she'd really relaxed. Leona probably wanted them to admire a new song or help choose an outfit for a performance.

Reluctantly, she and Tessa made their way to Leona's room. Before they could even knock, Scarlet opened the door, eagerly beckoning them inside.

Now that's surprising, Adora thought. *Since when does Scarlet get excited about anything Leona does?*

The rest of the Star Darlings were already there, gathered around the star-shaped platform as they'd been before Adora's mission. But now Leona stood in the center of the star, no microphone in sight.

She began to talk before Adora could even sit down. "You might have noticed I've been quiet lately," she told the girls. "I have been spending time on my own, thinking."

Adora waited for Scarlet to make a starcastic comment. But the loner Starling, usually so quick to put Leona down, just nodded.

"I found something the other starday," Leona continued, "when we snuck into Lady Stella's office. And I need to share it with all of you. Scarlet and I have already discussed it. And we feel exactly the same way."

"Did you see something in Lady Stella's desk drawer?" Cassie asked. "When you said you were startled by a rainbow orb spider?"

Leona nodded. "Yes. I didn't see a spider. I saw this."

She opened her hand. And there, in her palm, sat her old, blackenedWish Pendant.

The pendant had been a beautiful golden metallic cuff. Leona had worn it proudly on her upper arm, the star at its center glowing brightly. Now it was burnt and ugly.

Scarlet looked directly at Sage and Libby, Lady Stella's two biggest supporters. Then she turned to Adora. "There's your proof. Leona's Wish Pendant, hidden in her desk drawer. Lady Stella is guilty."

"That's right," Leona said, her voice fierce and serious. "She never brought it to the lab or had a wish scientist examine it. She never tried to figure out why it burned or what happened. And she said she would! She lied.

"You know," Leona continued, a note of pride creeping into her voice, "I did grant a double wish. So the pendant could still have had some energy. But now we'll never know."

"Why wouldn't Lady Stella try to fix the Wish Pendant?" asked Scarlet, sounding like Cassie's uncle's fictional detective. She moved to stand next to Leona. Then she actually linked her arm through the other Starling's. "Lady Stella wants the pendant to stay broken. She doesn't want the energy. That would help the energy crisis. And she doesn't want it to help because—"

"She's responsible for it!" Leona finished.

Some girls gasped. Some nodded. No one spoke in Lady Stella's defense.

Slowly, Adora stood up to join Scarlet and Leona. She'd thought and she'd thought; she'd gone over the evidence again and again her last night on Wishworld. And now she'd drawn a conclusion.

This was the final proof she needed. "I'm with you," she told them.

One by one, the other Star Darlings stood up to form a tight circle. Sage, the last to stand, looked grim. The Star Darlings linked arms, frowning, teary, determined.

"We know what we have to do," said Cassie. The girls all nodded.

Adora thought about lies and truths, about right and wrong. In the end, the evidence was clear. There were no fuzzy half-truths. No little light lies. Lady Stella was guilty.

And the Star Darlings had to turn her in.

Clover's Parent Fix

Prologue

Together we face the music.
Together we take a stand.
We're one for all and all for one.
We're the members of the band.

Clover paused, Star-Zap in hand, as she swung slowly back and forth on her hammock, composing a song.

At least, Clover was *trying* to compose a song. She was the main songwriter for the Star Darlings band, although—by her own choice—she wasn't an official member. Clover could play just about any instrument on Starland—from the keytar to the googlehorn—and had a true stage presence. But she was taking a break from the starlight. After all those staryears performing with her circus family—traveling with "The Greatest Show on Starland"—she wanted to concentrate on her real love: songwriting.

If only this song was coming easier! It was supposedly about Star Darlings the band. But it was really about Star Darlings the star-charmed group of students fated to save their world. And Clover was having a tough time with it, despite her strategies.

First: to set a goal. And that was to finish the song before the Battle of the Bands competition.

Second: to keep to a routine. And she did, working first thing in the morning, before breakfast, even if inspiration didn't hit . . . even if she'd stayed up late the night before and wanted extra sleep. *Even now*, she thought.

Across the room, Clover heard her roommate, Astra, tossing a star ball into a net. *Thump, thump, thump.* It was the perfect backbeat.

She returned to work.

Together we face the music.
Together we sing our song.

We've faced a lot of startrouble,
But we always stay starstrong.

Strength. Clover considered how strong each Star Darling had to be. Every mission they'd gone on had been riddled with problems: mixed-up Wisher and wish identifications, for starters, and Leona's Wish Pendant's burning up on the trip back. And poor Adora, whose Wishworld transformation hadn't lasted one starday. Sparkly and glowing, she'd had to hide in a bathroom!

Of course there was Scarlet, too, whose trouble had started before her mission even began. She'd been kicked out of the Star Darlings and replaced by a girl named Ophelia. Lady Stella, the headmistress, had claimed Ophelia was the true Star Darling. Luckily, Scarlet wound up collecting wish energy anyway. But had Lady Stella switched the girls to mess up another mission? Clover hated to admit it, but it certainly seemed that way. In fact, all the evidence pointed to Lady Stella as the evil mastermind behind the problems. And that included both the poisonous flowers that had made the Star Darlings bicker and the toxic nail polish that had made them act so strange.

Did she have an accomplice? There was that mysterious woman Astra kept spotting having meetings with

Lady Stella. What did it all mean? And what could the Star Darlings do about it?

Clover wanted a faster beat to match all those questions. Something with an edge. Astra began to bounce two star balls at once. Double time.

Clover picked up the rhythm.

What is Starland's fate, fate, fate?
It's time to lend a hand, hand, hand.
We're all in sync, sync, sync.
We're the Star Darlings band, band, band.

Fate. That was a powerful refrain, Clover thought—for the song *and* for the Star Darlings themselves. Tessa, Cassie, and Scarlet had discovered a secret underground chamber holding an ancient prophecy, a book proclaiming that twelve Star-Charmed Starlings were destined to save Starland. (And it was clear now that Starland was certainly in trouble and needed saving! Power outages and energy blips had become frighteningly common.)

Of course the Star Darlings figured out they were those very Starlings—just before getting trapped inside the chamber. *Thank the stars we found them*, Clover thought. But was that another evil act by Lady Stella?

Clover slowed down the tempo.

Oh, we believe in the truth.
Please don't tell us these lies.
We believe in the stars
Shining high above in the skies.

Hmmm. Clover considered the next lines. The Star Darlings had confronted Lady Stella, demanding the truth. But what would Clover write about that meeting? How Lady Stella had—

Clover's Star-Zap flickered and chimed with a holo-call. She glanced at the screen. It was her mom, hanging upside down on a trapeze. In the background Clover saw the circus big top, the view swinging wildly as her mom moved back and forth.

These trapeze calls could last for starhours. Each time her mom swung past another relative, she'd pass the Star-Zap. Clover bit her lip. She was just getting started on these lyrics. But it meant so much to her family, particularly her mom, to talk to her. She swiped the screen and a holo-image appeared in the air before her.

"Hello, darling," said her mother, still swinging. "We just set up the tent in Old Prism for tonight's show."

"That's great, Mom," said Clover. "How is it going?"

"Well . . ." Her mom's trapeze slowed as she thought things over. "We're running behind, actually. Our circus swift train had to pull over and recharge a few times."

Just then Clover's dad grabbed the Star-Zap as he swung from the opposite direction. "Nothing to worry about, Clover!" He jumped off at the platform, passing the phone to her aunt Cecile.

Cecile held the device with one hand as she grabbed the trapeze with the other. She soared through the air, and Clover saw a dizzying stream of colors. "The show will definitely be late," her aunt said chattily. "And our clown car lost its shrink/expand energy, so it can't hold a hydrong clowns anymore."

Aunt Cecile let go of the trapeze, aiming for Clover's mom's outstretched arms.

"Now that clown car can barely hold your great-grandfather Otto!" her mom said, neatly catching Aunt Cecile and taking the Star-Zap at the same time.

So the wish energy shortage is really everywhere now, Clover thought. The high-energy circus, seemingly immune to negativity, was the last place she thought would be hit. "But are you doing okay?" she asked.

"We're right as starshine," her mom said, delivering her aunt to another swing. "Just some minor inconveniences. Let me show you my new dive into a barrel of water."

But Clover's Star-Zap buzzed with a holo-text. The barrel dive would have to wait. She had received an all-school message marked READ IMMEDIATELY.

PLEASE REPORT TO THE AUDITORIUM AS SOON AS STAR-POSSIBLE FOR AN IMPORTANT ANNOUNCEMENT, it read.

In Clover's two years at Starling Academy, there had never been a major meeting called unexpectedly.

Whatever it was, it had to be big.

CHAPTER
1

An important announcement! The whole school had to be there! Would the assembly be about Lady Stella and her role in the energy shortage? About her sabotage?

Clover flipped out of her hammock, landing perfectly on two feet with her arms high above her head. The somersault was really just a habit. But still she glanced at Astra to see if her roommate had noticed.

Astra, a star athlete, had recently returned from Wishworld, where she'd helped grant the wish of a young gymnast and had gone to a competition. Now Astra was projecting a holo-sign with the score 999,999.5.

"Starf!" said Clover. "Half a point more and I'd have a perfect moonium."

"Better luck next time," Astra said. "And I'm sure there will be a next time."

"And I'm sure you'll be there to judge me," Clover shot back with a grin.

Acrobatic tricks, kidding around—it all came naturally to Clover. Growing up as part of the Flying Molensa Family, Clover had been surrounded by generations of aunts, uncles, and cousins—not to mention her own parents and siblings—who could walk a tightrope while juggling a glowzen ozziefruits and cracking jokes. Living with Astra had always been a breeze. But living in a dorm at Starling Academy was another story.

Before school, Clover had never stayed anywhere for more than a starweek. She and her family traveled year-round across Starland, living out of suitcases on the circus swift train.

Clover had shared a sleeping car with her sisters and she'd always had an upper berth. That was why she loved her hammock bed. It reminded her of the gentle motion of the moving swift train.

"So," said Astra, slipping into her sneakers, "I wonder who will be making this big announcement. Surely not Lady Stella."

Wouldn't it be starmazing, though, if Lady Stella called

the assembly and everything is back to normal? Clover thought with a sigh. She imagined the school day proceeding just as it always had, with no energy blips, no upheaval, and Lady Stella just where she should be.

"Starland to Clover! Starland to Clover!" Astra snapped her fingers star inches from Clover's face. "Come on. We'd better hurry. If the entire school is going to the Astral Auditorium, it will be crowded."

Clover nodded. She picked up her hat and placed it on her head, making sure it curved just right. The purple fedora had been handed down to her by her great-grandma Sunny, and Clover planned to pass it down to her own grandchild one starday. It set off her sparkly eyes and short bouncy hair, matching their deep purple shade almost perfectly. She rarely went out without it.

"Ready," she told Astra.

The two Starlings headed outside and jumped onto the already crowded Cosmic Transporter. All around them, girls chatted excitedly, making guesses about the important announcement.

"Hey, Clover!" a third-year student named Aurora called out. "Maybe Lady Stella is canceling classes because your family is performing."

Last staryear, Clover's family had visited, and Lady

Stella had announced a holiday so the students could watch their show. Everyone had agreed the best part was when Professor Dolores Raye had been invited into the star-ring.

Professor Dolores Raye was short—in size and temperament—and wore serious large-framed glasses. She was no one's favorite teacher. So when Clover's dad had offered her his arm and led her to a cosmic cannon, the students watched with interest. Clearly the humorless teacher hadn't wanted to become a Starling cannonball. But at that point, there was no turning back. Clover's dad lit the fuse with a wish energy snap of his fingers, and she'd flown through the air.

"There's no landing pad!" Lady Cordial had screeched in panic.

Everyone gasped. But Clover's dad slowed the flight with a wave of his arm, and Professor Dolores Raye landed safely on her feet.

It had been fun. But today's announcement had nothing to do with her family, Clover felt sure.

"No, no," she quickly said. "The circus isn't coming!"

"Well, maybe Lady Stella will hand out the Triple S award today," someone else guessed.

The Silver Shining Star was the highest honor in all of Starling Academy, given to a student who had received starperlative assessments in the classroom, in the school community, and in her hometown.

"Maybe," Clover said pleasantly. She'd be starprised if this announcement brought any good news. But she couldn't share her thoughts with anyone but a Star Darling.

Once they were outside, three other Star Darlings walked up behind Clover and Astra: first year Libby and sisters Tessa and Gemma. They all looked worried.

"Star greetings," Gemma said in a quiet voice—at least, quiet for Gemma. As the Cosmic Transporter moved along, she kept up a steady stream of chatter, touching on everything but Lady Stella and the announcement. She could hardly be blamed, Clover thought, only half listening. They couldn't discuss anything there, in public. Only sweet-tempered, pink-haired Libby paid attention to Gemma, nodding at every statement.

"Did you hear that noise?" Gemma said in a much louder voice. "That rumbling sound? Something must be wrong with the transporter! Remember when it ran out of power just the other—"

"Relax, Gemma," Tessa said irritably. "It's only my stomach. You do know breakfast is postponed because of this assembly, don't you? It's really not fair. Some of us need to eat on a regular schedule."

Clover understood the part about keeping a schedule. She liked to have a predictable timetable, too. But how could Tessa be concerned about food at a time like this? "Tessa—" she began to scold.

But then Piper slid into place beside her and put a reassuring hand on her arm. How did Piper do that, always appear seemingly out of thin air? "Relax, Clover," she said in a soothing voice. "Tessa isn't really worried about breakfast. It's just transtarence—'transference,' as Wishlings would say."

"Transtarence?" Clover repeated. Sometimes Piper had an intuitive sense of others' thoughts and feelings, but sometimes she was way off starbase. Which was it now?

"Yes. Tessa is transferring, or redirecting, her concern about Lady Stella—to food!" Piper finished in a whisper.

Ahead, the Cosmic Transporter was emptying, and Clover realized they had reached the auditorium. She linked arms with Astra and Piper and—with Gemma, Tessa, and Libby close behind—followed the crowd.

Just outside the auditorium doors, the rest of the Star Darlings waited.

"Over here!" Leona waved her arms dramatically, her golden curls bouncing. Cassie stood next to her, looking pale. She seemed to be holding on to the arm of her roommate, Sage, for support. The two had disagreed about Lady Stella—Sage supporting the headmistress, Cassie opposing her. Sage had a strong personality. But shy, quiet Cassie had stood her ground, convincing the Star Darlings that Lady Stella was the enemy.

Now, looking at Cassie's conflicted expression, Clover wondered if she might be having second thoughts. Scarlet, a short distance away from the others, looked defiantly at anyone who so much as glanced in her direction.

Meanwhile, Adora and Vega, their blue heads of hair almost blending into one, were huddled over one of Vega's puzzle holo-books. "Hey! Aren't there any science questions?" Adora complained. More transarence, Clover decided.

"Come on!" Sage said impatiently. "Let's go inside."

The Star Darlings stepped into the auditorium. At the very same starmin, a student named Vivica—just about the meanest girl in school, Clover thought—elbowed her way past, her own group of friends trailing her.

Vivica stopped abruptly and the girl directly behind her tripped, crashing into Clover.

"Star apologies!" the girl told Vivica, ignoring Clover. "I should have been paying more attention."

Vivica sniffed. "Be more careful next time, Brenna." Then she turned to Clover. "As for you, I suggest you try harder to keep up with the crowd. Those SDs," she muttered to her friends. "They really are superbly dense!"

Clover ignored her. The Cycle of Life was too short to let Vivica get on her nerves. Unfortunately, she wound up sitting directly behind her in the auditorium.

"I'm really wondering about this big announcement," Vivica was saying to Brenna.

"If it is the Triple S award," Brenna said, "you'll be a star-in."

"Me? Getting the Triple S?" said Vivica with loud false modesty. "Why would they ever give it to little old me? Yes, I was the champion light-skater at the Luminous Lake competition. And I earn all Is in my classes. Illumination, Illumination, Illumination. That's all my star report says! And of course, there's the band I put together. We're totally stellar. Still . . . the award?"

The lights brightened, signaling the students to be quiet. Then Lady Cordial shuffled to center stage. She gazed around nervously, gripping a microphone in one hand. She tucked a loose strand of purple hair behind her ear, and the mic hit her head. A loud screech sounded, reaching the last rows.

Clover, an old hand at performing in front of an

audience, squirmed uncomfortably. Lady Cordial was so awkward and shy Clover's heart went out to her. Clearly she wished she was light-years away—not standing onstage, about to deliver a major announcement.

"Ahem." Lady Cordial cleared her throat. "S-s-s-s-star greetings, s-s-s-s-s-students," she stuttered.

"Do you know she s-s-s-s-s-s-s-stutters?" Vivica said in a stage whisper to Brenna.

Clover groaned to herself. Why did Lady Cordial always choose words that started with the letter *s*?

"I will get right to the point," Lady Cordial continued.

Clover nodded encouragingly at the stage. Not one S-word in that sentence! That was a start.

Lady Cordial dropped the mic, and the thud echoed throughout the room.

"S-s-s-s-s-s-star apologies!" she cried.

Clover glared around the room, daring anyone to laugh.

"I asked you here today," Lady Cordial said, plowing ahead, a bright purple blush flooding her cheeks, "to relay important news."

Clover sat forward expectantly. This definitely had to do with Lady Stella. Did Lady Cordial know what had happened to her?

"Lady S-s-s-s-s-stella has been unexpectedly called away due to a family emergency."

A loud hum filled the auditorium. *Okay,* Clover thought. *Lady Stella is really gone. And the family emergency must be an excuse.* But Lady Cordial looked like she had more to say.

"As director of admissions, I am next in line," she went on. "S-s-s-s-s-so I will be temporarily in charge."

The room erupted with cries of surprise. Only the Star Darlings remained silent, exchanging worried glances.

Lady Cordial called for quiet. She waved her arms frantically, but the noise didn't subside. Finally, Professor Dolores Raye whistled for everyone's attention, and the students settled down.

Lady Cordial nodded, as if she'd called on the teacher to step in. "I hope everyone will be patient with me. This is a huge s-s-s-s-s-step, with a definite learning curve. It may take s-s-s-s-some time for everything to run s-s-s-s-s-smoothly."

Three S-words, Clover thought. Not quite a record. But she knew Lady Cordial's speech would end with a great big embarrassing double-S phrase. She waited a beat, then nodded as Lady Cordial finished with "S-s-s-s-star s-s-s-s-salutations."

The lights brightened once again. The assembly was over.

The Star Darlings, in silent agreement, stayed seated while the other students hurried out, eager to talk about the news. Not even Vivica gave the "SDs" a glance.

Clover pulled Astra to her feet. "We should talk things over," she told the group. "Astra, is it okay if everyone comes to our room?"

Just then their Star-Zaps buzzed with a group holo-text. Clover read it quickly: "'Please report to Lady Stella's office immediately.'"

"What?" said Libby, confused. "But she's not here!"

Their Star-Zaps went off again. "'Correction: Lady Cordial's office, formerly Lady Stella's.'"

"That makes sense," Vega said in her practical way. "Lady Cordial's old office was so small and cramped you could barely turn around without knocking over a holo-file. At least now she'll have space to get organized."

But they found that Lady Cordial's new office was anything but organized. It looked like a lightning bolt had struck. Holo-books lay scattered on the floor. Desk drawers hung open haphazardly. And Lady Stella's lovely silver table was buried under holo-files.

Lady Cordial was nowhere to be seen.

"That's strange," said Clover, peering around. "Why would she call a meeting if she's not even here?"

"S-s-s-s-s-sit down, girls." Clover spied two feet, clad in clunky purple shoes, sticking out from under the desk. "I'll be with you in a s-s-s-s-starsec."

If Clover had been in a different frame of mind, she would have burst out laughing. She watched as Lady Cordial squirmed her way out, took a deep breath, then stumbled to her feet.

"Can we help you?" asked Cassie.

She shook her head. "I've looked everywhere. It's gone."

"What's gone?" asked Leona.

Lady Cordial sighed. "Lady S-s-s-stella had a wish energy meter that she used to determine the balance of energy. It's nowhere to be found. Sh-sh-sh-she must have taken it with her," she finished, seating herself in Lady Stella's chair.

Clover sucked in her breath. It was silly, she knew, but she wished that space could stay empty, at least until everything was straightened out.

"I wanted to sh-sh-sh-share my thoughts with you, girls. You've already told me everything that happened when you last s-s-s-s-saw Lady S-s-s-stella. Now it's my turn." Lady Cordial leaned forward, knocking over one holo-file, two holo-books, and a galliope figurine.

While she reached down to pick up the items, Clover thought back to everything that had happened.

Right after Adora had returned from her mission, the Star Darlings had agreed they needed to confront Lady Stella. But they'd decided to talk to Lady Cordial first. She'd know exactly what to do, they thought.

"Of course I told you I'd s-s-s-support you when you s-s-s-spoke to Lady S-s-s-stella," Lady Cordial said now, following Clover's swift train of thought. "Unfortunately, as you know, my sh-sh-sh-shoe got jammed in the Cosmic Transporter and I had to ride around the s-s-s-school twice, missing the meeting."

At first, Lady Stella had been pleased to see them, Clover remembered. She'd been urging them to come to her with questions or concerns. And finally, there they were. But then Cassie and Scarlet took turns talking, Cassie looking torn even as she outlined all the evidence, and Scarlet not quite meeting Lady Stella's eyes. And Lady Stella's calm expression had turned stormy.

Finally, Cassie had finished, saying, "We believe you should not be the headmistress anymore."

Lady Stella nodded slowly. "Forgive me," she said, standing up. There was a glittery flash and a crackle and pop. The air filled with smoke. When it cleared, Lady Stella was gone.

One starsec she had been there, the next she had disappeared without any explanation. Clover had been holding out hope that they were wrong. That Lady Stella would laugh and have an explanation for everything. But then Clover realized that Lady Stella must be guilty of sabotage. Why else would she run away?

Of course, that was Clover's head talking. Her heart still said something else.

"That confirms it!" Sage had said firmly as the smoke cleared, her voice only trembling a bit at the end. "Lady Stella is responsible for everything."

Lady Cordial cleared her throat, and Clover was brought back to the here (Lady Stella's office) and now (Lady Cordial in charge).

"I believe I have it all figured out," Lady Cordial said. "Lady S-s-s-stella has been training Wish-Granters for s-s-s-staryears. It is known throughout the worlds sh-sh-sh-she is the best, the brightest, the most accomplished teacher. Future Wish-Granters have thanked their lucky s-s-s-stars to be her s-s-s-s-students."

Clover nodded. She'd learned so much from Lady Stella.

"But because of her role," Lady Cordial went on, "sh-sh-sh-she was privy to knowledge the rest of us weren't privy to. For s-s-s-s-stars know how long, sh-sh-sh-she knew there was a wish energy deficit! That we'd soon be losing power. And she kept us in the dark."

"Literally," Clover joked.

"Ahem." Lady Cordial frowned, and Clover felt bad. This was hard enough for the new headmistress. She didn't need a wise-star interrupting.

"At any rate," Lady Cordial continued, "Lady S-s-s-stella eventually left a holo-letter open on her desk. I read the warnings. I confronted her, and she had to confide in me then, along with a few other faculty members. But s-s-s-still, she wasn't concerned. S-s-s-s-still she did nothing about the crisis!

"Then one s-s-s-s-starday, I was exploring the underground caves and I came upon a hidden room. It was filled with ancient tomes. I s-s-s-spent s-s-s-starhours there, poring over rare old holo-books. And then I came across a s-s-s-s-s-special one." She cast a significant look around the table. "It was about twelve S-s-s-star-Charmed S-s-s-starlings who are fated to s-s-s-s-save S-s-s-s-s-starland."

Clover bowed her head, still awed by the responsibility.

Lady Cordial continued. "I immediately realized we

could use this information to help S-s-s-s-starland. Lady S-s-s-s-s-stella was very reluctant to pursue this. But I wouldn't give up. I persevered and took matters into my own hands. I combed through records and test s-s-s-s-scores and s-s-s-sat in on classes. I identified you twelve S-s-s-s-star Darlings. Lady S-s-s-s-s-stella appeared to s-s-s-s-support your group. But she replaced S-s-s-s-scarlet with Ophelia for a time. She was responsible for the poisonous flowers and nail polish, for interfering with missions . . . and for trapping you in that underground room!"

"We already know all that!" Scarlet said crossly. "The question is, why? Why would she do it?"

"Lady S-s-s-s-s-stella wanted the energy deficit to worsen," Lady Cordial replied. "She was working against me . . . against us . . . against our planet . . . the whole time. Clearly, she thrives on negative energy. It gives her power. There is no other explanation." She paused. "Who knows what she would have done with that power?"

Clover gasped. Stated so baldly, it was shocking.

"What happens now?" asked Cassie.

"Excellent question. I am hoping no further action will be required. Lady S-s-s-s-s-stella must have gone into hiding. Most likely, she will never return. S-s-s-s-s-so now we work to repair the damage sh-sh-sh-she caused.

We have two Wish Missions left." Lady Cordial's eyes rested first on Clover, then on Gemma. "Much can be done."

Clover's heart thudded. Everything depended on these next missions—one of which would be hers. She'd work tirelessly to find her Wisher, to help grant the wish. And if she couldn't do it? She tossed her head to shake off doubts. It was easier said than done, but she'd just have to prove herself.

"I still can't believe it," Sage said miserably, her glow dimming. Clover knew that it was one thing to *think* Lady Stella might be evil, but it was another to have your fears confirmed.

"If you s-s-s-s-see or hear from her," Lady Cordial finished, "you must alert me immediately. Her destructive behavior cannot continue. I will not let it."

These were strong words indeed from Lady Cordial, who was usually so sweet and indecisive. Now she seemed almost fierce. All of a sudden, Clover felt glad they were on the same side.

"That is all." Lady Cordial spoke in a milder voice. "For now."

Slowly and silently, the girls filed out of the office, then left Halo Hall. Outside, they stood uneasily in a loose circle, not sure what to do next.

"We can still make it to the Celestial Café in time for a quick breakfast before class," Clover said. She didn't feel very hungry. Still, maybe the others were and would want company. But shaking their heads, sad and upset, the other girls set off in different directions.

"Tessa?" Clover called, certain that at least she would want to eat. But Tessa just turned away. Even she had lost her appetite.

CHAPTER
2

The next starday, Dododay, began in the usual way. There was breakfast, morning classes, lunch, and afternoon classes. But a shadow hung over the school. Without Lady Stella overseeing the students, everything seemed slightly off, even though on the surface nothing had changed.

So just as usual, the Star Darlings met after regular classes for their lecture.

Clover was glad to go to that class, happy to follow the regular routine and know what to expect. But deep inside she knew it wouldn't be normal at all. Lady Stella wouldn't lead the lecture or introduce a guest professor.

"It all seems so strange without Lady Stella," Clover said quietly, sliding into a seat next to Adora. "And sad."

Leona crossed her arms. "Well, I think it's all for the best. At least now we know what's what."

"Knowing and feeling are two very different things," Piper said, her eyes half-closed in meditation.

Those were almost exactly Clover's thoughts!

"Well, I know *and* feel one thing for certain," Clover said jokingly. "Lady Cordial is not going to get up in front of this class and lecture us like Lady Stella sometimes did. She's an administrator, not a teacher. We'll definitely have guest lecturers from here on."

Everyone turned to the door expectantly.

"Well, whoever it is, is late," Scarlet said.

Starmins ticked by, and still no teacher came to the room.

"Maybe our lecturer is stuck somewhere," Clover said, thinking of the stalled circus swift train. "Energy outages are everywhere."

"It's true," Libby agreed. "My parents canceled their vacation when their hotel lost its fifty-star rating because of slow service. Meals were delayed because of faulty micro-zaps, and beach towels at the cabana stand weren't dried properly."

Libby blushed a bright pink shade, realizing she came off as a bit entitled. Of course, it wasn't her fault her family was wealthy!

"We know you're not spoiled, Libby," Clover said gently.

Libby smiled gratefully and continued. "Everyone has to tighten their belts now and start conserving energy. My parents said things are pretty awful, even though the holo-papers have been downplaying the crisis. And they're not just talking about wet towels! Businesses are closing."

"Well, the only thing we can do is go about *our* business." Clover smiled at her play on words, even though no one else noticed. "Just keep collecting energy to help save Starland. Hopefully, a Wish Orb will be ready soon, and Gemma or I can go on a mission."

Then she turned to Sage. "What does your mom think?"

Sage's mother was a wish energy scientist and would be sure to know the latest news.

"I don't really know." Sage shook her head and her long lavender hair swung back and forth. "Every time we start to talk, her Star-Zap goes off and she has to take a holo-call, or she's called into a meeting. I've only gotten a few holo-texts. You know, typical mom stuff: do you need a new toothlight . . . holo-call your brothers . . ."

"Well, I'm going to holo-call my family right now,"

Leona said with a huff, "instead of sitting here and waiting for a teacher who isn't going to show."

"Yes!" Scarlet stood and stomped to the door in her heavy black boots. "Class dismissed!"

★

Stardays passed without any Star Darlings classes and without a Wish Orb notification from Lady Cordial. Increasingly, lights flickered and devices slowed. Still, Clover kept to her regular routine: writing songs before breakfast, going to class, and working on a big Golden Days project. It was an oral history assignment, and Clover was collecting stories from older family members.

She'd just holo-interviewed her great-uncle Octavius, who'd been a wee Starling during the Great Circus Disaster of '08. He'd described how the train's creature car had hurtled into a deep lake and everyone had jumped in to rescue the galliopes and glions. The story had a happy ending. The creatures had all survived. And there was an amusing bit about her great-uncle losing his pants.

But somehow, Clover's story kept turning into a piece about loss and disappointment. Usually, her written projects had a few jokes or witty sayings thrown in for entertainment. Now, worrying about Lady Stella and the power outages, she couldn't manage it.

At dinner that night, the overhead lights turned off and on and no even glanced up. It was becoming alarmingly routine.

"Are you done with that noddlenoodle soup?" Tessa was asking Libby hopefully. Noddlenoodle was the special of the day, and Libby had just started to slurp the one extremely long noodle in the dish. It wound round and round the bowl and could take starmins to finish. Libby, still working on the noodle, could only shake her head.

Disappointed, Tessa turned to Clover. "Don't even think about it!" Clover joked, placing her arms protectively over her own dish. "Just ask a Bot-Bot for your own soup!" She pointed out several Bot-Bot waiters hovering throughout the café, taking orders and serving meals.

"Well," said Tessa with a harrumph. "I just wanted a taste. But if you insist . . ." She waved to a nearby Bot-Bot, on its way to deliver another bowl of noddlenoodle. The Bot-Bot paused to say, "I'll be right back, Miss Tessa." Then its eyes opened wide. A loud whirring sounded from somewhere in its body, and its feet moved uselessly back and forth.

"Uh-oh," it said in its robotic voice. "I . . . am . . . about . . . to . . . power . . . down." It sank, tilting crazily. The bowl tipped over.

"No!" cried Tessa as the soup poured into her lap, the noddlenoodle winding up in a coil on her head.

The Bot-Bot, now on the floor, its face blank, had nothing to say.

"Well, there you have it," Clover said with a giggle. "Your own bowl of noddlenoodle."

And then, thanks to self-cleaning technology, the soup and noodle disappeared, leaving Tessa's skirt dry and clean, her head free of the noddlenoodle crown. Even she had to laugh.

For once, they'd found something funny about the power failures. But Clover's good mood didn't last. That night she couldn't take a sparkle shower; for the first time ever, the sparkles had run out. And she realized her Star-Zap had failed to record her Wishling Ways lecture, so she couldn't study while she slept.

Everyone was complaining about power problems early the next day, Yumday, as Clover and the Star Darlings joined the rest of the school for the weekly assembly.

"I bet we'll talk about the energy crisis," Gemma predicted.

"It would be hard to ignore," Tessa agreed.

"Unless Lady Cordial wants everything to seem as normal as possible," Clover said. "Then there'd just be the regular announcements and presentations."

Sure enough, Lady Cordial stumbled onstage and began the assembly with the traditional Starlandian Pledge of Illumination, same as usual. She then recited a long list of updates: students celebrating Bright Days, a holo–book club meeting, a special presentation by the drama club.

"Don't miss out on that," Lady Cordial said, nodding approvingly. "It includes a holo-retrospective of their most talented alumna, a student named Cora, who s-s-s-specialized in villainous roles."

Lady Cordial went on and on until she came to the last order of business: a demonstration by the Ultimate Frisbeam club. The girls walked onstage, holding their disks of light, ready to perform.

A loud voice interrupted the assembly: "Starscuse me, students!" The Frisbeam team stopped, confused. "I don't mean to interfere with your performance, girls. But the assembly is drawing to a close, and we still haven't discussed a topic of utmost importance: the energy crisis."

A tall, thin imposing figure rose from the first row of teachers. Her bright red hair framed her narrow face like a sun's corona. "It's that new teacher!" Astra hissed to Clover. "Professor Honoria McHue. She just took over my Astronomics class."

The teacher stood, half facing the audience, half turned toward Lady Cordial and the stage.

She certainly has everyone's attention, Clover thought admiringly. All the students were sitting up straight now, alert and interested.

Lady Cordial stared at Professor Honoria McHue, flustered.

"What exactly is being done here?" the teacher demanded. "I've heard other schools have started conserving energy. Is that an option at Starling Academy?"

Lady Cordial nodded so vigorously her bun came loose. "Of course it is, Professor Honoria McHue. I was planning on addressing the issue, of course—at a more appropriate time. But I will get right to it now. I feel the best course of action is to establish committees to research those options."

While Lady Cordial continued, the students settled back in their seats. Scarlet yawned.

"Each committee can be tailored to focus on one aspect of the issue," Lady Cordial went on, "s-s-s-s-so the eventual plan will be s-s-s-s-stronger as a whole. For instance, the Rules and Regulations Committee can be headed by Professor Dolores Raye." Lady Cordial took a few steps toward the professor, as if to introduce her, and tripped over her own feet. She tumbled to the ground with a loud thud. "Oh, my s-s-s-s-stars!" she cried, holding her ankle. "Can s-s-s-s-someone call an EMB?"

The assembly ended in chaos. Emergency Medical Bot-Bots rushed to Lady Cordial's aid. But many didn't have the energy to reach the stage. They slowed, then stopped, blocking the aisles.

Finally, the Bot-Bots were rebooted. They carried Lady Cordial out on a stretcher and flew her to the infirmary. The assembly was officially over. Slowly, moving with the crowd, the Star Darlings made their way to the starmarble lobby.

"Should we just go to lunch?" Tessa asked the others. "It's early, but the café is open. If we're the first ones there, the Bot-Bots will still have plenty of energy to serve us."

"That makes sense," said Clover. They turned toward the Cosmic Transporter just as all their Star-Zaps went off.

"I have a feeling this is important," Piper murmured. She patted her pockets, then went through her big green bag, taking out a sleep mask, a dream journal, and other odds and ends as she searched for her device.

Clover watched Piper with amusement. She wasn't the most organized Starling around. Clover, on the other hand, liked to be fully prepared—always.

"Ready when you are" was, in fact, the credo of the Flying Molensas. The family was constantly on the go, with all their belongings in tow. *Hmmm*, thought Clover, *nice rhyme*. Maybe she could use it in a song.

Then she flicked her Star-Zap and read the message aloud to share with Piper. "'To all faculty and students.'"

"It's from Professor Honoria McHue!" Piper said, looking over her shoulder. "She sent a holo-mail blast to the whole school."

Nodding, Clover continued reading: "'Every Starling—here at the academy and across the planet—should be asking questions about the state of our energy supply. Why have there been power outages? Our energy is supposed to be continuously replenished! Are our Wish-Houses in order? Is negative energy affecting our Wish Orbs? And what can we do about our wish energy manipulation losing its power? If you have suggestions or would like to discuss any of these points, I am available. Starfully yours, Professor Honoria McHue.'"

"That's hitting the starnail on the head," said Scarlet, reading over the holo-mail on her own Star-Zap. She flicked to a news site. "And listen to this. *The Daily Moon* reports major outages in Solar Springs and Gloom Flats."

Tessa and Gemma were from Solar Springs; Piper was from Gloom Flats. *This is really hitting close to home,* Clover thought.

The sisters bent over their Star-Zaps, tapping furiously. A starsec later, Tessa and Gemma heard back from their mom. Gemma read the quick holo-text out loud. "'All farm creatures are fine. Hydro-energy system not working, so crops may be in danger. Garble greens in bad shape.'"

"No loss there!" Clover joked. Hardly anyone enjoyed eating the bitter green vegetable—except for Tessa. "Sorry, Tessa."

"'But Dad and I found some antique watering cans,'" Gemma continued, "'so don't worry!'"

Piper, meanwhile, had finally found her Star-Zap and sent off her own holo-text. "Oh," she groaned. "It keeps bouncing back. I can't get through!"

Piper's grandmother and brother lived in such an out-of-the-way place that their lines of communication were probably the first to go, Clover thought.

Piper took a deep breath, closed her eyes, and seemed to go to a different place for a moment. Clover had seen this happen before. So had all the other Star Darlings. They waited patiently.

"It's all right," Piper said, opening her eyes. "Gran is sending messages our old-fashioned family way. And mind-mail never fails! She and my brother are both fine."

"That's good," Clover said, relieved. Then she was filled with determination. "But we need to help any way we can—Wish Orb or no Wish Orb. We are the Star-Charmed Starlings."

Everyone nodded. Clover knew she sounded sure and in control. But what could they do without Lady Stella's guidance? They were just students, after all. And some were just first years, away from home for the very first time. Were they really prepared to take on Starland's fate?

Yes, she decided.

But maybe Lady Cordial was wondering the same thing! Maybe she was hesitant to send them on a mission.

"We need to see Lady Cordial," Clover told the others. "To the infirmary!"

CHAPTER
3

Clover, always in good health, had barely stepped foot in the Interstellar Infirmary during her two staryears at school. Now she noted the floor glistened with extra starpolish. A strong but not unpleasant antiseptic smell floated through the air.

She led the Star Darlings to the front desk. Smiling at the receptionist, she said warmly, "We're here to see Lady Cordial."

"Well," said the Starling, smiling back, "that's nice."

"Yes," said Clover pleasantly. "What room is she in?"

"I can't tell you that," the receptionist said, still smiling. "Lady Cordial has requested privacy. No visitors allowed."

Surely Lady Cordial didn't mean the Star Darlings! The receptionist had to let them in. Clover was doing her best to establish a bond with the woman—just like she'd been taught as a performer—smiling, speaking with friendly good humor. It seemed to be working. So she'd give it another try.

"I know Lady Cordial would be pleased to see us," Clover told the receptionist. If only they'd brought flowers—calliopes or chatterbursts. That would convince the woman.

"Take a seat," the receptionist said, waving toward the waiting area. "Lady Cordial is with the doctor. I'll see what I can do later. But right now I am swamped with work."

She whirled around to face a holo-keyboard, then examined her nails one by one.

"I guess we'll wait," Clover said, disappointed. Nodding, the girls sat down. Some flipped through old holo-magazines. Leona snickered, looking at the cover of *Starlebrity Journal*. "Look at this actor. He's so last staryear."

While everyone else crowded around, Clover decided to explore. In case the receptionist didn't follow through, she wanted to find Lady Cordial's room. She sidled down the hall, tiptoeing past empty rooms, until she heard voices in one room. She peeked through the door.

"We can't find anything wrong with you," a doctor was saying, her back blocking Clover's view. "But since you are in such pain . . ."

"Yes," said Lady Cordial in such a weak voice that Clover had to strain to hear. "I am in a great deal of pain."

"We'll keep you overnight for observation." The doctor turned and left. Clover jumped back, not wanting Lady Cordial to spot her. But it was too late.

Starf! thought Clover. What if Lady Cordial really didn't want to see them? Clover had gone and put her in an awkward position. And Lady Cordial wasn't at her best in difficult situations.

"Clover," Lady Cordial said falteringly, "you've come to s-s-s-s-see me."

"We all have, Lady Cordial, if that's okay."

"Yes," Lady Cordial said with a sigh. "But just for a few s-s-s-s-starmins. I don't have much s-s-s-s-strength."

Clover hurried to get the other Star Darlings and they all squeezed into the room.

Lady Cordial lay in bed, the sheet pulled up to her chin.

"How are you feeling?" asked Tessa. "Is it your ankle?"

Lady Cordial shook her head wearily. "At first I thought it was, but now I'm not s-s-s-so sure. The s-s-s-s-staff is running tests. It could be s-s-s-s-serious."

Maybe keeping someone for observation meant running tests. And "we can't find anything wrong with you" meant the doctor didn't want to frighten poor Lady Cordial.

Clover's glow flared with remorse. *We should have been visiting Lady Cordial because it's the right thing to do,* she told herself, *not because of our energy crisis.* But they were there now. So they might as well proceed.

Lady Cordial closed her eyes.

Clover edged closer to the bed. She'd better say something fast! "Since we're here," she said, "we thought we could talk about energy. We're hearing all sorts of reports about power outages."

"And it's been so long since we've had a mission," Cassie said.

"Yes," Clover said. "Maybe you're worried about Gemma or me not being ready, so you're holding off on sending us. But there's no need to worry. You can trust us."

Lady Cordial said nothing. She began to breathe evenly. Was she sleeping? Should they leave?

Then Scarlet stepped forward, bumping into the bed. Lady Cordial's eyelids fluttered a bit.

"It would be a very good time for a Wish Mission," Scarlet told her loudly. "Lady Stella isn't here to sabotage us. So we should be able to collect a starmendous amount of wish energy." She smiled. "I wish I could go back again. I really liked it on Wishworld."

"We can check the orbs!" Clover offered, thinking quickly. "Since you're in the infirmary, we can monitor them and see if one is ready."

Lady Cordial's eyes snapped open.

"Oh, good!" cried Leona. "Our visit is helping. You look wide awake now."

"S-s-s-s-sweet of you," Lady Cordial murmured, half closing her eyes again. "But I can keep track of the orbs remotely." She gestured at her Star-Zap on the nightstand, and it fell to the floor with a clatter.

Clover picked it up and put it out of Lady Cordial's reach, just for safekeeping. "I wish we could do something!"

"Maybe you can," said Lady Cordial. "I, too, have been following the reports." Her voice grew louder, as if relating her idea was giving her strength. "All the heads of s-s-s-s-schools are comparing notes on the energy crisis. I just heard about one s-s-s-s-school at the top of Mount Glint where they are making their own alternative fuel source. I don't know any details. But perhaps you girls could look into it? I can write you a s-s-s-s-starscuse note for missing class tomorrow. Why not take a trip and check it out?"

"That would be starmazing!" Sage said. "So we won't just be waiting for the Wish Orb!" She smiled at Clover. "Like you said, we'll be doing something!"

"Yes, something any old Starling could do," said Scarlet. "We should be concentrating on collecting wish energy. Remember, we're the chosen ones."

"And Mount Glint is so far away." Leona frowned. "It's really quite a hike."

"Oh, come now," said Lady Cordial. "You twelve are s-s-s-star-charmed. But who knows what fate has in s-s-s-store for you? What role the S-s-s-s-star Darlings will need to take?"

Piper nodded, and a dreamy expression crossed her face. Clover knew what would happen next. Piper would recount a dream and interpret it.

"I did just have a dream," Piper said, her forehead furrowed in concentration. "I was walking . . . walking . . . I couldn't tell where I was going. But I wasn't alone. And I needed to reach a specific destination. The fate of Starland depended on it."

She shook her head to clear it. "Maybe it means we should travel to Mount Glint."

"Well, count me out," Scarlet said crossly. "It doesn't make sense."

"I'm with Scarlet." Leona linked arms with her roommate. Clover blinked. More and more often lately, the two roommates—universes apart in every way—were in agreement. It was odd to see, but really nice. "It sounds like a lot of work and no payoff," Leona continued.

"But we all need to be together," Clover argued. "The oracle states clearly there are twelve Star-Charmed Starlings. Not ten." She looked at Cassie, the only Star Darling the other two would listen to. "Right?"

"We do need to stick together," Cassie agreed. "In the ancient book, the energy at the center of the holo-drawing comes from all of us working together."

"Yes!" Gemma grabbed Tessa's hand. "We stick together!"

Lady Cordial leaned back, looking exhausted.

"We'll go tomorrow," Clover said quickly, before Scarlet or Leona could say anything else. "And we should leave you, Lady Cordial, so you can rest."

Lady Cordial lifted her hand in a feeble wave. "Farewell and s-s-s-star s-s-s-speed," she said drowsily.

Walking on tiptoe, the girls filed out of the room.

"And bring your S-s-s-s-star Darlings backpacks," Lady Cordial called out in a surprisingly loud voice, "in case you need to carry the energy s-s-s-source back!"

★

Early the next starday, just as the moons were eclipsed by the suns, the girls met between the two dorms. They'd all had a bit of difficulty getting ready. Their manipulation energy was slowing down, and sparkle showers took forever to sparkle. But there they were, everyone except Clover and Gemma carrying a backpack as Lady Cordial had instructed.

Tessa handed out astromuffins, saying, "I hear Mount Glint's cafeteria can't hold a hololight to ours. So just in case we get hungry . . ."

"Star salutations," Vega said, placing the muffin in her backpack. "Now," she said, turning to Clover, "are you sure you have the route figured out? I checked some holo-maps and—"

"Vega! I said I could do it!" Clover interrupted. "We just take a few hover-buses, then walk a bit." She consulted her Star-Zap holo-map. "We can get the first one right at the gate. It's the number twelve bus."

"Twelve!" said Piper, delighted. "A wonderful sign."

And it did seem to be a sign. The bus was already at the stop, as if waiting just for them. The door lifted.

"No passengers!" the Bot-Bot said, hurriedly closing the door without further explanation.

The bus didn't move, and the girls stood there impatiently. "Maybe it will take us after all," Libby said hopefully. But then a sign on the side of the bus flashed: OUT OF SERVICE. OUT OF POWER.

"When will the next one come?" Adora asked.

"Right now," Clover said, pointing down the street. But that one was so crowded the Bot-Bot conductor poked its head out and said, "No room!" before the bus sped away.

A starhour later, the girls finally boarded the first bus, which was by then fully functional. "So," Clover said, checking the map, "we change buses at Starland City Hall."

"Starland City Hall?" Vega blinked. "We could have walked there!"

In no time at all, the Star Darlings reached Starland City Hall and changed buses, first to the number 593, then to the number .003, and finally to the number 6,672.

"Now, this one will take us right to the foot of Mount Glint!" Clover said triumphantly.

"If we ever get there," said Adora as the bus sputtered to a stop.

"We are having problems with the power steering," the Bot-Bot conductor announced. "All passengers must disembark. Another bus will arrive in one starhour."

Two starhours later, the girls finally reached their destination: the foot of Mount Glint. Clover gazed at her friends. They all looked grumpy and tired. And they still had to hike up the mountain!

"This way," Clover said cheerfully, leading them to a path. "We're almost there!" she added, though she really had no idea.

Luckily, Mount Glint turned out to be more of a hill than a mountain, and the path was smooth and wide. Still feeling responsible, though, Clover made up a marching song to energize the group.

Left, right, left right—
We're almost there, we're on our way.
Right, left. Right left—
Right in the middle of a star school day.

Before Clover knew it, they'd reached the top, having stopped only once, to eat Tessa's astromuffins. The suns were shining brightly, the grass sparkled with glow-dew, and multicolored glittery trees swayed in the breeze. Clover's spirits rose.

The girls walked a few steps more to a narrow walkway, which was marked with a sign: WELCOME TO THE MOUNT GLINT SCHOOL, WHERE LEARNING IS SUNDAMENTAL.

The path led directly to the campus, built on a much smaller scale than Starling Academy. Its low one-story buildings seemed a bit worn.

"They don't have a Cosmic Transporter?" Libby asked.

"I think we're on it," Scarlet said. "It's just not working."

"They must be restructuring it for the new energy source," Clover said determinedly. "Maybe they've discovered that energy can come from those colorful trees we passed."

"Or from that dirt road we took!" Scarlet smirked.

Clover sighed. Of course her guess was just a moonshot. And usually she was the one with the sarcastic one-liner. But if she dished it out, she had to take it, so she just grinned.

"Okay, enough joking around," Scarlet said, actually returning the smile. "I don't want to waste another starsec on this silly trip. . . . Starscuse me," she said, stopping an official-looking adult with large glasses on top of her head, holding back her dark green hair. "Can you tell us anything about an alternative energy source?"

The woman looked at her, baffled.

"Or at least direct us to the head of the school," Clover added quickly, not giving up. "She'd know what we're talking about."

"I am the head of the school, Lady Marissa."

"Star greetings, Lady Marissa," Clover said, politely bowing her head. "We're from Starling Academy. And we heard your school is using a new energy source. But we don't have any other details."

"That's because there are no details—and no energy source," the headmistress said. "I did send a holo-mail to headmasters and -mistresses across Starland, suggesting we spearhead a research effort. But no one thought I was serious. In fact, they thought I was joking. Here." She showed Clover the reply from Star Prep's headmaster, which Clover read aloud.

"'Star salutations for the laugh. If only laughter could be used for fuel, I would show your holo-letter to everyone.'"

Everyone's a comedian, Clover thought grimly.

Lady Marissa sighed. "I guess he's right. Our history holo-books tell us the founding Starlings tried everything before they stumbled upon wish-granting energy."

Clover sighed along with her. How disappointing. She hated to go back and tell Lady Cordial the bad news.

"And as you can probably tell," Lady Marissa continued, waving an arm to indicate the dim campus, "we are on energy rationing right now, saving our resources for overcast days and nights."

Clover nodded. Lady Marissa was trying to be helpful. Unfortunately, she couldn't give them what they wanted: a way to save Starland. "Star salutations anyway," Clover said as the Star Darlings began to retrace their steps. Now they'd have to make the long trip back empty-handed. Everyone was grumbling unhappily.

"Look on the bright side," Scarlet said, nudging her as they walked. "I see a Starcab stand right over there. There are three cabs hovering, so we can divide up into groups of four and just drive home.

"I have only one question for you, circus star: why didn't we do this in the first place?"

CHAPTER

4

Even with Starcabs, the trip back wasn't easy; the cabs had to stop to recharge again and again. Finally, as the first stars began to shine, the Star Darlings walked through the school gates, just in time for dinner. The girls ate quickly, then decided to go to the infirmary and tell Lady Cordial what had happened.

Unfortunately, it seemed the stars were still against them. Lady Cordial had checked out. They hurried to her office, but she wasn't there, either.

Clover felt terrible hauling everyone all over campus—especially after dragging them all around Starland. "I'll go to her house," she told the others. "Everyone else should just go to bed."

Walking alone, Clover made her way to the faculty

residences. She placed her hand on a scanner and walked through the entrance as the curtain of leaves slowly parted.

Clover recognized Lady Cordial's house immediately. The teachers' homes looked just like them. And Lady Cordial's was the same shade of purple as her hair, with an unkempt yard and a frazzled look. Clover strode to the door and knocked loudly.

She looked up and saw the curtains on the second floor ripple slightly, as if someone was peering out. But she must have been mistaken. Lady Cordial didn't answer the door.

I probably just missed her, Clover thought, disappointed. Maybe now she was back at her office, catching up on work.

Clover sighed. Another wasted trip. Quickly, she turned to walk up the overgrown path. *Wait, what was that?*

A newish home a little farther up the street had caught her attention. It was tall and narrow, imposing and no-nonsense, with a bright red roof and a silvery sheen.

That must be Professor Honoria McHue's house, Clover told herself. *I'm here. I might as well talk to her.*

The teacher had raised so many interesting questions;

maybe she actually had answers, too. But just as Clover reached the front steps, a holo-sign appeared.

ATTENTION, VISITORS! PROFESSOR HONORIA MCHUE HAS TAKEN A POSITION AT A WEE STARLINGS SCHOOL IN GLOOM FLATS, EFFECTIVE IMMEDIATELY. HER STARLING ACADEMY HOLO-MAIL HAS BEEN DISCONTINUED, AND THERE IS NO FORWARDING ADDRESS. WE WISH HER ALL THE BEST!

Well, that was sudden, Clover thought. She hoped the teacher was happier at her new job, but her absence certainly didn't help the situation at Starling Academy.

Standing by the leaf curtain a starmin later, she flicked her wrist to open the exit. Nothing happened. She was too low on energy to use her manipulation skills—that was the problem. Groaning a bit, Clover pushed her way through.

Would things keep getting worse?

★

Clover wasn't the only Star Darling who was worried. It seemed everyone's spirits were so dim that the sparkle had gone out of their eyes . . . and hair . . . and skin. And of course that was perfectly understandable. Nothing was going right.

Clover had eventually found Lady Cordial, to tell her about the Mount Glint fiasco. But the new headmistress, while feeling better, was too busy catching up on work to come up with more suggestions. Plus there was still no sign of a Wish Orb. Add to that the worthless, time-consuming trip to Mount Glint, and Clover felt her own energy level sink.

She felt responsible for cheering everyone up. *And what makes every Starling smile?* she asked herself. *A circus, of course!*

Excited by the idea, Clover sat at her desk to holo-type some notes. The atmosphere had to be fun and daring, bright and energetic. For starters, she could give star-swallowing lessons. She made a note: *order at least twelve stars.* And she'd need a cloud candy machine. What was a circus without that fluffy, sticky, sweet treat on a stick?

Then she had another idea. There was a galliope stable a couple of floozels away. She could bring over a few and work up a routine—standing on one galliope's back while it galloped, then leaping to another and swinging from the tip of its glowing tail to its sparkly mane.

Clover's mind raced with more plans. *Juggling! A clown act!* She could set up a starwire between trees. She could use the school's trampoline for a tumbling performance!

Clover designed a flyer announcing the circus to the Star Darlings: COME ONE, COME ALL! COME TO THE SHORES OF LUMINOUS LAKE AND SEE THE GREATEST SHOW AT STARLING ACADEMY! She added a date and time and grinned. It would be starmazing!

Next Clover placed orders for the cloud candy machine, the galliopes, the special starwire, and more. But the holo-request for the machine never went through. Another energy blip. The galliopes were already booked for a wee Starling's Bright Day party. And when the starwire came, Clover realized it was all wrong. The company had accidentally sent a firewire, a replacement part for micro-zaps!

How could she tell everyone the circus was canceled? She couldn't. The day of the big event, she trudged to Luminous Lake. Any starmin everyone would arrive, and all she had were some star balls to juggle and clown makeup and accessories her mom had sent by lightning delivery.

Clover was going to let everyone down—again. The circus would have proven she could do something besides lead them on wild glowgoose chases for energy. She'd been waiting and waiting for a chance to make a difference—to go on her own Wish Mission, to be a true Star Darling. And now she wasn't even a true circus performer.

"Hello, Clover." Piper appeared out of nowhere. "Where's the circus?"

Clover bit her lip. "You're looking at it."

"Really?" Astra said, walking over with the others. She kicked a star ball to Clover. Automatically, Clover ducked under the ball so it landed on her head. The ball spun around twice, then dropped into her waiting hands.

"That's starrific! Can you do more tricks?" Sage asked.

"Of course she can!" Astra said encouragingly.

So Clover juggled all the star balls. She bounced them off trees, off a fence, and even off the lake with a bit of energy manipulation. Then she showed everyone else how to do it, too. Soon all the Star Darlings were laughing and participating.

Meanwhile, Leona wandered over to the clown supplies and started playing around. Before Clover knew it, all the girls had big glowing noses and twinkling stars painted around their eyes, and were wearing suspenders and giant shoes. They pushed each other around playfully, tripped over their big feet, and tossed buckets of starfetti, pretending it was water.

Finally, they collapsed on the ground in fits of giggles. "That was more fun than Light Giving Day!" Libby said, still laughing. And everyone agreed.

★

Later that starnight, lying in her hammock, Clover couldn't fall asleep. She was very glad the circus had turned out so well. Who would have thought that star balls and clown makeup could be just as much fun as a three-star circus! But still, she felt like the event had been missing something—or someone.

Lady Stella.

Clover knew Lady Stella—or the Lady Stella she remembered, anyway—would have been pleased that everyone had fun and proud of Clover for pulling it off against the odds.

Clover had been close to giving up, just like when she had first come to school and had a starmendously tough homework assignment. It was a project for her Wish Energy Manipulation class, and the deadline was looming.

She was new to Starling Academy, and expectations couldn't have been too high. But Clover wanted to prove herself right away. She'd already spent starhours tinkering around with ideas for a basic manipulation demonstration. The assignment was to use a starsack of groceries. But the assorted fruits and vegetables were just so uninteresting! And she couldn't come up with anything special. So she'd moved to a picnic table outside the Illumination Library, hoping for a fresh perspective.

At the table, she'd set her Star-Zap to record. She was ready to take a holo-video to hand in. But ozziefruit? Garble greens? Plantannas? Dull, dull, dull.

The bag stood there doing nothing, totally uninspiring. She looked at it through narrowed eyes. Should she transfer the food onto dishes? Boring. Separate the groceries into food groups? Glo-hum.

"I can't do this!" she'd said out loud.

"Clover?" Lady Stella had said, gliding over in her graceful way. "Are you having trouble with homework?"

"Um." Clover was at a loss for words. The headmistress was so lovely and kind, and of course Clover wanted to impress her. But she couldn't even speak. All her circus training, and she was starstruck!

Finally, she'd managed to tell Lady Stella the problem. It helped to look into her eyes and feel her concern.

"Well," Lady Stella had said, "what's the worst that could happen with this project?"

"I'd get a D for Dim or G for Gloomy."

"I'd say the worst thing would be if you ate all the food and couldn't do the assignment at all."

Was Lady Stella kidding around? Clover couldn't be sure. But she felt her shoulders relax.

As if she'd read her mind, Lady Stella said, "I'm trying to help you relax, Clover, because I think you need to figure out a fun approach. I hear you like to joke around."

"Is that a good thing?" Clover asked.

Lady Stella smiled. "You make people laugh and you lift their spirits. Of course that's a good thing. Perhaps you can add more of your personality to the project."

While Lady Stella waited patiently, Clover thought about the groceries, funny things she could do with the items, and what would make her laugh if she was watching it on holo-video.

Finally, she took one plantanna—a curved tubelike glowing yellow fruit. She placed it on the table. Then she stepped away and, using her wish energy manipulation skills, peeled it completely in one long motion. Slowly, she guided the peel to the ground.

Whistling nonchalantly now, Clover walked closer to the plantanna, into the video frame. "Whoa!" she cried, slipping on the skin. She flew through the air, twisted her body into a flip, and landed with her feet solidly on the ground.

"Was that a-*peeling*?" Clover joked.

Lady Stella laughed and clapped. "I believe you nailed it, Clover."

Clover had, in fact, received an I for Illumination on the project, and her holo-vid was the hit of the class. Right after, she'd run to Lady Stella's office to show her the grade. The headmistress had been as delighted as Clover, repeatedly saying how proud she was of her.

But had Lady Stella really been proud and delighted? Or had she been pretending? How could someone who seemed so supportive, kind, and open have been secretly plotting against her students?

A purple-tinted tear trickled down Clover's cheek. It was all so very sad.

CHAPTER
5

"Come on, Clover! You're supposed to be lighting me up for the game! Not bringing me down."

"I know, Astra! I know! Star apologies!"

Clover and Astra were on their way to a special star ball game, held at night, under the stars. It was the Glowin' Glions versus their biggest rival, the Bright Horizons. Astra had asked Clover to walk over early with her, to help her drum up some energy.

Clover knew she wasn't doing a very good job. But now she was outside on a beautiful evening. The temperature was a mild ten degrees Starrius, and the stars twinkled brightly. Rainstorms were called for later. But if everything proceeded on time, the game should be over well before they hit.

And really, rain was a good thing, Clover remembered. With hydration machines not working properly, crops were drying out. But right then Clover wanted to push any thoughts about the energy shortage out of her mind. It felt good to look forward to a night of pure enjoyment.

"You'll knock those players' starsocks off!" Clover said encouragingly. "Who's the best? Astra's the best!" she cheered loudly.

Astra grinned. "That's way better."

Together, the roommates walked to the locker room, where Clover gave Astra a quick hug for good luck.

"Remember when all you did was hug me?" Astra said with a smile. "That was starmazingly annoying."

Clover smiled back. Her odd behavior—caused by the poisonous nail polish—seemed like ancient history. So much had happened between then and now. "Tell you what," she told Astra. "If you win—which I'm sure you will—I promise *not* to hug you!"

Astra disappeared between the rows of brightly colored lockers while Clover made her way to the stadium. It was still early. The stands were empty; Clover had her choice of seats.

She walked to the midfield, then up a number of

rows so she'd have a perfect view of the action. Then she counted off eleven seats, reserving ten for the other Star Darlings, and settled into one at the end. Immediately, it transformed into a swift train seat, the most comfortable chair Clover could imagine—one that always made her feel at home.

Slowly, the other seats filled up. In ones, twos, and threes, the rest of the Star Darlings arrived. A nervous-looking Cassie, clutching a large bag at her side, slipped in beside Clover, and the stadium seat turned into a reading chair, complete with headrest. Leona, next to Cassie, sat regally on a padded golden throne.

The stadium was packed now, every seat taken.

Shaking her head, Leona leaned over Cassie to complain to Clover. "Can you believe I won't be singing—I mean *no one* will be singing—the Starlandian anthem? They're just having a parade of athletes. Like that's appropriate!" She opened her glittery cropped blazer to reveal a microphone in an inside pocket. "I brought it along just in case there's a change in plans," she confided.

Cassie, meanwhile, kept looking inside the bag. Clover thought, *She has glow-ants in her pants*, as her great-uncle Octavius used to say.

"Are you okay?" Clover whispered.

Cassie nodded and closed the top of the bag, a guilty look on her face. "I just can't seem to settle down. I think it's because I miss Lady Stella."

"I know," Clover said sympathetically.

"I mean, I believed she was guilty. I guess I still do. The evidence is overwhelming. That's why I pushed everyone to confront her. But Starling Academy just seems wrong without her."

Cassie stopped talking as the teams ran onto the field for warm-ups. A cheer rose from the fans. Libby held up a holo-sign that read GLOW, GLOWIN' GLIONS! GLOW, ASTRA!

Thirty starmins passed, then forty, then fifty. The players were still stretching and taking practice kicks. "Why isn't it starting?" Cassie asked.

"We must be waiting for Lady Cordial," Clover said. "The headmistress always *kicks* off the games." She looked at Cassie to see if she got the joke. But Cassie was rearranging her bag again and hadn't heard.

Thirty more starmins ticked by; then an announcer said: "Attention, fans! Lady Cordial, head of Starling Academy, will now welcome the athletes and lead the parade."

And finally, there she was, on the field, in front of

the crowd, looking anxious and frazzled. The two teams lined up on either side of her.

"Oh, my stars," said Leona. "She's tucked the back of her skirt into her stockings."

Clover saw that sure enough, Lady Cordial's rumpled skirt was hiked up in a very unflattering way.

Leona started waving at Astra and finally got her attention. She pointed to Lady Stella. Astra shrugged, then took a closer look. Her mouth, in an O of surprise, said it all.

"S-s-s-s-s-star apologies for the delay in getting s-s-s-started," Lady Cordial said into a microphone. "It s-s-s-seems I had the wrong time on my S-s-s-s-star-Zap. But now—"

Astra had edged around the athletes, moving in back of the line until she reached Lady Cordial. Now she was whispering urgently in her ear.

Clover heard a loud gasp. Lady Cordial reached behind her to fix her skirt, and Astra slipped back into place.

"But now," Lady Cordial continued, her glow flaring with embarrassment, "I'd like to introduce the teams."

Somehow she got through the names, bungling only the longer ones and calling Astra Adora by mistake.

Finally, sighing with relief, she led the procession in an awkward but uneventful march around the field. With a wave at the audience, she took a seat behind the team bench.

"I'm glad that's over," Clover told Cassie. "But at least Lady Cordial remembered the game!"

The referee flashed a holo-star, and the teams got into position on the field. Another holo-star signaled the start.

Astra passed the star ball back to a defender, then sprinted forward, waving her arms to show she was open. She used her wish energy manipulation to control the ball, then raced toward the goal. The Brights' goalie bounced on her toes, ready to stop the shot. But Astra concentrated the ball high and into the corner of the net—impossible to deflect. Goal for the Glions! The crowd roared.

By the end of the second half, the Brights had come back with two goals, while the Glions had added one more. The score was tied. Now a girl on the Brights had the star ball and was making a run up the field.

Cassie gripped Clover's hand. "It's almost over!" she said, excited. "If they make this goal, the Glions won't have time for another attempt!"

The player was closing in on the net, with a clear

path ahead and no defender close by. Suddenly, the field lights sputtered out. Gasps and cries of surprise erupted throughout the stadium. The game came to a standstill.

The referee flashed a star. "Startime out!" she called. "Spectators, please set your Star-Zaps on flashlight mode so the game can continue."

They all pulled out their Star-Zaps. It was becoming common procedure in a blackout.

Clover flicked her screen, but nothing happened. "I'm out of power," she groaned.

"Me too!" said Cassie.

"Same here," Leona chimed in.

More shouts rang up and down the rows as everyone realized the same thing: none of their Star-Zaps were working.

Lady Cordial jumped up. "Don't panic!" she cried in a voice that sounded quite panicky. "As long as we have the s-s-s-stars, we will have light."

Just then a giant storm cloud rolled across the sky, dimming each and every star. A few raindrops fell, then more and more. The stadium was plunged into darkness.

Frightened and wet, girls rushed to the exits, pushing each other.

The Star Darlings stayed in their seats. Clover thought quickly. She knew the dangers of crowded venues: their big top tent had collapsed once, and the audience had barely gotten out in time.

"We have to do something," she told the others. "Leona! Does your mic still work?"

"Testing, one, two, three. Yes!"

"Tell everyone to return to their seats. The rain is letting up now, so that's better."

"Everyone," Leona declared into the microphone, "return to your seats!"

No one was listening. Instead, even more Starlings rushed into the aisles.

"Give them a reason," Clover ordered Leona. "And be louder."

Leona took a deep breath. "Starlings!" she said in a strong, commanding way. "Return to your seats. I will be raffling the chance to perform with the Star Darlings band by seat number." Leona spoke with such force that each Starling stopped in her tracks.

Some did turn around. But most, Clover realized with dismay, didn't seem all that interested in performing with Leona—at least when they were in the middle of a blackout. So Scarlet brought out her drumsticks to play a *rat-a-tat-tat* on the mic, and everyone stopped again.

At the same moment, Cassie opened up her bag and

lifted out something furry and glowing. *What* is *that?* Clover wondered.

"Now is as good a time as any," Cassie murmured. The creature lifted its head and Clover realized Cassie was holding a small pink glowfur. It was adorable, of course. They all were, with their big soulful eyes, delicate gossamer wings, and huggable plump bodies.

"She's yours?" Clover asked in starprise.

Leona glanced over. "Oh, my stars, is that a glowfur?" she cried.

Cassie nodded. "I've had Itty with me since the first day of school," she admitted. "I know we're not supposed to have pets. But I was so nervous coming to a big school and being with so many people I didn't know, I just had to have her close by."

Cassie paused as Itty nestled under her chin. "I brought her tonight because, well, you know how I feel, Clover. And she always makes me feel better."

Clover nodded.

"But I can't keep her a secret anymore. It wouldn't be right." Cassie held Itty close and whispered, "Sing the 'Song of Calmness.'"

Leona held out her mic, and the glowfur began to sing. Her voice was pure and tinkling, the melody soothing. The panic subsided immediately. Slowly, carefully, everyone returned to their seats as if in a trance.

"Give it all you've got," Leona instructed the glowfur, and Itty's song swelled. It grew louder and louder, and it became a call to all her glowfur friends. In starsecs, the sky filled with the brightly lit creatures, all singing the same lullaby.

A feeling of peace swept through the crowd.

"Now lead the way out," Cassie instructed, and the glowfurs flew to various sections of the stadium and guided the Starlings to the exits. The crisis was averted.

★

Later, swinging in her hammock when the events of the night had passed, Clover felt relieved. Everyone had gotten out safely. Astra was happy the game had ended in a tie, just before the opposing team surely would have scored. And in the commotion, no one but the Star Darlings knew where that first glowfur had come from. So Cassie's secret pet was, luckily, still a secret.

"You know," Clover told Astra, "I think we should offer to help Lady Cordial more. You had a team dinner, so you weren't at the Celestial Café tonight. But all the Bot-Bot waiters stopped working at the very same starsec. Remember Lady Cordial had sent that holo-message, explaining she'd be putting them on power-save mode to conserve energy?"

"Mmmm-hmmmm," Astra said sleepily.

"Well, it turns out that she accidentally switched them to hyperdrive instead," Clover said. "They all had to be rebooted. But everything's okay. At least for now."

She waited for Astra to say something—about Lady Cordial, about the energy crisis, about her lead-off goal. But Astra must have been running low on energy herself. She was already fast asleep.

★

Clover raced through dark streets. She was rushing to catch the circus swift train, not sure where she needed to go but fully aware she was awfully late. And if she missed the train? Clover's heart thudded in her chest. She'd never ever find it. Her family would be lost to her forever. She couldn't miss it. She just couldn't!

At the opposite end of the street, Clover glimpsed someone—she couldn't tell who—searching for her. "Clover?" called the figure. "Where are you?"

"I'm here!" she shouted. "I'm here!"

"I'm here!" Clover was still crying when she woke with a start. It had all been a dream!

She glanced anxiously at Astra. Luckily, her roommate, exhausted from the game, was still fast asleep. Clover reached for her Star-Zap, now working properly, and checked the time. She'd barely been asleep at all!

What an odd dream, she thought, sitting back in her hammock. She should definitely talk to Piper about it. Maybe it meant she was missing something. That she had to get to a certain destination before it was too late? And who was that Starling who'd been searching for her? Her voice was very familiar. . . .

"Clover?" called the same voice, coming from the other side of the door.

It was Piper, just outside her room!

Clover padded to the door and opened it quietly. "Piper," she whispered. "What in Starland are you doing here?"

Piper, her eyes closed, half nodded, then waved one arm languidly. *She's sleepwalking!* Clover realized. *And she wants me to follow her.*

Clover tentatively touched Piper's arm, but Piper slept on. Clover had read somewhere that you shouldn't wake a sleepwalker. So as Piper turned to go, Clover had no choice but to follow. She couldn't just let her wander around by herself.

Piper led Clover to the Big Dipper Dorm and opened

the door to a supply closet. It had to be the closet Scarlet used to go down to the caves. Clover hesitated. She really didn't like the idea of going underground with a sleepwalking Piper in the middle of the night—especially after getting trapped in a secret chamber just the other starweek.

But Piper was already inside, reaching for a trapdoor as if she knew exactly where it was. Soundlessly, she started down the steps.

Glad she was still clutching her Star-Zap, Clover set it to flashlight mode and followed. Moving quietly and quickly, the two went down the metal stairs—cool beneath Clover's bare feet—and into the underground tunnels.

The tunnels were a mazelike jumble. After a few starmins, Clover had no idea where they were. But Piper floated down the halls, sure-footed and confident, seemingly with a destination in mind. Then they turned left, and even in the gloom, Piper recognized the tunnel. It led to the Wish Cavern.

With a knowing nod, Piper stopped at a random spot and flicked a wrist at the wall. The hidden door whooshed open, and they stepped inside.

The Wish Cavern! Each time Clover saw it, she felt starmazed. They were deep underground, but starlight flooded the space as if they were standing in an open field. Golden waterfalls of wish energy still flowed down the cavern walls. But Clover noted the streams had narrowed and the current was sluggish. Then she turned to the center of the room, where a grassy platform stood, and she froze.

A Wish Orb was waiting.

"Piper?" she said questioningly. But before Clover could say another word, the orb floated through the air. It stopped, hovering star inches from Clover's nose. Without thinking, Clover reached for it and held it gently in her palm.

Now what? she wondered. Piper's eyes were still closed, and she was swaying on her feet as if in a trance. She'd be no help. But without Lady Stella—or Lady Cordial—to mark the occasion, there was no ceremony, no pomp, no starcumstance. Clover felt slightly disappointed. She was a circus performer, after all. She liked a bit of fanfare.

Then Piper spoke in a strange, sleepy, drawn-out voice. "The orb has been waiting for you to come, Clover. Time is running out for your Wish Mission."

Piper's voice grew more forceful. "You must leave right now!"

CHAPTER
6

Clover gasped. Leave right then? In the middle of the night? In her bare feet? Without a word to Lady Cordial?

Besides, did Piper even know what she was talking about? The Starling wasn't even awake!

It was all so unusual, and Clover didn't like it one bit. She should just go back to her hammock, pull up her blanket, and go back to sleep. Then she'd wake up, and maybe there'd be a group holo-text telling the Star Darlings a Wish Orb had been identified. There'd be the usual routine of the platform opening, the orb floating into the cavern, and the girls waiting for the orb to choose its Starling.

But right there, right then, she was already holding the Wish Orb—without the Star Darlings. Without Lady Stella. And she didn't know what to do.

Clover's Wish Orb trembled. Its sparkle dimmed. *Starf!* she thought. The orbs had notoriously short life cycles. Clover had to help grant her Wisher's wish before it faded away. And if she didn't do it in time? The energy would be lost forever. Not to mention her poor Wisher's dream would never come true.

Clover groaned in frustration. She was the eleventh Star Darling to be chosen. She'd waited so long for this to happen. (Not as long as Gemma, of course.) And now here was her opportunity, her chance to excel.

A flutterfocus darted by, and Clover gazed at it in wonder. It fluttered here and there, swooping around the platform as if searching for sweet-smelling nectar. It hovered for a moment, made up its mind, and landed lightly on Piper's nose.

Piper's eyes snapped open. She stared at the creature for a long moment, then held out her finger. The flutter-focus settled on the tip. "Hello, little one," Piper said softly. A moment later, the creature took off, disappearing behind a golden waterfall.

"Star greetings, Clover," Piper said with a calm smile. She gazed around the Wish Cavern as if it was exactly where she'd expected to be. All along, Clover had resisted the urge to shake Piper awake. Now she resisted the urge just to shake her. How could any Starling be so . . . so . . . unruffled?

"Aren't you starprised?" Clover asked a bit shrilly. "You're underground, in the Wish Cavern!"

"Of course I'm starprised," Piper replied. "But there must be a reason why I'm here—with you." She eyed the Wish Orb. Clover relaxed her grip. She'd been holding it a little too firmly.

"So tell me," Piper continued.

With a sigh, Clover explained how Piper had come to her room and led her underground. Piper nodded as if that kind of thing happened every starday.

"So what do you think I should do?" Clover's mind was racing like a runaway galliope, and at least Piper was composed and capable of clear thought.

"I already told you." Piper spoke with exaggerated patience, as if Clover was a wee Starling. "You need to go right now."

Oh! So she remembered that part! Clover thought. *How helpful!*

Clover knew Piper was right. Still, she hated to just leave! "Shouldn't we wake up Lady Cordial?"

"I don't think so," Piper said thoughtfully. "There's

no time. And I don't want to bother her. The poor Starling really needs her rest."

Clover definitely agreed with that. But there were other issues. "I don't have my hat! I'm in my pajamas!" she said.

"Your Star-Zap has a Wishworld Outfit Selector," Piper said reasonably. "And you'd have to change anyway."

"What about the Wishworld backpack? I need a place to store my shooting star!"

Piper thought for a moment. "I'll run back to the room and grab mine. We'll also need some safety star-glasses. Then we can go straight to the Wishworld Surveillance Deck."

Clover shrugged. "Okay," she said. She was out of arguments. Then she thought of something.

"My Wish Pendant!" she cried. "I can't go without that."

"It's right there, in your hair."

Clover reached for the purple barrette, decorated with three silvery stars. It was still there! Luckily, she hadn't taken it off before bed.

It was all happening so quickly. But that was the way it had to be, she supposed. The two girls left the Wish Cavern and made their way back to the dorm. Clover waited outside as Piper slipped into her room. She reappeared holding a blue backpack, the door sliding shut behind her. "Couldn't find mine," she said. "So I grabbed Vega's. I'm sure she won't mind." With a shrug, Clover grabbed the backpack and slung it over her shoulder. The two Starlings then headed to the Wishworld Surveillance Deck.

The girls kept to the shadows as they crept across campus. The Bot-Bot guards were on high alert that time of night, and the Starlings didn't want to be questioned.

They were just nearing the band shell when Clover spied a guard circling the Star Quad. She pulled Piper behind a statue of the mythical Atlight, holding up Starland. She'd always loved those stories. Her uncle Fabrizzio, the strongman at the circus, knew glowzens by heart.

Clover and Piper waited for the guard to pass. Then, breathing a sigh of relief, Clover stepped out from the safety of the statue—and bumped right into another Bot-Bot.

"Star greetings, Miss Clover and Miss Piper," said the Bot-Bot. Then he winked.

"Is that you, Mojay?" Clover asked. Mojay—MO-J4—was not your typical Bot-Bot. Sage had met him her first day at Starling Academy when he gave her family a tour. From then on, he had checked in on her now and again, and the two had developed a friendship. Sage swore the Bot-Bot had his own sweet personality. But Clover had never really talked to him—until now. And now wasn't a very good time. After all, she and Piper were roaming around campus at night, an activity that was strictly against the rules.

"Yes, it is I," Mojay answered. "I am on security detail tonight. It is a change of pace for me, and a little boring, I might add. But now I meet you two! How nice."

It was true that Mojay didn't talk like a typical Bot-Bot. But did that mean he wouldn't turn them in?

"Well, Mojay, we couldn't sleep," Clover explained, "so Piper and I are taking a walk."

"Yes," Piper added. "We're heading to the observation deck."

Clover nudged Piper warningly, trying to convey the message *Too much information! Not a good thing!*

"It is a lovely night for stargazing," Mojay said with another wink. "Please allow me to accompany you."

Clover smiled. With a Bot-Bot by their side, she and Piper wouldn't be stopped. "Star salutations, Mojay. Can we hurry? If we don't move quickly, we'll miss the . . . the meteor shower."

Mojay led the way past the band shell and Halo Hall, talking at full volume, as if it was the middle of the afternoon and the girls were going to class. When they reached the Flash Vertical Mover that would zip them up to the deck, he gave a little bow.

He turned to leave but stopped when Clover exclaimed, "Oh! The mover is turned off. Lady Cordial's orders to conserve energy, I guess."

"Please allow me to be of assistance," Mojay said. Using one of his tool-like fingers, he lifted a plate by the mover door and connected two wires. The lights flashed. The mover hummed. "There you go. I'll just wait here so I can turn it off when you're done."

What would Mojay think when Piper came down alone? "Don't worry about it, Mojay," said Clover. "Just turn it off after we reach the top. We can walk down the emergency stairs when we're ready."

Piper raised her eyebrows but said nothing. Mojay nodded and said, "As you wish."

"Of course you mean *I'll* walk down," Piper told Clover as they zoomed to the top. The mover doors slid open, and the girls stepped onto the deck.

"First things first," Clover said, trying to think of all the steps involved. "We need to put on our safety starglasses and find a star."

Piper put on her seafoam green glasses and handed Clover her pair. Clover slipped them on. It was funny to see the world through Vega's blue-tinted starglasses. While she preferred her usual purple, she did notice that she felt cool and a bit more relaxed.

Together, Clover and Piper scanned the heavens. "There's a bunch right there!" Clover pointed to a cluster of stars moving quickly across the sky.

The girls grabbed the wrangler ropes—strands of positive energy braided into lassos. They kept their eyes on the shooting stars. "That one is coming closer . . . closer . . . closer . . ." Clover shouted. "Now throw!"

They flung their ropes into space. Both fell woefully short.

"Another one is coming. Let's try throwing them like Frisbeams," Clover suggested.

"Okay," said Piper, planting her feet and changing her grip.

"Now go!" Clover cried. Piper let go, and her rope whooshed through the air—and settled over Clover. "Well, you did rope a star. A circus star," Clover joked. "But why don't you just watch me this time?"

Clover flicked her wrist—hard—and her rope sailed into space, falling neatly around a star. "Yes!" said Clover.

She tried to pull it in, but the star bucked and lurched like a wild galliope. "Help me, Piper!"

Piper reached to grab hold of the rope just above Clover's hands. They both held on tight. But the star jerked even harder.

"We're losing it!" said Clover breathlessly. Piper was not much help.

"I'm doing the best I can," Piper said calmly. She was panting and her knuckles had turned lightning white. Clover knew she really was trying. But how would they ever do this? She'd never realized how strong a Star Wrangler had to be. The most she and Piper could manage was keeping the star in place.

"Greetings again!" said a familiar voice. "I thought I'd observe the meteor shower, too. But this looks like much more fun. May I join in?"

Wrangling a star was definitely against student rules! But Mojay was already over the half wall, zipping into the inky blackness and tugging at the rope. Working together, all three towed the star to the edge of the deck, Clover and Piper stepping back farther with every tug.

Finally, the star hovered by the wall. It was ready to go. But was Clover?

"Now what?" asked Mojay.

"We strap Clover in," Piper answered.

By then Clover had stopped worrying about Mojay's reaction. She was just happy he was there.

Piper and Mojay quickly got Clover's legs in place, fastening the safety buckles tightly. But the waist belt wouldn't click into place. The whole thing was like a circus, Clover thought. A comedy routine the clowns would perform.

Even worse, there was no adult in charge, no one to give advice and reassure her or make her believe in herself. She missed Lady Stella.

Finally, Piper realized the buckle was upside down, and she fumbled the latch into place. "There," she said, satisfied. "Ready to go?"

"No!" The star was already pulling Clover over the balcony. But she hung on to the wall tightly, trying to stay a bit longer. She needed to feel this was an official mission. She needed to follow the regular routine.

"Let me practice my Mirror Mantra first."

"Sure," said Piper as Mojay struggled to keep hold. "What is it?"

"Keep the beat and shine like the star you are." Once she said it out loud, Clover felt better. Still, she needed a few parting words of wisdom.

"Piper, can you wish me well? Say something wise? I need some closure before I go!"

"Of course, of course," Piper said soothingly. She thought a moment. Meanwhile, Mojay almost lost his grip.

As she closed her eyes, Mojay's grip loosened even more. "Clover, may you always remember to—oh, *starf*!" Piper finished as the lasso slipped out of Mojay's hands.

"Goooood-bye!" Clover called as she rocketed away. That was not the way she wanted to go!

But just as Starland slipped out of sight, she heard a voice, speaking from close by, perhaps inside her very own head.

"Sometimes the simplest solution is the most powerful one."

It sounded like the headmistress. Not Lady Cordial—Lady Stella. The true head of the school, Clover still believed in her heart of hearts.

"Lady Stella?" she said aloud.

She held her breath, hoping for an answer.

Finally, she sighed. Of course Lady Stella—wherever she was—had no idea Clover had just taken off on a Wish Mission. And maybe no one had said those words at all; she was just being silly and sentimental.

Sometimes the simplest solution is the most powerful one, she repeated to herself. Then she pushed those words out of her mind. She still had to choose an outfit, change, ready herself for the mission, and, of course, take in the sights. All those streaming lights and planets! It really was starmazing.

In no time at all, Clover's Star-Zap signaled her to prepare for landing. Her journey was just about over.

"Wishworld, here I come!"

CHAPTER
7

"Ouch!" Clover landed on a hard surface, jarring her bare feet. She'd already changed into Wishworld clothes—a sparkly purple miniskirt and fringed jacket. Of course she'd chosen a hat, too—a cute purple cap with a brim that covered her face. But she hadn't been wearing shoes before, so she'd forgotten to pick a new pair.

Quickly, Clover scrolled through some choices and settled on a pair of purple flats. Instantly, they were on her feet. She took a tentative step and smiled. The landing hadn't been so rough after all; already her feet felt fine.

Before she did anything else, Clover picked up her shooting star, folded it up, and placed it carefully in the front pocket of her backpack.

That accomplished, Clover gazed around, trying to get her bearings. She seemed to be in some sort of open-air building. Parallel yellow lines were painted on the cement floor in neat rows.

Finally, she saw a sign: G2. That was a funny name for a building. But then again, maybe all Wishling buildings were called by letters and numbers and no other Star Darling had noticed it. She wondered if she should add it to her Cyber Journal. Then she decided against it. She wasn't sure, and anyway, right then she needed to get going. She most likely wouldn't even have time for observations on her mission, since she had gotten such a late start.

First step: find her Wisher.

Clover flicked her Star-Zap for directions. She followed the route, going around and around the building, walking down ramps separating floors marked F, E, D, C, B, and then A. *Hmmm, the letters must be for levels,* she thought, glad she hadn't entered the observation in the journal. That would have been slightly embarrassing.

Also, she noted the lined spaces were for Wishling vehicles. She recognized them from looking through the Starland telescope. But they seemed much more primitive up close, with clunky shapes and actual wheels. As

Clover went lower and lower, more and more spaces were filled.

Beep! A vehicle was coming right at her, honking like a glowgoose! Clover jumped out of the way just in time. *These Wishlings should slow down*, she thought, moving to the side, where she thought it would be safer.

She checked the directions again and found a door marked PARKING GARAGE EXIT. That's where she was! A parking garage. A sign below it read MALL ENTRANCE.

Mall, she said to herself. It sounded familiar. She'd learned about it in Wishling Ways . . . something about a place where teenagers "hung out" and shopped for friends. Basically, that was what she'd be doing. Making friends with your Wisher was the first step to finding out the wish. So the location seemed promising!

Stepping inside the mall, Clover was immediately surrounded by people. There were some teenagers. But the crowd was really a mix of all ages: some adults pushing little wheeled vehicles with wee Wishlings inside, Wishling kids holding their parents' hands, older Wishlings walking in pairs. They all held bags and rushed here and there with determined looks on their faces.

She peered around the Wishlings and realized store after store lined the walls. Clothing stores, shoe stores,

toy stores, many with signs that read BACK TO SCHOOL
SALE! *So this must be the end of the Wishling warm weather
break,* Clover thought. And teenagers didn't shop *for*
friends there; they shopped *with* them! Along with
everyone else.

A mall was really just a star–shopping center—only
not half as stellar. Yes, there were moving steps in the
middle, but it was nothing like the Cosmic Transporter.
Plus there was no Choose-Your-Sparkle Shop or Groom-
Your-Glowfur Corner. Not quite as useful a place—she'd
have to tell the other Star Darlings.

Still, it was interesting. The mall was one long rectangle. It had an open center space with moving steps
taking people from level to level and a very nice glass
roof that let in the afternoon sun.

Clover leaned over a railing so the rays hit her face,
then she moved on. *Wait!* Were those carts in the middle
of the floor? Vehicles with wheels? She jumped out of
the way, expecting them to come at her like the car in
the garage. Then she realized the carts weren't actually
moving. They were really mini-stores that specialized in
very odd items.

One, with a sign reading HEADCASES, had only
strange little statues with giant heads that bobbed when
you touched them. Another sold miniature scenes in

clear rounded plastic containers. She shook one that showed Wishlings wearing heavy coats, scarves, and hats, and tiny snowflakes fell on their heads. That made sense. But when she shook a beach scene, snow fell, too!

Suddenly, Clover noticed something familiar: Starland-like creatures!

Creatures that resembled glions and galliopes were grouped in a circle, just waiting to be petted. Clover rushed over, looking for starapples or some other snack to feed them. But when she got closer, she discovered they weren't real. In fact, they were part of a ride. Kids clambered on top of the fake creatures, which then moved around and around on a platform to sprightly music. Interesting.

Next Clover wandered into a hat store just for fun. She caught sight of her plain Wishworld self in a mirror. Even though she'd been expecting to see dull skin and Wishling-colored hair, it was still a bit of a starprise. Of course, she felt glad she could pass for any old mall visitor. And she did have a bright purple streak left in her hair, an occurrence many Star Darlings had already mentioned. So it could have been worse.

"Oh!" Clover cried as she spied a floppy purple hat. Maybe she could wear that instead of the cap! She plunked it on her head and checked out her reflection. It did look good. But then a sales Wishling walked over and asked, "Would you like to see more in that style?"

"No, ah, ah, thank you!" Clover said, hurrying out. How could she forget she had no Wishworld currency?

Not only that, but she'd been wasting valuable time shopping! *You're already way behind schedule,* Clover scolded herself. *Now get moving!*

Not even glancing at any other shop windows, concentrating only on her directions, Clover went up two levels and found herself following signs to the "Food Court."

Another oddity, thought Clover. Hadn't she learned that Wishlings played sports on courts, too? Did they eat meals surrounded by balls and nets and whatever other equipment they used? No, she realized as she stepped into the bustling space. There were only tables and small takeout restaurants. Most had food words in their names: Bongo Burger; Pizza, Pizza, Pizza; and The Smoothie Shack. Clover felt proud that she recognized most of the Wishling food names. But wait—there was one called The Sushi Spot. On Starland, Sushi was the most popular singer on the planet! Wait until she told Leona!

Again, Clover glanced at her directions. They ended there, at the entrance to the food court. So her Wisher must be at one of the tables or waiting in line. How could she possibly find her in this crowded place?

She took a few steps, moving closer to The Sushi Spot for lack of a better plan. Suddenly, she felt a slight vibration on her head. The Wish Pendant barrette! Good thing the cap was covering it. Otherwise, everyone would notice its glow.

Clover wove through the tables haphazardly at first, changing directions on the strength of the Wish Pendant's vibration. As she neared one table with a daughter and mother, the barrette pulsed so strongly that Clover stopped suddenly. The Wishling girl, staring with narrowed eyes at her mom, must be Clover's Wisher.

A couple was just leaving the next table, so Clover slipped into an empty chair. Immediately, her nose wrinkled in distaste. The Wishlings hadn't cleared their trays, which were covered with crumpled napkins and leftover food! And unlike on Starland, the mess would stay right there unless someone cleared it away. *That most certainly won't be me!* Clover thought.

She turned to her Wisher just as the girl, upset over something her mother had said, tossed her head. Clover grinned happily. The girl had a purplish streak in her hair—not quite as bright and shiny as Clover's, but it was a streak nonetheless, standing out in her long blond hair. They had something in common!

"I am not happy with you, Ruby Marshall," the mom was saying. "How could you go and dye your hair like that without asking permission? And purple of all colors. It looks ridiculous!"

Humph, thought Clover, a little insulted. Of course, it was different there. She knew that Wishlings had to add chemicals to their hair to make it look Starland-normal. *How sad for them*, Clover thought. And apparently, the procedure was frowned upon by adult Wishlings—at least when their children were involved.

"Stop it, Mom," the girl answered. "You are so old-fashioned. No one thinks a purple streak is a big deal anymore. Look around! Lots of kids do it!"

Clover took off her cap, expecting the mom to do what her daughter asked—look around. Once she spotted Clover, she'd realize her daughter was right.

But the mom just shook her head, glaring at the girl. The girl glared back, not noticing Clover's hair, either.

This was Clover's big chance to meet her Wisher. She needed to act quickly. She had to get the girl's attention so she'd see Clover's streak, realize they had lots in common, and want to be her friend.

Reining in her repulsion, Clover picked up the heavy food trays and carried them to the garbage container right next to the Wishlings. She made a big show of pushing against the swinging door to empty the tray.

The girl looked up. "Hey!" she called out. "I like your hair! See, Mom? I told you purple hair is not a big deal at all!"

Clover smiled at the mom. The mom frowned back.

"Did you use Splatter?" the girl asked excitedly. She held up a long lock of her streaked hair and examined it closely. "Yours is better," she said decidedly. "I definitely missed a few spots."

"You have to leave it on longer than the directions say," Clover said, as if she knew what she was talking about.

"Did your mom get mad when you did it?" the girl asked eagerly.

Her mom finally gazed up, meeting Clover's eyes. She didn't look angry now, just sad. She had a kind, open face—very similar to the girl's—with big brown eyes.

Clover shrugged, trying to be noncommittal.

"No, really. Is she angry about your purple hair?" the girl insisted.

"No," Clover said truthfully, stopping short of

saying her mother was actually thrilled. She and her mom had the same shade.

"See, Mom? I'm the only one who gets treated like a baby!"

The girl stared at Clover, taking in her outfit with approval. "And are you allowed to pick out your own clothes?"

"Yes, I am."

"I'm not," the girl said quickly, giving her mom a significant look. "My mother chooses all my clothes. Like I said, she treats me like a baby."

At this, the mom finally spoke. "Ruby Marshall! I only want you to wear clothes that are appropriate! You know I hate leggings and short tops that don't adequately cover your posterior!" She looked at her watch and stood up. "It's almost time for your appointment. I'm heading to the ladies' room and I'll be back in a minute."

With her mom gone, the girl deflated slightly. "My purple streaks are history. My mom's taking me to Snippy's to dye it back." She sighed loudly. "I wish she'd let me grow up!"

Clover felt a tingle run down her spine and her mouth fell open in starprise. She'd barely said two words to the girl, but she'd already discovered her wish. How easy could a mission be? *Thank the stars*, she thought, since time was of the essence!

Clover sat in the mom's seat and smiled. "I know I'm lucky. My parents talk to me like a . . . a person! Not a wee Star—I mean, little kid."

Clover couldn't even imagine her mom babying her. She'd always been treated like an important member of the circus family, with jobs and responsibilities. Even before she could walk, she had been crawling around to retrieve ozziefruit for juggling acts and sitting on top of spinning chairs. Once she could talk, she offered opinions about starwire performances. Poor Ruby Marshall. She really needed Clover's help.

"My name is Clover," she said in a friendly way.

"I'm Ruby."

Ruby slid her tray toward Clover. "Here, want some french fries?"

Clover realized she was hungry. She followed Ruby's lead and dipped the long objects into some red sauce. A smile spread across her face. They were delicious! Before she knew it, she had finished them all.

"Sorry," she said.

"No problem," said Ruby. "I'm kind of too nervous to eat, anyway."

"How come?" asked Clover.

"School is starting soon," said Ruby, clearly embarrassed.

"Where do you go to school?" Clover asked, knowing exactly what she'd say when Ruby answered.

"Westlake Prep." Ruby's eyes flashed—with excitement or nervousness, Clover couldn't tell. "It'll be my first year."

"Me too!" Clover said quickly. "I'll be a first year at Westlake, too!"

"That's so sick," said Ruby excitedly.

Clover frowned for a moment, then remembered that the word had two meanings, at least to young Wishlings.

"Yeah, sick!" she replied, feeling slightly silly.

"It's going to be so different," Ruby went on. "The school is really big and there'll be so many people I don't know! It would have been nice to have an older brother or sister who was going there, too, to show me around."

In Clover's circus family, there was always someone older to help you with a new act and always someone younger who needed your help. "Well, at least you can do that for your younger siblings," she suggested.

Ruby shook her head. "Uh-uh. I'm an only child. I

loved it when I was little. I had my parents' total attention. But now it's too much attention! My mom watches over me like a hawk."

Clover didn't know what a hawk was. But she guessed it was some sort of security system.

"I'm back," Ruby's mom—Mrs. Marshall— announced. "Time to go."

"M-o-o-o-o-m," Ruby said, stretching out the word. "Clover and I are starting Westlake together. We have to talk!"

"Well, I'm sorry, girls." And Ruby's mom did look sorry, Clover thought. "Why don't you make plans to get together before school starts?"

That was nice of Mrs. Marshall, given that she didn't approve of Clover's hair, and possibly Clover herself.

"Yes!" said Ruby. "Hey, want to shop for school supplies together? We can meet right here tomorrow. I'll bring the list."

Supplies for school? On Starland, students didn't really have supplies. They used their Star-Zaps for just about everything. Of course, here students had cell phones, which could only handle a bare minimum of tasks but still served Wishlings in a similar way. "What do we need besides our phones?" Clover asked.

"I know, right?" said Ruby. She laughed, as if Clover was being funny on purpose. Ruby insisted on exchanging numbers, just in case—so Clover input Ruby's number and called her, not entirely sure it would ring. Luckily, it did. But they promised to meet in the same spot first thing in the morning.

"Come on, Ruby!" Mrs. Marshall called, already outside the food court.

Clover waved good-bye. What should she do next? She had to fill the time between then and the following morning. She looked longingly at her backpack, where the invisible tent—complete with comfy bed—was just waiting to be used. Then she looked at her Countdown Clock. So much time had passed! Did she even have time for rest?

Yes, she decided. Realistically, she couldn't do any wish granting until she saw Ruby in the morning. She couldn't follow her now. Ruby would think she was weird. And what would her mom say? She'd tell Ruby she couldn't hang out with the strange stalking girl. Clover had to stay on everyone's good side for her mission to work!

That settled it. She was going to find an empty space somewhere, set up her tent, rest, and use the time to come up with a plan to help Ruby. The top floor of the parking garage would be a good empty place, she decided.

She hurried through the mall, retracing her steps to the garage: out the exit, up the ramps, straight to the top.

"Ugh," she groaned. That level was filled, too, and drivers were circling, looking for spots, zipping quickly up and down rows, tires screeching around turns. She certainly couldn't set up an invisible tent there. Wishling drivers were crazy! It wouldn't do at all.

But she didn't want to go far. Maybe she could find an out-of-the-way place where cars weren't allowed. She searched around corners and found a large empty space with a sign that read NO PARKING. EMERGENCY USE ONLY.

Well, this will do, Clover thought. As far as she was concerned, she was in an emergency situation. She walked to the far end of the spot, leaned against the wall, and unzipped the main compartment of her backpack.

It was empty.

CHAPTER
8

"What? There's no tent in the backpack?" Clover searched through the side pockets and the big front one, where she'd packed the shooting star. They were all empty, too, aside from the star. She turned the backpack upside down and shook it. Nothing. Had Vega forgotten her invisible tent on Wishworld, or were they one-time use only? In any event, it didn't matter. Clover was out of luck.

Why, oh, why hadn't she used mind control on Ruby's mom when she'd had the chance? She could be staying in a cozy, warm house, not in a drafty garage without a tent!

So what next? If she hurried to the hair salon . . . What was it called? Flippy's? Tippy's? Snippy's! That was it! If she left right away, she could still catch Ruby and her mom.

But the mall was big. Very big. Clover made several wrong turns before she discovered that the mall had a map. Finally, she located Snippy's, full of salon chairs and mirrors, and walked inside.

Someone was sweeping hair from the floor. *Yuck!* Another worker was talking into a device that looked a bit like a cell phone but had a cord that plugged into the wall. Stylists were snipping, washing, drying, and brushing their customers' hair. Clover peered around. She could only see the customers' backs. But one had long, straight blond hair. *Ruby!*

"Excuse me," she said, using the correct phrase, as she stepped between Ruby and the facing mirror. Only, when she was face to face with the blonde, she realized that it wasn't Ruby. It was a woman she'd never seen before—with big thick glasses and a wide round face, her mouth falling open in surprise.

Clover did the first thing that crossed her mind. "Here, I think you dropped something," she said. But when she bent down, the only thing she found was a long lock of blond hair. She handed it to the confused woman. Then she raced outside.

She kept running until she saw an empty bench,

where she sat down to think. Okay, she'd missed Ruby. So she could forget about staying with her. The night stretched in front of Clover, and she had nowhere to go and nothing to do. *What time does the mall close, anyway?* she wondered.

Just then a young woman walked over and handed Clover a flyer. She marveled at the feel of the paper, about to crumple it into a ball, just for fun. But a big word on top caught her attention: FREE!

Clover read on.

FOCUS GROUP: FREE MOVIE SCREENING! BE THE FIRST TO SEE THE NOT-YET-RELEASED FILM VAMPIRE'S KISS. FILL OUT SHORT QUESTIONNAIRE AFTERWARDS. FREE SNACKS PROVIDED!

Clover checked a big clock on the mall wall and realized the movie would be starting shortly. *Perfect*, she thought.

By then it was getting late, and the crowds were thinning. Clover found the movie theater, handed in her flyer, and walked into the lobby. A good number of people were already there. They were all Wishlings around Clover's age. *Too bad Ruby isn't here*, she thought.

She went to the concession center and decided on white fluffy food called popcorn, crispy chips with yellow sauce called nachos, and some root beer, whatever that was. Clover hurried into the theater, carefully balancing her treats. She settled into a seat in the back row. The snacks were good, she thought. But she wasn't so sure about the movie. A strangely pale teenage boy with two sharp teeth kept chasing people.

Was it supposed to be scary? Funny? Clover couldn't tell. She was more interested in the lack of technology. There was an actual screen, onto which flat moving pictures were projected. She thought how different it was from home, where everything seemed so real and solid, floating in the air right in front of your eyes.

After the film ended, she filled out the questionnaire as best she could. People around her had seemed to enjoy the movie, so she held back her own opinions. Maybe she couldn't be the best critic, coming from another world and all.

She wandered around the mall, thinking about a plan to help Ruby and wondering what to do next. And there, right in front of her, like a dream come true, was a furniture store with a bedroom display in the window. The bed looked so inviting and comfy that Clover wanted to crawl under the covers and close her eyes. And she could, she realized, with the help of a little mind control.

Quickly, Clover stepped inside.

"I'm sorry," said a woman with a name tag that read LINDA. "We're closing up."

"That's okay," Clover told Linda. "I'm going to stay overnight . . . as part of a focus group . . . to test the bed in the window." She looked deeply into the woman's eyes.

"You're going to stay overnight to test the bed," Linda repeated as if in a trance, "as part of a focus group." Then, in a more normal voice, she added, "I think I'll stop off at the bakery and pick up some chocolate croissants. For some reason, I feel like I can smell them right now!"

Clover grinned. It was hard to believe that adult Wishlings would do what you said just because you made them smell favorite treats from their childhoods. But clearly, it really did happen!

"I'll turn off the lights," Clover said.

"You'll turn off the lights," Linda said. Then she left, locking up behind her.

Alone in the store, Clover walked through displays of dining rooms, living rooms, and bedrooms. She stopped in front of a full-length mirror to say her Mirror Mantra to herself: "Keep the beat and shine like the star you are."

Immediately, her reflection began to sparkle and she felt more focused, ready to refine the plan she'd come up with earlier.

The goal: to get Ruby's parents to see she was a young adult so they would stop treating her like a baby.

The strategy: to help Ruby prove herself and show her parents she was mature and responsible. Being responsible herself, Clover knew exactly what was involved. And she believed that helping Ruby prove herself was surely the way to go. She was still a little fuzzy, though, on how to do it. Suddenly, her eyes fell on a picture frame for sale. It held a generic family photo—two parents, three young children.

That was it! Ruby could babysit. She would earn money, and then she could open her own bank account. Not only would she prove she was capable and steady, but she'd have money to buy her own clothes.

The plan was complete! *Now,* Clover thought, *I can rest.* She changed into a comfortable pair of violet pajamas with the help of her Wishworld Outfit Selector and slipped between the sheets of the comfy bed in the window. Within minutes, she fell fast asleep.

Clover slept soundly. Hours passed, and she stirred a bit, her eyes still closed. Then she stiffened. For some reason, she felt like someone was watching her.

"Astra?" she murmured. Then she remembered: She was on Wishworld. In a bed. In a store window. *Starf!*

Clover opened one eye. A crowd of people stood in front of the store, pointing at her. Linda was pushing past them, opening the gates by the door. "Here is the first tester from our focus group," Linda announced. "Let's see if she's satisfied!"

Clover hopped up, hurriedly straightening the blanket. She stood in front of the crowd in her pajamas, feeling slightly silly.

"I love the bed!" she said loudly as the crowd surged into the store. "You saw for yourselves! I slept better last night than I have in starweeks . . . I mean, *weeks*!" She smiled widely.

Linda beamed.

"I was watching that girl for over half an hour," one woman said. "She absolutely slept like a baby. I want to try it out."

"Me too!" called a man.

People pressed closer to Linda, eager to put their names on a list. Clover slipped away from the crowd with a final smile and a wave and ducked into the restroom.

She emerged in a new Wishling outfit of purple leggings, an oversized black off-the-shoulder sweater, and purple-fringed ankle boots. A black fedora completed the outfit. She stole a glance in a full-length mirror in a bedroom display. Perfect. Looking at the Wishworld clock on her Star-Zap, she hurried to the food court.

Ruby was already sitting at a table, her long hair entirely blond—not a bit of purple left. It was really too bad, Clover thought. But Ruby was smiling, happy to see her.

"I got us some muffins!" Ruby said.

The muffins tasted similar to astromuffins, and Clover had two. While Ruby chatted about her friends—which ones were going to Westlake, which ones to Eastlake—Clover checked her Countdown Clock. She gulped. It was really, *really* getting late. In order to succeed, she'd have to do everything in record time.

She only hoped it was possible.

CHAPTER
9

After breakfast, the girls headed to Take Note, which was the "dopest place to buy school supplies," according to Ruby.

"Not the sickest?" Clover asked.

Ruby nodded. "That too," she said.

Clover grinned. She couldn't wait to tell her fellow Star Darlings she'd picked up a new Wishling word!

At Take Note, Clover gazed around in astonishment. *Paper!* There were notebooks, pads, stationery, envelopes, and stacks of paper everywhere. *Unbelievable!*

And what about those things called binders? How did Wishling students fit them into their backpacks? They were so large and bulky. Everything in the store was strange and fascinating—especially those writing sticks called highlighters that, disappointingly, didn't even light up.

She and Ruby loaded up their carts, and Ruby declared they were done.

Mrs. Marshall met them by the checkout, where employees stood behind clunky machines and customers passed them small plastic cards to pay with. The line snaked almost to the back of the store. While they waited, Ruby's mom reminisced about her first day of high school—back before students used what she referred to as "laptops." Ruby rolled her eyes, but Clover noticed she was actually listening.

Finally, they were next. Clover, who had no Wishling money, had a plan. She faked receiving a text. "Look at that!" she said. "Good old Mom. She already bought all my supplies for me!" She turned to Ruby. "Now I don't have to carry them home. That's ill of her."

Ruby gave her a funny look. "I think you mean 'sick.'"

"Of course," said Clover. "Totally dumb."

"Dope," corrected Ruby's mother. She laughed. "Guess I've been paying attention!"

Mother and daughter checked out while Clover put

all her school supplies back. She wished she could have kept the pack of loose-leaf, with its straight lines and perfectly placed holes. Or the purple composition notebook. That was hard to return to the rack.

"Mom," said Ruby as they left the store, "can you take my stuff home so Clover and I can hang out a little here?"

Ruby's mom paused. "I don't think so," she said. "I have to get back and I don't want you to walk home alone. I'll just drive you back."

Clover got into the backseat, and Ruby slid next to her. "My mom won't let me sit up front," she explained. "Still! My cousins are allowed to and they're younger than me! I bet even the ones in preschool will beat me to the front!"

During the drive, Clover shared her idea with Ruby, whispering so Mrs. Marshall wouldn't hear: *babysitting, money, bank account.*

"Sounds good!" Ruby agreed happily, speaking in a low voice. "My neighbor Mrs. Howard has little twin girls. They're adorable! And she just told my mom that her babysitter moved away and she's looking for a new one."

"Sounds perfect!" said Clover.

Mrs. Marshall dropped them off in front of Ruby's

house, then went to run more errands. "At least she leaves me home alone," Ruby grumbled. "Finally!"

"Let's go talk to your neighbor now," Clover suggested, glancing worriedly at her Countdown Clock. "You can line up a babysitting job and then we can tell your mother your plan." Ruby agreed.

Mrs. Howard was in her backyard. She was holding a hose as two little girls in bathing suits ran around in the spray. They were about three Wishworld years old, Clover guessed, with short curly hair and little round bellies. They weren't identical, but they looked very much alike.

Ruby waved to Mrs. Howard. "Won't be too many more summer days!" the woman said as Ruby and Clover walked closer. "I want to get them outside as much as possible."

"Oh, sure!" said Ruby. She introduced Clover, then explained that they were available for babysitting.

"Great!" Mrs. Howard said, putting down the hose. "If you're free right now, I could really use the help. I need to go to the grocery store, and it's so much easier without the girls."

Clover looked at the wee Wishlings. The girls were little angels, really, playing together nicely and amusing themselves. The babysitting job would be a snap.

Moments later, Mrs. Howard left, while the girls—Joelle and Michaela—waved good-bye cheerfully. The first hour was a breeze. Ruby and the girls played games with funny names, like Red Rover, Freeze Tag, and Kick the Can. The girls then decided to run through the sprinkler, so Ruby turned it back on. The twins laughed and shouted with glee. One of the girls busied herself next to the sprinkler. Then Joelle stood up with the hose in her hand. "Let's play!" she cried.

The next thing Clover knew, the nozzle, which must have been loose, fell off. The hose began to snake and buck like Clover's shooting star. The little girl was having trouble holding on to it.

"My turn!" shouted Michaela, grabbing the hose, too. They both spun around as the hose twisted and turned, soaking first Ruby, then Clover, then spraying a stream of water right into the house through an open window.

The girls fell to the ground and rolled over each other, crushing a neat row of flowers and coating themselves in a thick layer of mud. The hose slipped out of their hands and continued to spray the yard.

Joelle and Michaela burst into tears. The yard was a muddy mess. So were they.

Clover and Ruby stood frozen in place, looks of

panic on their faces. It had all happened so quickly they hadn't even had time to move. And now Clover didn't have the starriest idea what to do. Her littlest relatives would be thrilled to have a muddy playground, and a little water never fazed them. They'd be laughing, not crying.

Suddenly, Ruby went into action. She raced to the side of the house and turned off the faucet. The hose slowed to a dribble, then stopped.

She scooped up both muddy girls, then held them tight and murmured comforting words. "There, there. It's all right. You're okay. It's fine."

The girls quieted, sniffled a bit, then stopped crying altogether when Ruby tickled them.

"Okay," Ruby said cheerfully, setting them on the ground. "Let's see what we can do to clean up around here!"

"Don't want to clean up!" Joelle opened her mouth to cry again.

But Ruby said quickly, "Did I say 'clean up'? I meant, what can we do to have fun around here? I say let's turn on the hose again—on low!—and watch all that mud disappear from your bodies."

She waved at Clover to twist the faucet and held the hose carefully away from the twins as she splashed water on them. They laughed hysterically. Then she moved the lawn furniture around so the muddy spaces would be in direct sunlight. "That should dry pretty fast," she said.

Next Ruby led Michaela and Joelle to the garden area, gave them shovels, and showed them how to pat down the mud and dirt while she replanted the flowers.

Clover edged over to Ruby and whispered, "What about all the water that went inside?"

Ruby nodded. "Now!" she said, standing up. "Let's check out your house and see what we can do there!"

Everyone wiped their feet on the doormat. Then they stepped through the door and into the living room. *It doesn't look good*, Clover thought.

Toys had been knocked over by the blast. Water still dripped from the open window, and there were puddles of water on the wood floor. The place was a disaster. Clover didn't even know where to begin, and meanwhile, the girls were racing around, making even more of a mess.

Ruby found some small towels in the linen closet and showed the twins how to "house skate" by placing their tiny feet on the towels and sliding around, mopping up the wet floor. They thought it was great fun.

Meanwhile, Clover dried and organized the scattered toys.

"Now what, Ruby?" asked Michaela as she handed Ruby her towel. "We skate in the kitchen? Wash that floor?"

"The girls want to clean?" Mrs. Howard said, walking in at that moment. "Ruby, you're incredible!"

"Ruby is a real *gem*!" Clover giggled, remembering Wishworld jewels, but she meant it, too. Her Wisher had taken charge, and clearly the little girls loved her.

Mrs. Howard paid Ruby with paper money, thanking her again while the twins begged her to come back and play. Smiling, Ruby and Clover left through the back door. They paused for a moment, admiring the good-as-new backyard.

"Now," Clover said, switching gears for the next step of her wish-granting plan, "we just find a bank, hurry over, and set up an account for you."

"Slow down!" Ruby laughed. "The nearest bank is about three miles away. And we can't just walk in and open an account!"

"You can't?" Clover asked. Ruby pulled up some information on her phone and showed it to Clover. "Oh, no," Clover groaned. "You need to be accompanied by a parent, with proof of address, plus identification.

"Can we manage all this?" she asked Ruby.

"Well, my mom could go with us," said Ruby. "But

we'd have to ask. And if we really need ID, I'd have to wait until school starts. They hand them out on the first day."

"When is the first day again?" Clover asked.

"Thursday."

That meant next to nothing to Clover. "Um, how many days from today?" Maybe if it was the next day, they could work things out.

"Today's Monday, so in three days."

Clover sighed. That was way too late. Her plan was too complicated. It would take too long to complete, she realized. Why did she always do that? Just like the circus idea and the trip to Mount Glint—she made everything too involved. She wanted so much to succeed, to prove herself! And she thought the more complicated the plan, the better and smarter it was.

Then Clover remembered the words she'd heard at the beginning of her journey to Wishworld: *Sometimes the simplest solution is the most powerful one.* She hadn't been thinking simply. But maybe she could now.

Simplify! Clover told herself. *Simplify.*

Just then Ruby's phone rang. She looked at the screen and then quickly put it away. "It's just my mom," she said.

"Ruby! Answer it!" said Clover. "Talk to her!"

Reluctantly, Ruby swiped the screen. "Hi, Mom."

Mrs. Marshall's voice came through the speaker loud and clear. "Where are you?" she said in a panic. "You're supposed to be at home!"

"Mom! Calm down! I'm just next door. I was babysitting Michaela and Joelle."

"What? Why didn't you ask permission? Why didn't you—"

"Mom! I'm hanging up. I'll be right home."

Ruby hung up and didn't move. Her mouth turned down in a pout. "I can't believe she doesn't trust me when here I am babysitting, earning my own money. She doesn't get it!"

Across the yard, Clover could see Mrs. Marshall peering anxiously from her back door.

This is definitely not helping! Clover thought. *Ruby is proving she's the opposite of mature and responsible. She should have told Ruby to ask her mom about the babysitting. And Ruby should have asked her about the hair color, too, before she dyed it. She didn't talk to her. So of course her mom got angry.*

Now she'd never get her wish—unless Clover could come up with another idea. Something simple and—

Ruby interrupted her thoughts, saying, "Let's go to

my room. I'll show you the outfit I want to wear on the first day of school. Of course, I'll have to show it to you online, because my mom won't buy it for me."

"Okay." Clover wouldn't give up! She'd stay on Wishworld with Ruby until the very last starsec.

Together, the girls went into Ruby's house. Mrs. Marshall was nowhere to be seen. But the door to the master bedroom was closed tight.

Ruby opened her door and walked inside, but Clover stood in the doorway in shock. Ruby's bedroom looked like a starclone had blown right through it.

Clothes littered the floor like a second carpet. Every surface was covered with papers. Clover could barely see the desk, dresser, or nightstand. Drawers hung half-open, with more clothes falling out of them. A jumble of shoes, blankets, and coats spilled out of the closet. The garbage can overflowed onto the rug. Dirty dishes were piled on the desk.

Clover couldn't even bring herself to walk into the room. Maybe she would just wait outside.

"Come in! Come in!" said Ruby. "Make yourself at home."

Gingerly, Clover took a step forward. She edged closer to the window, over to a teeny tiny clear space.

Peering outside, she saw a girl with bright orange hair walking down the street.

Could that be Gemma, here to help? Clover thought excitedly. She hoped against hope it was the Star Darling. She desperately needed her.

The girl drew closer, and Clover realized it was just an ordinary Wishling, not a transformed Starling. But now that she thought about it, she realized her Star Darling helper should be there any starsec. Her mission was definitely in trouble. Clover couldn't pull herself away from the window, just in case she spotted a Starling.

What was happening on Starland, anyway? Surely Piper must have told Lady Cordial about the mission. And Lady Cordial must know that it was going terribly wrong and reinforcements were needed. Then Clover's heart sank with a realization. Maybe Lady Cordial didn't know what was going on because of the lack of energy. Maybe Clover had to figure it out all by herself.

Clover slumped and yawned. Quickly, she recited her Mirror Mantra in her head—*Keep the beat and shine like the star you are*—twice. Even without a mirror, she felt a bit better. She was just about to think it a third time when Mrs. Marshall came to the door.

"Ruby Marshall," she said in a firm voice, "we really

need to talk. You need to tell me where you're going. Do you know how worried I was when I came home and you weren't here? It's important that I know your plans, in case of an emergency."

Then she turned to Clover. "You'll have to leave now, Clover. Ruby is grounded. She can't have friends over."

This was getting worse and worse. What was she going to do?

She turned and looked into the woman's eyes. "I can still stay here. It's okay."

"You can still stay here," Mrs. Marshall repeated in a dull voice. "It's okay." Then she sniffed the air. "Does anyone else smell chocolate fudge cookies?" she asked, then left before Clover or Ruby could answer.

"Wow," said Ruby. "That was weird."

"It doesn't matter," Clover told her. "And you know, don't you, that your mom is kind of right? She just worries about you, that's all. And she wants you to talk to her. Maybe if you did, she'd be more open to hearing about your ideas about your hair and clothes."

Ruby looked at her thoughtfully, considering. Giving Ruby time to think, Clover pushed aside some books and sat on the edge of the bed. She hadn't even had a starsec to come up with a new—*simple*—plan. How much time did she have left?

She opened her Countdown Clock. *Starf!* She was down to fifteen Wishworld minutes. She didn't see how the mission was even possible anymore.

Clover heard sounds from downstairs: voices raised in greeting, Mrs. Marshall saying, "Hello, dear." Ruby's dad must be home.

"Ugh," said Ruby as her phone vibrated with a text. "My mom's still not leaving me alone." She turned the screen so Clover could see the message: DAD AGREES. YOU'RE GROUNDED. AND DON'T LEAVE YOUR ROOM UNTIL IT'S CLEAN! THAT WOULD BE ONE WAY TO PROVE YOU'RE RESPONSIBLE.

Aha! Clover leaped to her feet. Cleaning the room would be a simple solution, an easy way for Ruby to show her maturity.

Clover didn't know whether to laugh or cry. She had the answer. But there wouldn't be enough time to clean up. The room was a wreck.

Clover sighed. It was really too bad. Ruby was so close to achieving her wish. She was a terrific, responsible babysitter. And she seemed to be seriously thinking over Clover's advice about talking to her mom. But Clover was out of time.

She turned, smiling sadly at Ruby. "I need to go home."

"Can't you stay longer?" Ruby pleaded.

"I wish I could!" Clover shook her head, upset. "If only I could make time stand still!" She laughed bitterly. "For everyone but us, of course."

For a moment she visualized time actually standing still, everything coming to a halt: cars and buses stopping; Michaela and Joelle standing in front of the sprinkler, still as statues, the water frozen in place.

"Good-bye, Ruby." Then, before Ruby could say a word, Clover slipped out of the room, leaving the wish ungranted.

CHAPTER
10

In the hall, Clover took a deep breath. Everything seemed oddly quiet. She turned toward the stairs, then gasped. Mrs. Marshall stood at the landing, her finger raised as if she was making a point. She didn't move, didn't blink as Clover slid past. In the kitchen, a man— Ruby's dad—stood unmoving by the table, pouring a glass of juice, the liquid frozen in an orangey arc.

What was going on? Clover peered out the window. A boy was riding a two-wheeled vehicle, flying over a bump. But the wheels weren't turning; the boy wasn't moving; and the vehicle hovered in midair, stuck in place.

A realization dawned on her. Just like she had imagined, time was standing still! And she'd made it happen—that had to be her special talent. Without Lady Stella's reminder, Clover hadn't given her special talent any thought. She hadn't spent a starsec trying to figure it out. But there it was, revealed, like a gift! And she was certainly going to take advantage of it!

But how long will it last? she wondered.

Hurrying back upstairs, Clover couldn't resist waving a hand in front of Mrs. Marshall's face. Clover giggled. No reaction.

Still laughing, she flipped just for fun outside Ruby's bedroom and walked casually inside. "Hey," she said.

"You're back!" Ruby said happily, sitting up in bed, her laptop open.

"Yup, change of plans." It felt good to be spontaneous for once; maybe things didn't always have to follow a routine. "And I'm going to help you clean your room."

"Oh." Ruby slumped back against the pillow. "Great."

"Listen, Ruby." Clover sat next to her, kicking aside two empty tissue boxes. "I've been thinking about your mom and your wish. About how you want her to stop treating you like a baby."

"Let me guess," Ruby said with a smile. "You think cleaning my room will help."

"Absolutely. Let me explain." Clover talked about a

vicious circle of stars—leaving out the "stars" part of the phrase—how Ruby complained about being treated like a baby but actually sometimes acted like one.

"You have to *act* like someone who deserves to be trusted," Clover explained. Hopefully, she didn't sound too much like a parent herself! She lifted a half-eaten chocolate bar off the blanket and added, "Ask permission. Be polite. Cleaning your room would be a good first step to gaining their trust. And then your wish could come true!"

"Maybe later," Ruby said, going back to her laptop. "Let's just—"

"No!" Clover interrupted loudly. It had to be done then, while time was frozen, so she could collect the wish energy and still be able to get back home. "Can you play music? That would help get us moving."

At that, Ruby jumped up, fiddling with her phone. Suddenly, music was pumping through the room. Clover couldn't quite make out the lyrics. She heard the word *baby* a lot and not much else. But the song had a danceable beat, and Ruby was clapping her hands in time with the rhythm.

Together, the girls danced around the room, filling garbage and recycling bags, making the bed, dusting the furniture, and folding clothes. They were just slipping the last books onto the shelf when they heard a knock.

Clover grinned. The spell was broken at just the right time!

Ruby went to open the door, but Clover stopped her. "Remember," she said, "you can't act like a little kid anymore. No whining. No surprises like dyeing your hair without asking. And keep your room neat." She paused as she spied a stray sock under the bed. "At least, neater than it's been," she added.

"Ruby?" said Mrs. Marshall from the other side of the door.

Ruby looked at Clover as she reached for the knob. So would she take Clover's advice or not? Clover still wasn't sure.

The door swung open. "Ruby!" Mrs. Marshall gasped when she saw the room. She flung her arms around her daughter. "Look at this room! I can't believe it! How is this even possible? I just—"

"We're fast workers," Clover interrupted.

Ruby laughed. "It is kind of awesome, isn't it? I forgot how much I actually like my room!"

"And you listened to me," Mrs. Marshall said. "That makes me feel respected. And it shows you're acting responsibly."

Meanwhile, Clover tried to make herself as invisible as possible, leafing through a book while the two talked.

"I know I was tough on you," Ruby's mom added.

"Not as tough as I was on you," Ruby said genuinely.

"I'm proud of you, honey."

"Does that mean you'll stop treating me like a pre-schooler?"

"Ruby," Mrs. Marshall said warningly.

"Okay, no attitude." Ruby smiled. "But really, will you trust me more now?"

"Yes. In fact, Mrs. Howard called earlier. She said you did a great job with Michaela and Joelle. She wants to offer you a regular position, babysitting every week."

"Wow!" said Ruby. "I'll make a ton of money! I can buy all the clothes I like—"

"Within reason," her mom said.

Clover held her breath. What would Ruby say to that?

"Within reason," Ruby agreed. Then she grinned. "And could my hair be within reason, too? How about just one teeny streak?"

Mrs. Marshall turned to Clover. "I do like the way Clover has it: very subtle, so it doesn't always show. Can you do it that way? I can help."

"Yes!" said Ruby. "Deal?" She held out her hand for her mom to shake.

"Deal," said Mrs. Marshall, pulling her in for a hug.

Clover let out her breath and felt a tingle travel down her spine. It was happening! She knew it. The wish energy would be released any starsec.

Just then a burst of colors streamed from Ruby straight into Clover's Wish Pendant.

She had done it! She had beat the Countdown Clock. Now all she had to do was hug Ruby good-bye to erase any memory of their meeting, unfold her shooting star, and ride it all the way home. There was just one question left.

What would she find there?

Epilogue

It was late afternoon when Clover landed back on Starland, right behind the hedge maze. Just a few star feet more and she would have been smack in the middle of the maze. And stars knew how long it would have taken her to find her way out.

Smiling, Clover checked her Star-Zap to see if Lady Cordial had called the Star Darlings together for her Wish Blossom presentation. *I can't believe it*, she thought. *I'm the only one to have completed a mission on my own!*

Sure enough, there was a Star Darlings group holo-text waiting. Clover hurried to the Cosmic Transporter. The transporter moved smoothly; the students seemed fine; and the lights were shining brightly. *Everything seems okay,* she thought, relieved. *Maybe the energy shortage is resolving itself. Wouldn't that be starmazing?*

"Hey, you!" Gemma was rushing around other Starlings to catch up to Clover. "I'm starmendously happy to see you!"

Clover grinned. "I'm happy to see you, too—and to be back."

"You have to tell me all about it," Gemma said excitedly. "I can't believe we didn't even know you went! But first, let me tell you what happened here when . . ."

Gemma kept up a steady stream of talk as they approached the headmistress's office, and Clover didn't end up telling her one thing about the mission. That was just as well. Why make her nervous? Surely Gemma's mission would go better. By then Lady Cordial would have everything under control.

"And Lady Cordial was in such a tizzy!" Gemma was saying. "Piper told her you'd left for your mission, and all of a sudden, she was rushing around her office like a bloombug during a full moon! I guess she was really worried about you, Clover, because as soon as she realized you'd taken the backpack and were better prepared, she calmed down a bit."

Clover was about to mention that the backpack had been empty, anyway, but they were walking into

Lady Cordial's office. Piper was waiting at the door.

"Welcome back, Clover!" she said. "I was sending you good thoughts from the moment you left the Wishworld Surveillance Deck."

"You were?" Clover exclaimed. "Just as I was leaving, I heard a voice giving advice! It said—"

Clover was cut short as the rest of the Star Darlings engulfed her in a group hug, chattering excitedly.

"Come, come, girls," Lady Cordial said, waving off the Star Darlings as she shuffled over to Clover and awkwardly placed an arm around her shoulders. "Job well done."

As everyone took their seats, Lady Cordial continued. "S-s-s-s-star apologies, Clover. I feel terrible you had to leave on your own. Your mission, while a s-s-s-s-success, was highly irregular. Everything about it, in fact, appears to be a bit off. Your Wish Blossom opened before you returned, and your Power Crystal has already been revealed."

Clover's heart sank with disappointment.

Stop it, Clover! she told herself. The most important thing was a successful mission—and she'd brought back wish energy. Besides, she reminded herself, she'd still get her Power Crystal.

"So will you just give it to me now?" she asked.

Lady Cordial shook her head sadly. "With every-thing going on, I s-s-s-s-seem to have misplaced it. I will continue s-s-s-s-s-searching, I promise you."

"It's fine, Lady Cordial," Clover said quickly. She didn't want to add one more worry to the poor woman's list. "It's all been so odd, anyway, the Power Crystal can wait. But why was my mission so difficult when Lady Stella hasn't been around to cause trouble?"

Lady Cordial stepped back, a strange look on her face. "What could it be?" she whispered. Suddenly, to Clover's shock, she grabbed a starstick from her bun and reached for the backpack. Then she stabbed the star key chain hanging from its loop.

A heavy black cloud spilled out from the star. It floated above the Star Darlings' heads until, bit by bit, it broke apart and disappeared. An icy cold shiver ran down Clover's spine so forcefully that her teeth chattered.

"Is that negative energy?" Clover asked with a gasp. She'd never actually seen it before, never realized it had a color, shape, and form.

"Negative wish energy, to be exact," said Lady Cordial. "Lady S-s-s-s-stella created those key chains. Again, s-s-s-s-star apologies, everyone. I should have realized those could be a danger."

Lady Cordial was so visibly upset that it looked to

Clover like she might cry. "Really, Lady Cordial," she said, "don't worry . . ."

Clover paused, staring at Lady Cordial's skirt. "Your pocket is glowing," she said. A small but bright purple light was beaming from inside.

"It's got to be Clover's Power Crystal!" Cassie rushed over, the other girls right behind her. Lady Cordial reached into her pocket, and there it was, shining for all to see.

"Oh, my s-s-s-stars," said Lady Cordial, turning the brightest shade of purple Clover had ever seen. "Imagine that! I've just been s-s-s-so distracted I'd forgotten where I'd put it!"

She handed Clover the crystal without another word. The whole thing was a bit anticlimactic, Clover had to admit. But she had her lovely Power Crystal, cone-shaped with magenta and mauve swirls and an exquisitely bright orb dangling from the bottom.

It felt smooth and powerful, and holding it gave Clover a sense of strength.

"S-s-s-s-see, girls? Everything is falling into place. We are well on our way to returning S-s-s-s-starland to its earlier brilliant s-s-s-s-state!"

The girls left Lady Cordial's office together, happily talking about the future. "And there's still Gemma's mission!" said Tessa. "That will make everything even better!"

"I know what we should do to celebrate!" Astra jumped up and down with excitement. "Let's hike up in the Crystal Mountains. The suns will be setting. It will be beautiful!"

Leona glanced worriedly at her sandals. "We'll only go to the foothills," Astra assured her. "We don't want to wear anyone out—especially Clover, since she just got back."

Tessa ran to the Celestial Café to pick up a picnic dinner, and starmins later, they were off. The girls followed the trail, talking and laughing and hugging Clover. *This is even better than a boring old ceremony!* Clover thought. She was having so much fun it took her a few starsecs to realize they'd reached the lookout point.

One by one, the Star Darlings took seats along the soft mossy ledge. Tessa handed out star sandwiches and glimmerchips as everyone gazed at the setting suns. Colors filled the sky like Festival of Illumination fireworks. Clover, filled with a sense of well-being, put one arm around Astra and the other around Piper.

Piper turned to her, a worried expression on her face. "I had a dream just like this. I have a strange feeling something's about to happen."

"Stop it, Piper!" Clover said, laughing. "You heard Lady Cordial."

"Look," Piper said quietly, pointing to the view.

Clover gazed over the city and towns spread below, and suddenly, she saw it, too. The lights were flickering. The Star Darlings' voices trailed off as one by one they noticed it. Then, suddenly, the lights were snuffed out. All was dark.

"Oh, *starf*," said Clover. "Things aren't better. They're way worse."

She had a sudden horrible thought. What if Starland faded so much that Wishlings stopped making wishes at all? What would happen then?

The temperature dropped, and she shivered. She'd keep her frightening thoughts to herself for now.

Sage jumped to her feet. "Everybody! Let's get out of here and go someplace warm. My room!"

The girls hurried down the hill, hugging themselves for warmth, relieved when they reached Sage's room.

Clover sat on Sage's comfortable round bed. The room was homey, decorated in soothing shades of lavender, with a holo-photo album running pictures of her life in Starland City. She saw Sage posing with her younger twin brothers.

"I'm more worried than I was before," Cassie said

with a shake of her head. "I just don't know what to think anymore."

"Well, I'll tell you," Scarlet said heatedly. "Nothing has changed. Lady Stella is evil. And things are getting worse even after Clover brought back all that wish energy."

Suddenly, Astra gasped, pointing at the holo-photos. "Oh, my stars. I just saw the woman who's been plotting with Lady Stella!"

"What are you talking about?" Sage asked. "Show us!" She rewound the pictures with a flick of her wrist.

"Stop!" Astra ordered. "There she is! That's the woman who's been meeting with Lady Stella. They've been working together for stars know how long!"

The holo-photo showed a woman in a purple cloak standing next to a laboratory table.

Sage stared at the picture, shaking her head wordlessly.

"What's wrong?" Cassie cried.

"We've made a big mistake," Sage said dully. "Lady Stella can't possibly be evil. I know that woman really well." She raised her head, and her lavender eyes glittered.

"She's my mother."

Gemma and the Ultimate Standoff

Prologue

"**Quiet, please, everyone!**" Gemma shouted.

She was immediately gratified when the room fell silent and eleven pairs of eyes—in varying shades of violet, rose, auburn, gold, green, and blue—looked up at her. Gemma wanted to make sure that all of the Star Darlings, who were sitting on the floor of Tessa and Adora's dorm room, were listening carefully.

Leona tossed her golden curls and grinned at Gemma. "That's rich, coming from you," she said. But her smile was warm and kind and Gemma grinned back at her. *It's funny, those could have been fighting words not so long ago,* Gemma thought. But the Star Darlings had been through so much since the school year began and they had learned so much about each other's personalities— their strengths, quirks, and foibles. Gemma now understood that Leona was just attempting to lighten the mood, not trying to provoke her. She smiled as she took in Leona and Scarlet, roommates who had once been at each other's throats (even before receiving the floral arrangements of negativity) now sitting side by side, almost leaning against each other. They still both possessed strong personalities, that was for sure, but they were learning to work together instead of against each other. And maybe even becoming friends in the process.

"Does everyone have a snack?" Gemma's older sister, Tessa, asked in a motherly tone. She was circling the room with a tray of pastries. Gemma knew that her sister had stayed up late the night before, making certain to prepare each Star Darling's favorite baked treat in her micro-zap.

"I'll take a moonberry tart!" called Cassie, her eyes glinting behind her star-shaped glasses.

"It's all yours," said Tessa enthusiastically. She took a step forward.

"*Starf!*" screeched Clover. "You're squashing my hand!"

"Oops, star apologies," said Tessa. Without thinking, she let go of the tray of delicacies and sent it floating toward Cassie.

"Hey, stop that!" said Adora. "You know we need to conserve all the wish energy we can!"

Startled, Tessa dropped the tray, which landed with a clunk on Cassie's head. "Ouch!" the tiny girl said, rubbing her head. Then she gave a cry of delight as she grabbed a pastry, oozing with moonberries, before it slid off the tray. She took a big bite. Her glowfur, Itty, once a secret but now known to all the Star Darlings, zoomed over for a cuddle and a bite of the treat. Itty's "Song of Contentment" filled the air and visibly relaxed everyone.

"Go ahead, Gemma," said Sage.

Gemma pulled up a holo-letter. It was a group effort, composed by all the Star Darlings after much discussion. Now they were ready to hear it read back to them. They would make any last-minute changes they deemed necessary and then send it out to its intended recipient.

"'Dear Lady Stella,'" Gemma read. "'We are writing to you because we have come to the terrible realization that we have made a mistake. . . .'"

Cassie raised an arm clad in a sheer silvery sleeve. "Can we get rid of 'terrible' and add 'unfortunate'?" she suggested. "I think it sounds a lot less judgy." Cassie's voice was clear but her eyes were downcast. Gemma knew that Cassie was feeling very guilty about spearheading the suspicion against their former headmistress.

Gemma looked over at Sage, who nodded. She started again: "'We are writing to you because we have come to the unfortunate realization that we have made a mistake. . . .'"

Vega raised her hand. "Yes, Vega?" Gemma said patiently.

"I don't think that's right," Vega said, her brow furrowed. "It's actually quite fortunate that we came to the realization that we made a mistake. Fortunate for all of us, including Lady Stella, actually. If we're going to change it, I think we should just say 'the realization.' Simple and effective."

Libby spoke up. "Why don't we call it a shocking realization? I mean, it certainly surprised all of us when we realized that Lady Stella was working with Sage's mom and that we were totally wrong about her."

"No, no, no," said Cassie, shaking her head emphatically. "I meant that we should get rid of 'terrible' and add 'unfortunate' before 'mistake.' The *mistake* was what was unfortunate, you see."

The girls started to chatter among themselves. Gemma made a face. They were never going to get the letter out to Lady Stella if they were going to deliberate over every word.

Then Astra stood up and gave a piercing whistle. That got everyone's attention. Itty's song came to an abrupt halt. Astra pointed to Gemma. "Let's just let Gemma read it through. We can comment when she's done. Go on, Gemma," she said.

Gemma cleared her throat and started over. "'Dear Lady Stella, we have come to the realization that we have made an unfortunate mistake.'"

Gemma looked up. Cassie nodded, and everyone else seemed okay with the change, so she went on:

"'We now know that you have been working with the noted wish energy scientist Indirra to come up with a solution to the wish energy crisis and are not causing it. We think we can help figure out who is the culprit: the same Starling who sent us the poisonous flowers that caused us to argue and provided us with the nail polish that made us act odd, and who has been controlling our missions and ruining our Wish Pendants . . .'"

Gemma made a point of not looking directly at Leona, who was actually the only Star Darling whose Wish Pendant had been ruined. She continued.

"'There is one Wish Mission left to come. We have been hearing reports from our families and friends that the shortage is worse than we realized. We are worried that this is our last chance to collect enough wish energy to help reverse the crisis.'"

Gemma's glow flared orange. It was *her* Wish Mission and she was both thrilled and terrified at the prospect. Talk about pressure!

"'Lady Cordial is trying her best, but it is clear that she is just not up to the job and may even be in denial about the severity of the shortage. We need your help and guidance. Won't you please come back and be our leader once more? Starfully yours, the Star Darlings: Sage, Libby, Leona, Vega, Scarlet, Cassie, Piper, Astra, Tessa, Adora, Clover, and Gemma.'"

She stopped reading and looked up. The group stared back at her silently and the mood suddenly felt tense to Gemma. Itty must have sensed it, too, because she gave a throaty purr and began to sing her "Song of Relaxation." Despite her anxiety, Gemma found herself calming down a bit as the comforting tune filled the air.

"I think it's ready to go," Sage finally said. "Is everyone in agreement?"

All the girls nodded and Gemma pressed the send button. As everyone stared at her expectantly, she felt like a few words were in order. But Gemma's mind began to race. Lady Stella was missing. It was their fault. There was a terrible energy shortage and only one mission—hers—left. She opened her mouth to say something reassuring, but nothing came out.

Well, that was a first.

CHAPTER
1

Gemma narrowed her eyes and scrunched up her face at her Star-Zap's screen, trying to use the sheer force of her will to make it chime and flash with an incoming message from Lady Stella. When she looked up, the rest of the Star Darlings were looking back at her oddly. *Must be nerves,* she thought. Everyone was on edge, waiting for the headmistress's response.

"Any starmin now," Gemma said encouragingly, at last able to speak. Her words came back to her in a rush. "Any starmin now I'm sure we'll be hearing from Lady Stella. Actually, she's probably holo-typing like mad right now, writing to let us know that there are no hard feelings! She's not one to hold a grudge. She's got to understand that all the evidence was clearly pointing to her. We actually had no choice but to believe she was the culprit." She caught her breath and thought for a moment, seeing the other side of the story. "Although, come to think of it, she actually could be quite angry. We *did* falsely accuse her of sabotaging us. And at the very least, she's most likely disappointed in us for not trusting her. I mean, she was our headmistress. What were we thinking!" Then, noticing the other Star Darlings' frowns, she did an about-face. "But . . . it's quite likely she will be simply relieved that we came around to believing in her. I mean, she just disappeared in a puff of smoke as soon as we started talking to her. What were we supposed to think? She could have explained everything, convinced us we were wrong. Instead, she vanished! Well, hopefully she's forgiven us and she'll have an idea about how we're supposed to save Starland that she'll share with us. We certainly haven't been able to figure that out on our own! Oh, my stars, I just hope she's not mad at us for doubting her. The truth of the matter is that we really should have—"

"Gemma!" said Adora in a warning tone.

"Yes?" said Gemma, turning toward the tall, slender girl with the sky-blue aura. Gemma had just been getting warmed up and, frankly, resented the interruption. So she had raised some uncomfortable points. They were all true, weren't they?

Adora's response was to put both index fingers to her temples in the classic Starlandian "zip it" signal. Gemma gave the girl a "What in the stars do you mean?" look. Gemma couldn't stand uncomfortable silences, and it looked like the rest of the girls were feeling the same way. Like Piper, for example. Although she had just begun to meditate, her long seafoam-green ponytail draped over her shoulder like a lovely ripple of seawater, her eyes kept popping open. And Cassie was taking off her immaculate star-shaped glasses and unnecessarily polishing them on the hem of her gauzy silver shirt for what was at least the fourth time. Upside-down Astra, who could effortlessly walk on her hands through an obstacle course with her eyes closed, had just clumsily bumped into Clover. This caused Clover, who was juggling three ozziefruits, to drop the fruit to the floor. Tessa absentmindedly picked one up and took a big bite. "Tessa!" snapped the usually starmazingly patient Clover. Tessa turned to her, her lips darkened by the indigo juice. "Sorry," she said. "I get even hungrier than usual when I'm worried." Clover looked like she was going to say something else, then picked up a substitute glorange from a bowl on the table.

But instead of returning to juggling, she sighed and sat down next to Leona, who was fiddling around with her microphone. These girls needed a distraction, and fast.

Gemma knew she was a talker. A chirpy, cheerful chatterbox. Gaps in conversation seemed empty and uncomfortable to her. Why stand there in uneasy silence when she could fill it with a joke, an interesting observation, or just some friendly chitchat? She had a lot to say about everything—and anything—under the suns, and she always had the confidence to speak up and state what was on her mind. It puzzled her to no end that this ability of hers could occasionally irritate those around her. (It was her observation that those who did not appreciate her ability generally had a lot less to say than she did or were lacking the confidence to speak up.) Gemma knew that her talkativeness could come in quite handy for her classmates. When Cassie, who could be very quiet, got called on unexpectedly in class and blushed a stunning shade of silver, Gemma would helpfully offer an opinion to give her a moment to gather her thoughts. And during those awkward lulls in conversation among acquaintances, when everyone was standing around, looking at their feet, searching for something to talk about, Gemma always knew exactly what to say. If she didn't, she made something up.

"You have the gift of gab, my starshine," her grandmother used to tell her. That was exactly how Gemma saw it, as a great gift. And now it was time to bestow that gift upon her fellow Star Darlings. With everyone about to go supernova with edginess, she felt in her heart of hearts that it was her job to make them all feel at ease. Plus, she thought she might burst if she didn't start talking again. The silence felt even more oppressive and heavy to her that day.

With a quick glance at Adora, Gemma opened her mouth, about to launch into some pleasant, distracting chatter. But just then she felt a slight tremble in her fingers as a message arrived in her Star-Zap's in-box. Her pulse quickened. This was it! As the phone began to chime and flash, there was a collective sharp intake of breath. Gemma squeezed her eyes shut for a split starsec, then opened them and read the words on-screen aloud to the group: HOLO-MESSAGE DECLINED.

Gemma's heart sank. The downcast faces of the other Star Darlings mirrored exactly what she felt. Disappointed. Scared. Guilty.

"This is terrible," Gemma said. "It means that Lady Stella has not forgiven us." She felt her face getting hot and she knew that her cheeks were probably bright orange. This was their fault! If only they hadn't turned on Lady Stella, she'd have been with them right then and there.

Sage looked sad. "We made a mistake," she said. "We took the evidence we were presented with and we made a decision—a bad one." But then she straightened up and spoke almost fiercely. "But we can fix it. I'm sure we can. We are the twelve Star-Charmed Starlings, aren't we?"

A few of the girls shook their heads. "Clearly she doesn't want to talk to us," said Tessa. "Not that I can blame her."

"Wait a minute," said Astra. "You mean you think that Lady Stella wouldn't accept our message? I'm thinking that it means she didn't receive it."

Clover nodded her head in agreement. "I don't think she's blocking us. If she was, it would have read 'sender rejected.'"

There was silence as they all tried not to look at each other, wondering why anyone would have seen fit to block a message from lovely Clover. But she wasn't offering an explanation. Perhaps that was a story for another starday.

Piper stood, her seafoam-green eyes misty and

faraway-looking. "Maybe Lady Stella isn't angry with us at all. Maybe . . . possibly . . . she needs our help. . . ." Her voice trailed off and she sat down abruptly.

Gemma stared. Sometimes Piper said things that were so odd that everyone just ignored them. But maybe there was something to that thought. . . .

"Our message probably just didn't go through," said Sage. "Otherwise we would have gotten her outgoing message. Like this." She stood, holding out her Star-Zap. A hologram of her mother, clad in a lavender cape, popped up. "I'm sorry," her holo-self said, "but I am away on a business trip and cannot be reached. Please try again." Even in hologram form Indirra was beautiful, an older and taller version of Sage with the same large violet eyes, pointy chin, and lavender hair.

"You're right," said Vega. "Lady Stella's Star-Zap should have an outgoing message." She peered more closely at Sage, who looked uneasy. "Is something wrong?"

Sage took a deep breath. "I know I shouldn't be worried," she said. "But I am. It's very unusual that my mom's message would come up for me. In the past, even on her most classified business trips, calls from the family would go through. This just doesn't feel right to me."

Cassie stood to put a comforting hand on Sage's

shoulder and Gemma noticed that it seemed to almost instantly calm the girl. Sage thought for a moment and brightened.

"Hey, I have an idea!" she announced. "We should go tell Lady Cordial the good news. She's been such a mess trying to hold this place together. I mean, it took her star ages to figure out how to start conserving energy on campus. And now she's totally fixated on planning Starshine Day when it's obvious it needs to be postponed so we can spend our time concentrating on coming up with new and better ways to save energy. I'm positive this will be a big relief to her."

"I like that idea," said Gemma, Piper's words disappearing from her mind. "I think that will make Lady Cordial feel so much better." Poor Lady Cordial. She simply wasn't headmistress material, and she had been thrust into the role after the disappearance of Lady Stella. She was obviously trying her best, but that wasn't cutting the ballum blossom sauce.

"Shall we go now?" asked Sage.

"Sure," said Leona, jumping to her feet. Gemma watched as Leona casually reached down to grab Scarlet's hand and hoisted her up. Sage pulled open the door, and she, Astra, and Leona led the way as the rest of the girls fell into place behind them, Gemma and Piper

taking up the rear. They stepped on the Cosmic Transporter and Gemma half expected it to start moving them
along, as it usually did. But the power to all nonessential
machinery had been cut after students had begun to pro-
test Starling Academy's wasteful wish energy practices
during the crisis. Now Bot-Bots were set in sleep mode
unless absolutely necessary, food choices were limited
in the Celestial Café (much to Tessa's chagrin), and
doors needed to be opened manually, to name but a few
changes.

CONSERVE WISH ENERGY: LEVITATE OBJECTS ONLY
WHEN ABSOLUTELY NECESSARY, a flickering holo-sign
read. Another proclaimed SPARKLE SHOWER WITH A
FRIEND, and showed two smiling Starlings showering in
bathing suits. That one made Gemma laugh, as it was
intended to. A little Starlandian humor in the face of an
overwhelming situation.

Gemma turned to Piper. "This is good," she said. "I
bet Lady Cordial will help us find Lady Stella now that
we know she can be trusted. Those two have been working together for a while now and seemed very close. Lady
Cordial could have an idea of where to find Lady Stella."

"Mmmmm-hmmm," replied Piper distractedly. In
the bright sunlight, her dulled appearance was more

apparent to Gemma. She didn't even want to see her own reflection. Sparkle shower rationing made everyone dimmer and less vibrant. It was disheartening.

The girls pushed open the heavy doors to Halo Hall. The starmarble corridors, usually crowded and bustling, were empty and quiet on this Babsday, the second day of the Starlandian weekend. Gemma even missed the roaming Bot-Bot guards, which she realized gave her a sense of security. The Star Darlings' footfalls echoed ominously in the empty hallways, which suddenly seemed full of looming shadows.

"This is weird," Gemma whispered to Piper, who stared straight ahead, not acknowledging that she had been spoken to.

Apparently the rest of the group felt the same. They had been chattering excitedly on the walk to Halo Hall, but suddenly their voices were silenced. Wordlessly, they walked to Lady Stella's old office. Leona raised her hand to knock, but Sage boldly slid the door open and stepped inside.

The rest of the girls filed in behind her. Gemma was right behind Piper, who slowed for a starmin.

Piper turned and grabbed Gemma. Her fingers felt icy cold on Gemma's bare arm. "Should we be doing this?" she blurted out. Her eyes seemed clouded and her brow was furrowed. "I—I'm just not sure about this." She bit her lip. "Maybe it will just confuse Lady Cordial more. Maybe we should handle this on our own."

Gemma considered that. But the girls were energized and positive for the first time in a while. It felt good to be doing something, taking action. And they were already there, for stars' sake. She shrugged. "It probably can't hurt," she said.

"Okay," said Piper, though she still looked a bit doubtful. She turned and glided through the doorway. With a deep breath, Gemma stepped inside and pulled the door shut behind them.

CHAPTER
2

"Halt! Who goes there?" shouted a robotic voice. Gemma felt a jolt of fear and jumped.

"We-we're looking for Lady Cordial," said Sage in an unexpectedly shaky tone. Clearly the Bot-Bot voice had startled her, too.

A shiny Bot-Bot zoomed toward them from a dark corner of the room, its eyes blinking and its voice loud and commanding. "State your purpose, Starlings," the Bot-Bot said.

Leona spoke up. "We need to talk to Lady Cordial," she said. Her eyes narrowed as she stared at the floating robot. "I thought all Bot-Bots were in sleep mode until further notice. What's going on?"

"Not guard Bot-Bots," said the Bot-Bot. "My job is to protect Lady Cordial's office at all times."

"Lady Stella's office," Clover muttered under her breath. "It will always be Lady Stella's office." Gemma silently agreed.

"Well, where is she?" asked Sage impatiently, having regained her composure. "We have some important news to tell her."

"Lady Cordial is on her way to address the student body," the Bot-Bot said in its clipped tone, "at the assembly."

"At what assembly?" said Gemma just as the Star Darlings' Star-Zaps all started vibrating. Looking down, Gemma saw that they had just received a school-wide holo-blast: GATHER IMMEDIATELY AT THE BAND SHELL FOR A QUICK UPDATE ON STARSHINE DAY FROM YOUR HEAD-MISTRESS. STARPRISE GUEST ENTERTAINMENT!

"Maybe she's going to announce that she's postponing Starshine Day until the energy shortage is fixed," Cassie suggested reasonably. "That would make sense."

"Does Lady Cordial ever make sense?" scoffed Leona. It was an unkind thing to say, but there was some merit to it. Lady Cordial was, in the best of situations, nervous and awkward. With Lady Stella away, she seemed to be making bad decision after bad decision.

The girls made their way to the band shell and plopped themselves down on the stargrassy area in front of the stage. They watched as the Star Quad began to fill with students. Some had brought blankets, which they spread on the ground, while others stood around, chatting with fellow students. The overall mood seemed to be slight puzzlement at the last-minute invitation, but pleasure nonetheless at being outside with friends. The sun was shining brightly and there was a slight breeze, which felt refreshing. Gemma closed her eyes and lifted her face to the sun, knowing the result would be a smattering of light orange star-shaped freckles across her nose. She caught snippets of conversations, which mostly seemed to be about news from home—Starcarpool regulations, newly added HOS lanes, and sparkle shower rationing. That made Gemma realize that she hadn't heard a star news report on campus in a while—or, come to think of it, seen a copy of a holo-newspaper. Very odd.

"What in the stars?" she heard Leona say. Gemma's eyes snapped open. Leona was pointing to the stage. A girl with a bright green aura was dragging out a drum kit. Leona stood, walked onto the stage, and started talking to the girl in green. Another girl, in a pale blue robe, hurried out to join them. It looked like Leona and the new girl got into a discussion that was not particularly friendly. Gemma watched as Leona turned, her face angry, and stormed off.

Scarlet, who had been lying on her back, staring up at the clouds, raised her head. "Where did Leona go?" she asked. Gemma shrugged and closed her eyes again. Vega was deep in a holo–crossword puzzle and Piper was, of course, meditating. Truth be told, Gemma didn't care if the assembly ever started. It was nice to just empty her mind and relax, to not think about anything. It had been far too long since she'd had the pleasure of doing that.

Just then Cassie grabbed Gemma's arm and Gemma snapped her eyes open. Lady Cordial was standing in the middle of the stage, staring out at the crowd. The students watched as she took a deep breath and pulled a purple microphone out of one of her voluminous pockets. Lady Cordial's face was pale and she looked as ill at ease as ever. "It's painful to watch," muttered Cassie, who knew a thing or two about feeling awkward. It was obvious that the responsibility that had been thrust upon Lady Cordial due to Lady Stella's abrupt depar-ture hadn't done a thing to boost her self-confidence. Someone jostled Gemma as she sat down next to her. Gemma gave a sidelong glance and realized it was Leona. The Starling didn't look angry anymore, and she was grinning wickedly. But before Gemma could ask what Leona was up to, Lady Cordial began to speak.

"S-s-s-star greetings, s-s-s-students," she said softly into the microphone. The students continued to talk. She raised her voice and tried again. "S-s-s-star greetings, s-s-s students," she repeated, and the crowd began to quiet down. "As you all know, S-s-s-starland is in a bit of an energy crisis. Belts have been tightened and we are now doing all we can to help conserve energy on campus. And don't think I haven't noticed the s-s-s-sacrifices that you have all made! You deserve to be commended! S-s-s-so with Lady S-s-s-stella s-s-s-still temporarily away, I have made the executive decision to keep S-s-s-starshine Day on the calendar, which, as you know, is coming up s-s-s-soon. This is an important celebration for us all and I am counting on all of you to pitch in to make this a resounding s-s-s-success. It will boost morale and foster feelings of hope and camaraderie among s-s-s-students and faculty alike."

The Star Darlings glanced at one another. Was she serious? Starshine Day was still going to happen despite all the uncertainty?

"The S-s-s-starshine Day committee has been hard at work, but now we must ask for your help to make this day go off without a hitch. In a few s-s-s-starsecs you will each receive an assignment on your S-s-s-star-Zaps."

Gemma's Star-Zap vibrated and she looked down. The screen read DECORATING COMMITTEE. She glanced over Tessa's shoulder. FOOD COMMITTEE. Figured. Astra was on the games committee, and Leona was entertainment. The other girls were assigned to hospitality, science fair, prizes, sports, animals, light shows, art fair, costumes, and the parade. Oddly, none of the Star Darlings were on the same committee.

"Are there any questions?" Lady Cordial asked after the general post-assignment hubbub died down.

Several arms shot up, including Sage's and Astra's. But Lady Cordial didn't notice. She squinted at the crowd and said, "Okay then, let's go s-s-s-straight to the entertainment! As you know, we will be having an exciting Battle of the Bands competition on S-s-s-starshine Day, with a gift certificate from Musical Madness for the winners! Today we have a s-s-s-special treat. Competitors Vivica and the Visionaries are going to give you a preview of their s-s-s-spectacular s-s-s-sound!"

The crowd clapped politely as Vivica and her bandmates ran onstage. They were all in sparkly outfits that matched their auras, and Gemma had to admit that

Vivica's light blue outfit, which looked like it was made of moonbeams, was positively stellar. As the drummer, keyboardist, and guitarist got into position, Vivica raised the mic to her lips. "Hey, everyone, I'm Vivica," she said, pointing to herself, "and these"—she pointed to her band—"are the Visionaries. And we're here to get you pumped for Starshine Day. We're gonna rock your starsocks off! The song we're going to sing is the brand-new anthem 'Starshine Day Is Coming.' It's a song written and composed by our very own headmistress, Lady Cordial. It's a great song that I am sure you will enjoy, and . . ."

As Vivica went on (and on), Leona turned to Gemma and placed something in her hand. Gemma looked down and blinked at the star-shaped orange devices. "Ear shields?" she said. "Really, Leona?"

Leona grinned. "I ran into Vivica onstage when I went up to check out the drum kit. She was so rude and called us embarrassing amateurs! Of all the nerve! So I ran off to the star emporium to pick up twelve pairs." She gave Gemma a pleading look. "Come on, put them on. It's just a little joke!"

Gemma bit her lip. "I don't know," she said. "Aren't we supposed to rise above others' petty behavior?"

Leona did not look at all convinced, so Gemma tried another tactic. "Don't you want to hear what the competition sounds like?" she asked.

"Nope," said Leona. "I've heard them play one too many times already."

"Maybe *I* want to hear them," said Gemma.

"Come on," begged Leona. "Humor me!"

"Fine," said Gemma with a sigh. She held them tightly in her hand as she watched Leona hand out the ear shields to rest of the Star Darlings. Some questioned her, but most of the girls just shrugged and placed them over their ears. Donning ear shields at a performance was an aggressive move, especially when your rival was onstage.

Gemma held off, curious to hear a bit of the music before sealing up her ears. Vivica turned to the band and said, "A-one, a-two, a-one, two, three . . ." and the Visionaries burst into song:

Starshine Day is coming
Time to celebrate
Starshine Day is coming
Hurry, don't be late

Not too bad, actually, thought Gemma. The tune was bright and bouncy, and Vivica, surprisingly, had a clear, sweet voice. Gemma suddenly felt startacularly excited about Starshine Day and started clapping along to the music. But after a sharp elbow to the ribs and a look of disapproval from Leona, she reluctantly fastened the ear shields over her ears. She was immediately engulfed in silence. It was a strange experience, almost like being underwater. She could see girls in the audience mouthing the lyrics, dancing, and jumping up and down. But because she couldn't hear anything at all, she felt like she was watching everything from a distance. The crowd had certainly perked up. She looked all around her. They really appeared to be enjoying the music. One girl even looked like she was about to cry with joy!

Leona, standing next to Gemma, jostled her arm. Gemma glanced over and saw Leona remove something from her pocket. She took a closer look. It was black and misshapen, but Leona cradled it in her hand quite lovingly. Suddenly, Gemma realized what it was—Leona's ruined Wish Pendant, a cuff bracelet, once gleaming and golden. Poor Leona! Gemma felt very sad for her friend and her dashed dreams. Leona would never get a Wish Blossom or a Power Crystal. The ruined accessory was a reminder of that. If Gemma were Leona, she'd just throw it away. Who needed a token of one's failure?

Gemma realized that Vivica and the Visionaries had finished playing as they took a bow and exited the stage. She removed her ear shields and put them in her pocket. The crowd wasn't moving, apparently hoping that the band would come back and sing some more. They lingered for quite a while. When it was clear that the band wouldn't be playing another song, the crowd reluctantly began to disperse.

Leona smiled at the other Star Darlings. "Star salutations for humoring me," she said. Scarlet gave her a look that Gemma could only translate to "I can't believe you asked us to do that" and possibly "I'm shocked that we all agreed," and Leona rolled her warm golden eyes back at her roommate. "And yes, Scarlet, I do know that I was being childish."

Gemma shrugged. It was no big deal. "You're welcome," she said. She was about to say more when she spotted Lolo, a girl who had a turquoise aura and was in her lighterature class, passing by. Gemma reached out an arm and stopped her. The girl blinked at her sleepily, as if she had just woken up.

"Hey, Lolo," Gemma said. "I was wondering if I could borrow your notes from yesterday's class. I can't find mine anywhere. It's like they disappeared."

Lolo smiled at Gemma as if she hadn't heard a word she had said. "What a startastic song," she said. "I'm so excited that Starshine Day is coming."

Gemma frowned. "But don't you think it's weird that we're still celebrating Starshine Day even though we're in the middle of an energy shortage?"

The girl looked back at her blankly. "No," she said, shaking her head. "Not at all. Starshine Day is coming."

A girl with bright pink curls springing out from under a knit cap stopped in her tracks. "Oh, yes," she gushed. "Starshine Day is going to be startacular!"

Passing girls began saying, "Starshine Day! Starshine Day!" until, to Gemma's starprise, it became a chant. Gemma turned to the rest of the Star Darlings, who still stood in front of the stage in a tight little group.

Clover's piercing purple eyes flashed. "Did you know that Starshine Day is coming?" she said sarcastically.

"So I've heard," said Gemma. "What's going on?"

"We're waiting for Lady Cordial," answered Clover. "We're going to tell her the news about Lady Stella."

"Startastic. That'll put an end to all this Starshine Day silliness," Gemma said.

Clover nodded in agreement.

Just then Lady Cordial emerged from backstage,

flanked by two Bot-Bots. She stepped off the stage and hurried past the Star Darlings, so focused on her Star-Zap that she appeared not to notice them.

"Lady Cordial!" called Astra. The headmistress turned and stopped.

"Hold it right there," said one of the Bot-Bots.

"At ease, RE-D7," said Lady Cordial. "You may proceed, girls."

Sage opened her mouth to speak, but Leona burst out with "Vivica and the Visionaries? Really?"

"Leona!" said Scarlet warningly.

Lady Cordial's eyes glittered and Gemma was afraid for a moment that Leona had angered her. But then her expression changed. "S-s-s-star apologies," she said. "But Vivica begged for a chance to practice in front of a crowd. It was thoughtless of me. Thoughtless."

Leona made a face and folded her arms tightly across her chest. "Fine," she said, though Gemma could tell she was still steaming. "We'll beat them fair and square. You'll see," she said, her words clipped.

"Is that all, girls?" asked Lady Cordial. "There's s-s-s-so much to do to get ready!"

"Actually, we have some great news to tell you," Gemma said.

"Great news!" echoed Libby.

"The very best!" said Cassie.

Sage and Astra both opened their mouths to speak, but Gemma felt like she was going to burst if she didn't say something. "We're pretty certain that Lady Stella is not the culprit!" she blurted.

Lady Cordial looked shocked. Then her expression grew soft with sadness. "Oh, you poor, poor girls," she said. "This is a very difficult s-s-s-situation for you. You're quite clearly in denial about Lady S-s-s-stella's involvement. Completely understandable."

Sage pushed forward. "Actually, we're almost a hydrong percent sure of it. We recently discovered that Lady Stella has been consulting with my mother," she explained. "You know, Indirra, the top wish energy scientist? So Lady Stella is clearly working with her on a solution to the shortage. She's not the one sabotaging us."

"Well, how do you explain that all the terrible things s-s-s-stopped as s-s-s-soon as she disappeared?" Lady Cordial asked.

"We're convinced it was a coincidence," said Cassie. "Or maybe the real saboteur stopped as soon as Lady Stella disappeared to make her look guilty."

Lady Cordial considered this. "I guess that's possible. . . ."

Gemma piped up. "It's such a relief to know she's on our side," she said. "We were all so worried!"

Lady Cordial opened her mouth to speak, then shut it just as quickly. She took a deep breath and appeared to be thinking. "Of course. How wonderful to hear this news. Did you also find out if she'll be returning s-s-s-soon?" she asked eagerly.

The Star Darlings' faces fell. "We . . . um . . . thought that you might be able to help us with that," Gemma explained. "We can't seem to find her."

Lady Cordial shook her head. "I'm s-s-s-sorry, girls," she said, "but I have no idea where she could be." She smiled at them. "Well, keep me posted," she said. "This is exciting news indeed!"

"So will we postpone Starshine Day?" Gemma asked.

Lady Cordial looked at her as if she had two auras. "Postpone S-s-s-starshine Day?" she said, her eyes wide. "On the contrary! We must s-s-s-step up the preparations in honor of Lady S-s-s-stella's return. This c-c-celebration is even more important than ever!"

CHAPTER
3

Starshine Day, Starshine Day. That was all anyone could talk about after Lady Cordial's impromptu
assembly. The Star Darlings were getting tired of hearing about it. Students and teachers discussed it in class.
They received holo-reminders about it every starday. It
was talked about in the echoing starmarble hallways of
Halo Hall, at the finely set tables in the Celestial Café,
and on the soft, comfortable couches in the Lightning
Lounge. It seemed that everyone, except for the Star
Darlings, had Starshine Day on the brain.

It was last period on Yumday, and the Star Darlings
had assembled in their secret classroom, waiting for
the guest lecturer to arrive. They were hoping it would
be Lady Cordial. There were so many unanswered

questions: Was there anything they could do to help with the shortage? Did Lady Cordial have any further thoughts about where Lady Stella could be? Could she offer them any help in trying to figure out who the saboteur was now that Lady Stella was no longer their number one suspect? And did she have any idea when the twelfth and final Wish Orb would reveal itself?

"I just don't remember Starshine Day being such a big deal last year," Adora was saying as they waited. "I mean, it's a fun day and all, don't get me wrong. I always have a great time and I especially enjoy the interactive science experiment exhibit. But this is a little over the stars, don't you think?"

"Totally," Clover replied. "Especially since we're in the middle of this energy shortage." The rest of the Star Darlings nodded in agreement.

"So what are the chances that our guest lecturer makes an appearance today?" Libby said as she twisted a strand of jellyjooble-pink hair around her finger.

Vega perked up. Now they were speaking her language. "Oh, I'd say it's one in—"

"It might as well be one in ten moonium," interrupted Scarlet in a bored voice. She was sprawled on the floor with her head leaning against the wall, tapping her big clunky boots together rhythmically. "Face it, Vega, no one's coming. We haven't had Star Darlings class in stardays. We keep showing up, but the guest lecturer never does. It's like everyone forgot about us or something. I say we shouldn't waste our time."

"Oooh," said Leona. "That's really bad. You mean, you think everyone has given up on the Star Darlings?"

Gemma grew irritated. She didn't like the sound of that at all.

Piper spoke up and her voice startled Gemma. "Maybe it's because we already know everything there is to know about being a Star Darling," she offered. "Maybe it's actually a star compliment!"

"Maybe," said Gemma. But she didn't really believe that. "Actually, I'm worried about my Wish Orb. When will it be ready?" Maybe Lady Cordial was too distracted by her duties and responsibilities and had lost sight of the importance of the final Wish Orb. Gemma desperately wanted to be sent to Wishworld. (She didn't want to say it out loud, but she was wondering if her Wish Mission—the twelfth and final one—could be the mission that would collect enough energy to save Starland, which she believed would fulfill the prophecy.) Then she had a scary thought and was seized with panic. Maybe

Lady Cordial knew something they didn't know. Maybe there wasn't going to be a Wish Orb for her at all.

"Let's try Lady Stella again," Cassie suggested. "We just have to keep sending messages until we reach her."

But the result was the same: HOLO-MESSAGE DECLINED. The looks on the girls' faces ranged from disappointed to sullen, teary to fed up.

Sage shook her head. "I haven't gotten through to my mother, either, but Dad and Gran keep telling me she's fine, not to worry. Of course, they have no idea about what's going on with Lady Stella."

Gemma wished she had the right words to help take the worried look out of Sage's lavender eyes. She was about to start trying when the bell rang for the end of class. Scarlet stood up and brushed off her black tulle skirt with hot-pink lining. She grinned wickedly and hopped up on the desk, where she perched primly. "Students, class dismissed!" she called out in a perfect imitation of Professor Lucretia Delphinus. "I hope you all enjoyed my fascinating lecture on the different types of Wish Pendant glows, though I did notice a few of you nodding off in the middle of my discussion of faintly bright versus somewhat bright, which could be considered quite rude! But perhaps you were overwhelmed by the sheer volume of information I provided today. Now if someone could just help me get down from this desk . . . Is there a Flash Vertical Mover around here?"

"Scarlet!" said Piper, shaking her head reproachfully. "Be nice!" But even she couldn't help smiling. Scarlet's imitation of the tough and tiny teacher had been starspot-on.

"Off to our Starshine Day committees," said Tessa with a sigh. "As usual." All after-school clubs, meetings, and sports had been put on hold until after Starshine Day so students and faculty could fully concentrate on the preparations, per Lady Cordial's direct orders. Her laser-sharp focus on this one event was troubling to Gemma, who wondered why Lady Cordial didn't seem concerned about who had been sabotaging them (since Lady Stella had been cleared), the shortage, or the delinquent Wish Orb. She'd ask her all those questions if she got the chance.

She waved to the other Star Darlings as the girls went their separate ways to their various committees and Gemma headed to her own—the decorating committee, which was made up of a group of students who were all startastically excited to have such a big part in making Starshine Day "the best it could be," plus Gemma.

"Star greetings, Gemma!" called a girl named Tansy. "It's so nice to see you this starday." Tansy had a sweet round face and a pale pink aura. Gemma smiled despite herself; the girl was so kind and gentle she deserved a warm greeting in return, no matter how grumpy Gemma might be feeling. "Star greetings, Tansy," she said as she settled into the stargrass next to her. They had been tasked with stringing what felt like floozels of briteflower garlands, which they would hang all over campus. Gemma picked up a half-strung garland and, with a sigh, began threading the small twinkling white blossoms onto it by hand, one by one. Every task, every preparation these days took an agonizingly long time, as everything needed to be done the old-fashioned way, which was the way many things were done on Wishworld—by hand.

Gemma's thoughts wandered back to her Wish Mission and she pricked her finger with the needle. "Ouch!" she cried. If this was what life was like on Wishworld every starday, she had no idea why Scarlet wanted to live there so badly. Everything was so much harder without the hands-free benefits of utilizing wish energy. But the rest of the girls laughed and sang as they worked and seemed so happy to be there. They never complained that they were bored or that their fingers hurt. They didn't seem to have a care in the world. *Why are they so excited about Starshine Day and I'm not?* Gemma wondered.

By the middle of the starweek Gemma felt more irritable than ever. Each and every one of her fingers was sore. And every time her Star-Zap vibrated, she snatched it up, hoping to find a message about Lady Stella or the Wish Orb. But it was always a useless Starshine Day update from Lady Cordial. And while the temporary headmistress was in constant communication via her Star-Zap, she was nowhere to be seen.

The hydrongs of briteflower garlands were finally done, and it was time to begin the arduous task of hanging them. Since the Starlings couldn't use their wish energy manipulation to effortlessly fasten the garlands, someone managed to find an ancient ladder from the old days and dragged it out. They carried it over to the first lamppost, set it up, and then stared at the contraption warily. It looked rickety and unstable and no one wanted to climb it. Tansy finally took a deep breath and ascended shakily to the top. Another girl produced an old-fashioned tool kit. Gemma rooted around in it until she found a sparklehammer and a solar-metal spike (both of which she was vaguely familiar with from the toolshed on the farm) and handed them to Tansy, who looked at the tools in confusion. "I . . . I'm not sure what to do," she said. Gemma took pity on the Starling and motioned for her to climb down, switching places with her. When she reached the top, she looked down—she was pretty far off the ground—and got a bit dizzy. She wasn't quite sure how to position the spike so she wouldn't smash her finger with the sparklehammer, but then, after some adjusting, she figured out the correct angle and did the job. *There!* She climbed back down and took a look. Her proud moment was cut short as the briteflower garland promptly fluttered to the ground.

Gemma sighed and climbed back up the ladder. From her vantage point she saw a passing Bot-Bot. They were programmed to help with all sorts of issues around Starling Academy, so she waved and called it over.

"Star greetings," she said as it got closer.

"Star greetings, I am JR-Y6," the Bot-Bot said.

"Would you help us hang this garland for Starshine Day, JR-Y6?" Gemma asked politely.

"Negative. I am currently solely in guard mode," said the Bot-Bot. "My directive is to serve Lady Cordial. I am not programmed to help you." He nodded briskly and zoomed off.

"*Starf!*" said Gemma. With a shrug, she climbed back to the top of the ladder and hammered in the spike again. To her relief, this time it stayed put.

She climbed down, carried the ladder to the second post, and climbed back up. She carefully positioned the garland, admiring it as it hung between the two posts, twinkling prettily. She was just about to pound in the spike when she spotted JR-Y6 heading off in the distance. That was when she realized that if a guard was around, Lady Cordial must not be too far away. Without hesitating, she put down the sparklehammer, jumped down from the ladder, and took off after the Bot-Bot.

"Gemma, wait!" called Tansy. It was only then that Gemma realized she was still holding on to the end of the briteflower garland. As she ran, the other end of it ripped off the first pole, scattering blossoms every which way.

"Star apologies, Tansy!" she called. "I won't be long at all."

The girl looked distraught. "But Starshine Day is coming!" she said.

Don't I know it, thought Gemma. "I'll be back soon! I promise!"

Gemma followed the guard all the way to the ozzie-fruit orchard, where it set off on a winding path through the trees. Eventually, to her astonishment, she discovered Lady Cordial sitting on a bench, about to bite into a star-sandwich, a fine picnic lunch spread out around her.

"Oh, Gemma!" Lady Cordial cried, jumping up to greet her. Gemma grimaced as the fine china plate that had been sitting on her lap smashed into smithereens on the stone walkway. "Oh, dear," Lady Cordial said sheepishly. "How clumsy of me."

Two Bot-Bot guards zoomed closer, then hovered nearby. To Gemma's starprise, one of them winked at her. Gemma realized it was MO-J4, otherwise known as Mojay—Sage's special Bot-Bot friend. She winked back.

"How can I help you, my dear?" Lady Cordial asked as the smashed china and lost star-sandwich disappeared, as messes always did on Starland.

"I need to talk to you," said Gemma. "I am feeling this tremendous pull to go to Wishworld, but my Wish Orb is still not ready." She looked up at the headmistress searchingly. "Or is it? Have you checked?"

"Every day," said Lady Cordial earnestly. "I'm just as anxious as you are. But I have this feeling, this very s-s-s-strong feeling, that we are all worrying and getting upset for no reason. I can't shake this feeling that everything is going to turn out exactly the way it is s-s-s-supposed to. And I also have this feeling, a premonition almost"—she leaned closer to Gemma, as if she was about to tell her a secret—"that it's *your* mission that will turn the tide for S-s-s-starland. That you, my dear, will be the one to return S-s-s-starland to the way it should be."

Gemma gasped and felt a glimmer of hope in her chest. "Do you really think so?" she asked eagerly. "That's exactly what I was hoping for!"

"I do," said Lady Cordial. "Just you wait and s-s-s-see. We just need to be patient." She closed her eyes, concentrated for a moment, and nodded. "Yes," she said, "I think it will all work out just in time for S-s-s-starshine Day."

"But that's only three days away!" Gemma said anxiously. She had a sudden realization. "So that means I'll be sent down on my mission any day now?"

Lady Cordial nodded. "It's almost ready, I'm sure of it," she agreed. "So rest up and s-s-s-start getting ready for the mission of a lifetime!"

Gemma walked back to the dorm in a daze, completely forgetting about Tansy and the decorating committee. She had to mentally prepare herself for this most crucial mission. Her mind was racing. *I'll keep this news to myself,* she thought. *No need to discuss it until it actually happens.* Yes, it would be good for her to sit on the information and digest it slowly. Everyone would know soon enough, at the Wish Orb reveal. She was pleased with herself for coming to that conclusion, which she felt showed great maturity and composure.

She bumped into her sister just outside of the dormitories.

"Hey, Gemma," said Tessa.

"I'mgoingonamission!" Gemma nearly shouted, all in a rush.

"Slow down," said Tessa. "Say that again?"

Oh, starf, there goes maturity and composure, Gemma thought. She looked around furtively to make sure no one had overheard, and repeated her message. "I'm going on a mission! Any day now. Lady Cordial just told me."

Tessa bit her lip.

"What's wrong?" said Gemma. "It's what we've been waiting for. This is good news for me—and for Starland."

"It's great news for Starland," Tessa replied slowly. "You, I'm not so sure. I'm worried. The last thing Mom said to me before we left for Starling Academy was that I should always look out for you."

"Really?" said Gemma. "She told me I should always look out for *you.*"

The two girls laughed. That was just like their mother—trying to make them both feel useful and trusted (and carefully looked after, of course).

"But seriously, Gemma," said Tessa, "we're having a crisis. Things keep going wrong. Adora's mission nearly was ruined because her secret Starling identity was compromised. It all turned out okay in the end, but it could have been a disaster. Not to mention Leona's messed-up mission. She almost didn't make it home."

"I'll be careful, Sis. I promise," said Gemma. "But I've got to go on this mission. The fate of Starland is hanging in the balance, you know."

"And on that dramatic note," said Tessa, "I've got to go. I'll see you later."

She turned and made a glitterbeeline toward her dorm.

"Wait a minute, where are you going?" Gemma cried. She had been hoping they could pick a few outfits together with the Wishworld Outfit Selector.

"Why, to my room, of course," Tessa called back over her shoulder. "To bake. You can't go to Wishworld without the proper amount of snacks, now can you?"

CHAPTER
4

It was a full starday later and there was still no message from Lady Cordial about Gemma's Wish Orb. So, as usual, the twelve girls assembled in the Star Darlings classroom. This time, anticipating the free hour they would most likely have, they decided they had no choice but to start preparing for the Battle of the Bands. They brought in their musical instruments, sewing supplies, and what seemed like mooniums of sequins, especially created by Adora, which they would sew onto their outfits—a striking golden pantsuit for Leona, its legs wide and flowing; a pink minidress with enormous bell sleeves for Libby; a flowy purple tunic over leggings for Sage; a bright blue bolero jacket and matching shorts for Vega; and a hooded black sweatshirt dress for Scarlet.

Gemma's sewing skills had improved dramatically after her experience with the briteflower garlands, and she chose to work on Scarlet's dress, adding hot-pink sequins to the dark material. It was going to look startastic when she finished. The only way to do it without wish energy was to pull a needle and thread through the center of each sequin, thread a tiny bead onto the needle, then push it back through the sequin, knotting the thread on the other side—over and over and over again. It was time-consuming, mindless work, but Gemma was finding it to be oddly soothing. It helped to calm her nerves. She was both bursting with excitement and trembling with apprehension, an uneasy combination. Being nervous made her chattier than ever. It soothed her a bit to keep up a constant stream of words, which she was sure entertained the other Star Darlings as they sewed on sequins, too. Meanwhile, the Star Darlings band members rehearsed. The room had been soundproofed to keep their special lessons private, so they didn't have to worry that they would be disturbing any classes while they rocked out.

After a while, the band took a break. Leona took the time to try to reach Lady Stella. Gemma held her breath as Leona holo-dialed, but there was no answer. Again.

Gemma turned to Sage, intending to ask if she had

heard from her mother. Cassie, sensing her question, shook her head and leaned over to whisper to Gemma. "No word yet," she said. "And when she last spoke to her grandmother and her father, she could have sworn that they sounded a little worried. But they assured her that everything was fine."

With break time over, Vega, Sage, and Libby picked up their instruments and Scarlet settled in behind her drums.

"Let's take that one from the top again," said Leona. "We have to be totally perfect." She looked determined. "I just *have* to beat Vivica."

Scarlet reached over and poked her in the side with a drumstick.

Leona jumped. "Oh, sorry. I mean the *Star Darlings* just have to beat Vivica and the Visionaries," she said, correcting herself.

Scarlet nodded. "That's more like it," she said.

★

That evening, as they walked back to their dorms after dinner, Piper spoke up. "I have an idea," she said. "We've been under a lot of pressure the past few days. Anyone want to join me for a little meditation?"

It was the last thing Gemma wanted to do. She was

envisioning herself slipping on a pair of comfy pajamas, crawling under the covers, and holo-calling her two best friends from home for a chat before she fell asleep. She glued her eyes to the ground and kept walking toward the dormitory.

When none of the Star Darlings responded, Piper pressed on. "We've all been working so hard. We're under a lot of stress. Some simple meditation will work wonders. It will center us, take our minds off our worries about Lady Stella and our concerns about this ridiculous festival. We'll all sleep really well afterwards, too."

Gemma was just about to politely bow out when she glanced over and noticed the disappointed look on Piper's kind face. She mentally changed her plans for the evening.

"I'm in," she said, a note of fake cheer in her voice. Her sister, with a barely audible sigh, followed suit. And before long, each and every Star Darling was on board. No one wanted to be the one to disappoint Piper. They made a plan to go first to their rooms and put on their comfiest clothes. Half a starhour later they were all knocking on the door to Piper and Vega's room. Gemma had dressed to relax in a silky bright orange pajama set with red trim and knotted buttons, and she had pulled her hair into two pigtails (adorable, if she did say so herself). She sniffed the air appreciatively as she stepped inside, enjoying the smell of glowball incense that wafted through the air. It brought a smile to her face, reminding her of the bouquets her father would handpick to star-prise her mother. She giggled, remembering the time her mom had leaned in to sniff a blossom and had come nose to nose with a glitterbee. The fuzzy little creature had taken a starshine to her mom and became her little pet, following her all around the house and settling on her shoulder as she read holo-books in the evening. Gemma looked over at Tessa, who also had a wistful little smile on her face, and Gemma wondered if she was sharing the same memory. Thinking of her parents, alone on the farm, struggling to keep things going in the face of the energy shortage, brought a lump to Gemma's throat. How she wished that Wish Orb would just start glowing.

Gentle music was playing and Gemma could already feel the tensions of the day easing from her tight shoulders. She lowered herself to the ground to sit on a soft orange cushion. There were colorful cushions in each girl's signature color scattered on the floor, and Gemma watched as her friends sank onto theirs gratefully. They all switched their Star-Zaps to silent mode and placed them within arm's reach, just in case. Gemma looked around and smiled. The lighting was muted and very peaceful.

Piper sat facing the girls on her own seafoam-green cushion. She wore a long sleeveless tunic in varying shades of green over a pair of knit leggings. Her hair was pulled back smoothly into a rippling ponytail. She smiled at the girls, looking quite pleased to have them all there together. Gemma admired Piper for her serene demeanor. She was suddenly quite glad to be there, and she hoped that this meditation experiment might bring her some inner peace to replace the anxiety that had been troubling her.

Piper pressed her hands together and brought them to her face, bowing her head at them in greeting. "Welcome," she said. "I'm so starfully happy that you all have chosen to spend your evening with me in meditation. Through meditation we learn to become calm and at peace with ourselves. We will learn how to be more focused, how to transform our minds from negative to positive."

Sign me up! thought Gemma. *I'm ready!*

"Now we'll begin. Everyone, please sit up straight, but still make sure that you are feeling comfortable. Not quite so tense, Vega . . . no, no, oh, yes, that's much better.

Are you all sitting criss-cross starapple sauce? Perfect! Now place your hands on your knees, palms up. Close your eyes and concentrate on your breathing."

Gemma had never really thought about breathing before. It just happened; it was something you never considered. She concentrated on the action. In and out. In and out. Wait—was she breathing too fast? Or too slow? How many breaths were you supposed to take in a starmin, anyway? Were there rules for breathing that she didn't know about? She had so many questions!

"Now don't change the way you are breathing, just pay close attention to the way that you inhale and exhale," Piper said, as if she had heard Gemma's thoughts. Actually, knowing Piper's many talents, Gemma wouldn't put it past her. "Think of your chest, rising and falling with each breath. Good! Now we'll do this for two starmins."

Gemma was trying really hard to just think about her breaths, but she found her mind wandering, not to energy shortages and missing headmistresses, as she might have expected, but oddly enough to briteflower garlands. Were they sparklehammered in properly? What if the night was windy? Would they fall? Had they hung them up too soon?

Piper's soft voice sounded in her ear. "If you find

your mind wandering, get right back to your breaths. In and out, in and out." Gemma's eyes flew open, but Piper was still sitting on her cushion at the front of the room. Her words had the desired effect, nevertheless, and Gemma was once again where she needed to be, at least in terms of meditation.

Piper's voice grew more distant. "Through meditation we will learn to free ourselves from unnecessary worries and achieve peaceful minds. This is the way to experience true happiness.

"Now," she said when the two starmins of concentrated breathing were up, "we are going to introduce a mantra. This is a simple word or phrase we will concentrate on that will really help you to focus your mind. We will all think of a simple word or phrase to focus on. We will repeat this mantra silently over and over to ourselves. I'll give you a moment to choose a word or phrase." Gemma felt a slight ripple in the air as Piper passed by.

"Has everyone chosen a mantra? Now it's time to think of your word," Piper said.

"Wish Orb!" said Gemma.

"Say it in your head, just to yourself," Piper corrected gently.

"Wish Orb!" Gemma repeated.

"Shhh," said Tessa irritably next to her. Clearly, her sister needed more meditation.

"No—Wish Orb!" Gemma shouted, holding up her Star-Zap. "Everybody check your Star-Zaps! My Wish Orb is ready!"

CHAPTER
5

The room broke out into excited chattering. Finally!

Gemma's eyes were shining. "The timing is perfect!" she said. "Lady Cordial said she had a feeling that everything would be straightened out in time for Starshine Day. I just know that this mission is going to collect a starton of wish energy!" she said confidently.

As Gemma stood, she noticed that Leona, who was still sitting on her golden cushion, slipped her hand into her pocket. Gemma knew exactly what she was doing—running her fingers over her ruined Wish Pendant and thinking of her own failed mission. Gemma wanted to tell her that it was okay, that hopefully her mission would more than make up for Leona's, but she thought the girl might take it the wrong way.

Gemma was all set to sprint to Lady Cordial's office when Sage stepped in front of the door and cleared her throat. "I just want to say that while you are off on your mission, we will continue to try to locate Lady Stella. Maybe we'll find her by the time you return and we can fix this problem for good."

"I hope so," said Gemma. "Can we go now?"

Slip-slap, slip-slap. Gemma walked so quickly to Halo Hall that she almost lost an orange slipper along the way. Only Astra was able (or willing) to keep up with her. When Gemma arrived at the office door, she paused.

"Are you okay?" asked Astra.

Gemma nodded, but inside she felt paralyzed. What if her mission went wrong and she didn't collect any energy? What if something went wonky with the wish energy and she got stuck on Wishworld? That would be fine for Scarlet, but Gemma liked living on Starland! And what if the girls didn't find Lady Stella while she was gone? So many what-ifs kept crowding her mind, all of them bad. She closed her eyes, and a voice, clear and strong, suddenly cut through the chatter. It said, "Just remember these words: while looking to the future, you must not forget the past."

Gemma's hands trembled. She turned to Astra. "Did you just hear that?" she asked.

"Hear what?" Astra said.

"Um, nothing," Gemma replied. She didn't want to say anything to get Astra's hopes up, but the voice had reminded her of someone very dear to her—to all of them. It had sounded a lot like Lady Stella. Emboldened, and with the rest of the Star Darlings' footfalls sounding in the hallway, she knocked and then slid the door open.

Gemma blinked. The number of Bot Bot guards in Lady Cordial's office had swelled to four.

"That's a lot of Bot-Bots," she remarked.

"Oh, better s-s-s-safe than s-s-s-sorry," Lady Cordial said offhandedly.

The rest of the Star Darlings filed into the room and took their seats around the full moon–shaped table.

"Welcome, everyone," said Lady Cordial. "I am sure you are as pleased as I am that the final Wish Orb has been identified. There's no question who it belongs to, s-s-s-so we will dispense with the dramatic reveal and s-s-s-simply open the box."

Lady Cordial reached behind the desk and produced

a large solar-metal box. She placed it on the table directly in front of Gemma. All of a sudden the sides fell away to reveal a smaller box. The wait was agonizing to Gemma as she watched this happen again and again. She kept a smile on her face, but she really just wanted to scream. Finally, there was a Wish Orb–sized box sitting in front of her.

"Open it, Gemma," said Lady Cordial.

Gemma lifted the lid, which was surprisingly light. She gasped as the orb—*her* orb—rose into the air. She blinked. Was it her imagination or was it moving a bit shakily? She reached out her hand, but the orb simply bobbed in place in front of her. She looked around. The rest of the Star Darlings were staring at the orb oddly, too.

"It looks . . . different," she said. It appeared to be much more sparkly than the other orbs, but somehow less glowing. And it was quite large and bulgy—almost like it was ready to burst.

"That's because it is the final orb. The most crucial one!" said Lady Cordial. She leaned over and whispered into Gemma's ear. "The most important mission of them all."

Gemma shivered with excitement as a tingle ran down her spine. The twelfth and final mission. The biggest one of all. It was quite an honor—and a great responsibility. She felt like making a speech to commemorate the occasion.

She continued to hold out her hand. Lady Cordial, perhaps unable to stand the suspense, bustled over and plucked the orb out of the air.

Gemma waited for Lady Cordial to place it in her hand, imagining the smooth surface against her skin, the warmth that would flood her hand and run up her arm and into her body. But Lady Cordial instead placed the orb back in the box and snapped it shut.

"Are you ready, Gemma?" she asked.

"I am," replied Gemma. "As a matter of fact, I just wanted to say a word or two about . . ." She then launched into a speech about last chances, bravery in the face of adversity, and the importance of support from one's peers. "And in conclusion—" she began.

Lady Cordial put her hands on Gemma's shoulders and squeezed, perhaps a little too tightly in Gemma's opinion. Gemma shifted uncomfortably. "S-s-s-star s-s-s-salutations for that inspiring s-s-s-speech, Gemma," Lady Cordial said. "Now it's time to prepare for the final Wish Mission. The fate of S-s-s-starland rests in your hands."

Gemma thought for a moment. As the voice had said, she had to look back into the future. She frowned. Or maybe it was that the future was in the past? In any event, her mission—the twelfth and final one—was about to start.

CHAPTER
6

By the time Gemma landed on Wishworld, her head was spinning, her hands were shaking, and her mind was racing. The trip down to Wishworld had been much more tumultuous than her previous journey, with dips and falls, near misses, and close calls. Whether an increase in negative wish energy in the atmosphere or an overabundance of solar activity was causing the disturbances, she did not know. The funny part was that all of the atmospheric activity had been positively beautiful, with flashes of light and colors so unusual that Gemma didn't even have names for them. Unfortunately, she hadn't really been able to enjoy it, because she'd had to close her eyes to avoid feeling sick. And this from a girl who loved starcoasters more than anything! While she wanted her mission to be a fast one so she could return home quickly, the thought of reattaching herself to her shooting star for the return trip was terrifying. Thank goodness for those meditation skills that Piper had shared with her; they came in very handy. By focusing on her breathing, she was able to keep calm on the trip.

Saying good-bye on the Wishworld Surveillance Deck had been quite a melancholy experience. Not only because she had always pictured Lady Stella sending her off, but because her sister had been positively teary. Tessa had hugged her so long and so hard that Gemma had had to gently push her away so she could take off. And Lady Cordial's final words to her—"always look ahead, not over your shoulder"—seemed to contradict the words she had heard in her head just before she had received her Wish Orb. Now she didn't know what to think.

Gemma had landed in a small wooded area, shielded by trees and bushes in fiery shades of yellow, orange, and red. After she folded up and carefully put away her shooting star, she pushed her way out. She realized that she was standing in the middle of a field filled with orange spheres that appeared to be growing out of the ground. It immediately brought her a sense of familiarity. A farm! A sign hanging nearby read HAPPY HALLOWEEN FROM MACDONALD'S PICK-YOUR-OWN PUMPKIN FARM. It was illustrated with an orange pumpkin (she presumed that was what it was, at least) with a scary face carved into it. A holiday that seemed to celebrate both the harvest and spooky things. How curious!

Gemma watched as families wandered about, looking at pumpkins, lifting them up, and sometimes carrying them off, but more often than not setting them back down and moving on to the next pumpkin. The chosen pumpkins were carried to a rustic-looking red building nearby. Gemma took a closer look at the structure and nearly screamed. The most enormous black spider she had ever seen was perched on the top, its colossal web covering the entire side of the building. How horrifying! Wishworld spiders were way uglier (and bigger) than their Starland counterparts, that was for sure. But then she noticed that families were walking into the building, directly underneath the horrible creature, hardly even looking up at it, and her pulse started to return to normal. Lady Cordial had warned her not to waste any time recording Wishworld observations in her Cyber Journal, but if she had, it would have been: *Mission 12, Wishworld Observation #1: Wishworld spiders are STARNORMOUS! But evidently, not dangerous. Or even noteworthy.*

Tentatively, Gemma took a step closer to the building, then another. She stopped and stared up at it. Had the spider just moved one of its eight spindly legs or was her mind playing tricks on her?

"Pretty scary, huh?" said a voice right behind her.

Gemma jumped. She whirled around to find two girls standing there, smiling at her. The taller one had short straight brown hair and green eyes that sparkled. The shorter girl had wavy shoulder-length blond hair and warm brown eyes. Gemma's hands flew to her ears as she felt a tingling sensation.

"Ooh, nice earrings," said the blond girl. "How do they glow like that?"

Is one of these girls my Wisher? Gemma wondered. *Could it possibly be that easy?* She hoped the answers were yes and yes.

"That spider has been in my family for generations," said the brown-haired girl. "As a matter of fact, my grandpa MacDonald used to hang it up with *his* grandfather, Angus. He was my"—she thought for a moment—"great-great grandfather."

"So you're a MacDonald?" Gemma asked, pointing to the sign.

"I'm Zoe," said the girl. "Welcome to MacDonald's farm."

"E-i-e-i-o," said the blond girl, thoroughly confusing Gemma.

"Don't you ever get tired of that joke, Cici?" Zoe asked, rolling her eyes. Gemma sensed a tinge of annoyance in her voice and wondered if Cici was insulted.

But Cici just laughed. "Nope," she said. Then she leaned in to look more closely at Gemma. "You didn't really think that spider was real, did you?" she asked.

"Oh, my st—I mean, goodness, of course not!" said Gemma. "How silly! I mean, of course it's fake!"

"So are you new in town or something?" Zoe asked. "I haven't seen you around at school."

"I am new and my name is Gemma," she said truthfully. "I just arrived. It was a long journey and it was quite eventful! What a ride it was. All the way from . . ." She paused. All the way from where? *Stop talking, Gemma,* she told herself. *Just stop talking!*

Luckily, Cici jumped in. "Well, you came at the right time!" she said. "We celebrate Halloween big around here. I hope you have a costume!"

Gemma vaguely recalled learning about Halloween in Wishworld Relations class, but the details were fuzzy. Maybe she had forgotten to put her headphones on that night and hadn't absorbed that day's lesson. She searched her brain for details. Was that the holiday when Wishlings ate a large roasted fowl with their family? Or the one when they pinched fellow Wishlings if they weren't wearing the color green, and had a big parade?

Suddenly, Cici's eyes widened. "Don't look now!" she said in a loud whisper. "But Maddie and Kaila are headed our way!"

Zoe looks both excited and nervous. "Do I look okay?" she asked.

"Are you afraid of heights?" Cici asked.

Zoe looks confused for a moment. "No," she answered. "What does that have to do with anyth—"

"Well, your zipper is."

Zoe seemed down in a panic, then realized she was wearing a skirt. "Cici, you nearly gave me a heart attack," she said.

"Sorry," said Cici. "I thought it was funny."

"It wasn't," said Zoe icily. Then she put a huge fake-looking smile on her face as the two girls stepped up to them. They looked almost identical, with long, straight light brown hair, off-the-shoulder oversized sweaters, and short shorts over patterned tights and tall boots. They both wore knit hats. Gemma looked from one to the other. Were they wearing some sort of uniform?

"Hi, Maddie. Hi, Kaila," said Zoe in a rush. "You know Cici, of course. And this is Gemma. She just moved here."

"Hi, Gemma," said one of the girls, her eyes flickering over Gemma from head to toe, taking in her ripped jeans, flannel shirt, and beat-up ankle boots. Gemma must have passed muster, because she nodded at her. "Cool earrings. So where are you from?"

Gemma opened her mouth. "Um, from . . . well, it's actually quite far away. . . ." Her voice trailed off.

The girl quickly lost interest and turned back to Zoe.

Gemma stared at the girls. Now which one was which? They were hard to tell apart. She wondered if she should ask them, but then she decided to keep her mouth shut. She was realizing that speaking as little as possible on Wishworld was the best way to go. It was a struggle and perhaps would be the biggest challenge of her mission.

"Is it always so dirty here?" asked one of the girls, grimacing at her dusty boots.

"Well, it *is* a farm," Cici offered. "Dirt is kind of necessary."

The girls glanced at Cici, then returned their attention to Zoe. "So my mom sent us here to get a pumpkin. Can you help us?"

Zoe smiled. "Sure," she said. She turned to Gemma and Cici. "Be back in a couple of minutes."

Cici sighed as she watched them walk off. "Zoe

really wants us to be friends with Maddie and Kaila. I guess it's okay. They're super popular and really into clothes and stuff. But they seem fake to me." She looked at Gemma. "Hey, what happened to your earrings?" she said disappointedly. "They're not glowing anymore."

What happened is that I just got confirmation that Zoe is my Wisher! Gemma thought triumphantly. She leaned in close to Cici. "So would you say that Zoe really wishes to be friends with those girls?"

Cici nodded. "Yeah. She talks about it all the time."

"Hmmm," said Gemma. She was confused. Friendship seemed like a positive wish. Based on Cici's comment about them seeming fake, Gemma wondered if they'd make good friends for Zoe. Perhaps they had positive attributes that she had not yet seen.

"Are they really fun or nice?" she asked. "Or smart, or maybe interesting? Do you like them?"

Cici shifted as if she was uncomfortable. "Well . . . they are very popular," she said slowly. "And fashionable, for sure. Nice?" She paused. "I wouldn't go that far. But if that's what Zoe wants, I'm fine with it."

"You're a good friend to Zoe," said Gemma.

Cici's smile lit up her whole face. "She's my best friend," she said. "Ever since the first day of preschool."

All right, then, thought Gemma. It seemed way too easy, but she had been counting on a quick mission, so this was working out just right.

"Listen, it's time for me to leave for my brother's basketball game tonight," said Cici. "Maybe I'll see you tomorrow at the carnival."

"Carnival?" said Gemma.

"Oh, that's right, you're new. There's this awesome carnival with rides and food and games. Then there's a parade and costume judging," explained Cici excitedly. "Zoe and I almost always win a prize. We come up with the best costumes! One year we were bacon and eggs and another year we were Bert and Ernie. And we make them all by ourselves."

"We don't have to decorate for it, do we?" Gemma asked warily, afraid she was going to be put on another committee.

"Oh, no!" Cici laughed. "We just show up and have fun." She turned to leave. "So, see you tomorrow?" she asked.

"You can count on it," said Gemma. "I wouldn't miss it for the worlds—I mean, world."

After Cici left, Gemma leaned against the wall of the barn and squinted down at her Star-Zap. *Starf!* There was only twenty-four hours left on the Countdown Clock! She knew that was one Wishworld day. Lady Cordial had said it should be a quick mission, but this was cutting it close!

She spotted Zoe and the two girls across the field, deep in conversation. *Is there that much to say about pumpkins?* she wondered. She headed toward them. As she got closer she caught a snippet of the conversation. She heard "It'll be fun" and "You'll look great," then "It's up to you. No pressure."

"So see you tonight," one of the girls said. She nodded at Gemma. "You can bring her if you want." The girls took off, carrying a medium-sized pumpkin between them.

"See you later!" called Zoe, waving after them. They didn't turn around. "Thanks for shopping at MacDonald Farms!" Then she slapped her forehead with her palm. "That was so lame. Ugh! Why did I say that?"

"So you want to be friends with those girls?" Gemma asked. It was pretty clear, but with time of the essence, she wanted confirmation from her Wisher herself.

"More than anything," said Zoe. "And they asked me to hang out with them tonight. I'm totally nervous. You'll come, right?"

"No need to be nervous," said Gemma. "I'll help you." A shiver ran down her spine so suddenly that it made the tiny hairs on her arms stand up. She guessed that was the confirmation she was looking for.

Her Wish Mission was under way.

CHAPTER
7

Zoe flipped through the pages of a glossy magazine. "It looks good. Now, you're sure this is cool?"

"I'm sure," said Gemma confidently. She had spent the afternoon wandering around town, making observations and collecting information she thought would help her Wisher on her quest to win over these new friends. They were obviously very into fashion, so she looked in all the store windows until she found a place selling clothes that looked trendy and cool. Luckily, the owner was bored and just as chatty as Gemma. She showed her the latest Wishworld trends and even gave her an extra copy she had of the cool new fashion magazine. "It's the first issue," she said. "This will really impress the little fashionistas!" Gemma left with a new admiration for Wishworld fashion. While it was certainly not as sparkly as Starland fashion, it was pretty startacular in its own way.

Zoe tucked the thick magazine into her backpack and the two girls wandered down the street side by side. The sun was beginning to set and the streetlamps started to turn on. Gemma had noticed that many of the stores were decorated with what she assumed were Halloween decorations—green-faced ladies with pointy hats, black winged creatures that looked a lot like bitbats, white-sheeted figures with dark holes for eyes. Gemma pointed to a pumpkin carved with a spooky face, flickering light shining through its eyes, nose, and mouth. "Spooky!" she said.

"They should know better than to leave that out on Mischief Night!" said Zoe, shaking her head.

"I thought it was Halloween," said Gemma, feeling thoroughly confused.

"Around here the night before Halloween is called Mischief Night," Zoe explained. "Kids go around smashing pumpkins, egging cars, TP'ing houses . . . you know."

Of course Gemma didn't know, but she nodded as if this all made perfect sense.

"My family hates Mischief Night," said Zoe. "One year someone took the giant spider off the roof and covered it with shaving cream. It took forever to wash it off. I'm lucky my parents let me out tonight."

"So was Cici invited to come tonight, too?" Gemma asked.

A cloud passed over Zoe's face. She shoved her hands into her jacket pockets and concentrated on a crack in the sidewalk. "No, she wasn't invited. Luckily, she had her brother's basketball game tonight, so she won't know."

"So Maddie and Kaila don't want to be friends with both of you," Gemma said slowly. She had an uneasy feeling and again wondered what made this wish—one that involved befriending not-so-nice girls and leaving out a real friend—a good one.

Zoe's voice sounded a little strangled as she spoke. "It's just really hard. Cici is fun and loyal and smart, but she's just not . . ." Zoe had a pained look on her face. "She's just not very cool."

"Cool is important?" asked Gemma.

"If you want to be popular, it is," Zoe said with a sigh. "I mean, look at Maddie and Kaila."

"What makes them so popular?" Gemma wanted to know.

"Well, they wear nice clothes, and they listen to the coolest music, and all the kids like them, and they get invited to all the parties, and everyone copies what they do," Zoe said in a rush. "I'm just . . . I'm just . . . tired of being boring. I really think I'd like that, too. And they seem to want to be my friends. So this is my chance. I can still be friends with Cici. We just won't be able to spend all our time together. She'll understand. It's no big deal."

Gemma shook her head. Was Zoe trying to convince Gemma—or herself?

Zoe stiffened. "Here they come," she whispered harshly. "Act natural." That made Gemma giggle a bit. How else was she supposed to act? The two girls crossed the street and stepped up to them, in two brand-new matching outfits—short dresses with cropped jackets and ankle boots.

Gemma wondered if Zoe was going to have to buy a brand-new wardrobe to hang out with these girls.

"Hi!" Gemma said. "Aren't you cold?" she asked, noticing their bare legs.

Maddie (Gemma thought it was Maddie, anyway) barked out a laugh. "Who cares, as long as we look great?"

Gemma nodded politely. "Of course," she said.

Zoe was rooting around in her backpack frantically. She pulled out a half-eaten bag of pretzels, three tubes of something called ChapStick, and, finally, the magazine.

"What do you have there?" Kaila asked curiously, pointing to the magazine Zoe was holding.

"The newest fashion magazine!" Zoe said proudly. "*Chic!*" But she pronounced it like *chick*. Gemma grimaced. She was pretty sure that was wrong.

The girls laughed. "Oh, Zoe, you're always so funny," Maddie said. "I've never heard of *Chic*, but it looks uh-maze-ing."

The girls flipped through the magazine. "Can we borrow this?" Kaila asked.

"Sure!" said Zoe happily. Gemma smiled. Her plan was working.

Gemma was all set for a fun time with the three girls. What would they do? She was excited to find out the fun things that Wishling kids—especially cool, popular ones—did for fun. But the evening was a bit of a disappointment. They wandered around, meeting up with groups of kids at different places around town. They went to the arcade, but they didn't play games. They went to the ice cream parlor, but they didn't order anything, even though the ice cream looked amazingly delicious. They waited outside the movie theater, but they never went inside. Then they headed to a long building called Lucky Lanes.

"Ooh! Are we bowling?" Zoe asked excitedly. "Cici and—I mean, I love to bowl!"

Maddie laughed. "Zoe, you have so much to learn. Nobody actually bowls. That's for losers. We hang out." She looked sharply at Zoe. "I mean, like I'm going to wear a pair of stinky bowling shoes with this outfit? Uh-uh."

Zoe laughed. It sounded forced to Gemma. Zoe nodded. "I was just kidding. Of course." She glanced at Gemma. "Is something wrong?" she said. "You look pale."

Gemma was feeling a bit weak. She excused herself and left to find the bathroom. It was empty, so Gemma quickly recited her Mirror Mantra. "Make up your mind to blaze like a comet!" she said, and she was instantly rewarded with the sight of herself in all her sparkly orange glory. She smiled at her bright orange hair, her glittering skin. She felt like herself again! She had renewed energy and a sense of purpose. She was going to grant this wish if it was the last thing she did. She just had to get past her negative feelings and help make this wish come true.

She pushed open the door and strode back out into

the bowling alley, its air filled with bouncy music and the crashing sound of large round objects knocking into pins.

She found Zoe leaning over, stuffing something into her backpack. Gemma was about to ask what it was when Maddie and Kaila rushed up, giggling excitedly. "Come on!" they said. "Now the fun is going to start. Eddie McNoonan has dozens of eggs and tons of shaving cream. Mischief Night has begun!"

Zoe's face fell. "Um . . . I . . ."

"Sorry, guys," said Gemma quickly. "But I have to get home and I promised my mom I would walk home with Zoe."

"Fine," said Maddie. She leaned in close to Zoe. "Now don't forget to meet us at the parade tomorrow."

"I won't," said Zoe. "Have fun!"

But one thing confused Gemma. Why had Maddie's message sounded more like a threat than a reminder?

CHAPTER
8

Gemma sat on the bed watching Zoe and Cici as they stood in front of the full-length mirror in Zoe's bedroom, giggling. Gemma couldn't help laughing, too. Cici was wearing a poorly fitting dress in a cheap, shiny material with a garish print. The hem of a white slip stuck out underneath the skirt. On her legs were black tights with runs in them, and she wore what Gemma could describe only as sensible lace-up shoes. She wore a pair of dark eyeglasses that were fastened together across the bridge with tape. Her hair was done up in a hugely unflattering three-ponytail style. Zoe wore slicked-back hair, a similar pair of taped-up glasses, a garish plaid shirt in shades of brown and blue, a clashing red-and-yellow plaid bow tie, and pants that were pulled up practically to her armpits, explosing her white socks. Black lace-up shoes completed her ensemble.

"You are both totally hideous!" said Gemma.

"Thank you!" they replied in unison.

"But . . . um . . . what are you supposed to be?" Gemma asked.

"Why, we're nerds, of course!" Zoe answered, still admiring her reflection.

The two girls turned and looked at Gemma. "Where's your costume?" Cici asked. "Go put it on!"

Gemma grabbed her backpack (which presumably held her nonexistent costume), walked into the bathroom, and closed the door. What should she be? The only costumes that came to her were Starlandian ones—a glion, a star ball player, a bunch of ozziefruit. Not exactly appropriate for Wishworld. She wondered if she could even access costumes on the Wishworld Outfit Selector.

"Hurry up!" called Zoe. "It's time to go to the carnival!" Gemma had to think fast. Then she smiled. She knew exactly what to do. She looked into the mirror and did her thing.

"Holy guacamole!" Zoe said as Gemma walked into the room. "You look amazing, Gemma!"

Cici stared. "Wow," she simply said.

The costume that Gemma had chosen to wear was

actually not a costume at all. It was Gemma's real sparkly Starlandian appearance. It made perfect sense—since
she was there on a holiday when Wishlings changed their
looks, she could revert to her true appearance. It was lib-
erating and fun.

"How in the world did you manage to get ready so
quickly?" Zoe asked, marveling at Gemma's sparkly skin
and glittery hair.

And Gemma simply answered, "Practice."

★

Gemma discovered that she was totally in love with
Halloween. Not only was the predominant color her
favorite, but it was just so carefree and jolly and fun.
Everyone was dressed up—babies in strollers, big kids,
little kids, and even some adults. One man was dressed
like a chef, and he held a pot with a little baby sitting
inside it dressed up as a bright red creature with big claws.
Some people simply wore white sheets with eyeholes cut
out. There were monsters, and ladies with green faces
and pointy hats. Even some pets were dressed up. Everyone was smiling and having fun.

As the girls stood in line for a deliciously airy and
sweet Wishworld delicacy called cotton candy, Maddie
and Kaila showed up. They were wearing high heels,

tons of makeup, slinky-looking gold dresses, fake fur coats, large sunglasses, and flowing wigs—one blond, one brunette. Gemma almost didn't recognize them under all the makeup.

"Wow," said Gemma, amazed by their fancy costumes. "What are you two dressed up as?"

Kaila tossed her head a little too hard, and her wig slipped to the side, covering half her face. "We're supermodels, of course," she said, yanking her hair back into place.

Maddie leaned forward and touched Gemma's arm, surprised that no glitter came off on her hand. "Where did you get that body glitter?" she asked. "It's awesome."

"Um . . . I brought it from home," Gemma answered.

"And look at you two!" Maddie said to Zoe and Cici. "Very funny!"

Zoe didn't answer, but Cici thanked her.

"See you later," Maddie said, looking directly at Zoe, who nodded, then looked away.

Gemma half expected the wish energy to pour off Zoe right then and there. The girls were obviously accepting her as a friend. And wasn't that just what she wanted? As much as Gemma was enjoying Halloween, it was time for her to return to Starland.

After Gemma, Zoe, and Cici went on rides (pretty tame compared to those on Starland), played several games of chance (Gemma won a large stuffed white-horned galliope, which she immediately gave to a little kid), and ate every treat there was to try (cotton candy was the winner, followed closely by something called fried dough), it was time for the parade.

The girls lined up with all the other costumed kids. Music began to play, and slowly, everyone began to march. It was a procession down the main street of the town, ending when they reached the town square, where a stage was set up for the costume judging. People lined the streets to cheer on the costumed marchers, who waved like they were starlebrities. When Gemma saw people pointing and cheering just for her, being herself, she felt very proud. For a second she thought she saw a familiar face in the crowd, but she figured she was just feeling homesick.

When they reached the end of the parade route, she had somehow gotten separated from Cici and Zoe in the mob of kids. She heard someone calling her name and turned around with a smile, expecting it to be one of the "nerds." To her surprise, Gemma saw Leona pushing through the crowd toward her.

"Oh, my stars!" Leona said when she reached Gemma's side. "How perfect! You can be your Starlandian self today because everyone is in costume! What a great idea!"

Gemma nodded proudly. Then she frowned. "Why are you here, Leona?" she asked a little testily. "I've got everything under control."

"Then I guess I'm just here for support," said Leona with a shrug.

"So what's been going on back home?" Gemma asked eagerly. "Did you find Lady Stella?"

Leona shook her head. "They're still looking. We went to Lady Cordial for help, but she was useless."

"So why did they send you?" Gemma asked again. "You've already been a helper on a mission. I was expecting Tessa, actually." If someone had to come help her on Wishworld, she would have liked it to be her big sister. It would have been startastic for Tessa to see her collecting her wish energy.

"It's kind of weird," said Leona. "The rest of the Star Darlings were concentrating on finding Lady Stella, but Tessa and I started getting worried about you. We hadn't heard anything from Lady Cordial, but we didn't trust her to be paying attention to your orb. So we decided that Tessa would make the trip to see how things were going. We brought Astra along, too, and headed to the Wishworld Surveillance Deck. Astra had just lassoed the star, and we were struggling to hold on to it so Tessa could get strapped in, when all of a sudden something told me that I needed to go instead. It was like a voice in my head. It said, 'It's your turn, Leona. Go and help Gemma!' So, um, I kind of pushed Tessa out of the way and strapped myself in. She was pretty mad, as you can imagine. She was yelling and shaking her fist at me as I took off!"

Gemma smiled a little, imagining her irate sister.

"So how much time is left on the Countdown Clock?" asked Leona.

"A half starhour," said Gemma anxiously. She took a deep breath. "But I have a feeling that the wish is going to come true when the girls are onstage during the costume judging." She smiled. "I'm pretty sure they are going to win a prize for best costume, and that's what will end up making Zoe part of the popular crowd."

"Your Wisher's wish is to become popular?" Leona asked. "That's a good wish?"

Gemma shrugged. "I know. It seems weird. But she's really a nice person, so I guess it's somehow got to be a good wish."

"Talk about taking it down to the starwire," said

Leona with a whistle. "Very dramatic. So what are they dressed as?"

"Nerds," said Gemma.

Leona looked at her uncomprehendingly.

"From what I can tell, nerds are unfashionable-looking Wishlings," Gemma explained. "Um, like they wear ugly clothes and broken accessories."

Leona made a face. "So why do Wishlings like to dress up as them?" she asked.

"Your guess is as good as mine," said Gemma.

The Star Darlings watched as Wishlings lined up, were introduced by the announcer, walked across the stage, and stood in front of the table of judges, who scored them. A group of Wishlings—a girl in a blue-and-white checked dress and sparkly red shoes (that would have fit right in on Starland); a woman with a green face and a pointy hat; a silver man with a pointy hat; a large glion; and a man who seemed to be made of straw in raggedy clothing—were apparently from a movie called something like *The Blizzard of Frogs.* A bunch of girls with bodysuits that matched their skin tones, jewels in their belly buttons, and big brightly colored wigs were something called trolls. The crowd loved them all.

Gemma grabbed Leona's hand and squeezed it as she

spotted Cici in the wings. "This is it," she said. "They're about to come onstage."

Gemma stood on her toes so she could get an unobstructed view of the wish coming true. She had to remind herself to breathe; she was hardly able to contain her excitement.

Cici walked onstage, followed by Zoe. Gemma took one look and gasped. Something was wrong. Very wrong.

CHAPTER
9

Leona shook her head. "I don't get it," she said. Cici was still in her nerd outfit, dangling slip and all. But Zoe had changed. She was in a costume that looked remarkably similar to the ones Maddie and Kaila had been wearing earlier. Makeup. Wig. Fancy shiny dress. Heels. The announcer called them onstage. Cici walked to the middle of the stage, then stopped short. Zoe bumped into her. The two girls began arguing.

Gemma clutched Leona's arm. "I don't like this one bit," she said.

"Whenever you're ready, girls," said the announcer.

Zoe took a few wobbly steps forward. She turned back and gestured for Cici to follow. Cici shook her head. Zoe motioned again, and then finally, reluctantly, Cici walked forward and stood next to Zoe.

Even the announcer looked confused. "And what are you two dressed as?" he asked.

Zoe hesitated for a moment.

"They're chic and the geek!" a voice called out from the audience. Gemma craned her neck to see Maddie and Kaila standing in the front row. They were laughing hysterically. The crowd laughed, too. "I'll say!" someone yelled.

"Chic and the geek?" said the announcer.

Zoe looked awkward and uncertain. Cici was clearly miserable.

"My Wisher just turned her wish into something really bad," Gemma whispered. "And I helped her do it. This is terrible."

Cici stood for a moment as the laughter washed over her. Then she bolted off the stage.

Leona and Gemma watched in horror as an arc of dark swirling colors invisible to everyone but them began to ooze from Zoe and sluggishly creep toward Gemma. She wanted to flee. But she was frozen in place as the horrible energy was sucked into her Wish Pendant. She suddenly felt very heavy and dull, as if she could barely stand.

Leona turned toward Gemma, her eyes wide. "That can't be good," she said. It was the understatement of the staryear.

"Oh, my stars," said Gemma. "What have I done?"

Leona found Gemma a bench to sit on. Gemma put her head between her legs and breathed deeply.

★

"We have to fix this," said Leona. "There must be a way." She paused. "Have you discovered what your special talent is?" she asked.

"No," said Gemma, lifting her head.

"Think, Gemma, think," said Leona. "We need to reverse this somehow."

Gemma buried her face in her hands. This was the twelfth and final mission. The last chance to collect enough wish energy to save Starland. And she had ruined things for everyone.

"I only collected bad energy!" she cried. "How bad is this for Starland?"

"It's pretty bad," said Leona. "While you were away, the wish energy scientists released some more information. It turns out that if the wish energy balance on Starland is shifted toward the negative, there won't be energy to do anything. No Starcars, no Star-Zaps, no lights. But that's not the worst of it. The worst thing is that as the negative overtakes the positive, everyone on Starland will lose their joy and become sad and mean. We won't be able to grant wishes anymore, so the Wishers will lose their joy, too."

Gemma shivered. "Maybe I'll just have to stay here. Keep the negative energy here with me."

"Maybe," said Leona. "But I'm not even sure it works that way."

Gemma thought about the possibility of never seeing her parents again and felt like her heart would break. She supposed she'd possibly be able to see her sister and the other Star Darlings if there continued to be missions. That was the one ray of starshine in a bleak future.

"There you are!" someone shouted. "You have to help me!"

Gemma lifted her head again. Zoe rushed up to them, her wig askew.

"What was I thinking?" she cried. "I made a huge mistake. I got so caught up in impressing Maddie and Kaila that I ruined the most important friendship I've ever had."

She sank down onto a nearby bench and thrust her hands into her luxurious blond wig. "Can you help me?

Please?" Zoe looked quizzically at Leona and back to Gemma.

"This is my friend Leona," Gemma hurriedly explained. "We really want to help you," she added fervently.

"Hi," said Leona. "You really were a bad friend to Cici."

Zoe couldn't make eye contact with either of them. "I know," she whispered.

"What happened to your new friends?" asked Leona.

"It didn't last too long," said Zoe with a wry smirk. "Right afterwards, I just felt awful about what I had done. Then Maddie and Kaila came over with all their friends and they started laughing at Cici and saying that she really was a nerd, and I thought to myself, 'Oh, yeah? Well, I am, too! And we nerds have way more fun than people like you, who just stand around making fun of people. You're so afraid of looking stupid that you never do anything!' And then I realized everyone was staring at me, because I had said it out loud."

Leona sat next to Zoe and grabbed her hands. "You have to realize that you made a selfish wish followed by a bad choice. And here's the thing—our wishes and our choices tell the world who we really are. So you've got to choose and wish wisely."

Zoe sniffed. "I know that now," she said. "And I'll never forget it. I learned it the hardest way of all."

She ripped the wig off her head and threw it to the ground.

Gemma blew out her breath sharply. "Poor you. Poor us."

Leona pulled Gemma to the side. She put her hand to her forehead. "Poor Cici," she said, pointing to the girl, who was standing alone in the crowd. Cici's exaggerated nerd costume made her look even sadder. Leona laughed bitterly. "She looks like she just lost her best friend."

"Thanks to me," said Gemma, her voice despondent. A ruined friendship, a missed chance to collect positive energy, and a Wish Pendant full of negative wish energy. Could things be any worse? This was a very grim future, indeed.

Suddenly, she remembered the words she had heard in the hallway back on Starland: *While looking to the future, you must not forget the past.* She said the words out loud, softly, and a jolt of energy went through her. She closed her eyes and concentrated on the past.

When she opened her eyes, she watched in disbelief as Leona put her hand to her forehead again. "Poor Cici," she said again, pointing to the girl. She laughed bitterly. "She looks like she just lost her best friend." Again.

Gemma grinned.

Leona gave Gemma a funny look as a realization hit. "Wait a minute! Did you just . . . ?"

"I did!" Gemma crowed. "My talent must be to turn back time! Oh, my stars, we just might be able to fix this after all!"

This time Gemma managed not to get separated from Zoe and Cici after the parade. She followed Zoe as she walked to the park bench where she had stashed her backpack. Stuffed inside was the supermodel costume that Gemma now knew Maddie and Kaila had handed her in the bowling alley the night before. Gemma grabbed the bag from Zoe's hand. "Don't do it," she said. "Embrace the nerd!"

Zoe looked as though she'd been caught red-handed. "But how did you . . . ?"

Gemma smiled. "Don't worry about it. Just know that you're better than this."

"But . . ." Zoe looked over at Maddie and Kaila, who stood in front of the stage with a group of friends, laughing and joking.

"You have a choice to make," said Gemma. "True friendship or popularity."

"Leave me alone!" said Zoe. She slung the bag over her shoulder and stalked off.

Gemma chewed her lip as she watched her disappear into the crowd. Which choice would Zoe make?

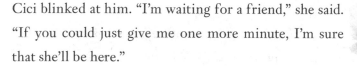

"So what happened?" asked Leona when Gemma joined her.

"I don't know," said Gemma. "I guess we'll know soon enough."

So Gemma and Leona watched as Cici walked onstage alone. "And what is your costume?" the announcer asked.

Cici blinked at him. "I'm waiting for a friend," she said. "If you could just give me one more minute, I'm sure that she'll be here."

Just then there was a commotion that sounded like someone pushing her way toward the stage. Gemma held her breath as she waited for the person to appear. It was Zoe.

The announcer asked, once again, "And what is your costume?"

And Zoe said, "We're nerds. Me and my best friend, Cici, are nerds."

Gemma felt as light as air. It didn't hurt that she was zipping through the heavens—not a meteorite in sight—on her way back to Starland. She was bringing back positive wish energy in her Wish Pendant. But she had collected an awful lot of negative wish energy, too. Would the positive energy win out over the negative? She didn't know. Despite her worry, she smiled as she recalled how Maddie and Kaila had thrown up their hands in disgust when Zoe showed up onstage in her nerd outfit, signaling to them that she had made a choice—true friendship over popularity. That had felt awfully good.

★

Gemma landed right behind the dorms and headed inside. The halls were completely empty and her footfalls echoed. Through a window she saw a fourth-year Starling Academy student passing by. She ran to the door, pushed it open, and followed her. "Hey! Where is everyone?" she called.

"Where have you been?" asked the girl. "It's Starshine Day! Everyone is in the Star Quad. It's almost time for the Battle of the Bands. You don't want to miss that!"

It was already Starshine Day! Gemma's stomach did a flip. Talk about cutting it close. She couldn't wait to tell Lady Cordial that it looked like her premonition just might be correct. That everything might turn out exactly the way it was supposed to. That her mission would turn the tide for Starland and return it to the way it was meant to be.

Lady Cordial had predicted that this would happen just in time for Starshine Day. And here it was, really happening.

Gemma took a deep breath, smoothed back her hair, and headed to the Star Quad.

When Gemma reached the quad, she could see the briteflower garlands draped from pillar to pillar, shining beautifully, and she felt a little swell of pride in her handiwork. There was a glimmerbounce house, bumper Starcars, even a mini starcoaster. The smell of grilled garble greens filled the air, and Starlings were walking around, laughing and chatting. It was as if everyone had forgotten about the shortage and they were just allowing themselves to relax and enjoy the day. And maybe that was the point.

Gemma heard Lady Cordial's voice over the loudspeaker. "Introducing S-s-s-starlight S-s-s-starbright, the first contestant in S-s-s-starling Academy's Battle of the Bands!" she announced. The crowd roared.

The quad was packed with Starlings, so Gemma took the long way around, past the hedge maze. As she passed the entrance to the hedge maze, she heard a sound. *Psst! Psst!*

Whoa! The next thing she knew, someone had grabbed her arm and she was being yanked backward into the maze. She spun around. "What in the stars!" she exclaimed. Vega stood there, looking grim.

"What's going on? Did you find Lady Stella yet?" Gemma asked.

But Vega just spun on her heel and started walking

quickly into the maze. Not wanting to be left behind, Gemma raced after her. "Vega! Say something! What in the stars in going on?"

"Just follow me," Vega hissed. In only a couple of turns, they were in the center of the maze. It would have taken Gemma forever if she had been by herself.

There, facing her, were all the Star Darlings, including Leona. Then they all took a step forward. And there, in all her regal beauty, was Lady Stella.

Without a word, Gemma ran toward her, throwing her arms around the headmistress. "Oh, Lady Stella, Lady Stella." It was all she could say.

The headmistress stroked Gemma's hair gently. "Oh, Gemma, I hope your mission wasn't too overwhelming," she said. "I heard it was a difficult one."

Gemma felt like she might burst into tears if she said a word. She took a step backward. She noticed that another adult stood nearby, her arms around Sage. They looked so much alike, right down to their pointy elfin chins. "Indirra!" said Gemma.

Indirra smiled gently. "It's so good to be here," she said.

"Tell her the story!" said Sage eagerly. "But quickly! We're due onstage soon, so there isn't much time!"

"Cassie, you figured it out. You tell the story," said Lady Stella.

Cassie smiled at Lady Stella gratefully. "Well, Sage and I were really getting worried. Neither Lady Stella nor Indirra was anywhere to be found. We called all the Star Darlings together but no one had any idea what to do, and everyone was getting really frustrated. Then Itty started singing. I scooped her up and tried shushing her, but she just wouldn't stop. I was about to put her in the closet when I stopped and listened to the words. She was singing the 'Song of Secrets'! And the song told the story of two beautiful women who were trapped in a cave at the base of the Crystal Mountains against their will! We were hoping against hope that it was Lady Stella and Indirra. But we weren't sure. Then we realized that the song rhymed 'star-protection suits' with 'forbidden fruits' and 'shovel' with 'on the double.' We grabbed those things and took off immediately, a little scared at what we might find."

Cassie paused to take a breath and Adora took up the story next. "When we got to the foothills of the mountains, we found a cave entrance blocked off by the hugest pile of the most beautiful crystal shards. But as soon as we got close, we all started bickering and feeling extremely tired and angry. They were clearly infused with negative energy! So we put on the suits and started digging. We dug and dug, and after what felt like forever, we finally reached the entrance. And there stood Lady Stella and Indirra!"

Lady Stella smiled at the girls. "You have no idea how happy we were to see you. I explained that when I was confronted"—here she placed a hand on Cassie's shoulder reassuringly—"I realized that someone had to be framing me. I panicked and disappeared in a flash and headed to the Crystal Caves. I contacted Indirra to meet me there so we could come up with a plan together. But as soon as we stepped inside the cave, disaster struck. There was a huge avalanche and we were trapped. My Star-Zap had gotten crushed in the avalanche and Indirra's wouldn't work. The negative energy was making us weaker and weaker. We were beginning to despair of ever escaping. Then, as we were drifting off to sleep one night, we heard the familiar 'Song of Comfort.' That's when we realized we shared the cave with a gaggle of glowfurs! Quickly we made up a song and taught it to them, knowing they would pass it on to every other glowfur they met, as is their tradition. I just hoped it would get to Itty quickly."

Gemma had to interrupt. "So you knew about Cassie's secret pet?"

Lady Stella just gave her a look and Gemma blushed. Of course the headmistress had known. She knew everything about her students. That was the kind of headmistress she was.

Sage's mother spoke next. "And then we waited. And then the Star Darlings came!"

"And we started talking and I discovered that my mom has known Lady Stella for a long time. She used to take me to campus when I was little, to hone my wish energy manipulation skills!" Sage said.

"They were off the charts," Indirra said proudly. "Even when she was a wee Starling."

"And that's why Mojay liked me so much!" Sage said. "He must have somehow remembered me from long ago!"

Leona stepped forward. "But why didn't you tell us you were working together? That we were the twelve Star-Charmed Starlings?" she asked.

"We didn't want to overwhelm you," explained Lady Stella. "We thought the pressure would be too much. We realize now we should have told you right away the true nature of your missions. I can promise you this, Star Darlings: there will be no more secrets going forward."

"We thought that once the twelfth Star Darling went on her mission the shortage could possibly be reversed," Indirra said. "And now you have returned, Gemma. Soon we will discover if the theory is true."

Lady Stella reached into her pocket and pulled out a

small solar-metal instrument. "This is the Wish Energy Meter. Right now it is exactly in the middle, right between positive energy and negative energy. Your mission should determine which way it will tilt."

"So, Gemma, how was your mission?" Indirra asked eagerly.

Gemma looked down at the ground. "It was terrible. Something went wrong and I collected negative wish energy."

Everyone gasped.

"But then she turned it around and collected positive energy, too!" Leona hastily offered.

Though Lady Stella looked calm, Gemma could tell she was worried. Very worried. "We'll see how things go. Stars crossed, my Starlings. Stars crossed."

Leona looked down at her Star-Zap. "Oh, *starf*, Lady Cordial is freaking out. The Star Darlings are up next!"

"Everyone, stay calm," Lady Stella commanded. She pulled her hood up over her head. Indirra did the same. "The saboteur could be out there," Lady Stella said. "We can't take any chances. We need to get that orb!"

A shiver ran down Gemma's spine. The twelfth orb. The final mission.

Had she succeeded—or had she failed?

CHAPTER
11

The Star Darlings stood in the wings—five ready to perform, seven there for emotional support—waiting nervously as Vivica's band finished its set. Leona had a grim look on her face, and Gemma wondered if it had the tiniest bit to do with the fact that the band actually sounded pretty good. A huge roar went up when they were done. The crowd apparently loved Vivica and the Visionaries.

When the crowd quieted down, Lady Cordial began to speak. "And now, introducing our final contestants— S-s-s-scarlet on drums, S-s-s-sage on lead guitar, Libby on keytar, Vega on bass guitar, and Leona on lead vocals. S-s-s-starlings, I introduce you to the S-s-s-star Darlings!"

The girls ran out to polite applause.

Astra peeked out at the crowd and gasped. "Oh, my stars! Leebeau is here! I don't think he has any idea what he is getting himself into. Who knows how tonight will end?"

Despite her nervousness, Gemma took a peek. When her eyes fell on the boy, she could understand Astra's interest. Leebeau, with his dark skin and shock of blond hair (not to mention his excellent bone structure), was stellarly cute.

Lady Cordial stepped offstage and smiled and nodded as she walked by the girls. A shiver—of either excitement or dread; she couldn't be sure which—ran down Gemma's spine.

The band began to play. The crowd was quiet at first, but as the music grew louder and faster, they began to get into it, dancing and cheering.

Each band got to play three songs. After playing "Together" and "Star-Crossed," the Star Darlings launched into "Wish Upon a Star," which turned out to be a real crowd-pleaser. When the girls were done, they took a bow. The crowd roared.

Lady Cordial scurried back onstage, clapping her hands. "Star salutations, Star Darlings, on a job well done," she cried. She shielded her eyes with her hand as she scanned the wings. "And now I will call *all* of the Star Darlings onstage. Come on, girls, don't be shy!"

Gemma started. What was Lady Cordial doing? The Starling Academy students only knew about Star Darlings the band. She wasn't the only one who was confused: the band members stood there, still holding their instruments, looking at each other.

"Yes, all of you," said Lady Cordial. "Gemma, Adora, Astra, Cassie, Piper, Clover, and Tessa, please come join us onstage."

Not sure what else to do, the rest of the girls walked out and stood blinking in front of the crowd. Lady Cordial smiled at them. "Before we name the winner of the Battle of the Bands, I have an announcement to make. Here before you stand the *real* Star Darlings. I don't mean the band. I am talking about twelve of your peers who were secretly hand-selected as the best of the best of Starling Academy. And believe it or not, these brave girls have all secretly gone down to Wishworld on missions to collect wish energy to help stop the shortage that has befallen Starland."

There was a loud gasp as the students took in this shocking news.

Gemma glanced at her sister, who looked as puzzled as she felt. Why was Lady Cordial doing this? Tessa reached over and grabbed Gemma's hand, which made Gemma feel a tiny bit better. Gemma stared at Lady Cordial. She suddenly realized something: Lady Cordial hadn't stuttered a single syllable since she had revealed the Star Darlings. And something else was different. Was it possible that Lady Cordial looked taller than usual?

What in the stars was going on?

Lady Cordial continued. "There were twelve missions in total. The last mission was taken by Gemma, who returned just starmins ago. Thanks to her hard work, the wish energy imbalance is about to be readjusted. Gemma, will you please step forward?"

Gemma gulped, dropped Tessa's hand, and did so.

Lady Cordial next reached into her pocket and pulled out Gemma's Wish Orb, still shiny and glittery. But then she did something strange. Lady Cordial blew on the orb, and the glitter fell away, revealing that it was dark and murky.

Everyone gasped. It was a Bad Wish Orb!

So that's what happened! Gemma thought. *It was a bad wish from the beginning.* She turned to Lady Cordial again and she suddenly realized that her eyes hadn't been playing tricks on her. Lady Cordial was transforming before their very eyes from the frumpy, awkward, and unremarkable headmistress to a tall and imposing presence.

Her neat purple bun had been replaced by lank gray hair. Her plump cheeks were becoming thin and sunken. And her skin, once bright and sparkly like that of most Starlings, was now dull and ashen. But Gemma could only focus on her eyes. They glittered coldly. It was hard to look away. But she did notice that the stage was suddenly surrounded by a squadron of Bot-Bot guards, all there to protect Lady Cordial.

"I, Rancora, in the guise of silly, stuttering Lady Cordial, tricked Gemma into granting a bad wish," crowed the villainess. "And now, thanks to her, the balance has been shifted—to negative wish energy—just as I planned!"

The crowd gasped again. Someone screamed.

Lady Stella, who had been watching from a distance, took a step forward. She stared up at the woman on the stage and a wave of recognition crossed her face. "Rancora," she whispered solemnly.

Gemma's stomach lurched. She could hardly believe what she was hearing. This changed everything. Her mission hadn't been a good wish gone bad at all. It was out-and-out, no question about it, a bad wish that she had granted. The negative energy she had collected would be too strong and powerful. Her mission had been a huge mistake. She had fallen for Lady Cordial's—er, Rancora's—trick. And now everything was ruined—forever.

Gemma wanted to run far, far away, but some terrible force held her in place. She watched in horror as the bulging, blackened orb lurched toward her, closer and closer. It hovered in front of her, mere star inches from her face, and she almost couldn't breathe.

What have I done? she thought, nearly overcome with despair. But then, as if in a trance, she held out her hand. The orb settled in her outstretched palm. A lovely warm feeling ran up her arm and coursed through her. And suddenly, she realized what had happened. By turning the bad wish into a good one, she must have reversed the orb!

Before Gemma's eyes, the orb transformed from a dark, misshapen thing into a beautiful glowing sphere. It felt warm and smooth and *good*. She felt strong and powerful as she held the orb above her head in triumph. "Yes, I was tricked into granting a bad wish. But what you don't know is that I turned that Wish Orb into a Good Wish Orb, Rancora! Now watch!"

Before everyone's eyes, the orb turned into a flower—a beautiful chatterburst, a vibrantly bright orange blossom, fairly bursting with energy. The Wish Blossom swiveled around to face Gemma as she inhaled its sweet orange-vanilla scent. As she stared at its filaments, hung with glowing stardust, it suddenly opened, revealing her Power Crystal—a lustrous egg-shaped scatterite, sprinkled with stardust on its perfectly smooth surface. It settled in her hand like it belonged there.

Triumphantly, Gemma held the milky orange stone up to Rancora.

But Rancora did not look scared, taken aback, or even slightly concerned. She just looked at Gemma's Power Crystal and laughed.

CHAPTER
12

"Silly girl," Rancora said mockingly. "Once a bad wish is granted, you can't negate its power entirely. I. Still. Win."

"It looks like she's right, Gemma," a voice said sadly. Indirra stepped out of the shadows, holding Lady Stella's Wish Energy Meter. The arrow had lurched toward BAD and was swinging wildly back and forth. The sky grew dark and the wind started to whip. Thunder rumbled and lightning flashed.

Rancora raised her arms to the heavens and lifted her face to the stormy sky. Her lips twisted in an evil smile. "How do you stupid Star Darlings not realize that you need *all twelve* Power Crystals to have any sort of power? You're the *twelve* Star-Charmed Starlings, after all! Without that final one, your crystals are completely useless on Starland! And I destroyed Leona's Wish Pendant! It will never absorb wish energy again!"

"*You* destroyed my pendant?" Leona shouted.

"Child's play, my dear," Rancora said mockingly. "Remember the star key chains you all took along on your trips to Wishworld? I infused them with negative wish energy in order to sabotage your missions. It worked differently, yet effectively, on each mission. And luckily for me, it caused *your* Wish Pendant to malfunction. All the things you blamed on Lady Stella happened because of me. *I* sent you the flowers. *I* created the nail polish. *I* switched Scarlet's and Ophelia's grades." She laughed. "I even hypnotized everyone with the song so they would all be happy about Starshine Day, knowing it was the perfect venue to make my announcement."

"But why?" Gemma asked.

"For power, of course," she said. "The rest of you thrive on positive energy. I thrive on the negative. By upsetting the balance, now I will rule Starland!"

"Wait!" called a voice from the back of the crowd. Lady Stella walked toward the stage, the crowd parting to let her pass. She looked exceptionally calm and regal.

"Lady Stella!" someone called out.

"Well, if it isn't our dear headmistress," said Rancora. "I see you managed to escape from your crystal cave. Well, I am glad you are here, old friend, to witness the destruction of all you hold dear!"

Thunder crashed, and lightning struck a nearby kaleidoscope tree. Gemma watched as the flowers drifted to the ground like multicolored snowflakes. *How beautiful*, she thought despite herself.

"Not so fast," said Lady Stella. She reached into her pocket and pulled out a golden orb, which floated up into the air. "I've held on to this orb in the hopes that it would someday transform."

Before everyone's disbelieving eyes, the orb floated through the air, right toward Leona.

Leona's eyes were wide. She reached into her pocket, as if in a trance. Gemma had a sudden realization. The positive energy that resulted when Leona helped her turn a bad wish into a good one must have been so strong that it repaired Leona's ruined Wish Pendant. And now her Wish Orb was glowing again. No wonder she had felt an impulse to push Tessa out of the way and join Gemma on her mission!

As Leona pulled the golden cuff out of her pocket, Rancora, realizing what was about to happen, raised her hand to the pendant dangling from her neck and, opening it, poured out a cloud of negative energy and sent it soaring toward Leona. The negative energy glanced off the orb and hit the sign that hung over the stage, which was draped in briteflowers. They immediately withered and drooped. The orb, however, continued on its path. Then, just as it was about to land in Leona's outstretched hand, Rancora shot another burst of negative energy, this time directly at Leona.

"Nooooooo!" Gemma heard herself scream.

Leona stood stock-still, unable to move. Just as the negative energy was about to hit her, a Bot-Bot lunged forward and absorbed the shot. It plummeted to the stage with a crash so loud it made Gemma wince.

"That Bot-Bot saved my life," said Leona in disbelief just as the orb settled in her hand. She held her Wish Pendant in the other. It now glowed with pure golden energy, burnt and blackened no more. The orb rapidly transformed into Leona's Wish Blossom, a golden roar, which then opened to reveal her Power Crystal, a rough-cut, yellow-gold glisten paw. Gemma instinctively reached for her Power Crystal and held it up. That was when she realized that all the other Star Darlings were doing the same thing.

Rancora shot another burst of negative energy at the

Star Darlings, but this time it was as if they were surrounded by an invisible force field. It glanced off and dissipated.

As if they were in a trance, the Star Darlings all let go of their Power Crystals, which floated in the air in front of them. They joined hands. The Power Crystals glowed so brightly that everyone in the audience had to shield their eyes and look away. Then the crystals began to spin, faster and faster, until they were a colorful blur.

"NO!" Rancora screamed.

Indirra was still holding the Wish Energy Meter. The arrow swung violently back and forth until it veered so violently to the good side that it flew right off! Then every light in Starland went on at the same time, flooding it with light once more. A wave of pure good wish energy swept over the crowd. The air was filled with positivity and light. The crowd cheered, overwhelmed with joy and relief.

Everyone but Rancora, that is. With a bloodcurdling scream of anger and despair, she opened her pendant once more, tapped out some of the powdery substance, blew on it, and disappeared in a puff of acrid smoke that stung Gemma's eyes.

Gemma ran over to the spot where Rancora had seemingly disappeared into thin air. She was really gone.

Just then Gemma heard a cry. She rushed to Sage to see her kneeling over the brave Bot-Bot who had saved Leona's life.

Sage turned when Gemma touched her shoulder. "It's Mojay," she said sadly. She turned back to his still metallic body and peered down at him. "Mojay, speak to me," Sage pleaded.

But there was no answer. His face was blank, his eyes empty. Sage began to weep bitterly, the tears coursing down her face in glittery purple streaks. "Oh, Mojay," she said. "You saved us. Please wake up!"

With a whir and a shower of sparks, the Bot-Bot sat up so quickly he bumped heads with Sage. She lost her balance and landed on her bottom.

"Why are you crying, Miss Sage?" Mojay asked worriedly. "I'm fine!"

Sage rubbed her head and laughed shakily. "Oh, Mojay," she said simply. Then she stood up and jumped into the air with joy. "We did it! We did it!" she shouted, grabbing Gemma's hand and raising it in the air.

Gemma jumped up and down with her. They had done it. They had rescued Lady Stella, turned a bad wish into a good one, saved Starland. Her sister ran over and swept her into a tight hug. Relief and happiness rushed through Gemma, leaving her shaking.

There was a roar and Gemma looked around wildly. "Gemma, look!" said Tessa, pointing to the crowd. Gemma looked down to see a sea of upturned faces calling out their names, hundreds of Starlings clapping, cheering, and pointing to a spectacular rainbow glittering in the sky. Gemma noticed the bright orange aura emanating from her body and gasped as she realized that she and her fellow Star Darlings were glowing so radiantly that together they formed the most beautiful glittering rainbow anyone had ever seen.

Lady Stella stepped forward and applauded right along with the crowd. Then she motioned for the Star Darlings to gather around her. When Gemma got closer, she was confused by the look of regret on the headmistress's face. Smiling at them sadly, Lady Stella said, "Star apologies, my Starlings." She raised her arms in the air and the crowd silenced.

"For what?" Gemma asked, but her words were swept away by the loud whooshing wind that ripped through her hair and tore the Starshine Day decorations off the stage, scattering them into the air. Gemma shielded her face with her arm. What in the stars was going on? Tessa put her arms around Gemma and the two sisters huddled together fearfully.

But their terror turned to awe as a shooting star

streaked across the sky, exploding into multicolored blossoms that fell toward their upturned faces, close enough to touch. "Ohhhhhhhhh!" said the crowd. Suddenly, the sky was dancing with colorful beams of light. The crowd and the Star Darlings were transfixed. Gemma was filled with an amazing sense of hope and beauty and pure wondrous joy.

It ended as quickly as it had begun. The Star Darlings stood blinking at each other in confusion. The air—and the mood—felt different. Something momentous had just happened—but what exactly?

Gemma looked down at the crowd. The faces were no longer looking at them in adulation. In fact, they looked confused. Some faces even looked irritated.

"Get off the stage, you Star Ding-a-lings!" someone called out.

Gemma felt her face grow slack with shock. And then, suddenly, she laughed loud and hard. The rest of the Star Darlings joined in. Their moment in the suns had been quite fleeting!

Lady Stella shook her head, her expression sympathetic. "I'm sorry, but everyone's memories have just been erased. Starland needs your special talents to remain under wraps, at least for now. I have a strong feeling this is just the beginning of your adventures. Your time in the starlight will come, Starlings. I promise."

Lady Stella turned to the crowd. "Attention, students! Now we will crown the winners of the Battle of the Bands. Will Vivica and the Visionaries and Star Light Star Bright please join the Star Darlings onstage?"

Gemma, Tessa, Cassie, Adora, Piper, Astra, and Clover moved into the wings to watch the judging. Gemma saw Leona grab Scarlet's and Libby's hands. From the pained looks on their faces she was apparently squeezing them very tightly.

"As you know, we use the Ranker in our competitions to ensure that the judging is fair and unbiased. The Ranker uses an algorithm that measures the level of crowd reaction, difficulty of music, and creativity of lyrics to choose the winner. And the winner of this year's Battle of the Bands is . . ." Lady Stella paused and consulted the Ranker. It seemed like she was moving in slow motion. Gemma realized that she was holding her breath. A Star Darlings victory would be so sweet at that very moment.

"Vivica and the Visionaries! Star kudos, Starlings, on a job well done!"

Gemma felt her heart sink down to her sparkly

orange flats. She saw the disappointed faces of the Star Darlings band, smiling bravely. But then she brightened. So they had lost the Battle of the Bands. They had won the battle for Starland—even if they were the only ones who knew it.

The Star Darlings gathered on the stargrass, where they stood in companionable silence. They were exhausted, ebullient, a tiny bit disappointed, and a whole lot proud.

"Don't look now," Gemma whispered to Sage, "but here comes Vivica."

The girls watched as the Starling made her way to them, her aura glowing pale blue. She was clutching the holo-statue she had received in her hand and had a huge smile on her face.

"Maybe she's coming to extend the kaleidoscope tree branch to us," said Gemma optimistically. "It could be now that Lady Cordial's negative influence is over, she'll be nice."

She smiled at Vivica.

"Hey, girls," Vivica said.

"Hey, Vivica," said Sage. "Star kudos on your victory."

The rest of the Star Darlings nodded.

Leona bit her lip but managed a smile. "Yeah, you put on a good show," she said.

Vivica looked down at the ground almost bashfully. "I just came over to say one thing," she began. Then she looked up and her grin turned nasty. "Beat you good, Star Dippers," she said, then spun on her heel and marched off.

Leona's mouth fell open. "Of all the . . ." she started. "I have half a mind to . . ." Her voice trailed off and she said simply, *"Starf!"*

Lady Stella glided over and gave the Star Darlings a sympathetic look. "Oh, my stars," she said. "That was certainly unpleasant, wasn't it? Talk about a sore winner!" She looked at Vivica's retreating back and shook her head. "We had better keep an eye on that girl. She seems like trouble."

Epilogue

A short time later, the Star Darlings stood on their own private section of the Wishworld Surveillance Deck. Lady Stella had brought them there for a confidential chat.

She smiled at them tenderly. "I want to tell you star salutations once more for saving Starland. You faced many challenges from a formidable foe. Rancora tried everything she could to make you turn against each other, but you persevered and stood together!

"You were strong, smart, and startacularly brave. Even what you thought was a huge misstep—accusing me of working against you—was actually beneficial, as we were able to get the real saboteur into the starlight." She glanced at Cassie, who was staring at her feet. "So no more feeling guilty, Cassie."

Cassie's glow deepened. "Star salutations, Lady Stella. That means a lot," she said earnestly.

Lady Stella continued. "The twelve of you were brought together for your strengths. Separately, you are strong and spirited, smart and talented. Together, you are an unbeatable team. Your differences could have been your undoing, but you managed to find ways to work together. And for that, I will be forever grateful."

Gemma noticed that the Star Darlings were all glowing with pride. They had grown to understand and accept each other and in the process had forged an unbreakable bond.

"Do you have any questions?" Lady Stella asked.

Vega spoke first. "What about Rancora?" she said. "Who is she?"

Lady Stella frowned. "It appears that she has been plotting the downfall of Starland for quite some time, and she infiltrated Starling Academy disguised as Lady Cordial in order to gain a position of power."

"What will happen to her?" asked Gemma.

"The authorities are searching for her right now," Lady Stella explained. "She will be apprehended in due time. You can be starsure of that."

"Will we be sent back down to Wishworld again soon?" Scarlet asked hopefully.

"Eventually," the headmistress said. "At the moment, we have plenty of wish energy. There will come a time in the not-too-distant future when you will be sent back down to Wishworld. But first I'd like you all to meet with our leading wish energy scientists for a debriefing. They have a lot to learn from you and your extreme success in collecting wish energy."

Sage grinned at the news. Gemma knew she was excited to spend some time with her mother.

"One more thing," Lady Stella added. "As the twelve Star-Charmed Starlings, you may have powers that have not been discovered yet. We'll have time to study and practice and determine exactly how charmed you all are."

Leona spoke up. "You said that someday everyone will know about what we did. When do you think that will happen?"

Lady Stella nodded. "I cannot tell you exactly when, but someday all of Starland will know just how special you are."

Leona stole a sidelong glance at the other girls, a funny half smile on her face. "I guess . . ." she began slowly. "I guess it would be nice, but the truth is that the twelve of us—and you, Lady Stella—knowing it, somehow that's enough for me."

Gemma stared at Leona in disbelief. Was she serious? Didn't she want the glory and the accolades? Gemma did! But then a feeling of warmth and joy flowed through her. Actually, it *was* enough.

Lady Stella pointed into the heavens. "Not to mention that, thanks to you girls, Starland is once again twinkling brightly in the sky, beckoning Wishlings to continue to make wishes."

The girls stared down at Wishworld, a bright beacon in the dark sky. Gemma imagined that she could feel the power of all the wishes —good ones, of course—making their way to Wishworld for granting.

Gemma could hold her tongue no longer. "We're the Star Darlings—one for all and all for one!" she shouted.

Leona reached over and gave her a quick hug. "You can say that again," she said.

Gemma grinned. "We're the Star Darlings—one for all and all for one!" she repeated.

Several of the girls gasped. Tessa grabbed her arm. "Oh, no, you're taking everything literally again!" She stared deep into Gemma's auburn eyes. "Are you okay?"

But Gemma just laughed and laughed. "Too soon?" she said. "Hold your stars, big sis. I'm just kidding!"

Glossary

Afterglow: The Starling afterlife. When Starlings die, it is said that they have "begun their afterglow."

Age of Fulfillment: The age at which a Starling is considered mature enough to begin to study wish granting.

Astromuffin: A delicious baked breakfast treat.

Azurica: Adora's Power Crystal—rectangular blue pillars of various sizes dangling from a golden dome.

Babsday: The second starday of the weekend. The days in order are Sweetday, Shineday, Dododay, Yumday, Lunaday, Bopday, Reliquaday, and Babsday. (Starlandians have a three-day weekend every starweek.)

Bad Wish Orbs: Orbs that are the result of bad or selfish wishes made on Wishworld. These grow dark and warped and are quickly sent to the Negative Energy Facility.

Ballum blossom sauce: A sweet sauce made from the fruit of the ballum blossom tree and used to add flavor to Starlandian food, somewhat like Wishworld ketchup.

Big Dipper Dormitory: Where third- and fourth-year students live.

Bitbat: A small winged nocturnal creature.

Bot-Bot: A Starland robot. There are Bot-Bot guards, waiters, deliverers, and guides on Starland.

Bright-burner: A heating apparatus used in chemistry experiments.

Bright Day: The date a Starling is born, celebrated each year like a Wishling birthday.

Briteflowers: Small white twinkling flowers often used for decorations.

Celestial Café: Starling Academy's outstanding cafeteria.

Chatterburst: Gemma's Wish Blossom—an orange flower that turns to face whoever is near to capture attention.

Cloud candy: A fluffy, sticky, sweet treat on a stick, similar to Wishworld cotton candy.

Cocomoon: A sweet and creamy fruit with an iridescent glow.

Cosmic Transporter: The moving sidewalk system that transports students through dorms and across the Starling Academy campus.

Countdown Clock: A timing device on a Starling's Star-Zap. It lets them know how much time is left on a Wish Mission, which coincides with when the Wish Orb will fade.

Crystal Mountains: The most beautiful mountains on Starland. They are located across the lake from Starling Academy.

Cycle of Life: A Starling's life span. When Starlings die, they are said to have "completed their Cycle of Life."

Dododay: The second starday of the school week.

Druderwomp: An edible barrel-like bush capable of pulling up its own roots and rolling like a tumbleweed, then planting itself again.

Flash Vertical Mover: A mode of transportation similar to a Wishling elevator, only superfast.

Floozel: The Starland equivalent of a Wishworld mile.

Florafierce: A red flower with a ring of longer petals that surround a center mound of small, tightly packed leaves.

Flutterfocus: A Starland creature similar to a Wishworld butterfly but with illuminated wings.

Frisbeam: A disc-shaped piece of sporting equipment that flies through the air when thrown, like a Wishworld Frisbee.

Galliope: A sparkly Starland creature similar to a Wishworld horse.

Garble greens: A Starland vegetable similar to spinach.

Glion: A gentle Starland creature similar in appearance to a Wishworld lion but with a multicolored glowing mane.

Glitterbees: Blue-and-orange-striped bugs that pollinate Starland flowers and produce a sweet substance called delicata.

Glorange: A glowing orange fruit. Its juice is often enjoyed at breakfast time.

Glowball: A pink fluffy flower with a sweet scent that promotes relaxation, often used in incense.

Glowfur: A small furry Starland creature with gossamer wings that eats flowers and glows.

Glowzene: A chemical substance used in chemistry experiments.

Goldenella: A tall slender tree with golden blossoms that pop off the branches.

Good Wish Orbs: Orbs that are the result of positive wishes made on Wishworld. They are planted in Wish-Houses.

Googlehorn: A brass musical instrument that resembles a Wishworld trumpet.

Halo Hall: The building where Starling Academy classes are held.

Holo-text: A message received on a Star-Zap and projected into the air. There are also holo-albums, holo-billboards, holo-books, holo-cards, holo-communications, holo-diaries, holo-flyers, holo-letters, holo-papers, holo-pictures, and holo–place cards. Anything that would be made of paper or contain writing or images on Wishworld is a hologram on Starland.

HOS lanes: High Occupancy Starcar lanes; only vehicles with four passengers or more are allowed to use them.

Hydrong: The equivalent of a Wishworld hundred.

Illumination Library: The impressive library at Starling Academy.

Impossible Wish Orbs: Orbs that are the result of wishes made on Wishworld that are beyond the power of Starlings to grant.

Jellyjooble: A small round pink candy that is very sweet.

Kaleidoscope tree: A rare and beautiful tree whose blossoms continuously change color. When someone is said to extend the kaleidoscope tree branch, it means that they are making peace with someone else.

Keytar: A musical instrument that looks like a cross between a guitar and a keyboard.

Lightentific method: The scientific protocol that Adora follows when conducting experiments.

Lightning Lounge: A place on the Starling Academy campus where students relax and socialize.

Lightyard: A braided or woven length of material, like a Wishworld lanyard.

Little Dipper Dormitory: Where first- and second-year students live.

Lumin: A unit of liquid measurement used in chemistry.

Luminous Lake: A serene and lovely lake next to the Starling Academy campus.

Mirror Mantra: A saying specific to each Star Darling that when recited gives her (and her Wisher) reassurance and strength. When a Starling recites her Mirror Mantra while looking in a mirror, she will see her true appearance reflected.

Moogle: A very short but unspecific amount of time. The word is used in expressions like "Wait just a moogle!"

Moonberries: Sweet berries that grow on Starland. They are Lady Stella's favorite snack.

Moonium: An amount similar to a Wishworld million.

Old Prism: A medium-sized historical city about an hour from Starling Academy.

Ozziefruit: Sweet plum-sized indigo fruit that grows on pink-leaved trees and is usually eaten raw or cooked in pies.

Panthera: Clover's Power Crystal—a cone-shaped jewel with magenta and mauve swirls and a bright purple orb dangling from the bottom.

Plantannas: A curved tubelike fruit encased in a glowing yellow peel, somewhat like a cross between Wishworld bananas and plantains.

Power Crystal: The powerful stone each Star Darling receives once she has granted her first wish.

Pricklepine: A spine-covered animal similar to a Wishworld porcupine.

Purple piphany: Clover's Wish Blossom—the petals of this flower are surrounded by five rings of pale purple light.

Radiant Hills: An exclusive neighborhood in Starland City where Adora's parents own a clothing store.

Radiant Recreation Center: The building at Starling Academy where students take Physical Energy, health, and fitness classes. The rec center has a large gymnasium for exercising, a running track, areas for games, and a sparkling star-pool.

Reliquaday: The first starday of the weekend.

Scatterite: Gemma's Power Crystal—an orange egg-shaped stone with a smooth, sparkly surface.

Shooting stars: Speeding stars that Starlings can latch on to and ride to Wishworld.

Skywinkle: Adora's Wish Blossom—a blue flower that sparkles as if dusted with diamonds.

Solar metal spike: Similar to a Wishworld nail.

Sparklehammer: Like a Wishworld hammer, but it sends out a shower of multicolored sparks whenever it strikes something.

Sparkle shower: An energy shower Starlings take every day to get clean and refresh their sparkling glow.

Star ball: An intramural sport that shares similarities with soccer on Wishworld, but star ball players use energy manipulation to control the ball.

Starcar: The primary mode of transportation for most Starlings. These ultrasafe vehicles drive themselves on cushions of wish energy.

Star Caves: The caverns underneath Starling Academy where the Star Darlings' secret Wish-Cavern is located.

Starf!: A Starling expression of dismay.

Star flash: News bulletin, often used sarcastically.

Starfuric acid: A potent chemical used in chemistry experiments.

Star Kindness Day: A special Starland holiday that celebrates spreading kindness, compliments, and good cheer.

Starkudos: An expression used to give credit to a Starling for a job well done.

Starland City: The largest city on Starland, also its capital.

Starlings: The glowing beings with sparkly skin who live on Starland.

Starmin: Sixty starsecs (or seconds) on Starland, the equivalent of a Wishworld minute.

Star Quad: The center of the Starling Academy campus. The dancing fountain, band shell, and hedge maze are located here.

Star salutations: The Starling way to say "thank you."

Star-sandwiches: Elegant star-shaped sandwiches with various tasty fillings.

Starshine: An endearment used by loved ones, similar to "sunshine" or "darling."

Starshine Day: A special holiday when students get the day off from school and celebrate with food, music, games, science and art fairs, light shows, parades, sporting events, and more.

Starwire: A cable stretched between two high points that circus performers walk across, like a Wishworld tightrope.

Staryear: A time period on Starland, the equivalent of a Wishworld year.

Star-Zap: The ultimate smartphone that Starlings use for all communications. It has myriad features.

Stellation: The point of a star. Halo Hall has five stellations, each housing a different department.

Supernova: A stellar explosion. Also used colloquially, meaning "really angry," as in "She went supernova when she found out the bad news."

Time of Letting Go: One of the four seasons on Starland. It falls between the warmest season and the coldest, similar to fall on Wishworld.

Time of Lumiere: The warmest season on Starland, similar to summer on Wishworld.

Time of New Beginnings: Similar to spring on Wishworld, this is the season that follows the coldest time of year; it's when plants and trees come into bloom.

Time of Shadows: The coldest season of the year on Starland, similar to winter on Wishworld.

Toothlight: A high-tech gadget Starlings use to clean their teeth.

Twinkelopes: Majestic herd animals. Males have imposing antlers with star-shaped horns, and females have iridescent manes and flowing tails.

Twinkle-oxide: A compound used in chemistry experiments.

Wish Blossom: The bloom that appears from a Wish Orb after its wish is granted.

Wish energy: The positive energy that is released when a wish is granted. Wish energy powers everything on Starland.

Wisher: The Wishling who has made the wish that is being granted.

Wish-Granters: Starlings whose job is to travel down to Wishworld to help make wishes come true and collect wish energy.

Wish-House: The place where Wish Orbs are planted and cared for until they sparkle. Once the orb's wish is granted, it becomes a Wish Blossom.

Wishlings: The inhabitants of Wishworld.

Wish Mission: The task a Starling undertakes when she travels to Wishworld to help grant a wish.

Wish Orb: The form a wish takes on Wishworld before traveling to Starland. There it will grow and sparkle when it's time to grant the wish.

Wish Pendant: A gadget that absorbs and transports wish energy, helps Starlings locate their Wishers, and changes a Starling's appearance. Each Wish Pendant holds a different special power for its Star Darling.

Wishworld: The planet Starland relies on for wish energy. The beings on Wishworld know it by another name—Earth.

Wishworld Outfit Selector: A program on each Star-Zap that accesses Wishworld fashions for Starlings to wear to blend in on their Wish Missions.

Wishworld Surveillance Deck: A platform located high above the campus, where Starling Academy students go to observe Wishlings through high-powered telescopes.

Zing: A traditional Starling breakfast drink. It can be enjoyed hot or iced.

Acknowledgments

It is impossible to list all of our gratitude, but we will try.

Our most precious gift and greatest teacher, Halo; we love you more than there are stars in the sky . . . punashaku. To the rest of our crazy, awesome, unique tribe—thank you for teaching us to go for our dreams. Integrity. Strength. Love. Foundation. Family. Grateful. Mimi Muldoon—from your star doodling to naming our Star Darlings, your artistry, unconditional love, and inspiration is infinite. Didi Muldoon—your belief and support in us is only matched by your fierce protection and massive-hearted guidance. Gail. Queen G. Your business sense and witchy wisdom are legendary. Frank—you are missed and we know you are watching over us all. Along with Tutu, Nana, and Deda, who are always present, gently guiding us in spirit. To our colorful, totally genius, and bananas siblings: Patrick, Moon, Diva, and Dweezil—there is more creativity and humor in those four names than most people experience in a lifetime. Blessed. To our magical nieces—Mathilda, Zola, Ceylon, and Mia—the Star Darlings adore you and so do we. Our witchy cuzzie fairy godmothers—Ane and Gina. Our fairy fashion godfather, Paris. Our sweet Panay. Teeta and Freddy—we love you so much. And our four-legged fur babies—Sandwich, Luna, Figgy, and Pinky Star.

The incredible Barry Waldo. Our SD partner. Sent to us from above in perfect timing. Your expertise and friendship are beyond words. We love you and Gary to the moon and back. Long live the manifestation room!

Catherine Daly—the stars shined brightly upon us the day we aligned with you. Your talent and inspiration are otherworldly; our appreciation cannot be expressed in words. Many heartfelt hugs for you and the adorable Oonagh.

To our beloved Disney family. Thank you for believing in us. Wendy Lefkon, our master guide and friend through this entire journey. Stephanie Lurie, for being the first to believe in Star Darlings. Suzanne Murphy, who helped every step of the way. Jeanne Mosure, we fell in love with you the first time we met, and Star Darlings wouldn't be what it is without you. Andrew Sugerman, thank you so much for all your support.

Our team . . . Devon (pony pants) and our Monsterfoot crew—so grateful. Richard Scheltinga—our angel and protector. Chris Abramson—thank you! Special appreciation to Richard Thompson, John LaViolette, Swanna, Mario, and Sam.

To our friends old and new—we are so grateful to be on this rad journey that is life with you all. Fay. Jorja. Chandra. Sananda. Sandy. Kathryn. Louise. What wisdom and strength you share. Ruth, Mike, and the rest of our magical Wagon Wheel bunch—how lucky we are. How inspiring you are. We love you.

Last—we have immeasurable gratitude for every person we've met along our journey, for all the good and the bad; it is all a gift. From the bottom of our hearts we thank you for touching our lives.

Shana Muldoon Zappa is a jewelry designer and writer who was born and raised in Los Angeles. She has an endless imagination and a passion to inspire positivity through her many artistic endeavors. She and her husband, Ahmet Zappa, collaborated on Star Darlings especially for their magical little girl and biggest inspiration, Halo Violetta Zappa.

Ahmet Zappa is the *New York Times* best-selling author of *Because I'm Your Dad* and *The Monstrous Memoirs of a Mighty McFearless*. He writes and produces films and television shows and loves pancakes, unicorns, and making funny faces for Halo and Shana.

Check out an excerpt from
the next Star Darlings book,

Good Wish Gone Bad

Starling Academy was positively glowing. The buildings, the fountains, the trees, and even the moving Cosmic Transporter sidewalks looked more dazzling than they had in recent memory. Off in the distance, the Crystal Mountains also appeared to stand a bit taller, prouder, and brighter as the reflection of their multicolored peaks bounced off the shimmering azure surface of the Luminous Lake below. All signs of the negative wish energy that had been plaguing everything from the fruit orchards to the Starling Academy students themselves had faded away, almost as though it had been nothing more than a bad dream—and it was entirely thanks to the twelve star-charmed Star Darlings!

"Have you ever seen the campus look more beautiful?" marveled Sage. Her long, lavender braids were also shinier than they had been in quite some time, and they bounced behind her as she and the other Star Darlings hurried past classmates who were heading to the Celestial Café for dinner.

Instead of going to their own evening meal, however, the girls were on their way to Lady Stella's office. The head-mistress had summoned them on their Star-Zaps, instructing them to join her right away for an important meeting. In spite of the urgent tone of the holo-text, Sage felt certain that Lady Stella simply wanted to congratulate the Star Darlings on the successful completion of their top-secret wish missions. Together, they had collected enough positive wish energy to help ensure that everything on Starland would be powered for countless staryears to come.

"I've never seen the *world* look more beautiful," said Sage's roommate, Cassie, her eyes widening with delight behind her star-shaped glasses as the girls continued along the Cosmic Transporter.

"It *is* super celestial—but how long do you think this meeting is going to last?" Tessa wondered. "I'm hungry!" Just like her gourmet chef mother, the emerald-haired third-year student was almost always thinking about food.

"Do you think she's got more wish missions for us?" asked Libby. It had been a long while since she'd gone on her journey down to Wishworld and, as exciting as it was to know that all twelve Star Darlings had completed their missions, she couldn't wait to go on another one.

"I doubt it. We've already done all we can," scoffed Scarlet, shoving her hands into the front pocket of her sparkling red hoodie and rolling her eyes as the girls made their way into Halo Hall.

A few moments later, they arrived at the door to Lady Stella's office, which was cracked open in anticipation of their visit.

"Girls!" The elegant headmistress stood up from her desk, breathing a sigh of relief as she smoothed down the fabric of her sparkly silver gown. "I thought you'd never get here. Come, let's go down to the Wish-Cavern at once."

"I knew it!" Libby tossed her long, bubblegum-pink hair proudly and shot a triumphant smile in Scarlet's direction as Lady Stella opened the hidden door in her office wall. Why else would they be going to the Wish-Cavern unless she had more missions for them?

The girls followed their headmistress down the secret staircase to the dark caves beneath the school, shivering as they made their way through the chilly air, past the dripping rock formations and toward the door to their own secret Wish-House. It was a special room that had been built exclusively for the Star Darlings and their uniquely powerful wish missions.

But unlike the times they'd been in the Wish-House before, this time, at the foot of a large golden waterfall in the gleaming light-soaked room, a round table had been set up with all sorts of treats—including an enormous zoomberry cake and fancy crystal glasses full of sparkling puckerup juice at each place setting. Above the table, a giant holo-banner floated in mid-air, emblazoned with large, glittery gold letters that spelled out the words CONGRATULATIONS, STAR DARLINGS!

"Well, girls, this is quite a momentous day, indeed," Lady Stella began as they all settled into their chairs, which immediately adjusted to their respective heights and weights for optimum comfort. The headmistress raised her long, delicate glass. "I cannot begin to tell you how pleased I am with what you've each accomplished. Thanks to your hard work and diligence in completing your wish missions, there is now more positive wish energy on Starland than ever before!"

The girls all exchanged excited glances, beaming with pride as they too raised their glasses and each took a sip. "Star salutations, Lady Stella!" they replied in almost perfect unison.

"And to you," Lady Stella said softly as she cut into the cake, serving each girl a generous slice and encouraging them to eat—which they were more than happy to do. After all, it was highly unusual for young Starlings to be permitted to have dessert before dinner!

As the girls happily chatted, reminiscing about some of the best parts of their missions, Lady Stella glanced around the table at each one of them with a faraway look in her eyes.

"Why aren't you eating?" Tessa asked the headmistress between bites.

Lady Stella pressed her bright red lips together before attempting a smile. But it was no use. She couldn't pretend with them. "Star Darlings . . ." she said, inhaling deeply and closing her eyes for a moment, "we do have much to celebrate—but I suppose I should also tell you that even greater challenges may lie ahead for us all."

The celebratory mood in the air suddenly became thick with nervous energy. What was the headmistress referring to, exactly?

"As you know, everyone at Starling Academy was completely deceived by Lady Cordial, who was our Director of Admissions. She was someone I trusted and valued as one of my closest confidantes." Lady Stella sighed and shook her head as she stared down at the table. "I genuinely believed that she was our friend—but, in fact, she was not Lady Cordial at all. She was Rancora in disguise."

As soon as Lady Stella mentioned that dreaded name, the golden light in the Wish-Cavern flickered and dimmed ever so slightly, and the Star Darlings all felt an icy chill run down their spines. They frowned and nodded solemnly. Although they had managed to avoid discussing Lady Cordial for the past week, they of course knew that at some point her name—and the far more terrifying name of Rancora—would come up again. They had simply hoped it wouldn't be quite so soon.

"But she's gone now," Gemma pointed out, her wavy orange ponytail glimmering.

"Well, yes, she has left Starling Academy—that's true," Lady Stella acknowledged. "However, we don't know *where* she's gone or what she might be planning to do next. So, although I'm hopeful that she'll keep her distance and stay far, far away from the school grounds, I believe that she may be planning something bigger—something that will place Starland in even greater danger."

"Wh-what could be more dangerous than the negative energy she was releasing?" asked Cassie, who began trembling so much that she had to set down her fork.

"Yeah—and how much more can she really do?" Vega wondered. "You said that there's more positive wish energy on Starland than ever before—plus, we already defeated her, when we united our twelve power crystals. Won't that be enough to stop Rancora again, even if she tries to do something else?"

"That is my hope—but I'm still trying to find the missing page that I believe Rancora, or, rather, Lady Cordial, stole from the oracle," Lady Stella replied, referring to the ancient text that foretold of the twelve girls and the role they would play in saving Starland in the first place. "While I spend the next few days continuing my search, I suggest that you all put this out of your minds and get some rest. You've been through so much and will be needing your energy—not only for your studies, but in the event that I require your assistance again. Of course, that will depend on what I'm able to find out."

While the girls quietly pondered everything Lady Stella had said, she tried to encourage them to continue their celebration, offering them more cake and juice. But Tessa was the only one who still had any sort of an appetite left.

"I'm sorry, girls," Lady Stella said with a frown. "I hadn't intended to bring this up with you today—but it's important for you to be aware of the potential challenges that may lie ahead. Try not to worry too much. I *will* come up with a solution."

"We know you will," said Libby, her bright pink eyes gleaming with positive energy. "And we can help as soon as you need us!"

"Yes!" agreed Clover, lightly tapping the rim of her purple fedora. "We'll do whatever it takes. Right, Star Darlings?"

"Right!" the girls all cheered.

But as they got up from their comfy chairs and shuffled out of the Wish-House, the mood was anything but cheery.

The next morning, every last one of the Star Darlings woke up early. In fact, most of them had hardly slept at all. Vega had been especially restless, plagued by nightmares about Rancora, with her piercing purple eyes and ashen skin and hair, the blazing pink collar of her long, tattered gray gown rising behind her head like the fiery flames of doom. Sitting up in bed, Vega leaned back against her headboard and began to record holo-notes on her Star-Zap about everything she had observed about Lady Cordial. She still couldn't believe that the frumpy-dumpy director of admissions had been the evil Rancora in disguise all that time!

"You couldn't sleep, either?" Piper asked in a soft ethereal voice from her side of the room as she pushed off her cozy aqua comforter and pulled her long seafoam-green hair up into a high ponytail.

"No." Vega rubbed her blue eyes and shook her head. Her chin-length cobalt bob looked perfect as ever, in spite of the fact that she was still in bed. "I can't stop thinking about

Lady Cordial—or, you know, *Rancora*. I should have realized that she might still be plotting something terrible."

"I know." Piper slid on her fluffy slippers, closed her eyes, and took several deep, cleansing breaths. "I've been having visions ever since Lady Stella mentioned her name yesterday."

Vega wrinkled her nose. Sometimes Piper's visions could be kind of out there—but other times they had proven to be right on target. "What kind of visions?"

"Well . . ." Piper took a few more deep breaths. "It's kind of scary."

"Tell me!" Vega demanded.

"All right. I saw Rancora in a big dark cloud—but she kept changing into Lady Cordial and then back into herself," Piper recounted. "Every time she changed into Rancora, she tried to pull us into the cloud, too, and she kept saying she wanted us to join forces with her."

"Us—who is *us*?" Vega's eyes darkened with worry.

"All twelve of us—the Star Darlings," Piper said.

"Oh, my stars!" Vega jumped out of bed and began pacing around the room. "What if you're right? What if she tries to turn us into her negative energy minions? Her toxic trainees! We need to figure out exactly what Rancora is planning and find a way to stop her—like, *now*."

Piper widened her eyes, mystified by Vega's words. "But Lady Stella said she was going to search for the missing page from the oracle and *then* figure out what needs to be done. She told us we needed to wait to hear from her. She said we needed to rest up so we could get our energy back."

"I know," Vega said tersely. "But I don't want to sit around waiting—or resting—when we could be helping. We don't want to be caught off guard, right? The more prepared we are the better!"

Piper shrugged and sat back in bed while Vega raced around her side of the room, grabbing her toothlight and rushing out to take a sparkle shower. Within minutes, she was back and getting dressed in a shiny blue blazer over a matching tunic, with sparkly tights and ankle boots.

"What are you going to do?" Piper asked.

"We need to go to the Illumination Library!" Vega informed her.

"The library? Why?" Piper looked blankly at her roommate.

"So we can try to figure out exactly where Rancora came from," Vega explained. "There's *got* to be a holo-book there that will point us in the right direction! Hurry up and get ready. I'll holo-text everyone to meet us there!"

"Okay," Piper agreed reluctantly.

A few of the Star Darlings were already out in front of the Illumination Library when Vega and Piper showed up, some looking more awake than others.

"What's this all about?" asked Adora, who was flawlessly styled, as usual, in shimmering indigo leggings with knee-high boots and a chic fitted dress, her pale blue hair piled high in a fashionably messy updo.

"Yeah, what's happening?" echoed Adora's roommate, Tessa, stifling a yawn as she popped the last bite of a glorange-spice muffin into her mouth.

"I'll tell you when the others get here," Vega replied, tapping her foot as she stared impatiently across the Star Quad. Finally, she could see the rest of the girls moving toward the library on the Cosmic Transporter.

"What's up?" Libby asked when she arrived. "We got here as fast as we could!"

"Piper and I were up all night, thinking about the whole Lady Cordial—or Rancora—situation," Vega explained as the others all gathered round. "Piper had a vision that Lady Cordial kept turning into Rancora and was trying to pull us into some sort of dark cloud, insisting she wanted us to join forces with her or something."

"Seriously?" Scarlet crossed her arms in frustration. "You called us all the way here to tell us *that*?"

"No." Vega glared at Scarlet, whose short fuchsia hair was slightly messy from sleep. "I called you here because obviously there's a lot more to Rancora than any of us realize, and we need to know more about her if we're going to figure out what she might be planning to do to us—or to Starland—next. Lady Stella may be doing her own research, but I think we should start doing a bit of our own, too!"

"What kind of research?" asked Libby, always eager to help in any way she could.

"Well, for starters, we should see what we can find out about Lady Cordial, since that's who Rancora was in disguise," Vega proposed.

"That's not a bad idea," Sage noted. "There's got to be some information about her in the faculty pages of the school staryearbooks."

"Exactly!" Vega agreed.

"I don't see how that's going to help," Scarlet protested. "What are the staryearbooks going to tell us that we—and especially Lady Stella—don't already know?"

"I say we give it a try," Leona chimed in, giving her shiny golden curls a confident pat. "If we *do* find out something useful, Lady Stella will think we're even bigger stars than we already are."

"I agree," said Sage.

"Me too." Tessa nodded.

"Ugh. Fine." Scarlet rolled her eyes, giving in only after all the others had voiced their support.

"Excellent," Vega said with a smile, leading the way into the library.

With most of the Starling Academy campus still asleep, it was even quieter inside than usual. The twelve girls made their way through the vast stacks of holo books and up the winding staircase to the section where the staryearbooks were located. The tomes contained holo-images of every student and faculty member who had ever been at Starling Academy, along with detailed records of everything that had happened during each school staryear since the very first class had enrolled.

"So what are we looking for, exactly?" asked Gemma, accessing the holo-pages of a recent staryearbook as she sat down on a plush orange couch and began scanning through them. "This says Lady Cordial has been at Starling Academy for two years and she's helped to make the school what it is today."

"Ha—only because nothing's been written about *us* yet!" Leona grinned proudly while Vega sat down next to Gemma and tapped on the image of Lady Cordial, eager to see if anything more useful might pop up.

Alas, all she saw was the director of admissions shuffling from her office to Lady Stella's office, then back to her office, with an occasional moment where she spilled something or tripped. *That* was helping to make the school what it was today?

"There has to be more information about her than this," Vega said with a frown, taking the book from Gemma and scrolling through it some more.

"I'm kind of with Scarlet—even if we found more information about Lady Cordial, what would it really tell us?" asked Adora, sitting down next to Vega. "Isn't *Rancora* the one we need to investigate?"

"Yes, but they're one and the same," Vega pointed out as she continued to scroll through the pages, moving farther and farther back in time.

"True, but we might find something more informative—something she was hiding—if we go to her office, or maybe even her old residence in Prof Row," Adora pointed out.

"Adora's probably right," Sage agreed.

"She's *totally* right!" Scarlet said.

"Oh, my stars!" Piper suddenly called out. She had wandered off and found a much older staryearbook, which she was now gazing at in wide-eyed wonder.

"What?" Vega asked, leaping up from the couch and racing over to grab the holo-book from her roommate before returning to the couch with it.

"What is it, Vega?" Sage asked, positioning herself behind Vega so she could get a better view.

"It's . . . it's . . . Lady Stella!" Vega gasped as she glanced over at Piper. "Right?"

"Uh-huh." Piper nodded.

"So?" Scarlet huffed.

"No—I mean, it's Lady Stella when she was *our* age," Vega elaborated. "When she was just . . . *student* Stella."

That was enough to distract everyone from the task at hand, at least for the moment.

"Oooh! I want to see!" Gemma grabbed the book from Vega and studied the holo-page intently.

Even Scarlet leaned in a little closer to see the photo of two teenage girls with their hands clasped. The tall sophisticated one with long golden-pink hair and a Bright Day crown on her head was most certainly a younger version of their headmistress.

"Holy stars," exclaimed Adora, reaching over to grab the book from Gemma. "Look how super celestial that dress is! And those boots! She was so beautiful, even back then."

"She and her friend look so happy," Gemma noticed.

"C'mon, guys," Scarlet said. "Looking at old holo-photos of Lady Stella won't help us figure out anything about Lady Cordial or Rancora or whatever you want to call her."

"I'm actually getting a strange feeling this staryearbook is really important," murmured Piper.

"Piper thinks this is important. Let's take a quick look," Adora urged. "Then we can go check out Lady Cordial's office. It's not like we have to be in class for a while, anyway."

"Actually, I think we should do more than take a quick look," Vega said. "As long as we're going into this old star-yearbook, I might as well holo-hack into it. That way, it'll automatically link us to any important info from any other relevant holo-document, like a journal or letter."

"Wow, that's so cool, Vega," said Cassie, impressed with Vega's tech skills.

So, as the girls all gathered around, Vega tapped on the image of young Stella, and a holographic video detailing her time at Starling Academy—long before she became headmistress—began to play before their eyes. . . .

Join the **Star Darling** girls on their adventures to **save Starland!**